Force Majeure

Gift of Yale University

Bruce Wagner

FORCE MAJEURE

Random House

New York

Portions of this work were originally published by
Caldecot Chubb, Los Angeles, in 1988.

Grateful acknowledgment is made to the following for
permission to reprint previously published material:
HENRY HOLT AND COMPANY, INC.: Twelve lines from
"From Kleine Nachtmusik" by Jacob Glatstein from *A
Treasury of Yiddish Poetry* edited by Irving Howe and
Eliezer Greenberg. Copyright © 1969 by Irving Howe
and Eliezer Greenberg. Reprinted by permission of
Henry Holt and Company, Inc. PENGUIN USA: Excerpt
from footnote on page 434 of *The Penguin Book of
Modern Yiddish Verse* edited by Irving Howe, Ruth R.
Wisse, and Khone Shmeruk, published by Penguin
Books. Reprinted by permission. UNIVERSITY OF
CHICAGO PRESS: Excerpt from "Vowels" from
Rimbaud Complete Works, Selected Letters edited by
Wallace Fowlie. Copyright © 1966 by University of
Chicago. Reprinted by permission.

Library of Congress Cataloging-in-Publication Data
Wagner, Bruce.
Force majeure / Bruce Wagner.
p.– cm.   ISBN 0-394-58261-6
I. Title.
PS3573.A369F6   1991   813'.54—dc20   90-53840

Manufactured in the United States of America
Typography and binding design by J.K. Lambert
98765432

for Charles Mool

18. Force Majeure. If Producer is prevented from or materially hampered or interrupted in preparing or producing motion picture productions by reason of any present or future statute, law, ordinance, regulation, order, judgment or decree, whether legislative, executive or judicial (whether or not constitutional), act of God, earthquake, flood, fire, epidemic, accident, explosion, casualty, lockout, boycott, strike, labor controversy, riot, civil disturbance, war or armed conflict, act of public enemy, embargo, delay of a common carrier, inability to obtain sufficient material, labor, transportation, power or other essential commodity required in the conduct of Producer's business, or by reason of any other cause or causes of any similar nature; or if production of the Picture is suspended, interrupted or postponed by reason of any such cause of similar causes, or the death, illness, disfigurement or incapacity of any member of the cast of the Picture, or the termination or suspension of an agreement for the financing or distribution of the Picture; then, following any such event or any similar event(s), Producer may suspend this Agreement. During and for a reasonable time following any such event(s) or by written notice during or following any such event(s), Producer may terminate this Agreement. Writer shall not be entitled to any compensation whatsoever during any such suspension . . .

Contents

Force Majeure

1. The Best Years of Our Lives

daydream: Bud Wiggins was awash in clay. Mrs. Kent's smudged face presided over legs jammed into scudded black pumps that tacked the plangent clay of the corridor. He watched himself watch those heels like they were a force of nature, so focused he might have been a prodigy noting his first axiom, melodious and movably sensual, finally ordering the world. Little Bud stared at the foot in the shoe (CAMERA PUSHES IN TO EXTREME CLOSE-UP OF BOY) with the marooned intensity of a Truffaut urchin martyring himself on an image. He *communed*—

The torpid screenwriter turned over in bed and thought: *Jesus.* That was a fetish. Some kind of shoe fetish, that's what that was, at seven years old. Back in the Arbor. Or was it the Heights? Bud blind, the sound of the clack telling him everything, throwing back the contours, minutiae and mystery, the voluminous personality, the womanly smells, some kind of roaring sonatina in his ear and his eye; the teacher's heel made its supreme flat ruddy perfect report and the little boy listened, its echo Mrs. Kent's musk, her tough mannequin's makeup, her extracurricular life, life out of school, her *husband*-life. The sound was language to him and his heart sped up like an exhibitionist's. A coarse and resilient *klope,* chalkily hollow, gaudily efficient, like a WAC storming Woolworth's (there it was: a synthetic image, fake old reference, what was a WAC but a steal from the best years of his parents' lives). *Klope klap klop kleep klop klope klope klop,* a sound that was the world and Bud circled the drain of its plenitude. The hallway of the grade school like a cloister, the white hoseless calves working, the unimpeachable pump pounding its beat-up stem in locomotion around the calloused grown-up's heel.

There was a girl in there somewhere. He put her chair atop the desk, the custom when class was over, like closing up a restaurant. The teacher smiled at this chivalrous rehearsal; the little girl was sweetly embarrassed. Her name was Cora.

Twenty-five years later Bud shifted on the sheets and thought about the park across from that school and the boy-created bramble labyrinth there—a natural playhouse and combat games habitat—another fetish, a fetish of space and branches, secrets and burrows, the wet brows and musculature of little boys. Then the elder Bud fled magically to the private suburban garden, faded and abandoned like some grandmother's sitting room, opiate and golden, dolorous with suburban middle-day heat. Was that even a real memory? Or was it a pastoral cliché, a fairy tale Bud's lassitude made? No—there *was* a leafy hidden place he went as a child. Before they broke up—was it a year already?—Jeanette gave him *The Secret Garden* and he never read it because he had his own with its dim, mystical, inviolable memories; the famous lost bower had a bushy, fractured entrance and he always entered illicitly, through a broken trellis, crawling on rapturous roughed-up knees. You were a fag if you didn't have scarified knees, a taut yellow-white worm of a scar at the joint. He wondered if he ever took Cora there. He was sure there was a fountain . . .

Where was Bud Wiggins anyway? Daydreaming in Dolly's den,
his room for the past six months. He lived there almost twenty
years ago and now he was a boarder amid his mother's orderly
clutter. There was an exercise bike and racks of Adolfo suits,
a doctor's scale and a few silver dumbbells. Thus, his old room
had been mundanely violated. The books he stole as a teenager
were still in the shelves Dolly bought from the Danish place on
Wilshire that wasn't there anymore.

He fussily straightened the paperback spines, just like the
teen Bud did. It was a pretentious, canny group, ripped from
local bookstores, a time-capsule library whose selections ceased
at the end of the sixties. He hadn't read most of them—that
wasn't so much the idea. The idea was to possess and to sanc-
tify, like a connoisseur. The absorption would come by *osmosis,*
as the stale teacher's joke went around those days. Bud would
see an edition he needed, and the two of them—him and
Brian—would go out like pirates, shoving books in their underwear, cocks dumbly smudging the covers, breathlessly sharing
their booty blocks away from the crime. Real *Guide to Kulchur*
vultures.

What was he doing writing for the movies? How had it
happened? His plan was always to bypass, to *transcend* the
business of his father. He'd taught himself to type as if he were
a boy of noble birth learning to fence or hunt or horseback; one
night his father drunkenly mocked his efforts. Bud cried, and
Morris said, It's Little Lord Fauntleroy. *Go ahead, cry a little.*
In the middle of the night he came and sat on the bed and said
he was sorry. Moe called him his Only Son. Those were his
terms of endearment: he was the Father Image and Bud the
Only Son.

What had he been doing with all those books if not arming
himself for an assault on *Literature*? He'd made a few incursions, but never sustained anything beyond a few pages—meandering prose poems and short short story O. Henry rip-offs. His

father died and the Doctor drifted away; Bud dropped out of school and worked in a bookstore in Century City. At lunchtime friends came in and saw him behind the counter. They thought it was a prank.

One day he left work, bought a three-hundred-dollar leather vest, threw his wallet away and hitched north. He headed for the now-mythic boyhood suburb called the Arbor, dreaming of the lost bower. He got stuck in a halfway house near the Heights instead. They called it the Foundation; Bud was classified a "character disorder." They shaved his head and gave him a set of unfashionable clothes from a warehouse full of donated things (one of the "counselors" got his vest). In this zoney time he worked as a busboy in the Foundation-owned restaurant. Dolly found out where he was and flew up there, walking into the place in her Adolfo. Seeing each other like that was weird and awful.

Tucked away in the back of Dolly's closet were ornate trophies from the Paul Henreid Dance Cotillion, the one Bud attended at the Beverly Palm Hotel when he wasn't shoving fiction down his pants: first place in Waltz, Swing, Cha-Cha, Fox-Trot. Mr. Henreid always hung around the ballroom with his camera—the kids knew he was famous for inventing something having to do with cigarettes. Morris never went to the yearly Trophy Ball and Bud and Dolly always won the Mother and Son competition. She was petite and knew how to follow.

There was a shoebox of old photos and he looked at some of Brian. He even had the laminated med-school I.D. clip-on. An unopened package contained the Doctor's .357 and all his alarm clocks and the thing that allowed you to answer the phone when it rang simply by saying "Hello?" into the air. Bud hadn't figured out how that one worked yet. It was funny, but he'd never had friends over, not even the Doctor. He was always ashamed at living in an apartment, instead of a house—you were marked if you didn't have a house. Dolly never seemed to care about meeting Bud's friends; though when the Doctor died, she wept, and he was touched. When Dolly and Brian's mother met at the funeral, the woman shrieked: "Bud has a mother! Bud has a mother!"

He'd moved back with Dolly to finish *Toy Soldier* without the pressure of rent. It was a new script and he was high on it. Now that Bud had finished the third act, he'd be able to work more limo hours and get his own place again. After he sold the script to one of the studios, he'd mention in interviews the emotional ordeal of coming back to his mother's house to live, as old already as Dante was when he entered the woods. There would be no shame.

He was supposed to meet Dolly at the old Bellagio Road house, in Bel Air. God, that was going to be strange. Morris was probably haunting around it somewhere. Twenty-five years since they'd lived there.

Bud had a little headache and went to her bathroom for the pills. He inherited Dolly's migraines and sometimes had to go to the emergency room to get a shot to stop throwing up. Today it wasn't so bad, but he knew if he took the codeine, his appetite would go away. He wanted to lose about twelve pounds. Being overweight made him unhappy. Maybe he was just telling himself he had a headache so he could take the pills. He took so many pills with the Doctor that he learned to swallow them without water, even the big orange Darvons.

Brian was fat in the coffin. Bud hadn't seen him for two weeks and got the call that he was dead; he looked at him in the mortuary and thought, boy, he really ballooned. There was a twenty-four-hour Jack in the Box near the County General dorm where the two gorged themselves. When each put on twenty pounds, the Doctor got out the amphetamines and they stayed wired for a week. The drug companies used to send the dope gratis to young residents while they waited for their BNDDs, the codes that allowed them to write "triplicates" for the serious stuff. The Doctor also had coarse yellow powder that burned the sinuses and made your ticker hammer for about eighteen hours. You could take a ton of Valium to slow down, but about forty minutes later the heart started marathoning again. When all failed, there was a giant green pill that could knock it down; if you bit into it, the fluid inside stung your mouth. The Doctor always joked about "taking the edge off" and "circling the drain"—later he realized Brian was shooting up something the anesthesiologists used to put people under. Bud was never like the Doctor, he was a pussy with drugs because he didn't have a death wish. He hadn't taken anything for months the day he learned the Doctor was dead.

Bud swallowed the pills and sat down on the bowl. It was a crampy space and there was a white fluff rug around the toilet. He felt too big, like an interloper in a dollhouse. There were enormous bottles of perfume all around. One of them, a Chanel No. 5 that Dolly had for years, was actually a display window prop. Maybe she stole it, like she once stole dinner plates from the Beverly Palm. He picked up a magazine and flipped to an article about broke yuppie children unabashedly returning to the parents' nests. Downstairs, his phone was ringing. He caught it as the man was leaving a message.

Peter Dietrich introduced himself as a writer for the *News*. He said he met Bobby Feld at a party and the agent gave him Bud's number. He was doing an article on the movies and was interested in talking to screenwriters.

"Would you be available for lunch?" the reporter asked.

"When?"

"Thursday next week?"

Bud was driving the limousine Thursday.

"Thursday's bad. I'd say meet me out in Burbank, but I have to crawl back over the hill to Lorimar for a lunch," he lied. "How about Friday?"

"Friday's great."

Bud felt the slow warmth of credibility returning to his limbs.

"You're in the Hollywood area, aren't you?"

"I can meet you anywhere."

"No, no. How about the Old World? Or Mirabelle's?"

"Too weird. Let's go to Hugo's," Bud said cockily. "Do you know where it is?"

"It's on Melrose, isn't it?"

"Santa Monica."

"Oh, sure, Hugo's! On the corner. I've been there for breakfast. Great."

"Friday at noon."

"I'll make the reservation."

"See you then."

"Looking forward to it, Bud."

᙮᙮᙮

As the limo went through the car wash, he wondered what he was going to say to Peter Dietrich of the *News*.

He felt as much a part of the Business as a tourist on a studio tram. It was almost two years since someone had hired him, giving him a thousand dollars for jokes a cable special never used. It wasn't always that way. Once upon a time, in the post-Foundation days, a druggie director he met while working at Samuel French hired him to write a soap opera spoof that flukily went into production ten months later. Like a dream. It was financed by Australians and picked up for distribution by one of the majors before it even started shooting. Bud never needed an agent because his hairless boyhood pal Don Bloom handled the contract.

Then the big boys came after him—CAA, William Morris, ICM—and all the snazzy boutiques full of Young Turks. He was so hot even restaurant parking valets sensed his charisma, flashing ratty kiss-ass smiles like he was Bill Murray. When he went to meet his suitors, their secretaries were coy and careful, as if briefed on the seriousness of the courtship. They drowned him in cappuccino, crudités and cranberry sparklers, and Bud made them laugh. The ease of his delivery, always full of innuendo, made him feel legendary—savvy, blessed, sanguine. That was the way the world should be, *forever and ever*. He remembered what an agent said to him at the end of a superheated gang bang in which he was extolled by the entire staff of CAA with the felicity of a strong and sensitive lover: "They're going to start throwing money at you and they're never going to stop."

Bud chose not to go with CAA.

The Talent Agency was a spin-off formed by a trio of perspicacious renegades that included Bobby Feld. Feld wasn't a veteran, but the Industry's perception of him as a future power was undisputed. He already had a stable of clients slightly outside mainstream Hollywood, a sexy group who wrote quirky, quality films and were sought for interesting projects. None of them were hacks, though none were beneath doing a quick job for money—Feld orchestrated both worlds for them well. They were mordant and they were rich and that was enough for Bud. It was a smart, unexpected choice and no one faulted him. He made the phone calls to the losing agents like a potentate, thanking them for their interest.

His "Australian" movie (he no longer called it a spoof—it was a *satire*) hummed along in preproduction and on the first day of principal photography they gave him sixty thousand dollars. The money might have bought him time to write a spec script, an original, something the studios could bid for. Instead, he acquired an old two-tone Mercedes and a twelve-hundred-dollar Claude Montana pigskin raincoat. He traveled to Marin County to watch Pauline Kael debate Jean-Luc Godard and stayed at the Mark Hopkins, Morris always liked the Mark, then he cruised Pacific Heights in a rented yellow Fleetwood, like a cinéaste pimp. He sat in the car in his raincoat, leather on leather, across from the bramble labyrinths of his boyhood parks, dreaming of the Secret Garden, indulging in a little bittersweet how-far-I've-come melancholy-movie moment. Maybe he'd make the trip to the Arbor, if he had the time. He should probably get back to L.A. *After all, I have a picture in production.* He thought about boyhood things, coin collections and stamps from Zanzibar, Mickey Mantle and Orlando

Cepeda and Roger Maris and Willie Mays trading cards. There sat screenwriter Bud Wiggins in the plush, rented seat, a man with a *life*.

Six weeks later, his very first feature wrapped. He knew that once it appeared in the theaters, his price would go up. That was a rule of thumb. Bud sat back, savoring hubris. He attended parties and dinners, marked by the special iridescence of those with something "in the can." Then one day there were funny rumors. The director-addict's editing period was protracted (even allowing for the postproduction Genius Syndrome); Bud heard the picture was a shambles. The Aussies didn't return his calls—the director had fled to New York. Bobby Feld told him the distributors had arranged a number of marketing previews and the audience response, scribbled obscenely on ratings cards, had studio executives upchucking on their suede Theodore Man trousers.

Feld got him some fast rewrite work for undistinguished producers and Bud waited for his movie to appear. It would . . . *somehow*. It *had* to. Why wouldn't it? He told himself none of it mattered. It was a *movie*, it had been *made*, he had *written* it—that's what was important. The more he heard about its poor health, the less he cared, so long as they dumped it into the domain. He started openly trashing it, as if the whole venture were an ex-wife who'd gone mad and was setting fire to bags of shit left at his doorstep. The trades kept a steady stream of grim, laconic updates, the way newspapers write about chronically comatose dictators.

Whenever Bud heard something hopeful, he knew it was like calling a coronary "indigestion." The *News* even did a piece about a crop of in-trouble movies, referring to his own as "an apparently failed comedy." He imagined Dolly saving the clippings for a great Gothic memory album, a mausoleum to keep beside the Adolfos and dance kudos. Bud thought of writing a literate memoir on the unmaking of the movie and selling it to one of the prestigious film magazines. He'd call it "An Apparently Failed Comedy" and would name names. But he worried a piece like that might backfire. It was important to be perceived as rising above it all. Maybe he'd hire a publicist. Maybe the thing would come out and make a hundred million anyway.

Bud was cavalier and tried to dissociate himself from the ugliness. With crafty sangfroid, he told people he was thinking of having his writing credit removed. He never had a chance to: the film was shelved. The script that had been passed from hand to hand like a black-market curio, the script that agents gave their clients as an exemplar of state-of-the-art ensemble black comedy, offbeat characters and raucous sex—well, it was very suspicious now, like something Klaus Kinski used to haul around the rain forest.

Bobby Feld's attentiveness decayed. He didn't like it when things went poorly for his clients; he couldn't sow crops with water from a bad well. The agent was frustrated by his efforts, his frustration turned to contempt and soon he wanted to piss on Bud. The screenwriter remembered the day the transference was complete. Every now and then Bud read an article somewhere about a young director or indie producer and phoned TTA to have one of his scripts sent out as a writing sample. Once he called to double-check a request and Feld's assistant snapped that Bud didn't have to tell him things more than once and hung up. That night the miffed writer called the agent at home and Feld asked how he got his number, forgetting he'd given it to Bud himself. Before Bud said a word about it, he was told that no one could deal with a client calling five or six times a day. Bud shouted at Feld that he only called twice and didn't need a fag secretary hanging up on him and the agent shouted back that Bud was getting crazy. That was that.

So Bud Wiggins became the tawdry vaudevillian who never hears from his agent, and he didn't mind that much. Let it cool. Having a nonagent was better than having no agent at all. He checked in every few months with Feld's office, making sure they knew how to reach him. His contracts were long expired, but still Bud preferred to think of himself as represented by Bobby Feld of TTA. The call from Peter Dietrich had confirmed the erratic relationship's durability. Maybe it was Feld's way of burying the hatchet; it might even be a sign he was about to throw something Bud's way. After all, Feld was in the business of making money. Bud felt sure if the agent could fill a slot with an old client, he would. It was a business. He'd sell scrap as quick as sterling.

Then it came to him: he would give *Toy Soldier,* his just-finished stateside Vietnam script, to his old agent.

MMM

He was nearing the Bel Air gate and got a flutter thinking about the old house. Someone honked. A stretch limo pulled up beside him. It was a Chilean chauffeur from the Beverly Palm. Ramón Rivera was one of the drivers who actually owned their limousines, and Bud sometimes worked for him. He was an eccentric, with a thick, sensual accent. He was stout and goldly melanous and reminded Bud of the salt shakers they used to sell at the Luau restaurant gift shop on Rodeo Drive.

"Almodóvar, what's happening!"

"*¿Qué pasa?*" Bud said, unenthused.

"I am going to the *aeropuerto,* Almodóvar, to pick up a Jewish cocksucker like yourself."

He used to call Bud Orson Welles, because of an incident that happened years ago, when Bud and the Chilean first met. The name had metamorphosed; Ramón was one swarthy, squirrely, topical hipster.

"You're really freaky, Ramón." Bud waited for the light to change.

"I am *Freaky Friday,* starring Jodie Foster. Don't be thin-skinned, Almodóvar, like a girl." Ramón smiled weirdly, like a Day of the Dead doll. "Don't be defensive, like a *maricón.* "

Bud sped away.

Bud drove past it at first because the house was hidden by unfamiliar hedges. He made a U-turn and entered the driveway where Dolly's car was parked.

The mansion, with its spiral staircase and open spaces, had awed him as a boy and was still formidable. It was the first place they lived in Los Angeles, before the bad times and all the apartments. When Bud was a baby, they owned the house in Georgia and after that, the Arbor house, and the house in the Heights. Then Morris got the job offer at Goldwyn and the studio helped find them the rental in Bel Air. Dolly thought the place was ostentatious—it suited a family of five—but Morris convinced her they would be entertaining, they'd have houseguests, they might even have more children. It was all a write-off. Dolly said it was time to buy again, but Moe Wiggins refused, he was done with owning houses. He wanted the show-case. Moving backward—so senseless! Her husband had de-moted them, just to bankroll his spendthrift ways, to hit town like a big man. And worse, she'd acquiesced, lost her nerve. Had she threatened to divorce him, history might have been changed. So Dolly steeled herself in her own cowardice and suffered the shock of recognition: herself, beached in a world of rented things. It was calamitous. Bud had heard it all before, and braced himself.

"Buddy, can you believe it? When I found out they were showing it, I had to call you. Come: hug your mother!"

Dolly Wiggins's thin arms stretched out from Chanel sleeves. She hugged her son in the empty living room of the enormous house on Bellagio Road. Bud thought his mother looked pretty good, just like the rich women she waited on at the store—she still worked part-time at Hoffmann-Dougherty of Beverly Hills, a job held from before Moe's death. Dolly was trying to break into the real estate game, where she said there was crazy money.

"Don't think I'm getting a commission, are you kidding me? I'm helping Maureen, one of the agents, a client at the store for years, a real bund leader, that one. A German. But I have to eat her shit. I'm just sitting, waiting for that Nazi cunt. Do you think they'll give me a dime? The *fucks.* I'm working at the store tonight, the big sale, they're closing at ten, can you believe it? From here I go right to the store. I'm killing myself, Buddy."

He scanned the room. "The place looks great."

It was empty and white and ready to be filled with beautiful things

"Do you remember this house?"

"Of course I remember it."

"You were eleven. Your father was working for Goldwyn. We could have bought this house, it was a hundred and ten thousand in '66. Do you know what they're asking, Buddy?"

Dolly's mood swooped down like a plane on a dark tarmac, bellicose, gathering speed.

"Three-five, Bud! Three and a half million! I'm showing it to the Japs as a teardown! Because that fuck your father had to *rent,* like a pimp! I begged him to buy it Bud, literally begged your father!"

"Mom, stop—"

"I sit in that apartment on Rexford Drive with the carpet they won't clean and the shitty drapes for fifteen years and I'm afraid to move! Every dime I get pays off that piece-of-shit-your-father's creditors, for twenty years, Bud! You don't know! You don't know your father was a gambler, with Vegas and the gin clubs over on Robertson—thousands, he lost. His friends laughed at him, they had millions! They *still* have millions. And here I am choking from debt and he is laughing in hell!"

Bud saw it would probably be all right—"laughing in hell" was a stock, wiggy phrase that rarely foreshadowed anything too heavy. It *telegraphed,* as they said in script parlance, that her heart wasn't in it. Which was welcome, if a little strange, given the place's Chekhovian potential. Maybe that was it—the setting was too perfect, too tragic; Dolly didn't have her usual ironic distance. The air was so rich, her wild shopworn soliloquy couldn't breathe.

It was a good house. His mother used to call it a *pavillon,* with a sad, funny French accent. After they moved out, when things fell apart at the studio for Morris, they had a series of apartments, whorish approximations of a home. Dolly would canvass the new space and kill the heartache of rental by worshiping the clean white carpets of the new place, setting her white gold-freaked antiquey cabinets on the posh fabric's lunar cushion. Of each new place, Bud heard her stagey, heart-eaten braggadocio on the phone to inquiring friends: "It is *sprawling.*"

Moe was drinking and grandiose, a paper general planning his assault on moviedom. He had failed as a development executive and was going to be a producer now. A demonic Eloise, he imagined the apartment as a vast "suite," sitting on the white plains of Dolly's precious carpets in his skimpy black underwear from the West Hollywood fag shop Ah Men, his papers fanned before him like a lunatic's deposition. Each time they moved—every two years, two years was the most Moe could stand of one place—he needed a penthouse. They'd have to go into the savings, "digging into the principal," as Dolly put it, because Moe liked getting into the elevator and pressing PH; he needed a penthouse with its instruments of war—the wet bar, the prairie of white carpet, the wraparound fireplace—mise-en-scène for the domestic Armageddons, taunts, howls and hysteria, invasions, explosions, skirmishes, betrayals and sexual roughhouse. From his distant bedroom Bud tried through roaring heart to descramble pounding feet, yelps, strangled respirations, scary secrets, frauds and friendly fire. He wasn't the worst of soldiers; he was a prodigy of wakefulness.

He thought about his old room. If Dolly'd shut up a minute, he could even take a little tour. A carom shot might get her off the Old Subject.

"When are you going in the hospital?"

"Friday." She brightened. As they walked through the hexagonal breakfast room, runway lights appeared; her wings steadied. From the tower Bud would talk her down. "Your mother has to get up at four in the morning. Dr. Naugawitz is giving me a price because I leased out his Malibu home. Thirty thousand dollars a month, Buddy! Right on the sand, next to Dyan Cannon." She leveled a beady eye at him. "Jesus, you look handsome. You got so fucking thin. *Gorgeous.*"

It was time for Bud Wiggins, lothario and son, to get out of there. He was meeting Wylie Guthrie, King of Story Structure, at the Commissary and didn't want to be late. The screenwriter was starting to feel creepy anyway. It wasn't his house. It wasn't anyone's. It was depressing—his mother's remorseful harangues made him feel like a homeless person with AIDS.

Dolly followed him outside, waving her credit card. She wanted him to use it until he was on his feet again. Bud said he didn't need it and she said not to tell his mother what he didn't need. She shoved it in his pocket.

"You'll pay me back with a mansion. Did you know your mother was writing a book, like a Judith Krantz?"

"You always said you could write a best-seller."

"When I read the shit they write—your mother's gonna do it, Buddy, she's writing the Real Estate Novel! Your mother was a journalism major, top in her class." Her jaw clenched and she darkened like a totem, a clairvoyant getting a signal; Bud feared she'd speak in tongues. "Tutoring that *fuck,* with tears in his eyes, afraid he'd fail. I pushed your father through college, are you kidding me, Bud? Sitting up with him all night so he would pass his exams. Your father was not a bright man."

"I have to go. I'm meeting someone at the Commissary."

He opened the door of the limo and got in.

"Why don't you write something for television? They're making fortunes. You don't even have to write, you can have a 'created by' and still get the royalty."

"Ma, I finished my script," he said, calmly dignified, as if reminding her he'd recently taken the vows. "It's for the movies. You know I don't write for television."

"God forbid!" Her eyes blazed blue in her pale head. "Who cares about Vietnam, we've seen so much already! Why don't you do a *Home Alone,* you're so brilliant. Who are you meeting?"

"A famous writer."

"You could be meeting a Billy Quintero. Your mother would like him to be in the miniseries of *Beverly Hills Adjacent.* "

"What's that?"

"Your mother's book!"

"Billy Quintero doesn't do television."

"Then you two should meet!" She laughed at her little joke and Bud smiled, then grew concerned.

"What about Friday? Are you going to stay in the hospital overnight?"

"They send you home, same day. They drive you. I got a nurse for two days, the insurance pays."

"You won't need me for anything?"

"Nothing," she said, with a flourish. "Only to kiss your soon-to-be-gorgeous-mother's swollen cheek. Do you think I'd ask my son to nurse his mother? Even though I used to hold your head while you vomited." Dolly stretched her neck to the sky and crowed, *"E-zih-zinee!"*—the peculiar cry from the Language that he'd heard before memory, meaning glee and good tidings. Its origin was murky but might have had something to do with the Zizanie cologne his father used to buy, Zizanie and Schimmelpennincks from Dunhill's, down the street from Romanoff's. The phone inside was ringing and Dolly went to the front door. "You'll win an Academy Award, you'll see," she shouted. "Next week I want to introduce you to a Brazilian millionairess! *E-zih-zinee! Fahr fahr carmintrate!"*

⁓⁓⁓⁓

Bud felt the pills work as he went through the studio gate. He was excited about his lunch, getting that old integrated feeling again. Feeling *a part of.*

About six months ago, he took a story structure class and had kept in touch with its instructor, Wylie Guthrie. Bud bounced ideas off him—together they'd find the stuff of $2.5 million spec scripts. He was flattered the teacher had taken an interest. At first, the screenwriter was embarrassed to be in class at all because it was like a confession he couldn't write. The truth was, he was having trouble with the third act of his script. He'd heard that well-known people with good credits often took the course as a refresher and that mitigated his shame. Wylie Guthrie himself was a rich TV writer trying to break into features; he had an office on the lot and was going to be the first person to read *Toy Soldier*.

Guthrie wasn't in the Commissary. Maybe he was running late. Bud doubted he was being stood up—they'd left him a drive-on pass. He got some juice from the machine and sat down. He'd wait a few minutes, then take a brisk walk around the studio. That would give Guthrie time to arrive, then Bud could come in a little breathless, like someone on the move.

Then he remembered there was a dining room with a separate entrance. He'd eaten there a few times, back when he was hot. It was mostly for executives and chummy above-the-liners; there were linen tablecloths and you needed a reservation. Bud decided to have a look.

He was sitting at a table with a bookish-looking woman, and beckoned Bud over.

"Who said it, Wiggins?" he asked eagerly. "Who said it is not enough to succeed, but our friends should also fail? La Rochefoucald or William Goldman?"

"I think it was Merv Griffin."

Guthrie laughed raucously, full of counterfeit life. He was in his fifties and had an affected, street fighter sensibility.

"That's Wiggins!" He turned to the woman. "Funny man. *Very* talented writer. Genie Katz-Cohen, meet Bud Wiggins— who you should know."

He shook her hand and she smiled like it was costing her money. Then she stood to leave.

"Order something, Wiggins. Have a decaf Al Pacino." Guthrie walked her a few steps from the table, lowering his voice. "So, will you move on this, Genie? Because tell them, as you know, my plate is getting full and once they come in me, I'm gonna be pregnant. I'm very fertile."

Then he mumbled something in her ear and she left. When the master of story structure returned to the table, he looked crestfallen.

"One of my agents. Just got a terrible piece of news—guy she broke up with has AIDS."

"Gay?"

Guthrie nodded grimly. "In a hospice. Kept it from her. So, Wiggins," he said, suddenly cheery, "you been writing?"

"I got a first act of something."

"The road to hell is paved with first acts! But that's *good,* you're *writing.* I like my kids to write. Otherwise, I feel like I'm stealing your seven hundred bucks." Bud casually laid his script on the table. "What's this?"

"This is it. *Toy Soldier.*"

"Bravo, Wiggins!" He baptized it with a slap, then slid it into a leather portfolio. He got a sly look. "I hope there's more than just a first act. I'll read it the weekend. What else you got?"

"An idea for a psychological action picture."

"You have a contradiction in terms." He threw a vapid wave to someone across the room.

"It's a mystery movie about incest. A lady cop who had a thing with her father."

"It's a little Canadian. I mean, watch it—it could be Canadian. I'm bored with incest, but explore." He stared off into the room. "Jesus, look at Quintero."

Bud turned and saw the famous star sitting at a table with Joseph Harmon, the red-haired head of the studio. Between them was a man with a luxurious white mustache whom Bud didn't recognize.

"He's got total approval—script, director, everything. A *fuhcocktuh* actor! The studio wanted me to exec-produce a picture of his. I said no way! You work for Billy Quintero, you got to kiss his ass so deep you go home each night wearing a turtleneck. And it isn't cashmere."

"Do you know Harmon?"

"What's there to know?" He smirked and leaned into Bud.

"You know what the difference between Joseph Harmon and a refrigerator is?"

"Tell me."

"A fridge don't fart when you take the meat out."

Guthrie laughed hard enough to start a coughing jag that made Bud want to run. He had to leave soon anyway because he left his chauffeur's cap in the TV room of the hotel garage. He was working today and the dispatcher wanted him to get it before he went out on a call.

"What else you bring me, Wiggins?"

"I took one of those tours through Beverly Hills."

"I like it already."

"I thought: what if there was a fugitive on the bus with all the tourists and when they pass Bette Midler's house, he gets out of the bus—"

"How does he get out of the bus? Do they allow that?"

"Haven't worked it out yet. The guy holds Midler hostage—"

"Wasn't that an *I Love Lucy*?"

"Maybe Midler plays someone who's trying to make a comeback and she milks it. Maybe there's a crooked business manager and Midler's got some crazy relatives visiting from the bayou or Miami or something. Or a delinquent stepson from a first marriage. The whole thing takes place inside this mansion she can't afford anymore. It becomes a media circus."

"A comedy."

"Yeah, but with reconciliation."

Guthrie sat there, lost in thought. Then he looked straight into Bud's eyes for the first time and said, "Not there yet." When Bud started to talk again, Guthrie said, "Focus." Then he said it again, like a life-lesson mantra.

"What about doing *Lord of the Flies,*" Bud said, "but with the guys from Drexel? You know—arbitrageurs stranded on an island—"

"This, I like! But now I gotta go." He snapped his fingers toward one of the waiters. "*¡Hombre! ¡La Cuenta!*"

While they waited for the check, Guthrie did his intellectual raconteur guru shtick, a fractious discourse on his favorite "big theme," the War Between Men and Women. It was apropos of nothing—that was his prerogative. Wylie Guthrie was a great gaudy, galling book, a roiling work-in-progress, and now and then he privileged you with a peek amid the pages. He karate-chopped the space in front of him into segments as he spoke: men looked at women and saw Martians. Men were very pissed off at women—the epidemic of serial killers proved it. He kept saying serial murders were "endemic" and "pandemic," not just an aberration. "An aberration is a"—he groped for a word—"an aberration is a . . . *cold.* Something you get *once in a while.* These murders of women are going on every week in fifty states!"

He'd been married for thirty years; Bud met his wife once at the end of one of the workshops and she struck him as a mommy type. The check came and Guthrie signed it. He shook Bud's hand as he left.

"About *Toy Soldier,* Wylie—I need you to tell me if you think it's too black."

"You know what they say about black comedy, don't you, Wiggins? It's a gray area!"

He retrieved his cap and the dispatcher gave him an airport pickup: Mr. Robert Feld. The agent was arriving from New York in an hour and a half.

On the way down, Bud stopped at home to get another copy of his script. He'd planned on registering it at the Writers Guild first, but that could wait.

His client stood beside the baggage carousel with a willowy, husky-voiced woman. Bobby Feld was thirty-two now and looked like some kind of savvy dagger. Bud breathed deeply and approached, deciding to leave on his cap.

"Hi, Bobby. It's Bud Wiggins."

Feld shook Bud's hand as if he were expecting him, then introduced him to Krizia Folb. He asked how the writing was going and it was all very pleasant. The agent was masterful—elisions were his sustenance. Bud got the car from the lot and by the time he brought it around, they were waiting at the curb with a porter. As they pulled into traffic, Krizia Folb was in the middle of a story.

"So he's under there—"

"Where'd you say he picked her up?" Feld interrupted.

"Jesus, Bobby, you're not listening! Mortons, at the bar."

"And she's a hooker—"

"No, she's an investment banker. Of course, she's a hooker! So he takes her back to the Bel Air—"

Feld suddenly talked to the back of Bud's head. "We're going to be dropping off Miss Folb first. Do you know where the Towers are?" Bud said he did and Feld thanked him. He hadn't used Bud's name yet and the screenwriter felt a little deflated. Maybe Feld needed the distance.

"Would you let me for chrissake *finish*, Bobby?"

"He takes her back to the Bel Air—"

"And they have a drink and they get in bed. And he feels under there . . . and it's *long* and it's *hard.*" Feld said *Jesus!* and the woman started to laugh, then pulled herself together. "So he says, 'What's this?' And she looks at him—and he's starting to see the cheekbones and the acne pitting—she looks at him and says, 'That's my *clitoris*'!"

They howled awhile, then spoke in undertones. Bud felt the distance again. The agent made a phone call while Krizia Folb stared into the night. When they dropped her off, the screenwriter handed the bags to the doorman and waited beside the car.

"You should come and make movies for me, Bobby."

"I'm an *agent*, Krizia. Spielberg sends a card on my birthday, Billy Quintero calls me back *same day.* Bertolucci confides in me, Michelle Pfeiffer has me to barbecue, I'm in fucking heaven. Okay? And I wake up in the morning and don't have to think what studio I'm working at today."

She kissed him on the cheek. "All you need now is a wife.

To meet someone nice. Someone who'll say those three wonderful little words: *that's my clitoris!"* She screamed and ran inside.

Finally alone together, Bud told the agent how he'd laid low and written an original. Feld was gracious and inquisitive, and Bud decided not to elaborate; best to tantalize. With some eagerness, he promised to read *Toy Soldier* and Bud knew he wasn't bullshitting because a finished script was still the most valuable of commodities.

ᴀᴀᴀᴀ

When he got home, Dolly was cleaning out the downstairs closet. She was into one of the shoeboxes, full of snapshots of her and Moe from the forties and fifties.

"Your mother once had a house, in Macon. Do you remember the house in Macon?"

She was 105 pounds and wore a baby-blue jogging suit. She was drinking wine; Bud guessed she was nervous about the surgery. His mother handed him a picture of a black mammy in a smock.

"Do you remember Trudy? Fat black Trudy? A fat black pig, a real *shvartzeh.* I shouldn't say that." She told for the hundredth time the old "cute" story about Bud asking Trudy if she was a Jew. "I'm *Nih-gro,"* she said, and the mammy laughed so hard she almost had a heart attack. Dolly burrowed through the boxes and his mind's eye saw Trudy trucking through the overwaxed linoleum halls on blubbery legs, all perspiration and Lysol. What were they doing in Macon?

Moe Wiggins was a campus DJ in Illinois, that's where he and Dolly met, he had a good radio voice and an aptitude for Broadcasting. He liked talking into a mike. Bud remembered that whenever his father used a tape recorder at home, he always gravely intoned, *Testing one two three, test one two three, this is a test,* like he was about to announce where to find the fallout shelters. Out of college, he worked for a local station owned by Jerry Fairchild, who became his big broadcasting boss. Handsome Jerry Fairchild. Everything was Fairchild-this and Fairchild-that and Moe didn't particularly like it but was starting to make good money and even offered stock, so he didn't complain. When Bud was born, he dubbed Fairchild to be Godfather, a kind of obsequious homage *(your father was a kiss-ass)* that carried with it no obligations whatsoever. Fairchild owned a string of radio stations and sent his boy Moe down south to fix one of them that was in trouble. Bud was four years old. They stayed in Macon awhile with Trudy the *shvartzeh.* The house was set way back and Bud could remember their mailbox stuck on a road, wide as a river, its gutters choked with honeysuckle. He learned how to suck the fluid out and this was a kind of divinity. It became part of the traveling Garden he carried with him for all time.

When he got the Macon station on its feet, Fairchild sent him to San Francisco and Moe commuted to the city from the Arbor, across the bay. Dolly didn't enjoy moving around so much, but Moe didn't mind, he couldn't stand still anywhere too much. The only part that bothered him was having Fairchild tell him where to go, like he was a whore.

Moe swooped down on these fucked-up stations like an angry messiah. He was good at it, even though Dolly said his efforts always made him a "hated man." He was sometimes a vicious, abrasive *Communicator;* had to be, to get the job done. Morris Wiggins really liked to *communicate,* that was his college major, Communications—how he loved that word and its promise, it was his *field,* he used to say—Broadcasting and Communicating and promoting, ad sloganeering and jingles, *selling people on people.* He even formed a company, Morris Wiggins Communications, Inc., paying someone five thousand dollars to come up with a sovereign, swaggering logo *(your father was a little Hitler).* He brought Bud to his new office and the employees cooed over the little boy as he peeked from the big desk like John John Kennedy. Yes, *Communication* was the thing he knew through and through—he sermonized his son with it, an endless alcoholic rhapsody, and the word eventually acquired for Bud a bland and totalitarian occultism that encompassed everything from smoke signals to early Torah studies.

Bud flopped on the sofa bed and watched Dolly, cross-legged on the floor, sort through the pictures. She stared at a photo of a house as if it were a child long dead. "The place in the Arbor was the last home your mother owned." She had jumped to California, land of the *pavillons,* and was getting a little declamatory. So be it: the sermon of Houses. Let it ride, he said to himself. She passed the old Kodachrome to her son.

"With the gorgeous lanai, and the trampoline. Do you remember? He couldn't live in the city, no. Your father had to live in the Arbor with the luaus and the thousand-dollar sandboxes. Custom-made, that sandbox! Are you kidding me, Bud? Custom-made and paid for by Morris Wiggins Communications, Inc!" *Sandbox:* it was like remembering a Model T, a glorious extinct thing. He could feel the dense heat packed around his burrowed little boy bones. "A gorgeous house. We could barely afford the payments. I wanted to work, he wouldn't let me. Do you know who lived in the Arbor? The Gettys. That's right. Your father had to live with the Gettys, that was his sickness. Some of those homes had a hundred rooms, like Versailles. Smelling of shit." She smiled wickedly to herself. "I remember from college, tutoring your fuck father. Do you know Versailles, the palace? They had no plumbing back then, *e-zih-zinee.* Can you imagine, your mother remembering her studies from college? Brilliant, your mother! *Fahr fahr carmintrate!"* She pulled out a beatific charcoal drawing she'd done of Bud when he was fourteen. "The Young Scholar" was written below.

They stayed there for two years. They stayed everywhere for two years. The thing the screenwriter remembered most about the Arbor, like the way he remembered Macon's wide road with its honeysuckle, was its eucalyptus trees. They drove him to a private mysticism that he eventually linked to the Secret Garden. He could call up the eucalyptus trees at any time, but the Garden and its fountain remained elusive. He was always trying to place them; he knew they weren't part of any backyard.

Morris got tired of commuting and they moved to a lavish apartment in the Heights, on the hill atop the city, within a stone's throw of the Gettys'. Always the Gettys. Then he decided he didn't want to be in radio anymore—it couldn't contain his talent and ambition. It was too small-time; he wanted to work in the movies. They had a friend from college who was an up-and-comer in the Business. He got the studio to offer Moe a job in marketing and the Wigginses moved to Bel Air.

"Your father quit Jerry Fairchild without consulting me!" She had begun noodling with the needle and almost found a vein. "Your father was a *radio man,* he didn't know from movies! Are you kidding me? But Joe Harmon had a thing for him."

"Joseph Harmon?"

"We went to school with that fag, in Chicago."

Bud couldn't believe what he was hearing.

"Harmon got Dad the studio job?"

"He always had a crush on your father. We all *joked* about it together. He gave your father the movie bug and helped him get a little nothing job in publicity. Then your father—the talker—wangled his way into an executive office. But Moe didn't like to work for anyone. He had *personality clashes* with the brass. Your father was a hated man."

"Why didn't you ever tell me this?"

"No reason! Oh, Bud, Harmon would never do anything for you! Don't you think if I thought Harmon would do something for you I would have told you years ago? *Nothing,* Bud! Oh no, Joseph Harmon—'she,' we used to call him 'she'—"

Dolly unearthed a photo of her husband standing with a younger, thinner Harmon, he of the exuberant trademark red hair. Bud gawked at it while she spoke of the time Moe started to drink too much, quitting his job at the studio to become an independent producer, blowing potential investors to fifteen-hundred-dollar dinners at Perino's. A world of senseless dinners, Fabergé sandboxes and doom.

"The big man! And I would go into the bathroom and puke, literally puke on the fur I hadn't paid for. And these men and their wives and their mistresses—your father fucked around plenty, believe me—Moe hardly knew them, Bud! They were names Harmon gave him. Harmon had money, he didn't care. His family was very rich and his position at the studio was secure. He told Morris that he was going to leave the studio, that he'd go into partnership with him once your father tested the waters. A *lie!* He never had any intention of leaving the studio, Bud! He just wanted Morris around so he could . . . *jack off.* Your father was *naïve,* he got played for the *fool,* are you kidding me? He bought the caviar and these 'investors'—they weren't investors, they were *leeches*—they all said, *We really got somethin' here.* When your father was in trouble, Harmon cut him off! Are you kidding me? Nobody likes a loser, and your father was a *loser.* And the money was running out and I was dying. So I went to work at Hoffmann-Dougherty's while your father was taking 'investors' to the whorehouse on the hill. Circus Maximus, do you remember? Oh yes. Your father was a pimp. Always at the 'Losers Club' on La Cienega—*perfect!*"

She closed her eyes; her lids lit up as the blood entered the syringe. Bud went to the toilet and the words turned, as they had countless times before: his father had been played for a fool. He was a *mark,* they *set him up,* a real shakedown at *the whorehouse on the hill.* His mother was Thelma Ritter.

"You don't know how it hurts me not to have a house!" he heard her scream through the door. "I never spent a *dime.* And there was your father with the cigars—they kept them in a special humidor at Dunhill, with Milton Berle's—and the dinners at Romanoff's and Frascati's and the six-hundred-dollar hairbrushes from Milton F. Kreis—oh, yes! The hairbrushes and the preening in the mirror and the faggy underwear from Ah Men. Maybe he and Harmon had something going, I wouldn't put it past your father." Then, sotto voce: "He had to be fucking *some*body 'cause it sure as hell wasn't me."

Bud came back to the room. Dolly was on her feet now, a narcotized chanteuse.

"If he'd played it right, he could have at least got some money out of it! And now I'm running around that store, Buddy"—she welled up—"I don't even have time for lunch, and the women come in, thirty years old, one of them just put in a two-hundred-thousand-dollar tennis court with pagodas—Chuck Connors plays there—and I listen to them and I am dying! Three, four, five, six dresses at a shot and their old creep husbands say, 'Go! Spend!' and these are not cheap, Bud, these are couturier, some come straight from Europe and haven't been shown yet, and I smile and I'm carrying the heavy boxes and they say 'Thank you, Dolly!' and inside, I am dying. And they're flying off in their private jets—one of them has a five-thousand-acre horse farm in Kentucky—"

"Mom, come on! That kind of life—"

"It's a life! That people *lead*. I used to see them in the dressing rooms with their dirty bras and their bodies. Bud, their bodies! You wouldn't believe, *gorgeous*. And filthy, some of them, *crawling*. And not a care in the world."

"I thought you were quitting the store. What about the real estate thing?"

"It's impossible. You can't get in, it's like the Mafia. Your mother got a license for *nothing*. Million Dollar Club *bullshit*. I am going to *fuck* them, you'll see."

He stood up and walked toward her. She let him hold her, then broke away.

"Fuck him! Fuck him! A sick, sick man, your father! May he rot in hell! *Rih-meen!*" she crowed, exultant. "*Rih-meen, e-zih-zinee!* I'm your *mothra, fahr fahr carmintrate. Rih-meen!* Without you, I'd kill myself!"

It got him thinking.

Joseph Harmon had started a prestigious program for first-time directors called Daedalus. Each year the studio financed four or five short, ambitious films as a kind of penance for greed and general bad faith. Anyone was eligible to submit a script. The idea of writing a play had always appealed to Bud, but he lacked a venue. Theater in Los Angeles was a game for Ahmansons and masochists. He decided to write a play-for-film and give it to Daedalus. It would give him something to do while *Toy Soldier* was out there, a cool-down after a long, strenuous run. He'd take some risks—make it dense and loony and operatic, a Strindbergian turn. The deadline was six weeks away and he knew that once he got started, it would pour out of him. The stories were half-hours; compared with the feature length he'd just finished, it would be a breeze. The freakish connection between Harmon and his father certainly couldn't hurt. It would definitely get the powerful man's attention. That's all Bud wanted—his work to be *noticed* by people who mattered. If he got their attention, his talent would do the rest.

He would be practical. The script would take place in one location. For inspiration, he took another ride to Bellagio Road.

Bud parked a few houses down and walked.

At dusk, after a day at the playground, he pedaled his green Sting-Ray home down these leafy streets, ecstatically exhausted, that evocative hour when night starts to fall. He got a ten-speed with fashionably upturned handlebars that were carefully wound with special tape, softening them to the grip. All the boys wrapped their handlebars with care, like master weavers.

Bud slowed as he passed the neighbors' houses. One used to belong to a family who owned a bakery. They were called the Bakers, like an old-country joke (Dolly used to say they were from Hunger); they each weighed half a ton and barely spoke English. The Bakers had sweet, morbid sons and were always inviting the Wigginses over for pool parties—they were the first on the block to have a slide that curled into the deep end. Dolly hated being in the sun. So her husband the Communicator went over to be neighborly and partake in a little freebie sun-worshiping. He'd loll in a floating chaise with a martini while the rays blackened him. He loved getting *dark* and Bud winced when he saw the Baker boys titter at his father's tiny swimsuit.

The next house was grander and belonged to a famous actor. He used to appear at the Wigginses door in midmorning with a snifter, wearing a silk robe, a blasted old lion. He had a sullen, ruined tribe of stepchildren and a young actress wife who overdosed and died when Bud was eleven. On Monday nights Moe went over there to play gin. Once Bud was wheeling his bike into the driveway, back from the supernatural schoolyard, when Nick Adams jumped from his sports car and waved on his way to the game. That moment was fixed for Bud as perfect elysian early-sixties, like the photo he once saw of Russ Tamblyn "tumbling" on Rodeo Drive.

Bud peered at old Casa Wiggins through the hedge and wondered if he'd have trouble getting in. There weren't any cars, so he was certain it was empty. There was one of those big cartoony realtor padlocks clamped on the front door, so Bud went around toward the back. Maybe Dolly left a window unlatched. He tried a side door and it was open. Dolly was really getting *fuhdrait.*

As he stood in the foyer, the idea came to him, like a ball being rolled to his feet: his film would be the story of a woman who finally has her dream house. One day, while her husband is at work and the children at school, she's visited by a stranger. The stranger tells her he lived in the house as a boy. He is passing through town for the last time, he says mysteriously. He wants to come in for a final look. Nice and pragmatic—one location, two actors.

Bud crossed the open space of the living room, once rich with white carpet. As a boy he wasn't allowed to set foot on it. There was a breakfront there, the biggest piece of furniture he'd ever seen. He was always afraid it would topple over. The screenwriter passed the place by the picture window where he relentlessly practiced scales on the white and gold Kawai, his father's splashy gift to Dolly one Christmas. *Your father the parvenu, your father the arriviste, your father* King Shit. She went for anything white and gold. Liberace was big then, so Dolly stuck a garish candelabra on top, next to a menorah. When Bud was through practicing, Moe would spread his papers out on the floor and work on big deals while listening to the hi-fi hidden in the breakfront—"Moulin Rouge," "Some Enchanted Evening," "Bali Ha'i," "The Street Where You Live." He hated his son's arpeggios, his Czerny and Scarlatti; he bought him the sheet music to "Charmaine" and "Moon River" and "The Theme from *The Apartment.*" Bud stuck them deep down in the piano seat.

He went into the den, where Moe smoked cigars and made phone calls on the WATS line. Bud used to brag to his friends about his father's special phone, the one you could call anywhere in the world on and never have to pay. It didn't even have a dial, like it was from the White House or something. On the walls were award plaques for producing jingles, framed articles from *Broadcasting* magazine, photos of Morris Wiggins shaking hands with Phil Silvers and Jerry Fairchild and Dinah Shore and probably Joseph Harmon. Bud first heard Moe say "fuck you" in that room, right over the WATS line, and it spooked him, like watching someone get beat up. He could have been saying fuck you to someone in Thailand and it wouldn't have cost him a penny.

Climbing the spiral staircase to the second floor, Bud had a funny, disconnected memory: being sneezed on by a girl at school and smelling the core of the girl's cold, a sensual musky smell. Was it Cora? He reached the walk-in closet in the hall. Dolly used to sit in there when she was depressed, like it was a chapel. He remembered hearing her cry, muffled by the rows of woolly dresses, her own Secret Garden.

He entered his old bedroom and stared out over the trees. It was the room in which Bud came of age with the dark, learning about his aloneness. In the middle of the night he would hear his parents' faraway voices and, when they stopped, the creaky burglar sounds of the house itself. If it was windy, he strained to listen until his ears felt brittle and achy—murderous movements of imaginary intruders on their way to the foot of the spiral stairs. An hour of this became unbearable; he'd creep to his parents' door, knocking pathetically, ready to burst inside when the killers ascended. Dolly would finally open the door and watch him climb into the enormous bed, where he'd listen some more, the wind only wind now, the maneuverings downstairs untraceable, benign. The bodies snored beside him, each exhalation an anesthetic flooding the room.

Bud thought he heard something downstairs and laughed to himself. It was time to go. He'd grown up and the house had no more to give—it was a curiosity rather than a revelation, as it should be. His visit was a success. He was stoked, ready to begin an outline. Joseph Harmon would know about him soon enough.

The next morning Bud got a call from the office of Bobby Feld.

"Hey, big guy." The old appellation.

"Hi, Bobby."

"Listen, I read the script and I think it's great."

"*Toy Soldier?*" Bud asked incredulously.

"No, *Chinatown.* Of course, *Toy Soldier.* You wrote it, right?"

"I didn't expect you to get to it so fast—"

"I can read a script in ten minutes—yours took two. I'm kidding. It grabbed my heart by the short hairs. What happened to you, Wiggins? You write shit for years—I mean, not shit, but not *thrilling*—you disappear, then bam! you come back out of the blue with a killer. Have you showed it to anyone?"

"No. I just finished it."

He'd been waylaid by Feld's response; he felt like he was overhearing someone else's conversation.

"Good. Don't let anyone see it. We got a sale here, big guy."

He heard a click that meant Feld had moved a switch on the phone so he could say something to his assistant without being heard. The agent himself had shown Bud the gimmick in palmier days. It clicked again and Feld resumed.

"Listen, there's a project over at Universal I think you might be right for. It's for Joel Levitt, you heard of him?"

"No."

"He's a player, lots of stuff in development. I sent your script over and I want to set a meeting."

Bud's stomach flipped over. "You sent my script over? I didn't register it yet."

"Who are you, Art Buchwald? Joel Levitt is a personal friend of mine and your script is coming from TTA. We have a proprietary interest. Look, you haven't worked in about a thousand years and it looks like the ball's starting to roll again for you. So would you please not be a cunt?"

Bud couldn't help but like Bobby Feld. He'd actually missed the banter.

"What do you mean, the ball's starting to roll?"

"A few people have asked what you've been up to."

"Who?"

"Who, who, Gordon Schmoo," he mocked. "At the staff meeting. People still remember the movie you wrote and know it wasn't your fault it didn't come out. So cheer up. I'm going to put Marcus on to give you a time. Levitt's going out of the country, so I think it has to be Friday. Okay, big guy?"

"The reporter called me."

"What reporter?"

"The one from the *News* you gave my number to."

"Right."

He heard the clicking again and Feld said he had to go. Bud impulsively asked if he knew anything about Daedalus and the agent said it was a nice calling card, but if he wanted to direct, why didn't he let Feld try to get him a *real* gig? He had to go again and put him on to Marcus, who got his address and gave him a time for Friday with Levitt, right after his scheduled lunch with the reporter.

A script from Universal came late that afternoon and it was

the first time anything had been messengered to Bud in four years. Someone had torn the title page off. There was a note from Feld attached that said Bud was to read it and pitch his "take" on a rewrite at the Friday meeting.

He treated himself to some Darvon, and drove over to the little subterranean coffee shop at the Beverly Palm for a twenty-five-dollar breakfast. He brought the script with him but wound up making notes about his Daedalus project instead. He wasn't going to be an instant slave to Joel Levitt or Bobby Feld or anyone else. Friday was still a few days off. He knew he had to keep his balance, not get too excited.

tttt

When he got back from the Foundation, Bud lived for a while in a section of town the realtors called Beverly Hills Adjacent. He was depressed. He would go to sleep at four or five in the morning, wake up in the afternoon, order food from the local deli-mart and eat in front of the television. He'd watch the tube until he dropped off. He maintained this schedule for six months. It was during these small-screen vigils that Bud discovered a film which aroused an almost religious fervor in him: *The Best Years of Our Lives*. The story evoked something elegiac and beautiful that strangely soothed him. He loved inserting himself into the schema of this dead forties melodrama, a visit to Shangri-la.

Fredric March and family lived in an apartment that Moe Wiggins could relate to—spacious and too expensive. Sprawling, as Dolly would say. March had a lion's heart and a patriarchal charisma that was sensual and invigorating. His wife, Myrna Loy, was toughly tender, lucid and elegant. In the phraseology of the Children of Alcoholics meetings that Jeanette used to drag Bud to, Loy was March's "codependent," "cosigning" his alcoholism, grooving on its ambience and hard times and mood changes, standing by her man, loving him, Bud thought, the way you'd love a John Cheever or a Bill Styron. And it worked—it was a real *marriage*. It had heart and muscle, heat and historicity. Bud lusted for that family and its opalescent world of morality and epic promise, War and Enterprise, the creamy gateway to the fifties. The Class of '46: when he was eight, he went to Moe's Midwest college reunion and saw the zeitgeist of the era in all the yearbook eyes.

> This will be my shining hour
> calm and happy and bright.
> In my dreams your face will flower
> in the darkness of the night.

When Bud thought of the movie, it was like having real memories from that time. He swallowed the analgesia of all the fake old references; they became his own. He hoped one day to make a son-in-law worthy as Dana Andrews would be to Fredric March.

He scribbled some notes for the short film, using the Bellagio Road house as the stage: the couple with the little boy buy a home they can't afford, but the future is bright. A stranger knocks at the door, a youngish man, Dana Andrews type, casualty of an unnamed war. He tells the woman that he lived in her house when he was a kid and asks if can he please take a look. He says cryptically that it's the last chance he'll have. Something about the stranger disarms her. She lets him in.

Bud took another pill. He had a good beginning. He was on his way now, it was all making sense—he would make his own version of *The Best Years,* compressed, empurpled, dramaturgical, like some experimental Polish theater group's vision of that American time. He might even call the characters Fred and Myrna and Dana, take it right from the movie, "appropriate" it, as the avant-garde hacks say. Maybe there'd be a laugh track in places and warped eruptions of applause, a gaga homage to Bud's favorite sitcom *Father Knows Best,* which was really just a juvenilization of the March/Loy saga. A laugh track, with some Rachmaninoff or Bruckner or Vaughan Williams thrown in, a little postmodern Sirkian transport. Bud knew about Buñ-

uel and Sirk years ago, now all anyone could talk about was Sirk
and Buñuel, Sirk and Buñuel. Bud was hip to those guys when
he was eleven years old. Now it was Sirk and Buñuel and
Lynch. Jeanette would just say he was sour grapes. At least
Lynch knew how to promote himself. Bud needed to get better
at self-promotion.

He wasn't sure what was going to happen inside the house
yet, but maybe after the stranger leaves, the woman feels differently about her life. A sea change. That wasn't a bad title,
especially if the stranger was some kind of sailor. *A Sea Change.*
Too soft. Somebody had already called something that. *Other
People's Houses* was good, but someone had used that, too.

Maybe Bud would have the woman sleep with the stranger,
then pick the son up from school, make the husband dinner, go
for a walk and never come back. Or maybe blow her brains out
or defenestrate herself or choke on something during dinner
like Dolly once did in a public restaurant and the little boy
would run from the table in horror as the husband did the
Heimlich. Another title came to mind and Bud blushed with
enthusiasm: *Bringing Down the House.* He was pretty sure that
hadn't been used.

Bud needed a real structure now; even Lynch needed that. It
would come. He'd dip into the stolen library and absorb some
Strindberg and Tennessee Williams.

He took a nap.

Most of the limos at the Beverly Palm were owned by worka-
holic Chileans who occasionally needed stand-in drivers when
they felt like time off with the family or when they got demoral-
ized from too much exposure to the rich. Bud liked the work.
The hours were flexible and on a good day he could clear a
hundred dollars, cash.

There was time to think about his projects during calls. That
week, while he waited for clients outside expensive offices and
restaurants, Bud sat in the car reading the script Feld sent over.
It was awful but had some funny bits and was structurally

sounder than it first seemed. It could be salvaged. He wouldn't have to do that much work, which was good because lately Bud found it hard to concentrate—on anything, really. *Toy Soldier* had depleted him. He never wanted to spend two years writing a script again. He needed the time-frame discipline an assignment provided; Bud needed to work and be paid. It sounded like a joke, but he thought he got more creative when someone was paying him for his efforts.

He had a few days off and went to the cafeteria at Cedars-Sinai to hone the Levitt pitch. The hospital comforted him; it was where Brian might have wound up working, with a high tech suite of offices in the adjoining medical building and Percodan for everyone. That would have been good times. Anyway, Dolly was in there somewhere having her face fixed and would soon be ready to go home. Bud had offered to pick her up, but his mother was adamant about making her own arrangements. She hated being vulnerable, hated being a burden. On birthdays and holidays, she *ordered* him not to buy a gift. Don't spend your money. He guessed it was all some childhood thing, cold fish parents or something. Her parents died young and from all the stories he ever heard about them, they were stiffs. One day, when he had some money, he'd help Dolly out and spring for some Reichian therapy. That woman had more armor than a Russian tank. He thought about his poorly loved, well-defended mother's armor under the knife and had trouble with the details of his pitch. He got that scary blocked feeling and decided not to bother making too many notes for the meeting at Universal.

The screenwriter sat there in the cafeteria, letting the ideas percolate to the surface. He disliked working from outlines; it squelched his creativity. He agreed with himself to spend the next few days "unconsciously" working on the fix and felt the burden lift.

As he fumbled with his keys, a Jamaican nurse opened the door. He heard moans as he entered. When Bud switched on the light in Dolly's bedroom, he recoiled.

"Buddy!" she wailed, holding an arm out weakly. "Buddy! What did he do? Why did I let him? Why! Why!"

Her face was swollen and unrecognizable. Bud turned and gaped at the nurse.

"What did they do to her?"

"Cut her," she said laconically.

"That fucker, Bud, cutting and peeling! They wouldn't put me out. My nerves are on fire!"

Bud went toward the phone.

"We have to call him, what's his number—"

"No!" she shouted. He restrained her.

"Jesus, Ma, don't try to get up!"

"Only codeine he gave me, that fucker. Can you imagine!"

The stain-blotched sheet around her chest fell to the floor and he saw the thick bandages around her breasts. Everything was smeared with bright orange antiseptic.

"What happened to your tits?" he blurted out.

"They put silicone in there," the nurse said dryly.

Bud reeled back onto a chair, nauseated. The nurse helped prop Dolly up with a pillow.

"Your father was the tit man," she said, slurring her words. "I'd find Polaroids of the girlfriends, always with the D cup and the pancake nipples. Did you know your mother's writing a best-seller, *Beverly Hills Adjacent*?"

"Ma, don't talk."

"She gonna be all right," said the nurse.

"How long will you be with her?" he asked her.

"Trudy's going to stay right here and watch the shitty soaps."

The nurse smiled and said she wasn't Trudy, she was Carmen, but she'd stay no matter what Mrs. Wiggins called her because Mrs. Wiggins was a good woman in pain.

Dolly coughed, then winced and hovered her hand above her breast like a healing spatula.

"The day your father died, I went straight to Hoffmann-Dougherty for a pedicure, that's how much I hated him!"

Bud stood up. "Bobby Feld liked my script."

"Give me the basin," Dolly importuned. "I'm gonna throw up!" The nurse brought her a kidney-shaped emesis dish and Dolly rested it on her cheek, a cool savior.

"Breathe through your mouth now, girl."

"Trudy—Carmen," she corrected herself, "get me a rag with some ice in it." Dolly focused valiantly on Bud. "Bobby Feld, at TTA? I almost sold him a house."

Bud moved closer. "I have a big meeting the end of the week, at Universal. And they're interviewing me for the *News.*" He just wanted to make her feel better.

Dolly seemed to take it in; the whole thing sounded dream-like enough for Bud to wonder if she really understood. His mother beckoned him closer and whispered softly in his ear. "Would you do something for me, Buddy?"

"Do you want me to call Naugawitz? Do you want some water? Tell me what you want."

She put her frail hand on his.

"Would you write a hit movie for your mother and get an Academy Award? And buy a house for your mother in Holmby Hills? Because I'm tired, Buddy! You don't know how tired your mother is!"

She let go of him and immediately fell asleep.

ʍʍ

Bud was sitting in Hugo's going over the Levitt script when an eager man holding a knapsack approached.

"Are you Bud?"

Peter Dietrich introduced himself and sat down. He was around thirty, with a soft blond beard and easy manner. He groused about the traffic, set his tape recorder on the table and ordered some tea. Bud felt impressive; he was reasonably sure it would be obvious to anyone who looked over that he was being interviewed. After they ordered, he graciously asked Dietrich how he came to be a reporter. The young journalist went through the predictable personal data: Ivy Leaguer who came from wealth, girlfriend of nine years (a physician), unfinished novel. He was also related to a famous painter—just to spice up the résumé.

Dietrich turned his attention completely to Bud. He put on the recorder, then took out a little reporter's notepad and held it like a prop. It seemed more like a quaint emblem of his trade than anything else, like a pharmacist's mortar and pestle.

Bud spoke of his bygone unreleased film like an honored strategist whose campaign had failed not for want of heart and design, but arms and men; he'd delivered a brilliant, much-praised script that was destroyed by the hands of derelict strategists. He sounded very Zen about dropping out of Hollywood for a while because he "tired of the game." Bud Wiggins had cannily taken his probable "fuck-you money" and gone on sabbatical. He mentioned *Toy Soldier* and stressed the importance of taking charge, unshackling oneself from the yoke of what the tired town pundits called Development Hell. The reporter liked it when Bud told him he did his best work in a hospital cafeteria. Good copy.

Halfway through lunch Bud had a brainstorm. He told the reporter he happened to have a meeting at Universal at three and would he like to come along? Dietrich immediately agreed, hardly containing his excitement at the prospect of Babylonian fieldwork—Bud knew the interviewer's "serious writer" side was particularly engaged. After all, the sanctum sanctorum of Hollywood dealmakers was the stuff of great Literature. Potential great Literature anyway. Bud could kill two birds with one pitch: he'd come across as a hot "scripter" in the *News* profile while simultaneously impressing the hell out of Joel Levitt. Here was a writer noteworthy enough to be profiled for a day-in-the-life—and he's got the chutzpah to bring the reporter to a meeting! His balls alone might land him the gig.

"You should try and write a script," Bud said as the reporter paid the check. Dietrich blushed.

"I've thought about it."

"It's easier than writing a novel," Bud added. "But maybe not."

The guard at the gate took forever to find Bud's drive-on. Bud stared at the poster of *Banana Republic,* the ape movie that came out of nowhere to gross two hundred million. Dietrich smiled vacantly and the screenwriter got a sinking feeling. He wondered if Levitt's office forgot to leave him a pass.

"Bud Wiggins," he enunciated again, firmly.

"Relax." The guard was one of those sardonic leatherskinned crackpots indigenous to studio lots. "A guy goes to his shrink and says, 'Doc! I'm a teepee! I'm a wigwam! I'm a teepee! I'm a wigwam!' " He finally taped a pass to the windshield, then leaned over intimately to Bud. "The shrink says, *'Relax:* you're *two tents.* ' "

He waved them through.

As they drove to the executive building, Bud wondered if he was doing the right thing. What if his plan exploded in his face? He figured the worst they could do was make the reporter wait outside the room. He was suddenly calm now that the worst was all right. He got a second wind and began to psych himself up by "unconsciously" thinking about the pitch.

Feld was waiting in the anteroom when Bud appeared with his Boswell. The agent was euphoric. After a moment he recognized Dietrich and pumped his hand vigorously. Bud explained the situation and Feld didn't seem to have a problem with it.

"If it's okay with Joel—and I don't see why it shouldn't be. No, it's *great!*" He shivered with overconfidence. "I got these guys very *wet.* Do your homework?"

"The script is really bad, Bobby—"

"What'd you expect, *Sophie's Choice*? I've positioned you on this, big guy." Dietrich took it all in, beside himself. He looked like a starstruck rube who'd won a radio contest walk-on for *Speed-the-Plow.* "Let's go in there and do some serious felching."

Joel Levitt appeared at the heavy walnut doors to his office and gestured them in. He was the man with the white mustache whom Bud saw sitting in the Commissary with Joseph Harmon. Levitt was deeply tanned and either ten years older or ten years younger than he looked. When Feld told him Dietrich was doing a story on Bud and would he mind, Levitt shrugged; he couldn't have cared less. Bud was trying to think of something funny to say when Feld made a joke about Levitt's office actually being a new stop on the tour, so the public could see a producer in action. Levitt said something hiply nihilistic about wanting to blow up one of the trams. They filed past him to the big room.

Bud took one look and almost fainted. There were ten people, all seated, eyes trained on him.

"This is worse than the sale at Maxfield's," he blurted. Everyone laughed, and it pushed away his vertigo. Still, he thought he was going to vomit. Levitt made a few perfunctory introductions that ended with Bud shaking hands with none other than Billy Quintero. The screenwriter blanched, then recovered.

"Jesus, you look a lot like Billy Quintero." The star smiled at Bud and it was a nice smile; he was always written up as a shy man of few words. Quintero asked how he was and Bud said "Intimidated." He was a fan. The gracious star smiled again, sweetly awkward.

Bud liked him and that helped his nerves. The first few minutes of a meeting were crucial. If the chemistry was wrong or there were too many interruptions, it had the wrongness of a bad dream—he'd start to feel disembodied, like his soul had floated up to watch the goings-on from the ceiling. When a pitch soured, time got hammered down like an endless loop, all numb seconds of lurid, sweaty colors, vivid and alien. If they didn't like what you had to say (for whatever sane or irrational reasons), you became the personification of what they feared and hated most: waste, and the horrendous metaphysical implications of its courtship.

"Billy's looking to do a comedy," Levitt said, "so we brought him in on this project."

"I'm not sure he's right for it," Bud said coolly. The moment hung in the air, then the room broke up again and Quintero smiled. Levitt asked Bud if he wanted some coffee and Bud said how about a decaf Al Pacino. This time Quintero cracked up.

The reporter had the dangerously exhilarated look of a prize-fighter on peyote, and the screenwriter knew instinctively not to say a word. Dietrich would inhale the stink and hear the roar firsthand, feel the franchise of respect accorded a writer like Bud Wiggins. Yes, his career was not where he had hoped. But he'd had a film produced and that it did not come out wasn't his fault. He had done his part. What had Billy Quintero worked on, before getting the recognition he deserved? How many Equity waivers? How many taxicabs, how many bars? And what about Joel Levitt? He certainly wasn't born getting two hundred phone calls a day. He wasn't born with a Maserati Quattroporte, his own restaurant and accountants who took full-page ads out in the trades just to thank him for being alive. No, he was a schlep in a mail room, you better believe it. Like his father and his father's father before him, forever and ever. And he could be nothing tomorrow and was smart enough to know it. Quintero knew it, they all knew it—they could be nothing tomorrow. So they had to search all the time for the thing that would keep them rich and famous and powerful and their search invariably led them to Writers. If the writer had the hook, the take, the fix, *the vision,* they would pave the streets with gold for him. Because they were not covetous of the fame or fortune of a writer.

"Have you read the script?" Levitt asked.

"Bud had some problems with it," Feld interjected.

"That's why we're here," said the producer.

The screenwriter took a breath; it was time. "The body exchange stuff has been done to death," he said soberly. He was careful not to be cocky. No matter how bad the script was, there was invariably a minefield of hidden agendas. For all he knew,

It might have been the idea of Joel Levitt's dying seven-year-old daughter. Or maybe Quintero came up with it—why else would he be here? The material didn't warrant his presence, if only because the two leads were barely out of their teens. Quintero was almost forty. He hadn't done a film in two years. He was choosy, picked his shots well. The studio could never force him into a room like this; he had to be seriously interested. Joel Levitt aside, Bud *had* read somewhere that the star wanted to do comedy. But Quintero was too old for this project and Bud knew he had to address that—it was a test.

"I'm not so sure they should be teenagers."

"Go on," said Levitt. *You're getting warm.*

"Can we back up?" Bud said, buying time. He was starting to blank.

"Bud has some general notes," the agent offered.

"As I said, we've seen the body-exchange stuff before." No one could argue with that. He decided to play it out.

"That was one of Billy's concerns," said the producer.

Bingo.

"Still, it's been awhile since *Big.* If it's handled right, that's something an audience always loves. So I'd combine it with the subplot about the guy who gets made into the pope."

"Combine it," Levitt echoed flatly.

"Right." Bud tried to gauge the room—they were still listening. "The way it is now, the guy is made pope by mistake. That just couldn't happen. I mean, when they pick the dalai lama, *maybe.* But the pope—it's a process: with the *cardinals* and the puffs of *smoke.* . . ."

Levitt straightened up like he'd slapped himself with aftershave. "So, you'd have the guy from Newark wake up inside the pope's body?"

Bud nodded, an old safecracker passing on his secrets. "It's cleaner. Also, Jeremiah's too passive—which I don't particularly *mind.* It's just that I think there's a *Field of Dreams* element that needs to be drawn out—"

Bobby Feld squirmed a little in his seat. "That may not be

the perfect analogy, Joel." The producer mulled the title aloud. "I had some problems with that film," the agent added, for safety.

"I *love Field of Dreams,*" Levitt pronounced. Then, to Bud: "But Costner was passive. Or am I wrong?"

"He was more *benign* than passive," Bud said lucidly. "And he was the motor."

Feld quickly agreed. "If anything worked for me, it was Costner. I didn't like the wife and the black." Someone on the couch said, "James Earl Jones."

Levitt suddenly switched gears. "Bud—and I know this is one of those dumb questions, but hey, ask around, I'm a dumb producer. I think it has some validation to it, so I'm gonna ask it anyway: if one movie comes to mind for this project, a *flavor,* a *spirit*—"

"It could be more than one, Joel," interrupted the agent.

"More than one. Five, *ten*—I mean, if you could pick a movie, a *direction.* If it's a *Mad Mad World,* if it's a *Parenthood,* whatever comes to mind. If it's a *French Lieutenant's Woman*—" The producer eyeballed someone on the couch. "Jesus, where did that come from? I know where—it's been on cable all week."

"Amazing movie," said Feld respectfully. "Pinter."

"Are you kidding me?" Levitt yelled. "I fucking *hate* that! I go on live television, I cut his English head off and vomit down his neck!"

The agent's wheels spun in the sand. "The script is great—I had problems with the *movie.*"

"I fuck Harold Pinter's ass with a bullwhip in front of his whole fucking family!" There was laughter from the group and Feld smiled with relief. Levitt turned back to Bud. "So what do you think, for a *spirit*—"

"I'd say *Field of Dreams,*" he began, "and *It's a Wonderful Life* . . . Penny Marshall and Ron Howard and Rob Reiner . . . the Barry Levinson of *Diner* . . . *Broadway Danny Rose* . . . *Look Who's Talking,* but *smart* . . ." He wanted to stop but somehow couldn't find the way out. *"Batman* and Lubitsch—"

Someone from the back said, "Is that like 'Batman and Robin'?" and there was laughter. Levitt indicated for Bud to continue.

"The films of Preston Sturges—"

"Who?" the producer grunted. Bud looked to Feld for help.

"Joel," said the agent, "Bud's given us a lot."

The producer agreed and backed off.

The rest of the meeting was a downhill coast. Bud hadn't given them too much story, and that was good. Better to play it safe—to work with what was there, what was familiar. Nobody was paying him yet anyway. He never forgot the story Morris told him of the advertising agency that came up with a name for Carnation's new instant breakfast: Carnation's Instant Breakfast. What people wanted was often right in front of their faces. Don't rock the Quattroporte.

At the end of the meeting two Vice-Presidents in Charge of Production appeared at the door in Yohji Yamamoto suits. Their lives were defined by stealth and subterfuge—they walked, talked and breathed secrets. They looked giddy, antsy, like satanic interns auditing their first murder spree. One of them was Feld's old assistant, who once hung up on Bud. The men were thrilled to see Quintero and even interested in shaking hands with the potential script doctor. They didn't stay long; Bud felt like he was acting in one of those plays where the audience wanders from room to room.

He felt good as hired. If they wanted him to come in again with details, no problem. It would be like rearranging gifts under a Christmas tree. That would be an easier meeting, with only a few key production people.

He decided to wrap it up. "Those are basically my thoughts," he said magisterially. "Give me two weeks and you'll have a shooting script."

"One thing, Bud," Levitt offered. "Tell us a little about yourself. How you got started, how you work. I know Billy's curious."

Bud nodded, then glanced at the sphinxlike star. "Before I forget: if we keep the ghost of Freud, we can have Jeremiah say to him, 'Sigmund, I'm a teepee! I'm a wigwam! I'm a teepee! I'm a wigwam!' . . ."

Bud read an interview once with the driver Jackie Stewart about heightened senses during a race. He hit a certain stretch at two hundred miles an hour and suddenly it smelled like someone dumped a wheelbarrow of fresh-cut grass onto the seat beside him. Now he knew just what that meant; Bud felt exquisitely attuned.

"That was amazing," Dietrich said on their way back to Hugo's to get his car. He was wild-eyed, like a virgin bungee jumper.

"Was it like you thought it'd be?"

"It was heavy," was all the drained reporter could muster.

"Paper business don't run like that, huh?" Bud said, doing a little of his Dean Martin. Or was it Crosby.

"You were really funny."

"Yeah," Bud said casually, cool veteran of the wars. "You know, I could go home and never hear from those guys." He was lying, of course. "That's the Business."

Dietrich was astonished at such a possibility and shook his head at Bud's alien fortitude, marveling at the writer's crazy stomach. He was still high and starting to get on Bud's nerves. It was all so specific and brutal, he waxed, so esoteric, like combining the art of flower arrangement with police choke-holds. When Bud heard that, he started worrying about the *News* profile. The reporter humbly thanked him and left the car, wobbly from all the legendary action.

Bud went to the Writers Guild to register *Toy Soldier.* On his way in, he passed a homeless woman on a pay phone. She was singsonging *Hello* into the receiver, as in *Hello, it's been good to know you.* All she sang was the "hel-lo" part, over and over.

There was a roomful of applicants. He sat down beside a

plainly pretty young girl with curly black hair. She held a long manila envelope in her hand and looked eagerly at Bud's script.

"Is it a play?" She had a sunny smile.

"Screenplay," Bud said reticently. There was always something vaguely embarrassing about registering a script, like you were paying sucker-tax for being a dreamer. He knew most of the people in the room weren't even members; the Guild took your money anyway. He never really understood the whole "registration" racket. It was equivalent to having your car blessed by a priest.

"What genre?" she asked. The girl seemed thrilled to be there, as if they were all unlikely finalists in the Big Time.

"Screwball, I guess."

"Contemporary?"

He took a closer look. She wore French designer glasses and weird yellow vinyl boots. Her jaw was a bit pronounced and Bud sensed she might be playing down some kind of natural beauty.

"It's sort of about Vietnam."

"And *screwball,*" she said, quizzically. "Interesting! What's it called?"

"*Toy Soldier.*"

"I love that!" She repeated the title soundlessly. "Mine's more like *Moonstruck.* I'm an actress. No one would write me a part, so I decided to write my own."

Bud said that was smart. She asked if he had "representation." He mentioned Bobby Feld and she seemed impressed. She told him she didn't have an agent for writing but a few were interested in her acting. She'd probably sign with one for commercials and voice-overs soon. The clerk behind the counter called Bud's name and he went over.

"I'd like to register a script."

"Are you a member?"

He nodded and she punched his Social Security number into the computer. She said he wasn't showing current with his quarterlies, so it would be twenty dollars. (It was only ten if you were "in good standing.") He wrote a check and she took his script, sealing it in an envelope. Bud hated himself for making a comment about giving his business manager hell for not mailing in the dues.

He waved good-bye to the actress on the way out.

Bud called his agent the next day to thank him for the Levitt connection. Feld said he hadn't heard anything and would call as soon as he did. The screenwriter was debonair, in keeping with the new, improved Bud Wiggins. He wasn't going to worry. He felt rooted and mature, in the Now.

mm

A story broke about Dr. Naugawitz's being sued by some former patients; he was rumored to have checked himself into a detox unit. Dolly would require more surgery. She had to spend a few days in the hospital because of a high fever and her new doctor was worried about infection. She was already looking for an attorney to file a malpractice suit and talked animatedly about using Naugawitz as a character in her novel.

Bud worked steadily on his Daedalus submission. He began the scenario in the form of a short story, instead of a play. It was flowing that way; he'd adapt the script from the story when he finished. He had the stranger arrive in a rented emerald-green Lincoln. At first the housewife didn't want to let the guy in, but he begged. "He seemed to go limp, his imprecations little hemorrhages," Bud wrote, and was pleased. Maybe he'd submit it to a literary magazine—*The Daedalus Project: Bringing Down the House.* Or maybe he'd just call it "Scenario for a Short Film." He could even publish the story himself just to see how it looked, bound together, a thing with its own life.

For now *The Best Years of Our Lives* concept was fading—it was thrilling and mysterious the way characters came to life, if you didn't fight them. The piece had become a taut, two-person drama. The housewife wore capris and Capezios, with a Jackie Kennedy bob. She followed the stranger into the living room;

he had beautiful hands with long, slender fingers (Bud wondered if he could find an actor with beautiful hands). His eyes looked weak, with white flakes on the lower lids. While the young man looked around, the purified water people phoned and the housewife got queasy having to talk to one stranger while keeping an eye on another. That was a good moment—Bud hoped it would translate to film. When she told the visitor he had to leave, he protested.

"I've only seen two rooms."

"I have to pick my son up from school," she said, suddenly nervous.

"But it's not even two o'clock. School gets out after three. Besides, you live so close he could walk."

The stranger started for the sliding glass doors that led to the garden (Bud wanted to work a Secret Garden in there somewhere), and she put her hand on his shoulder. He spun around and stared deep into her eyes, and the woman felt the way trainers of wild animals must, right before being killed by the very things on which they lavished so much time and affection. It would be silly to feel betrayed because something black and unfathomable as, say, a panther, had violated one's notion of rapport. But she was an amateur—all she could do was smile, the wan postcard smile of an unlucky tourist turning to gaze at an avalanche.

He would FADE OUT, and FADE IN: the housewife awakening atop her bed. The stranger had carried her there, up the spiral staircase to the second floor. He'd removed her shoes and put a designer washcloth on her forehead. As she looked up at him, a few ridiculous phrases repeated themselves in her head, in VO: "I'm a town girl. I'm towering. Town-towering." From her fugue state, the woman noticed the tattooed letters above each knuckle of the stranger's hands, one H-O-R-E, the other C-U-N-T. The screenwriter wondered how much of it was usable or too bizarre or if it was going anywhere. He decided not to censor himself; he was enjoying the process.

Bud had hoped that by the time Dolly got home from the hospital he would have found an apartment. Outside of the rentals section of the trades, he hadn't done much looking. He told himself that as long as he was writing, there was no hurry. That was the main thing, to be generating product. He hadn't heard a word from Feld in two weeks. That wasn't necessarily good or bad; people went out of town, priorities got shuffled, deals fell apart. It was a troubled project from the get-go and everyone knew it. Still, Bud was reasonably certain that if Universal moved forward, they would want his involvement. He'd lay low—there was other business at hand. When he finished the Daedalus script, he would put in a call to Feld and ask about *Toy Soldier.* He wouldn't even *mention* Joel Levitt. They'd all probably call, at once: Feld, Levitt, Guthrie. In Hollywood a few weeks was nothing. He reminded himself that *Hurry up and wait* was the town maxim.

᠊᠊᠊᠊

This time he picked his mother up from the hospital. She'd lost weight and had a little shunt in her cheek to drain discharge from a wound; her mouth drooped a little on one side. She was taking antibiotics and anti-inflammatories, tranquilizers and pain pills. She slept a lot and let Bud take care of her. He felt closer to her than he had in the twenty-something years since Moe's death. He read to her from best-sellers, and when he got headaches, Dolly shared her Percodan. It made her feel good to dispense to him, to ease his inherited agonies. Partners.

A few months after they moved to Bel Air, when he was nine years old, Bud started hyperventilating and she gave him Miltown. He had trouble catching his breath and had a twitch and vomited all the time. She was worried he had an ulcer or would get a hernia from all the heaving, but the doctors did the tests, the upper and lower GIs, and couldn't find anything. Dolly began waking him up and dragging him from his bed, screaming that Moe was trying to kill her. Bud would enter the all-night telethon of their bedroom, his father in Joseph Harmon–approved bikini underwear, leering at him like a hellish odalisque. *Your mother's a very sick woman,* he'd say, and she'd beg little Buddy to do something because Moe had hit her. *Would I hit your mother, Bud?* he asked. *I'm black and blue, you bastard!*—she'd show Bud the marks way up on her thigh. Once Moe asked with a drunken ogle if he liked the way his mother looked, and Dolly shoved Bud out of the way, attacking her husband's head with a flurry of swats. He took the blows like they were doing slapstick cabaret. The scenes always wound down when Moe started to crash—a bored, testy *bundido* who only wanted a quiet place to sleep. Bud's room had two beds, and it was there that Moe would finally make his retreat. The Only Son softly pleaded with the Father Image to please be good to Dolly, until he heard the snores that came from some dead place within.

After their little Late Shows, Moe liked to check into a hotel for a few days—the Beverly Terrace or the Beverly Carlton or the Beverly Crest—then send roses. That was all Dolly ever needed to have him back. Once, the night after the worst fight they'd ever had, the thirteen-year-old Bud was rocking himself to sleep when he heard voices in the living room at the wrap-around fireplace. *Get out!* his mother shouted, and pounded to the bedroom, slamming the door behind her. Then Bud did the hardest thing: he pleaded with them to divorce, or at least separate. Moe asked why and Bud said, Because it's so bad between you. If it's so bad between us, why did your mother beg me to come over tonight and fuck her? *Communication.* If you're not part of the solution, you're part of the problem. *All I hear from you is the fucking problem. Aside from the problems with fucking*—an added quip—*those your mother and me ain't got. Or is it your mother and I?*

After a few days she'd let Moe back and the fights began, wresting Bud from his rock-a-bye oblivion. His father at his bedroom again, apologizing to the Only Son. The screenwriter remembered the man's heaviness on the sheets, the boozy for-give-mes in his ear, the dead gamy weight, and wondered: maybe something wasn't . . . *kosher*. Maybe Morris pimped him to business friends and Dolly whored him out for Miltown. Maybe Buddy had been set up for a shakedown, traded for caviar and breakfronts, wet bars, spiral staircases and free WATS-line time.

Only Thelma Ritter knew for sure.

Bud never saw the streets so full of water and debris.

He was driving the limo the long holiday weekend and was on his way to an assist; one of the cars had broken down. The winds shimmied the trees and the rain came down so heavily that when he glimpsed other drivers, they looked loopy and moonstruck, crazed children at millennium's end. Bud suffered tiny disconnected jolts of remorse, spasms of terror and regret, nostalgia and dread. He pushed the feelings away.

When he pulled up to Chasen's, Ramón was standing beside his stretch, its hood up.

"Almodóvar, you have come!" He looked wild in the rain, aboriginal. "For doing this for me, I am going to make love to you long and hard."

"What's wrong with your car?"

"It is the starter, Almodóvar. Three times I have replaced it. I am going to bloody the asshole of the mechanic who has dared to fuck with *Ramona*. And then I will bloody your ass, Al-modóvar, but with tenderness and love."

Ramón's quondam party suddenly emerged from the restau-rant, and the doorman frantically signaled the two drivers.

"Where are they going?" Bud asked.

"To Peralvillo!" shouted the stranded chauffeur, in delirium.

Bud drove forward while Ramón jogged alongside the car like berserk Secret Service. The doorman, umbrella gripped fiercely, ferried the five men across the sidewalk and into the limo, a contingent of holy men.

As Bud pulled away, he saw the receding caballero through his mirror, waving madly. He had a vision of Ramón removing his shoes and painting his face with dyes, then vaulting into the viscous, healing mud of the Hollywood Hills to forage for the sacred mushroom.

He heard voices from the dark cave of the carriage and with sudden horror realized who his drunk, wet passengers were: Billy Quintero and Joel Levitt. He also recognized some faces from the pitch meeting. Before he nudged the rearview so as not to be seen, Bud thought he saw one of the secretive vice-presidents. A fifth wheel, an unfamiliar crony, sat beside him in the front seat.

"Let's see, where we going?" said the crony to the boys in the back room. "You want to get a drink somewhere, Billy? Meet some girls?"

"The Bel Age, driver," said Levitt coldly. "You know where the Bel Age is?"

Before Bud could answer, the crony said, "You never told me what picture you're doing, Joel."

"I only talked about it for an hour and a half," said Levitt. "Where the hell were you?"

"I told you, Meg Ryan got ahold of me and wouldn't let go."

The curmudgeonly producer snickered. "Meg Ryan, my ass."

"Well, if you won't tell me," said the crony, "maybe Billy will."

"Billy doesn't feel like talking about it," Levitt said.

Quintero smiled his famous street-sphinx smile.

"Tell him," said another voice from the back, possibly one of the vice-presidents. "Joel, it's too fucking funny the way you tell it. He told Eddie Murphy, at Dominick's."

Levitt brightened at the memory. "He had blood in his stool, he was laughing so hard. And you know what that nigger's laugh sounds like."

Someone said, "Jesus, Joel!" in token outrage, and someone

else muttered not to pay attention, the producer was drunk. Whatever he was, he was ready to tell the story.

"Billy and I are readying a picture. From an idea by me and Billy." Quintero cleared his throat comically. "Okay, from an idea by Billy and me. Is that better, wise guy?" Everyone laughed. "Kind of a *Tootsie,* except about a screenwriter. That's what Billy's gonna play. Now, not only can this screenwriter not get arrested in this town, but he's a—Billy, what is he?"

"Schmuck," Quintero deadpanned, and the whole limo laughed the gravy-train laugh of sycophants who hear something genuinely funny.

"This thing is going to make a hundred million," said a putative vice-president.

"What's a hundred million?" the producer bitched. "The sequel to my daughter's nanny's *tuckus* made a hundred million. It's gonna make *four* hundred million. You know you really are stupid, Jonathan."

The boys beat up on Levitt a minute to get him back on the rail; the producer gripped Quintero's leg to get some control back, and the star clocked it with a raised comic eyebrow, like Levitt was a fag. The others laughed, but he was already too committed to his story to acknowledge it.

"So you know what a maniac this guy is for research, don't you? So I talk to Bobby Feld, over at TTA. Bobby's great—he's coming on the rafting trip, by the way. We tell Bobby what kind of guy we're looking for and he sends out this putz."

"You mean," said the crony, "you take a meeting with a real writer, just so Billy can watch him?"

"A 'real' writer," snickered Levitt, the mafioso trickster. "We get him a script—"

"Like a decoy," a voice said from the back.

"Tell him what script," said another voice.

"This is the fucking coup d'état. Are you ready? It's a draft of the new Caitlin Wurtz."

The crony gasped, enthralled.

"Which is structurally perfect," said a voice.

"They gave him the script and he doesn't know who wrote it," summarized the alleged vice-president. "And they ask him for notes, just so Billy can see him pitch."

The crony shook his head. "This is a classic."

Levitt started to shake with hilarity; a great cough welled up like a demon lozenge, and he shoved it down. "And he's tearing it a new asshole, the stupid shit—a *Caitlin Wurtz,* who's gonna be up for another Academy with that fucking monkey picture she did—"

"*Banana Republic—*"

"He's giving dissertations about structure," Levitt wheezed, "like he was Harold fucking Ramis!"

Suddenly Quintero boomed, "I'm a teepee, I'm a wigwam!"

The mob became quiet, startled by the star's sudden verbosity. It was an aberration which they finally decided not to register.

"This is marvelous," said the crony. "You have to put it in a movie somewhere."

"I'm a teepee! I'm a wigwam!" the star croaked again, and this time the men in back spontaneously joined in. The crony smiled, dismayed.

"I'm a teepee! I'm a wigwam! I'm a teepee! I'm a wigwam!" they crowed, Freemasons all.

"Re-lax," said the producer, holding an imaginary conductor's baton in the air. The cough welled up again and he shuddered with its bewitchment, then brought the baton down with a flourish as the men chorused.

"*You're two tents!*"

The downpour dumped a bucket of rain onto the windshield as the producer's strangled cough erupted and filled the car with something akin to electronic noise.

A week later Bud got a call from Peter Dietrich. The piece turned out great and he wanted to tell him everyone was given an alias, an editorial decision to avoid legal hassles. "So I guess you'll have to tell your mom who's who," he joked.

Bud asked the reporter if he was still interested in writing scripts after having seen the whole thing close up. Dietrich said more than ever. He wanted to know how the Quintero deal was going and Bud told him he had to pass, he was doing something for Warner's instead. Dietrich said he had to run. Before they hung up, Bud broached the idea of collaborating on something with him down the line. Maybe something about the newspaper business.

Late that night Bud went down to the newsstand to get the early morning edition. On the front page of the *News,* a banner in red ink read: HOLLYWOOD HI'S AND LOW'S, This Week in Style! He flipped to the Style section.

There was a Charles Addams–like drawing of the gates of Universal Studios. The caption read: "Abandon Hope All Ye Who Enter Here." There was some kind of logo incorporating a movie camera and dollar signs at the top, then:

HOLLYWOOD HI'S AND LOW'S:

PART I—AMBUSH!
by Peter Dietrich

(The following article is the first in a series of exclusive stories of Hollywood winners and losers. All names have been changed—Ed.)

Bill Wogans was excited. His former agent had called that morning with the news: a big-time producer wanted to see him over at Universal. He wondered if it was a dream, and for good reason.

The failed screenwriter had been working on a Vietnam script for years and living at home with his . . .

WWW

A month passed and Bud settled into a comfortable routine with his mother. They told her she would have some permanent disfigurement, and Dolly seemed to be taking it well. She was in generally good spirits, working on her book again. A lawsuit against Dr. Naugawitz was in the offing, and this quickened her blood.

When he wasn't working on *Bringing Down the House,* Bud took long walks through Beverly Hills, like a cushy retiree. He strolled past the movie theater he had frequented as a boy, now a savings and loan. It still had a dome like the Taj Mahal. They used to have Saturday morning matinées there, where he first saw *The Time Machine* and *Journey to the Center of the Earth.* Like the Arbor sandbox of his past, the idea of a free matinée made him feel ancient.

He went to his first one with a hairy-armed girl, a preteen date sponsored by the parents. The girl's mother drove them over. She had sunken cheeks and long, lacquered fingernails; Bud sat in the bucket seat, watching her nails clack the steering wheel of the Thunderbird, watching with the same fortitude he'd summoned for Mrs. Kent's clopping marches down the hallways of the school in the Heights. Inside the theater, he tried to touch the little girl's hand. After impossible trembling effort, he managed to brush the knuckles during final credits. She snatched her hand away.

When he first signed with Feld, the agent got him an assignment at Paramount working on a comedy western. As part of "research," the studio gave him carte blanche to screen old cowboy movies. Instead, he ordered *Journey to the Center of the Earth.* He got a hamburger from the Commissary, brought it to the screening room and made himself comfortable. Then, in time-honored tradition, he bent over the speaker, pressed a lever and said, "May we run it now?" The projectionist answered with an affirmation of static and the lights darkened. He considered himself a lucky man.

As he watched, the boyish intoxication he had when he first saw the movie was still there: the aboveground prefatory intrigue, the gathering of equipment for the expedition, the descent into the earth, the revelation of the underground sea that always left him breathless—someone rounds a rock and there it is, roaring, mystic, its dark finite underworld cope an agoraphobic's nightmare. There was a boat in the ocean, trapped in a vortex. Bud tried to recall whom the boat belonged to, but his memories commingled: Neptune and his trident, Jason and his Argonauts, Cyclops and sirens and time machines and dinosaurs staccato-dancing their strobed Claymation battles on the final beach, the tiny, undignified figures of the men running for cover. And there he was through it all, the last tycoon, eating his french fries in homage to the Year of the Matinée. The Year of the Vomiting.

Emboldened, he screened more movies, bingeing on *Dino* and *Look in Any Window,* Sal Mineo and Paul Anka as JDs. Paul Anka was a teenage Peeping Tom whose father was a lush and a coward. His mom wore white short-shorts and made out with Jack Cassidy at backyard luaus in the dark corners of the pool, right in front of soused Pop. Anka was sweet and wore tight T-shirts. He put on a Halloween mask when he stared with his bedroom eyes through the bedroom windows of the bedroom community. The family had a trampoline and the cops finally took him to Juvie, and nobody was home when Dino came back from the reform school in his skintight undershirt. He leaned against the fridge and seethed, sucking from a big milk bottle. Dino forced his brute father to slap him, and when the bastard complied, his lip swelled up sensually and the apoplectic dad backed away from him, shocky, blood on his hand, muttering, "He's crazy . . . crazy . . ." "You can't hurt me anymore!" Dino shouted at him, in triumph. Dino got a girlfriend (hot, brainy Susan Kohner), a shy girl with glasses who was always mooning at him and clunking into things and excusing the sadism of the neighborhood kids. They went to a dance together, a slummy version of the cotillion. Paul Henreid would have turned over in his grave.

ıɪɪɪ

Bud finished his Daedalus short story.

After the housewife wakes from her faint, she finishes the tour of the house in a weird fog. The stranger leads them to her son's room and comments on the funny stillness, like everything was waiting for the kid to come home, whereas in adults' rooms, the furniture waits for them to leave. He sees a closet and remembers a secret passageway there. He parts the hanging clothes with his beautiful hands, then walks into the room beyond, his steps muffled by the housewife's dresses, which close behind him like a breaker of dark trees, snubbing her, allies of the enemy.

He takes her back to the master bedroom and lays her down again, putting pillows beneath her feet. He picks up the damp designer rag that slapped to the floor when she first stood and refolds it, laying it across her forehead. The housewife brushes it off indifferently, like a feverish child. He takes her shoes off, and she feels her feet expand into the air, sweetly rank. The stranger places the shoes on the floor, neatly beside the bed. He removes her dank blouse, pulling it over her head. He undoes her jeans and her waist breathes. He pulls the jeans off with the underwear, gently disentangling, then folding them even though he was careless with the blouse. She lifts slightly, arching her back as he pulls the quilt down from under her, gathering it at her feet. Just before covering her, he puts his long hands on her shoulders and lays his head sideways in her bush. Like a lamb, he nuzzles the hairs, keeping a grip on the shoulders, exhausted. The woman stares at the ceiling, unfeeling. Then he kisses her there, firm, quick, like you'd kiss the crown of a child's head good-bye. The stranger leaves.

Bud brought the housewife's little boy into it at the end and wondered if that was a mistake; working with minors was a bitch. He'd overcome it. The thing was becoming a bit of a fantasia anyway, and he wondered about its producibility. He had the husband and the boy come home and the housewife makes dinner for them but isn't herself. She doesn't say a word about what went on. She chokes on something during dinner and the boy runs away, terrified. After she spits out the chunk of food, the father calls the boy back and slaps him for running away, *your mother could have died.* The boy stands there trembling, the muscles of his face making him look awful. He runs to his room and cries himself to sleep. That night he wakes up late. He hears noises and goes to his parents' door, shivering in the hall. His mother finally lets him in and he falls easily asleep.

"If the killers came tonight," he reasons (in a possible voice-over narration, one of those timeless *Days of Heaven* deadpan-kid VOs that can work so well), "and it didn't sound like they would anymore, tomorrow someone would discover the three bodies together. Together. And how it would happen wasn't even worth thinking about because nothing could scare him now." He'd end it like that. He wasn't sure if it would be the boy talking or what. The words were the important thing. He read the last sentences again out loud, and was pleased.

He'd make the call to Joseph Harmon himself.

That evening he sat at the bar and thought of his next labor—adapting the story for the screen. He might have to "open it up" a little and lose some of the subtleties. Still, the right actor could add, just when you thought you were taking away. The hardest part was over.

It was good being seen at Mortons—people assumed you were up to something. It made him feel as if he were part of the game. Every once in a while Bud got up to use the men's room or check his phone messages. If he stayed too long with his drink, it might smell like he wasn't really waiting for anyone.

On the way to the lavatory he passed a girl in a black off-the-shoulder cocktail dress, part ingenue, part wolf.

"Hi," she said, clear and open, her face like a taunt. *"Toy*

Soldier, right? I met you at the Guild." Her glasses were gone and she was fairly swaggering, a brazen debutante.

"You've got an amazing memory."

"Have to. I'm an actress, remember?" Then she laughed. "You don't remember much, do you?"

"What's your name?"

"Raleigh Wolper."

"Bud Wiggins." He shook her hand. It was small, like his. "I remember. You were registering your script. *Moonstruck.*"

"Very good."

"Are you here for dinner?"

"Lunch *and* dinner. Would you excuse me?"

She turned to greet a couple at the door, smiling at Bud as she walked them to their table. He wondered if she was flirting.

The screenwriter stood at the urinal, plotting how to give her his number when Bobby Feld stepped from the stall, buckling his belt. When he saw Bud, he was effusive. As he washed up, the agent said that Levitt was about to hire Bud when Caitlin Wurtz, of all people, expressed interest in doing the rewrite— the studio couldn't turn her down. They walked out together and Feld asked whatever happened to that war script of his, the one he gave him in the limo that night. The one about Vietnam, what was it called? *You tell me,* Bud said, making a little joke of it, and Feld was a blank, just like he never read it or raved about it or said it was a shoo-in spec sale. He let him off the hook and said *Toy Soldier,* and Feld said, "Right, good title." Bud said he was showing it around, and Feld urged him to call if there was anything he could do. He returned to his table.

"I see you know Mr. Feld," Raleigh said, back at her station. She was impressed.

"We shared a limo once—he's been trying to sign me ever since."

Bud asked if he could call her sometime, but before she could answer, more people arrived to be seated. Raleigh grabbed some menus.

"Call me *here,*" she enunciated, pointing to the floor as if talking to someone who was slightly deaf. "Wednesday through Saturday."

₦₦₦

On the next Sunday Bud decided to drive to the beach. The sky was brilliant and cloudless. He felt good. Dolly was letting him use the Cadillac.

He was afraid to swim in the ocean but loved it like a real California boy nonetheless, loved the whole surf mythology. On weekends, in seventh and eighth grade, Bud and his friends caught the bus at seven in the morning to get to the water. The boys stayed blissfully until dark. They let you ride the *83 Wilshire* barefoot back then.

He felt himself unwind as he passed the Bel Air gate, ingress to the house on Bellagio. He was hungry to see the ocean. Maybe he'd go to the pier, visit some of the old haunts. Bud thought of Tee's Beach and Pacific Ocean Park and St. Christopher medals and the swirly art he made in the beach arcades by squirting paint from ketchup bottles onto rotating cardboard squares. That was back in the sixties. It would be nice to do a script that used some of those memories.

On the road in front of him, in his trademark white Bentley convertible, Bud recognized the celebrated red head of Joseph Harmon. He was startled, then began to muse, like the guide of a secret tour.

Though Bud had only seen him twice in person (the other day in the Commissary and once, outside Mortons), he knew him well enough from photographs. Harmon and his trademark hair were as likely to turn up in *Variety* as they were in *Forbes, The Wall Street Journal, Vanity Fair* or the economic section of the *News.* He'd been the low-profile head of one studio or another for years and, it was guessed, currently raked in from thirty to eighty million a year in salary, stock options and bonuses from a hydraheaded parent corporation—all this apparently accomplished without involving himself in day-to-

day business affairs. He seemed to spend most of his time mountain climbing in distant continents, raising money for politicos
and socializing with megastars, Nobelists and bluebloods. He
had transcended; someone like Joseph Harmon probably had to
make only one or two key decisions per tenure. Bud wondered
if his real function was simply to *be:* a magic paradigm, a
sun-god, a golden icon of pure energy, pure power.

Harmon cruised Bud in his rearview mirror and the screenwriter stared back perversely. The gaze of the studio chief was
bold yet faintly coquettish.

"Beautiful Bentley," he found himself saying at a red light.

"Thank you. It's wonderful. I like your Caddy."

"I don't think it has too many miles left."

Bud knew his smile was not without charm.

"Oh, come on, it's a classic."

The light turned green. Bud didn't know what to say, so he
put his foot to the pedal. Harmon looked as if he were about
to speak, then closed his mouth awkwardly. Bud thought he
should have waited to hear what he was going to say. *Fuck it,
the ball's in his court.*

He caught up to Bud and heaved it.

"Do you want to get some coffee?"

It was a bold move, but Joseph Harmon wasn't Joseph Harmon for nothing.

"Sure," said the blushing screenwriter.

The powerful man pulled in front of him, showing the back
of his trademark skull.

He led them to a little place in Brentwood, off Barrington.
They slid into a booth.

"Were you on your way to the beach?" Harmon asked as the
waiter brought them coffee. Harmon liked his black—*the way
he likes his USC interns,* Bud thought, laughing to himself.

"Yeah, I was thinkin' about it," he answered, white trash to
Harmon's chicken hawk.

"Well, it's a beautiful day."

"What do you do?" Bud asked.

"I'm a businessman," Harmon said, "on sabbatical. What about yourself?"

"Salesman." His inner voice said *screenwriter* loud enough that for a second he thought Harmon must have heard.

"Do you carry what you sell?" Bud looked confused. "I mean, with your arms."

"No. I sell ink and toner for copy machines."

"You look like you work out."

"I do," he said, and gave it a beat. "I work out of my car."

Harmon laughed. He said he was house-sitting at a friend's in the Colony and invited Bud over. The screenwriter remembered reading in *M* or *W* that Harmon kept an unpretentious home in Malibu where he did most of his "brainstorming." *When he wasn't butt-storming,* he thought. No laugh this time.

Bud wondered what he was getting himself into. He didn't have a plan anymore; all was fate and impulse. Now that the famous executive was forcing his hand, he found the alchemy of both the playacting and the real knowledge of who Harmon was made it hard to resist. Bud wasn't sure exactly what he'd hoped to gain at the coffee shop. He hadn't copped to being a writer *or* knowing about Harmon, so he couldn't very well start talking Daedalus. Not yet, anyway. So far they'd only used first names. If he went along to the Colony, Bud could work it in that he was an occasional writer for the movies. The screenwriter would find a way to drop his last name, then gauge Harmon's response. If all went well, the Wiggins connection would be made. He had to be careful; he didn't want to embarrass the man. After all, the big studio boss had already lied about the beach house with the hokey house-sitting story. Maybe that was just habit. Harmon wasn't exactly hiding in the closet, but a man of his influence was probably immensely paranoid and secretive by nature. The more Bud mulled it, the less he thought Harmon could help with *Bringing Down the House.* Even if all was revealed, what could Harmon do? If Bud pushed the Daedalus issue, it might seem like a crass, uninformed plea. Harmon would just give him some bullshit promise anyway. Bud felt irrelevant and diminished, then his spirits suddenly lifted: he would ask nothing of Joseph Harmon, that was the key. He would try to be honest about his avocation, that's all. Harmon would make something happen, or not. Definitely Bud's best shot. The burden lifted; he felt like a peer.

Outside the coffee shop Harmon said he'd left something important in Bel Air that he needed to run back for. Bud asked just how many places he was house-sitting. Harmon laughed and said he'd recently bought the Bel Air place but hadn't fully moved in because of construction. It was only a few minutes away, and he suggested Bud leave his car in the lot and hop in the Bentley for the drive. They'd swing back for the Caddy on the way to the beach.

A Range Rover stopped beside them at the light on Beverly Glen and the driver shouted Harmon's name. Bud recognized the man as Dick Whitehead, a famous hack director whose last two pictures grossed half a billion dollars. Genie Katz-Cohen watched Bud from the backseat with a vapid smile, trying to place him. They waved and sped away.

Harmon drove the Bentley through the Bel Air gate and was about to pass Bud's old house when a funny thing happened: he pulled into its driveway. In the weeks since he'd been there, the *pavillon* had undergone a radical transformation. They weaved through about a dozen pickup trucks and parked. A houseman in white answered the door and Bud followed Harmon inside. The mogul disappeared, stranding the screenwriter a moment in the weirdly familiar entrance hall before calling him to "come on back."

Moe's old den had been enlarged, the back wall replaced by French doors that opened onto the yard. Harmon handed him a drink while Bud gave the room a cursory look. Where his father's sad memorabilia used to be, hundreds of books lined the shelves. A Lucian Freud hung over the fireplace. A giant dog appeared on the deck outside the doors, shook itself violently, then peered through the glass at Bud, barking rhythmically as if trying to tell him something. The dog ended its outburst and vanished.

"The dogs bark, but the caravan moves on," Bud said involuntarily, fairly cringing at the phrase he'd cadged from a paperback. Harmon laughed.

"You read," he said, the way handsome cavalrymen in the movies used to say, *You're Cherokee,* to exotic love interests who were leading double lives. He liked that Bud "read." They talked about books and films, and when Bud mentioned one of his favorites was *The Best Years of Our Lives,* Harmon enthusiastically retrieved a cassette from a paneled cabinet and stuck it in the VCR. Then he freshened Bud's drink and sat down to watch. Bud took a sip and shivered—more alcohol than tonic. There was "offscreen" laughter and the hammering of nails.

The tape began somewhere in the middle. Fredric March and Myrna Loy had just learned their daughter was determined to torpedo Dana Andrews's faltering marriage. Bud stared dumbly at the screen. Harmon's hand grazed his thigh, then lightly massaged it. After a modicum of moves, he went down on him. Bud kept his eyes on the set, feeling only the warmth of the trademark mouth while watching his favorite scene.

"I'm going to break that marriage up!" blazed the daughter. "I can't stand it seeing Fred tied to a woman he doesn't love— and who doesn't love him. Oh, it's horrible for him! It's humiliating and it's killing his spirit. Somebody's got to help."

Myrna Loy tenderly probed her wounded daughter. "Are you sure he doesn't love her?"

"Of course I am."

"Did he tell you?" Myrna asked. The girl wavered. "Did *she*?"

"No," the daughter said glumly.

Fredric March entered the fray. "So you just jumped to conclusions—"

"He doesn't love her," she retaliated, "he hates her! I know it! I know—"

"Who are you, *God*?" he bellowed. If she wasn't God, March

was Zeus. "How do you get this power to interfere in other people's lives?"

Myrna Loy, gently: "Is Fred in love with you?"

"*Yes.*"

"You've been seeing him!" said March.

"Only once—today. Oh, it was all perfectly respectable." She directed that much toward her father. "But . . . when we were saying good-bye, he took me in his arms and kissed me—and I knew."

March boiled. "And you think a kiss from a smooth operator like Fred—you think that means anything?"

"You don't know him! You don't know anything about what's inside him. And neither does she—his wife. That's probably what she thought when she married him. The 'smooth operator' with money in his pockets. But now he isn't smooth any longer and she's lost interest in him!"

"Whereas you're possessed of all the wisdom of the ages," he said. "You can see into the inner recesses of his soul!"

"I can see because I love him!"

"So you're gonna break this marriage up. Have you decided yet how you're gonna do it? You gonna do it with an ax?"

"It's none of your business how I'm going to do it! You've forgotten what it's like to be in love!"

"You hear that, Millie? I'm so old and decrepit, I've forgotten how it feels to want somebody . . . *desperately.*"

"Peggy didn't mean that. Did you, darling?"

Peggy was thoroughly flummoxed. "No." She took a breath. "It's just that everything has always been so perfect for you. You loved each other and you got married in a big church. You had a honeymoon in the south of France. You never had any trouble of any kind. So how can you possibly understand how it is with Fred and me?"

At this, the alcoholic and his codependent wife looked at each other with the wisdom of mature love as the music stirred, symphonic and melancholy. It was Millie's turn now.

"We never had any trouble," she said, sensually ironic.

Myrna Loy stared into the rheumy eyes of her soul mate; she never looked more radiant. "How many times have I told you I hated you and believed it in my heart? How many times have you said you were sick and tired of me, that we were all washed up—"

Then came the clincher, the line that always made Bud cry, the line that collapsed the daughter into a storm of confused, self-pitying tears . . .

"How many times have we had to fall in love all over again?"

They drove back to the Cadillac, which now looked derelict, a marooned mockery. Harmon seemed at one with himself, placid—*well balanced* was the phrase that gallingly came to mind. He didn't ask for Bud's number, didn't offer to see him again. Bud felt hurt; he liked being pursued better.

"Look, I know who you are," he blurted out. "You're Joseph Harmon. I'm a screenwriter. My name is Bud Wiggins." Instead of being angry or embarrassed, Harmon did a Warren Beatty—all coy bafflement.

"But why didn't you say?"

"I don't know," he said sheepishly. "I was nervous. I never did something like this."

When Harmon didn't acknowledge the "Wiggins," he got in the Cadillac and started the engine. Maybe the mogul just didn't catch it; or he did, but chose not to pursue. Whatever the reason, Bud was actually relieved—nobody liked loitering around a parking lot. The name probably meant nothing to him. How many light-years away was the apocryphal Moe Wiggins to a time traveler and make-over artist like Joseph Harmon?

"See you, Bud. Good luck with the writing."

It felt good to hear Harmon use his name so personally. Pure energy, power and light. *The dogs bark—*

"See you," Bud said, and pulled away.

〰〰〰

A month or so later Bud went to a gallery opening on La Brea. A woman approached and stuck out her hand.

"Genie Katz-Cohen," she said. "Wylie Guthrie's agent— *former* agent."

"Oh, hi!"

"I *thought* that was you with Joseph Harmon. Wasn't it?"

"When?"

"We saw you—on Sunset. I was with Dick Whitehead."

"Oh, yeah." She smiled knowingly. He knew what was going through her head. "He's interested in a screenplay of mine— *Toy Soldier.*"

"How *wonderful.*"

She wanted to know if he'd spoken to Wylie, and Dud said he'd been underground working on a new script and hadn't talked to "anyone." The truth was that Guthrie had never returned his calls. He asked what she was up to. Genie Katz-Cohen told him she'd left TTA for the independent production side. They talked some more about *Toy Soldier,* and she said to call her if he had any low-budget horror scripts in the trunk or "anything Joseph Harmon doesn't want"—this, without innuendo. She gave him her card.

Bud passed Mortons on his way home from the gallery. It was late and there were only a few cars. No trademark white Bentley convertible—only sulky valets, eager to go home. He thought of going inside to see Raleigh but decided to phone her instead. She wouldn't be there that late anyway. He wondered why he hadn't followed that up.

At home in bed, Bud watched the old film on the late late show. Dana Andrews had just walked in on his wife and a sullen lothario—an "old friend," she lied. The two were on their way to dinner. Andrews ordered the man out, but his wife said she was leaving too, whether he liked it or not. She preened in the mirror, adjusting her hat.

"I've given you every chance to make something of yourself," she said peremptorily. "I gave up my own job when you asked me. I gave up the best years of my life and what have you done?

You flopped! Couldn't even hold that job in the drugstore! So I'm going back to work for myself and that means I'm going to *live* for myself too. And in case you don't understand English, I'm gonna get a divorce. What have you got to say to that?"

Bud slept.

2. The Portable Henry James

Bud finished the screen adaption of his story. The little boy turned out to be the stranger by way of a chilling reveal at the end. Considering all the foreboding and queasy lyricism, a supernatural twist was effective. If Daedalus wasn't interested, maybe he'd sell it to one of the cable networks that were always doing pseudosophisticated retreads of Poe and the ghost stories of James. Besides, he could always lose the reveal if someone thought it was too much of a stretch.

An item in *Variety* caught his attention. Penny Reich had been promoted to vice-president of the Circle Group, a savvy young agency attracting a lot of talent these days: Academy Award-winning cinematographers, famous French scenarists, first-time directors with Park City sleepers. She'd courted Bud years ago and was wrathful to be spurned for Bobby Feld.

He remembered being attracted to Reich from their first meeting. She was around twenty-four then, the new kid at ICM, a young Anne Bancroft. She took him to expensive restaurants and laughed extravagantly at his jokes. She told him about her Holocaust-survivor parents and her old boyfriends and her schizophrenic sister. When they waited for their cars at the end of a meal, Reich slipped her arm through his. It was like they had an arranged marriage and were in the first weeks of learning how lucky they were to have been chosen for one another.

Bud never told her much about himself. He didn't need to—his movie was in production and that was enough of a past. The unfamiliar attention of agents was thrilling; Reich's design was to swamp him with openness. He listened to her wry, sporty confessions with the engaging benevolence of a chieftain. Could she really be interested in him romantically? She was a tease—everyone in the town was—but he had an important decision to make and didn't want to muddy the waters with sex. He liked her but knew Reich was capable of leading him on just to get him to sign. On the other hand, he felt if they were going to pursue a relationship, it might be better for him to seek representation elsewhere. She'd said all along it wouldn't matter where he signed—if he chose another agency, it would be "no biggie."

The day of the decision she invited him to a screening. They sat kissing in the dark of the Directors Guild theater. She stroked his leg, nudging his cock. At dinner, Bud finally told her he was going with Feld. She was spiteful and primitive.

He decided to call her. Why not? People like Penny Reich had short memories. They had to—they got beat up every day. It was like a line he remembered from *Prince of the City,* about corrupt cops wanting in their hearts to be caught. It was the same with agents: they *needed* to eat shit, to bob like buoys in the cloacal tide. What had he done to this woman anyway? Her reaction to his choice had been naïve and inappropriate—he sensed that even Reich had been embarrassed by her rancor. The bottom line was that her feelings had been hurt; she'd confused them with business. Bud could understand that. He might have a little work to do when he phoned, that's all. He would call to congratulate her on the Circle Group promotion, a voice from the past. He'd pull out a big gun right away, to disarm her: did she know Joseph Harmon? Bud would say he thought he saw her leaving the "house on Bellagio" the other night as he was arriving for a party. She'd say he was mistaken, then ask how he knew Harmon and Bud would say, "family friend." He'd add that he was developing something for the studio head, just so she wouldn't get any wrong ideas. If it turned out that she actually did know Harmon (unlikely), he might even leave a note on the sun-god's door that Penny Reich of the Circle Group was interested in representing him and if she called, would JH please say something nice. That was a little uncool, but you never knew. Bud would make the note funny. Maybe he'd phone Harmon at the studio (something he was thinking of doing anyway) and leave word Bud Wiggins was calling regarding the *"Best Years of Our Lives* sequel," something sly to get his attention. Harmon would be happy to do him such a small favor.

In his conversation with Reich, Bud had to be more than a name-dropper. He'd quickly segue to *Toy Soldier* and the Gothic script for cable—he didn't want her thinking he'd been asleep all these years either. *You sound very busy,* she'd say, with respectful approval, peer to peer. He'd ask if she wanted to have a drink so they could get caught up. She'd say she couldn't because a colleague was dying or she was too busy or she was going to Bora Bora, and he would say there was something important he wanted to talk about. He would make her laugh and she'd give in and when they met at Chaya Brasserie, the old chemistry would still be there. He'd casually let drop that he didn't have an agent, he used "the lawyer Don Bloom," he didn't like the experience he'd had with Bobby Feld (Bud would let her give him his comeuppance). She would soften and commiserate on what a crazy time that must have been for him and how sorry she was that his movie wasn't released. *The town is really insane,* she'd say. She would glowingly reaffirm her instincts about him. He'd ask her to read his new material and she would tell him to send it to her office. Or better, she could send a messenger to pick it up—no, that was doubtful, she wouldn't want to appear too eager. She'd already been burned once. They would finish their drinks. Standing by her black BMW, he would lean to kiss her and she'd sultrily back away, saying, a little breathless, *I have to be careful about you.* She'd smile like a drug was starting to work, and give him those tango eyes before she sped away.

When he called the next morning, she wasn't in. He gave his name to the secretary, adding he was an old friend wanting to congratulate Penny on the new job.

The screenwriter parked the limo and walked to the entrance of the Beverly Palm. The doorman sometimes threw him business, for a percentage. An airport run was the best. It only took about thirty minutes to get to LAX from the "front door," and that was cash in the pocket. Once he was down there, Bud cruised the arriving flights and usually found someone to take back to the Beverly Hills area—more cash. It was illegal but you could get away with it.

"Hey, Wiggins!"

The doorman had a dirty-blond mustache and was wearing a mauve top hat.

"Wanna make fifty bucks?"

"You better believe it."

"Then get your ass over to the kitchen."

Bud wondered what it was all about. On the way over, he thought about something that happened a few years ago. The dispatcher called him in the limo and asked if he wanted to make a thousand dollars, without saying how. The only catch was, Bud had to be back at the hotel in ten minutes. He was half an hour away and had to decline. Later he found out a cosmetics tycoon wanted a partner for his girlfriend, the old *he-likes-to-watch.* They supposedly got some other driver; he never was able to confirm the story but didn't disbelieve it. He got a blow job once as a tip and another time screwed a girl in the back of the limo on her prom night. Shit happens, as the annoying phrase went.

In the kitchen he encountered about twenty ragtag recruits, mostly embarrassed Mexican busboys in the act of dressing up as clowns. A shushing, nervous maître d' presided, handing Bud a colorful suit from a vast cardboard box.

"Form one line at the door, please!" barked the maître d' in exasperation. "When you are given your trays, you will wait for me to tap your shoulder. Then you will proceed into the ball-room. *¿Comprende?*"

Bud spotted Ramón beside a giant freezer, wriggling into a satin blouse. "What's happening?"

"Charity lunch, Almodóvar," he said, grinning lecherously. "It is an *excelente* opportunity for you to make a Best Film in the Short Subject category. Although, Almodóvar, when you aim the video camera at your prick, this is the *profoundest* short subject!"

Ramón cackled as an aide-de-camp stuck a bulbous nose on his face. A helper tried to put a fright wig on Bud, but it ripped apart at the seams.

There was a great fanfare from the ballroom and the busboys lined up at the exit like parachutists in a plane. They were handed dessert trays by the kitchen staff and struggled not to laugh while the maître d' gave them a final once-over. He pointed to Bud.

"This one has no makeup!"

There was a chilling trespass of applause as the lead busboy inexplicably pushed through the doors and into the ballroom without warning. The baffled maître d' held the rest back for a beat, then had no choice but to wave them through. The men were solemn now, shocky, and proceeded with the gravity of Toltecs at a sacrifice. When the screenwriter neared the door, the aide-de-camp grabbed some lipstick from an underling and smeared it crazily on the writer's mouth. Then he fussed Bud's head with the torn wig until the boss shouted, "No time! No time!" and pushed him out after Ramón.

While the orchestra played "Send in the Clowns," the maître d' shepherded the men to their posts in front of each table, mugging and rolling his eyes as he scampered. Like Gale Gordon chasing Lucille Ball, he went after a busboy who overshot his mark; the Mexican split-grinned as the ringleader pantomimed helplessness, shrugging his shoulders to the audience and smiling apologetically at the high jinks of the mischievous dancing bears. Everyone howled.

Bud took his post and watched the goings-on with a detached, avuncular eye. Fifty bucks was fifty bucks. When he turned to study the clients at his table, a familiar face gaped at him from a few feet away. Raleigh Wolper. Her expression went from dismay to the hilarity of recognition. The screenwriter froze, and the maître d' came over and forced him to put down the tray. While the desserts were being passed out, Bud made funny faces to show he wasn't ashamed. Raleigh was now laughing so hard that her eyes were shut. He left the table to join the others in the percussive march back to the kitchen, trays at their sides like useless tambourines.

An hour later he caught up to her at the front door of the hotel. She was standing with the pudgy girl who'd sat beside her in the ballroom. Bud was capless and wore a sweater he found in the trunk of the limo. After the ballroom debauch, he needed to look civilian.

"What were you *doing* in there?" She was grinning like a loon.

"I'm writing a *script,*" he explained. "Like *Shampoo.* Except instead of doing hair, the guy drives a limo at a hotel."

Raleigh looked at her girlfriend incredulously, then turned back to Bud. "What are you *talking* about? You were a *clown,*" she said with preposterous emphasis, the effect beguiling rather than cruel.

"They needed help, so they were asking drivers—"

"I see," she said. "That's really kind of funny. Because you know that job at Mortons I have? It's really research I'm doing for a play about a restaurant hostess!" Raleigh laughed outlandishly, elbowed her friend, then realized she'd gone a little overboard. "Oh, I'm sorry," she said wearily, abruptly fed up with her own antics. She focused on Bud's mouth. "You still have lipstick."

The actress smudged his lower lip with her pinkie, then drew it back and wet the finger in her mouth, reapplying it again. The procedure suddenly struck her as funny, and she started to laugh. The girlfriend looked bored and annoyed.

"This is Esmeralda," Raleigh introduced, finally taking her finger from his lip. "Esme, meet Bud Wiggins."

They shook hands as the car was brought around. Esmeralda made a show of taking the keys from Raleigh's hand and power-walking to the driver's side.

"I'm inebriated," the actress added.

"Will you be at the restaurant tonight?"

"Yes," she said. Then, roguish: *"Research."*

ʬʬ

It was dusk. The hotel was slow and the dispatcher sent him home. Bud thought about Raleigh and was gearing up to stop by Mortons later on or at least call. He didn't think he'd blown it; she really seemed to like him.

On the way home he stopped at the dry cleaner's. He noticed a white-haired woman bent over a pay phone. He wondered whom she was talking to. It was an image out of Beckett, this homeless old woman, body bent against an unseen wind, grimacing at the receiver. She could have been talking to a bureaucrat at the Department of Sanity, the Department of Death.

He went over and pretended to use the phone beside her. She spoke in undertones. It occurred to him there was no one on the other end; it was a charade, a ruse so the cops would leave her alone. That seemed a little elaborate. Anyway, the police didn't hassle the homeless around there unless they were prone to assault or defecating on the sidewalk—that didn't seem her style. Bud Wiggins, storyteller and storefront psychologist, theorized that using a pay phone *socialized* the woman, the banal act satisfying a nostalgia for the days before her big fall. He strained to hear but couldn't make out what she was saying. Then he heard a "Hel-lo," then another and another. Hel-lo. Hel-lo. *Hel-lo*—

"That's insane!" the old woman suddenly bellowed into the receiver, her voice full of bile and contempt. "You tell them we'll go someplace else in about thirty seconds! I mean it! The pieces of shit—tell them that the chandeliers in the palace burn on, despite the changing of the guards. And that if they think I'm interested in taking snapshots of the soldiers, remind them I'm no fucking tourist!"

Bud's face flushed with her words. The sudden eavesdropped awareness of an intelligence, a *presence,* flustered and humbled him. He felt like a pickpocket who realized his target was a master thief, an auteur. He struggled to find a context for her weird harangue. To whom was she talking and what of? What was all that about the palace and the guards and the chandeliers? Was there really anyone on the line? The pauses, the way she listened, were all too real. Only the wiliest of madwomen, encouraged perhaps by Bud's audience, could have pulled it off. No, it was unlikely. He was sure she was talking to someone after all; at least that had *dramatic* potential. As a writer, where could you go with no one on the other end?

That night Bud awakened at three in the morning. His hair was wet, as if someone poured a glass of water onto the pillow. He toweled it dry and was wide-awake, craving a Mars bar. He got dressed and went out.

On his way to the 7-Eleven, he passed the dry cleaner's, and the old woman was there again at the phone, this time sitting on a plastic dairy crate as she talked. Bud parked and watched. What was eccentric before was now seemed uncanny—like something out of *The Twilight Zone.* For a moment, it seemed *he* was the crazy one. Why should he be so drawn to this pathetic, dispossessed figure? The woman hung up the phone and turned to the store, then hesitated, woeful and vulnerable. Bud left the car and impulsively strode past her.

"Excuse me, sir," she said, everyone's grandmother. "Can you give me money for an espresso?"

Bud pulled out some bills and handed them to her. Her face lit up like a hag's—a caricature of gratefulness. Suddenly he got the feeling she was playing to the house. He noticed her leg was bleeding.

"Can I help you with your leg?"

"Yes," she said matter-of-factly. "You can give it a hand. Please give my leg a hand!" She laughed, hurrying into the store. "Listen, baby, I'm hurt, but it wasn't you. Lose your self-importance."

卅卅

The next morning, Bud showed up for work. He was tired. The greasy dispatcher sat in his office, a toxic plugged-in Humpty-Dumpty.

"Wiggins, you got a call."

"What is it?"

"Mulholland. Some lady wants to look at orchids."

"What do you mean?"

He looked like he wanted to jape at Bud but couldn't be bothered.

"The nurseries—up the coast. Hey, you working Academy Award night, Wiggins?"

"Can't afford not to."

"Good. You probably know all the nominees anyway."

"I'll know a few people," he said humbly.

"Sure you will," he said. "Maybe you'll get Best Driver this year."

The Mulholland address was in a four-year-old gated hillside development. The houses looked like New Age mortuaries, monstrous mansionettes with spookily coy, perpetually leased-looking façades. As he pulled into the home's driveway, Bud wondered if its dollhouse flatness, glittering stucco, beveled glass and outdoor chandeliers were some kind of deliberate parody, the in joke of a dying architect. The huge dimensions, coupled with an aesthetically retarded and unfinished look, made him feel stupid and light-headed; it was something a child might dream up if he was a god. They started at three million.

There was a batch of ninety-thousand-dollar cars parked in front. A black chauffeur was cleaning the windows of a limousine with newspaper. Bud didn't recognize him from around town.

"Go ahead on," he said with fatal cheer, nodding at the open front door like a Judas, all snitches' largess. The screenwriter guessed he was a live-in. They were both of the service class yet still subject to hierarchy; as a rented driver Bud had lower status. The chauffeur's tricky, honey-drip, homeboy-easy manner was a way of asserting that, and Bud didn't mind playing along. If some poor indentured bastard wanted to feel superior, so be it. He liked observing these types anyway. They were full of bizarre traits adopted over the years to fend off the humiliation of boredom and sometimes made good characters for scripts. *Go ahead and meet the sick motherfucker I got to deal with every goddam day,* he seemed to say. *Go ahead on in and deal with it.* Then he shook his head at a private joke and chamoised a fender. *You better believe the rich are different, baby, uh-huh.*

On stepping into the vaulted marble entryway, Bud was greeted by two Spanish housekeepers in faded pink-striped smocks. They motioned him to stay put, then disappeared. He removed his cap. There were voices from another room, then violent laughter.

"Krizia, I gotta go. With the shit traffic, it's gonna take me an hour to get to Lorimar."

"Well," said a second voice, "if she ain't gonna show, she ain't gonna show."

Bud peered around the corner and saw the following, heading toward him like a boisterous death squad: Joel Levitt, Dick Whitehead, Bobby Feld and a self-effacing man he didn't recog-

mize. Bringing up the rear were Krizia Folb and a TTA trainee
with a retro cascade of hair that ended in a flip, like one of
Superman's girlfriends.

There was another eruption of laughter and Bud took to the
stairs. The housekeepers reappeared to open the door for the
departing guests. They looked futilely for Bud, shrugging their
shoulders like amateur actors. They vanished again as the
screenwriter found a vantage on the landing where he could
watch the loitering guests without being seen. Bobby Feld
pointed to a stain on Levitt's silk shirt.

"Jesus," said the ubiquitous agent, "you're such a fucking pig."

"Only in bed, Bobby—just like your mother."

"Classy guys, huh, Dick?" said Krizia to the hack director.

"Beautiful, beautiful men. Hey, Joel, I need to go to the
beach. Can the driver take us to the beach?"

"He'll take us where we tell him to."

"Is that your limo out there?" Krizia asked. *You naughty,
powerful man.*

"Fucking Ferrari died in the driveway. No more, I'm telling
you. No more."

"So, Joel," Feld said, "I thought I was gonna sign her today.
I'm disappointed."

"You I don't mind disappointing," said Levitt. "It's the director and the studio I don't like to disappoint." He turned to
Whitehead. "Dick, has Ms. Wurtz disappointed?"

"Four in the morning, she read me pages," he answered,
biting into something held in a napkin. He smelled of beach,
cannabis and good times. Bud knew the director had begun his
career in television and now was the darling of the DGA—if
Dick Whitehead was lobotomized, what was left would still
make it onto the studios' A list. "I'm telling you, it's the best
rewrite I've ever seen."

"Or heard," said Feld grumpily.

Whitehead laughed, and some wet crumbs flew onto Krizia's
slacks and the actual lip of the junior agent, who brushed them

away so not to be impolitic. It would take more than stray offal to dampen her ambition. The secure director dared comment on the airborne faux pas, causing another round of scary roof-raising guffaws. From his aerie, Bud mused on the laughter of the powerful; it was Olympian and secretive, a kind of black-belt comic ardor, the sound track of sadists at Happy Hour.

"Some *amazing* third-act shit." The director shook his head, smiling. "She kept me awake all fucking night."

"No!" said the trainee, with forced disbelief. The hack coolly affirmed it was true, like someone talking about hair-raising adventures in wartime Kuwait. The screenwriter wondered if the director and the trainee were doing it. Whitehead turned to the man Bud didn't know.

"Jake is disappointed, I know."

"I'm fine," said Jake. "Don't worry about it."

"It ain't over till it's over, Jakey. We'll see her in action—one day. Guarantee it."

"The director has spoken," Levitt said, turning to Folb. "Krizia?"

The executive gathered herself for an official reply.

"Joseph's a little anxious," she said with offhand authority, "but we trust Dick. If Dick's happy, we're happy—*for now.*"

"How much you paying her, Krizia?"

"Bobby Feld don't know a *price*?" said Levitt, pretending to be stunned. "I can't believe it." Folb picked up the slack.

"Four hundred thousand a week. And that will go up if she gets the Oscar."

"She's worth every fucking dime," said Levitt. "You know what her last three movies have done?" There was a hush as he paused; the room became a prayerful sanctuary. "Four hundred eighty million." Another moment of silence.

"Well," said the weary warrior-agent, "I'm glad *some*body's happy."

"Do me a favor, Bobby, and stop pissing," said Levitt, bridling. "Jesus Christ, we're here on *production business* and I say to you: 'Come. *Meet.*' I'm doing you a *fucking favor* bringing you here!"

Levitt's temper was legendary, and Feld saw a potential "situation." Time for a little rimming.

"I know that, I know that, Joel, and don't think I don't appreciate it."

"I *talked* to her about you—you think I didn't *talk* to her about you? Jesus! You think I give a *fag's ass* about who you sign or don't sign? I'm making a forty-five-million-dollar *movie* here!"

The agent climbed into his shit-storm mode; the skin of the producer's neck looked suety and hot to the touch.

"I know that and appreciate it, Joel."

"You don't think I talked to her about you?"

"I'm sure you did."

"You're 'sure.' Don't treat me like I'm fucking pixilated!"

"What is that, Joel, what is 'pixilated'?"

"Wurtz don't *like* agents, she doesn't *need* agents, but I told her I'd known you for years. You can't *press* with this woman, Bobby!"

"Joel's right, Bobby," said Dick Whitehead. The director was very *there* except for the eyes that were reddish and turbid like a dog's.

"I'm taking a risk bringing you here today at all!" the producer shouted.

As quickly as his tantrum began, Levitt realized he'd gone too far and began coddling the agent, assuring him the elusive Wurtz could be—would be—signed. It just needed to be finessed. Everyone breathed again. The jig of reward and punishment formally ended with a remark of Whitehead's that was just out of Bud's earshot; the guffaws began again when the group got outside the house, the door slamming behind them.

Bud stood and took a deep breath. His shirt was soaked. Why couldn't he get away from these people? Suddenly he was thrown against the wall by an enraged woman in a bathrobe.

"Get out of my house, you flaccid prick!" He covered his face as she struck the top of his head, trying to escape without cartwheeling down the stairs. He felt like Marty Balsam in *Psycho.* "You thought I wanted to meet you?" she stormed. "I'd rather kiss cancer than shake hands with Bobby Feld!"

When they reached the bottom of the stairs, the buzzing housekeepers appeared, forming a wedge between Bud and his combatant.

"Rosa, what the hell are you doing!"

"He is the limousine driver!" she answered.

Only then did Bud get a good look at her, and made the connection in an instant. She was on the far side of fifty, with white hair and translucent skin. Caitlin Wurtz, the woman of genius being courted, worshiped and reviled just moments ago, was none other than the homeless, hebephrenic pay phoner of the night. He'd been thrown off from the start; the name on the dispatcher's order was "Milly Theale," an alias.

Rosa retrieved Bud's trampled cap from the bottom of the stairs, and the mythic rewrite artist took it from her.

"You're the limousine?" she said tentatively.

"I'm the driver," he answered. "From the Beverly Palm Hotel."

She turned to the maids. "How could you have let them stay so long?" she implored, as if it had been in their power. Caitlin rushed at a bowl of flowers on the entrance table and inhaled. "They're gorgeous!" Rosa caught Bud's eye and tittered.

It seemed to Bud as if he'd known Caitlin forever but someone had played a cruel trick: she didn't recognize him. That made for a strange vertigo. There he was, a *driver,* comically introduced, shoved in line with who knew how many hundreds of aspirants for her approval. Yet he knew himself to be a peer, plain and simple, a king trapped in an iron mask. He had to find a way to give her a sign.

She grabbed the flowers from the bowl and went into the living room. Rosa and the mute one followed, giggling like slumber-party girls. Caitlin lifted an enormous dying arrangement from a cobalt vase and heaved them onto the erstwhile company's gutted meat-stuffed hors d'oeuvres. The housekeepers went for the offending blossoms while the great lady shoved the new bunch into the container.

"Don't throw them out!" she shouted. The women ran from the room like players in a harem farce, their hands under the stems so they wouldn't drip on the carpet. "Where's the morbidity in dead flowers?" Caitlin demanded, recinching her bathrobe belt.

If he hadn't given her bag lady self money the night before—if just one more day had passed—Bud might have wondered if he was hallucinating. He knew he had to seize the moment, it was too perfect to pass up. Still, he had no idea what the nature of her insanity was. Perhaps he'd witnessed something terribly private and should (literally) write it off to the realm of anecdote. If he "confronted her"—well, she could just deny the meeting ever happened. What if she became violent? Wurtz had already demonstrated her imperiousness; if she could grind down Levitts and Felds, what might she do to Bud?

He took the plunge.

"We met—last night. You asked for money." She looked at him with a bewildered smile, as if they were onstage and he'd given her a wrong cue. Bud's voice began to quaver. "For an espresso. Outside the Seven-Eleven."

Caitlin's face scrunched up, a horrible squall about to beat down on his loosely seeded field. Then she screamed and threw her arms around him.

"You! I don't believe it!"

Bud felt himself shaking.

"My God, it *is* you!" She fell back on the couch shrieking, containing her bosom like it was a house pet trying to escape. "Rosa, please prepare lunch for myself and Mr.—what's your name?"

"Bud Wiggins."

"Well listen, Senor Seven-Eleven; you bought me spaghetti last night and now you're gonna eat it!" She clapped her hands loudly as Rosa entered the room again. "Spaghetti, *por favor—al dente. Vite!*"

Bud was enthralled.

Caitlin Wurtz thought in "story" with the native ease of a great athlete. Here was someone he could learn from. Now that the hardest part was over, he boldly resolved to push for another get-together. That was unlikely. Unless you were famous or had something very special to offer, getting a second meeting in this town was dicey, especially on a social level. Unions in Hollywood were like fever dreams—you bumped into strangers in a house of mirrors, squealed with delight from the garish intimacy, then moved on through the labyrinth. He was too jaded to think Caitlin Wurtz would be different. Besides, she was *nuts.*

They ate lunch on the terrace beside the pool. Caitlin wanted to know all about him, and for the first time in years, he didn't lie. They had met in nakedness—she in mania, he in livery—and as Bud told his story, he realized how tired he was from keeping up appearances for so long. All he had known were hustlers, shits and shallow men. He'd become the worst of them because his slow mortification made him put on an act to betray his best self. He began as Bud Wiggins the self-made dropout and halfway house alumnus, the up-and-coming screenwriter, the eligible bachelor, the aesthete, different from the pack. But that was then, and now he was resting on scary laurels; it was autumn and the laurels had been raked and they were burning. The façade didn't fool anyone. It was as useless and unwatched by the world as a billboard above a dead motel.

In the days of his career when it looked like he was going to be someone, he remembered going house hunting—with realtors at first, then finally alone. He'd be careful to show them his old Mercedes, even after it stopped running, so they'd know he was legit, that he was worthy. As they walked him through the hillside houses Bud was cheerful, his delusion insisting the money would arrive any day. Didn't he have the *right* to look at these houses, the *birth*right? As a boy he amazed his friends by entering stores on Rodeo Drive and telling the clerks he had five thousand dollars to spend on his parents for their anniversary. The salespeople never called his bluff: he was a glib child of the Arbor who'd come of age in Bel Air. Wasn't he cotillion royalty? Didn't his father keep cigars in the humidor at Dunhill's?

The money never came, and the maestro of promise began wandering from table to table with his fucked-up fiddle and shabby tux. He'd been feeding on himself for years. If he could just *own* what had happened to him, there might be hope. The radical insight made Bud wince; he'd been like a compulsive gambler who couldn't admit the disease. If he'd only face his disappointment, it might force him to change course, to write his way out of it, to deliver the script the town was waiting for. He needed to "reinvent" himself, that's all—time to shed his skin. If he was to succeed, he had to do more than fail; he had to *embrace* his failure. That was all part of the journey. Bud was amazed at his sagacity.

With Caitlin, he was able to break the mold and drop the pretenses. She had met him, unthinkably, as a limo driver, a stooge. And he had met her on the streets in the shame of her empty fortress, an orchid yanked and thrown. His healing had begun.

Late that afternoon he drove her to a drugstore on Roxbury Drive. While he waited outside, Bud looked up from his crossword puzzle, jolted by a bald-headed girl who was peering through the front window.

"Anybody? Julia Roberts? Anyone famous?"

He said, "Nobody," and the girl went away. Caitlin came out of the pharmacy with a white bag and got in the car. They headed up Sunset for the Pacific Coast Highway.

"I was on lithium for years—gave me cysts. They got me on Tegretol now. But sometimes I say fuck you and don't take it and I wind up on the pay phone. Jesus!" she exclaimed. "It's too funny, this business of bumping into you—phenomenal.

Very screwball, what they call a 'cute meet.' *Acutely psychotic!*"

"Sturges could've done something with it, huh."

"You know I lived with him, in Paris."

"You lived with Sturges?"

"In '55. I was young. Terrible time for him. You know, I was supposed to look at stud plants today. We're talking thousands of dollars for these things. You feel like going up to Santa Barbara, Wiggins? Good bookstores up there."

"Sure."

"You want to take me to the Academy Awards, Wiggins?"

"I'd love to."

"You know what 'orchid' means? Testes. You know what the medical term for removing a testicle is? 'Orchidectomy.' Isn't that glorious?"

"Really kind of sweet."

"I think I like you, Wiggins." She smiled, then squinted into his eyes. "Just don't get an attitude."

She agreed to see him in a few days. They could maybe go to a movie, she said.

Bud went over everything he'd ever learned about the great Caitlin Wurtz. She had been in and out of hospitals most of her life, with the kinds of difficulties he imagined often plagued a mind much finer than those around it. She was married more than once to men as famous as herself, all Europeans—until about ten years ago, she was pretty much an expatriate. Her most prolific period was late fifties/early sixties (Bud was a boy, in the Arbor), when she wrote novels and plays and directed a movie that won an award in Venice. She was sculpted by Giacometti, photographed by Man Ray, set to music by Paul Bowles and memorialized in various experimental French novels—reviled, worshiped and gossiped over in a dozen languages. There was even an unauthorized bio which Bud decided to avoid. The last thing he wanted to do was regurgitate some petty falsehood; she might hate him for that. An encounter of this sort demanded no prefixed notions.

She was hot this year. *Banana Republic*—her proficient comedy about a talking ape—had just been nominated for five Academy Awards, including Best Screenplay. Bud didn't know the details of her ascent, but she was current script doctor nonpareil and Hollywood was busy paying homage the only way it knew how: cash. A veritable stampede of the afflicted limped, rolled and dragged its way to the basilica of Caitlin Wurtz, speaking in tongues, imploring to be healed. The lucky ones she laid hands on fell into seizure, then threw off the crutches, their newfound legs earning grosses that made believers of the most egregious cynics. Because her services were prohibitively expensive, producers hoped to work grimy miracles of their own and often waited until the victim was comatose before dialing 911: that's when Caitlin stormed the death house, shoved aside the yes-men, grabbed the paddles and shocked the shit out of the third act. The outpatient's postoperative bloom was always universally ascribed to the swift, skillful intervention of our surgeon and the wonder of her technique.

Bud stopped at Bookz to see if there was a copy of her memoir *Inappropriate Laughter.* Derek, a pretentious young playwright who worked there part-time, began to hover solicitously.

"Caitlin Wurtz! She's great!" Bud was annoyed that he knew the book. "We haven't had that one for a while. Might be out of print. If it isn't, we could probably order it for you. Wild lady! Do you know her?"

"No. I'll go to one of the used bookstores."

"It's a wonderfully informed book," he went on. "Very cynical, very crazy but full of insights."

"You'd make a good reviewer."

Derek laughed, a glutton for the screenwriter's contempt. Bud always played it cool around him, prowling around the Lit Crit sections of the store like he was Paul Schrader not wanting to be bothered. Ever since Derek found out Bud once had a movie produced, he considered the two of them fraternity brothers, hotshot belletrists, fellow toilers in the word game. Bud hated him because he was seven or eight years younger.

"Did I tell you I'm going to Mexico?"

"Vacation?"

"I'm doing a rewrite. They're shooting at Churubusco, where Buñuel did his stuff."

Bud thought: Stuff *this.* There it was, again—everyone was a Buñuel fanatic. He remembered there was something about Derek and Mexico, he'd lived there as a boy or his father was a consul or something. It was his "specialty" area. If a film project had anything remotely to do with Mexico, he was in there lobbying for work.

Bud was supposed to get all excited about the news but preferred thwacking him with the mean wood paddle of sunny indifference—Derek would have to continue pledging through the eternal hell week of their dead, dumb-ass relationship. Bud didn't believe this wimp was on his way to the dry cleaner's, let alone Mexico to work on a script.

"Hey!"

He turned around and was startled to see his ex.

"How are you?"

"Great!"

Jeanette looked terrific but had that cheerleader energy that usually meant her defenses were up. Running into each other was always a little weird; Bud guessed it had been ten months or so since the breakup. She was looking for a book of acting class monologues.

"Want to get some coffee?" he asked.

She smiled at him blankly, as if wondering about opening a door better left shut. They'd finally broken it off, after three and a half stormy years. This time it was really over. She said yes; she could talk from a window.

Jeanette Childers was a smart hillbilly from Tennessee, a coruscating blonde with a temper. They'd formally met at a Rodeo Drive AA meeting (before the Doctor died, Bud had coerced him to attend) and the screenwriter had vaguely remembered her from high school in Beverly Hills, a wild girl who moved in a fast, rich-kid crowd. She was an occasional television actress, skittish, sexy, sober a few years already when they met, an alcoholic who'd used the needle a few times way back when. She really got his attention. They were vigilant about the past (they both had "abandonment issues," she liked to say) and ruthlessly shared old emotional humiliations. At that time Bud's movie had been defunct for only a few years—he knew his beaten-up credibility appealed to her. Jeanette liked his scripts, liked that he was a writer altogether. She was tired of dating actors and musicians. They started going to lots of Children of Alcoholics meetings together and for a while, as Jeanette once said, it was "beautiful."

Indeed, it was—grave, intimate groups that gathered in shabby community centers and solemn, stony churches. They called it the Program. Someone spoke of old domestic horrors; then others joined the weave, sharing the opera of abuse called Childhood. Bud envied the ones who seemed to be professional rememberers, torch singers with poisoned psalms sung from the heart. If one's memory was pure, one's speech invariably had the ring of authenticity. It was a valuable lesson for a writer, and he sat there spellbound with his new love. Each Meeting was petty, splendid, infuriating, sublime. There were loose rules of order that always managed to work, karmically balancing the room, tribal and benevolent. God was there, not as Father or Mother, but as the room created Him: God was anger and love, death and unspeakable acts, God was coffee, donations, fold-up chairs and recitations. He was grandly, blandly there, the homogeneous God and Godlessness of the new Healing. Bud loved to listen. He was in a writing slump then and felt his ear come alive again in the rooms. If you listened closely, you could hear a thousand crummy *Oresteia*s. It was great for Story.

He was shy; at first, he couldn't bring himself to "share" before the others. When someone commented on his reticence, Bud said, "Will sharing make me a good boy?" He was half joking, but a woman there was impressed with his response, even working it into her *pitch* the next night (that was another word for "sharing"; everything devolved from the Business). "These rooms are safe houses," she said to the darkness, like Mother Courage, "where boys and girls don't have to be 'good' anymore, where they can show their pain and vulnerability."

That woman was Jeanette.

So their courtship began in a church. Jeanette loved that, thought it "appropriate." That was one of her favorite words. The world could be divided in two: the Appropriate and the Inappropriate, the "impeccable" and the out of control. "Powerlessness" was a major Meeting theme—we are *powerless* over heroin and alcohol, *powerless* over psychotic siblings, abusive spouses, toxic parents and mewling infants. Once you admitted *powerlessness,* the burden began to lift. One man who was tortured in the cellar as a child stood up and said he was powerless over basements. That really got to Bud; his eyes welled up and Jeanette put her tiny hand on his. Another time a three-hundred-pound woman announced she'd made a pact with herself not to say "I love you" to anyone she picked up for sex—at least not for ninety days. The room thundered with applause. The couple found it fabulously poignant, comical, grotesque. There were people who were choked, stabbed and raped by their parents; others who decorated their chests with wounds, drawing razors across them with the deliberation of farmers plowing fields. There was a woman whose baby drowned in her arms as she nodded out in the tub. There were single survivors of suicide pacts, ecstatic bulimics, molesters and agoraphobics. There was a man whose cell door was welded shut by penitentiary guards and an angel-faced girl trying to break from a family porn dynasty and a man who changed his name by the hour.

What *material:* it seemed the worst disease of all was people addicted to *people*—"codependents" they called them. He saw this in his relationship with the Doctor. Bud had shown his codependency by lifting Brian off the floor of restaurants and cleaning up his puke. Bud was a codependent and Bud was an "enabler"; he *enabled* the Doctor to get loaded, he *cosigned* the Doctor's addictions. He was reenacting childhood scenarios, with his sick friend as dysfunctional parent. But Brian wasn't ready to stop using, let alone look into himself. By that time he was already circling the drain.

At the coffee shop Bud covered up the awkwardness by talking nonstop about Caitlin Wurtz. It was a good story, but he could tell Jeanette was seething, her anger triggered by his chatty, presumptuous familiarity.

"You've talked for twenty minutes without asking how I am."

He felt the old twinge, she was coming in for the kill.

"I'm sorry," he said, "I'm just a little nervous."

"It's so typical! So passive-aggressive! It was always you, you, you!" Disgust darkened her face. "I don't even know why we're—I don't know what I'm doing here, what I expected."

It always came to this. For almost four years he had abused this woman: one week proposing, the next week suggesting a hiatus, begging her to bear his children, then declaring he needed to see "other people." He wanted marriage and babies and thought Jeanette was the one, but whenever she lowered her guard and envisioned a future together, the bottom dropped out of Bud's feelings for her; she became galling and papery and he walked out. Months would pass before he realized what he'd thrown away and felt a terrifying remorse. He'd feel her in again, and she would let him—people who needed to repeat childhood abandonment traumas had a kind of sixth sense when it came to finding partners for the dance of death. So said Jeanette and the Meetings and the articles in *Mademoiselle* and *Us* and the *News:* the lovers watched themselves stuck in the tar pits of passion/aggression, "cunning and baffling," like alcoholism itself, and Jeanette kept saying how *brave* they were. They went to a shrink and tried to get to the bottom of it.

He walked out on her again.

When she wouldn't take him back, he sent her flowers, telegrams and love letters, baskets stuffed with fruit and potpourri,

miniature dolls, silverware and symbolic mementos. She re-
sisted, hiding away from him like a Muslim woman; he wore
her down until all that was left was a veil through which he saw
her nakedness. At last, she let him draw it away for intercourse.

"You know, you have a mother problem," Jeanette said as
she got up. He despised himself when he was with this woman.
"I wonder what went through your head each time you left.
You *know* you're just going to do it again, with someone else.
You're dangerous!"

He waited a moment, then asked how her job was going. She
laughed at his incongruity, shaking her head like he was certi-
fiable.

"Maybe your new friend will 'fix' it for you. She's about
Dolly's age, isn't she? Maybe now you can make a real commitment!"

Bud put down some money and followed her out.

"Well, I guess I'll see you around," he mumbled as she got
in her car.

"Not unless you come to Italy!" she yelled. Jeanette's eyes
blazed, fanned by a spiteful second wind. She would have that
family, that *life,* and shove it down his throat.

"What do you mean?"

"I'm moving to Italy."

"When?"

"In three weeks!"

Then Jeanette backed away, smiling toward him, her eyes
about to stream, unable to look at the man who had hurt her
so terribly. She started the car, then reached into the glove
compartment.

"Oh—here's your book."

She threw him *The Portrait of a Lady.* She used to ask Bud
to recommend books—why had he given her that? He saw for
the first time the cruelty in giving her a book about a woman
with so many chances to marry—to marry well—who perversely overthrows them all. He was that woman.

He was over her. Then why the rabbit punch feeling of abandónment when Jeanette said she was moving to Italy? Funny. Maybe he'd go back to Meetings or see her shrink again. They used to be in Conjoint, but Jeanette eventually demanded he begin individual therapy too, to speed everything along—like doubling up on classes toward a degree. He did that for a while. When the relationship became too much work, the shrink actually offered to help him end it, if that's what Bud wanted. Trouble was, he didn't *know* what he wanted. He knew one thing, though: he didn't want to go to Conjoint anymore. Therapy together was never that great, anyway. He would sit there feeling like a serial killer and Jeanette would cry and bolt into the toilet with the shrink shouting after her, "Don't run away, Jeanette! Don't run away!"

Bud knew she was going to Italy to wash the taste of him away. She had a rich father. He thought of what she said about him being "dangerous." Old Bluebeard Wiggins. *Right.* He suddenly got angry—anger was good for him. That's what the shrink used to say. As he watched her drive away, a mordant little voice inside him said, "They'd all better have rich fathers."

That night he was full of nervous energy. He called Raleigh at Mortons and made a date. When he hung up the phone, Bud felt the warm winds of destiny stirring. Weren't the cypresses nodding at his window? The fence of trees—only their woolly green waists were visible—was the best thing about his old room at Dolly's. For years the trees said nothing to him; now they shimmied with cool, cosmological elegance. He had arrived at a door, and felt like a novitiate. He remembered all those English novels, filled with cypress alleys, about the struggle to live with Art. Well, he'd meandered to the concourse and was waiting to be buffeted in the starry dark.

MMM

He took Raleigh out to dinner. On the way, she asked—a little ironically—if he was done with the "Shampoo" script and Bud said he was on the third act. He wanted to know what she was doing at the infamous hotel lunch. Raleigh said it was a fund raiser for Kidz with Kancer, an organization that granted last wishes to dying children. Her friend Esme worked for them.

"You know what was really sad? One of the sick little boys was supposed to meet Calabash—that monkey from *Banana Republic*. But he died before it could happen."

"The monkey?"

"No, silly. The little boy."

"Well, apes have busy schedules—you know, personal appearances, product endorsement, visits to the shrink."

"Very funny. I think it's *so sad.*"

"I'm sort of friendly with the writer."

"What writer?"

"Of *Banana Republic.*"

"I know about that person. What's her name?"

"Caitlin Wurtz."

"She's supposed to be crazy."

"Like a fox."

"Interesting woman. How do you know her?"

"We're friends."

"You're friends with a *lot* of people, aren't you, Wiggins?" Raleigh watched him shrug his shoulders. "*Writers,*" she said, and shook her head. "So *sensitive.*" She squinted through the windshield and changed tack. "What an *amazing* thing, to be a writer. I looked in a quotation book before you picked me up, under 'Writers.' " She pulled a crumpled paper from a pocket. "Listen to this! 'I have cultivated my hysteria with joy and terror.' Isn't that great!"

"Yeah. That's from the Writers section?"

"Uh-huh. Charles Baudelaire, have you heard of him?"

"Works for Touchstone."

"Listen to this one: 'A woman must have money and a room of her own if she is to write fiction.' I *love* that."

"Jackie Collins?"

Raleigh laughed. "God, you're silly, Wiggins. Virginia

Woolf. You are really a silly man. I mean, I've always kept journals, but writing my script was *so hard*—and it isn't even *good*. I don't think of myself as a writer. I'm an actress. I get paid to be with people—*sometimes* I get paid, anyway. But poor writers get paid to be alone." She scrubbed his head with her fingers. "You're really cute, you know. Like a dog. Look at this hair, it's like a *pelt*." She scrubbed harder. "Ooh, just look, just look! Like a *puppy pelt!*"

They went back to her Fairfax apartment and drank wine. They kissed and she pulled him to the bedroom. Bud got hard enough to put a condom on, but that was it. He started to go down on her but Raleigh didn't want that. They kissed some more. After a while he got hard again, but by then the condom was dry and she didn't have any lubricant. Bud pretended he wasn't at all bothered. He reassured himself that sometimes he just didn't feel sexual; that was normal. Listening to the pathetic "sexaholics" at Meetings had helped, had given Bud *permission* to be nonsexual. Not being able to fuck was no big deal. Happened to everybody. The trick was to let it go. If you didn't start obsessing, it wasn't so bad.

Raleigh microwaved popcorn and they watched television. An hour later they tried again, but it wasn't any good and Bud wound up telling her he was on antidepressants, that the booze probably wasn't a good mix. The fabrication had the right effect on her—she seemed moved, impressed, saddened. Maybe it was just relief at being exonerated.

"What's it called?"

"Prozac."

"I've heard of that. There was a whole *Donahue* about it. Does it help?"

"Sometimes," he said, nobly laconic.

"I think Esmeralda might be taking that, too."

Raleigh thoughtfully munched some popcorn, as if trying to solve a complicated math problem. Then she turned to him and cocked her head.

"Was Clifford Odets on antidepressants?"

He didn't know. They fell asleep for an hour with the TV on, then Bud left. She smiled in her sleep as he kissed her cheek on the way out.

When he was fifteen, Bud went to summer school in Canada and was impotent with a girl he met. He told Morris, who then sent him to a real Freudian son of a bitch in Beverly Hills, over on Bedford Drive. Dr. Jurgen was a psychoanalyst whom Brian was seeing after his kid sister got killed by a car right outside the house. Jurgen gave him pills that Bud looked up in the *PDR*. There were about a million listed side effects and the young patient got nervous. When he refused to take them anymore, the analyst looked at him coldly and said, "Listen to me: if you stop taking the pills, *you're going to be depressed.*"

Jurgen's breath was foul; every doctor's breath stunk, even Brian's.

≈≈≈

Bud waited for the shoe to drop, but instead Caitlin's interest in him grew. She messengered over rare books and tapes of old movie musicals, left dirty messages on his answering machine, sent flowers and balloons and sweet doggerel dispatches. What was it she needed from him? Didn't this woman have any friends? He wanted to be more than a mascot. How could he be worthy of taking so much of her time, what could he give her? That was negative thinking; he wanted no part of it. Why *not* worthy, why *not* Bud Wiggins? If this was Destiny, he would rise to the occasion.

A few days after his date with Raleigh, he took Caitlin out to the desert. She kept bringing up Death Valley and Bud told her about Badwater, the hottest spot on earth. She couldn't believe such a place was only a few hours away. Driving soothed her, and the screenwriter enjoyed their time on the road. The long drives had other benefits, too; he was making money. He could even exaggerate the hours on the invoice—the studio paid for everything.

As they neared Palm Springs, Caitlin marveled at the swarms of metal windmills on the hills. Bud had seen them for years, without ever knowing why they existed. Something to do with energy. He drove off the freeway and onto a dirt road to get a closer look.

"Phenomenal, aren't they? Do they really *do* anything, Wiggins? Do they have a purpose?"

The things had proliferated since he'd last seen them. Bud pulled the car over in the midst of the aluminum forest of petaled, whirligig contraptions.

"I always thought it was like some kind of land scam," he said, "with an environmental twist. You know: guy sells you stock in a wind farm in California . . ."

"Eerie, though, aren't they?"

They got out. She leaned back on the dusty limousine and lit a cigarette, looking up at the unattended gyrating mills like an artist taking in a canvas. The ones on flatland lined long, thin pools of water. Some of them twirled furiously while others were motionless, dormant.

"It's Dust Bowl sci-fi. Reminds me of something I once wrote, before I started spying in the enemy camp." She laughed bitterly. "I learned how to look like the enemy, talk like the enemy—too bad I forgot what my mission was."

"You can write what you care about, Cait—if that's what you want."

It was the first time Bud had offered such an opinion and he braced himself for abuse.

"Hope dies eternal." Caitlin snorted, stubbing her cigarette out in the sand. "That sounded 'written,' didn't it? Jesus." She smiled, warmly. "You know, I had a kid once called me Cait. I like that. We lived in a villa in Cuernavaca. He called it the Casa Que Pasa. Sweet boy."

"Are you close?"

"He lives in Europe, so it's hard. We rendezvous in Mexico every couple years."

"Is he in the Business?"

"No way. No sense of story, thank God."

"Does he know you're up for an Oscar?"

"I sure as hell hope not. He'd give me some shit. It's a far cry from the Prix Goncourt."

"What's that?"

"I wrote a novel in my twenties, sold it to Gallimard. Almost got the prize. Cocteau was on the committee—*outraged* I didn't win. Couldn't sway them, because I was *l'Américaine.*"

She chewed on some dried fruit and nuts they'd picked up at Hadley's, then swallowed some pills and sat in the limo. Around Indian Wells, the heart went out of her and she wanted to go home. She sang softly to herself but he couldn't hear the words.

When they got back to Los Angeles, Caitlin pointed out an anonymous low-slung building with a gravel roof, surrounded by a pale green concrete fence. It was a private psychiatric hospital, right there on Olympic. Bud said he had a morbid interest in such places and that it was strange he'd never noticed it.

"Oh, they don't like you to notice them," she said, a little sly. "I was there in '68—no, '65. Six weeks in '65. I oughta go back and break a few heads. I wasn't writing for money then— proof of insanity!" She laughed wickedly, then grew solemn. "I just wanted to die, die, die."

Bud kept his mouth shut. She mentioned her roommate at the time, a famous first name long dead.

"She wanted to, too—and she did. Boy, did they screw her up. She was pretty nuts by then without anybody's help. She had these long nails she used to like to *burn.* And she had this big old bra she wore—a Howard Hughes Special—twenty-four hours a day! And reading, I mean, *really* reading, all the time. She was a bright girl. Not dilettante-bright but bright-bright. Had some kind of obsession with Henry James. Can you believe it?"

"What kind of an obsession?"

She dragged on her cigarette like she was in a dusty drama,

then laughed, exorcising smoke. "I don't know where she picked that up. But there they were, in the room—*The Complete Tales of Henry James,* twelve volumes! A sad, sad little girl. She'd been so hurt one way that she swung the other, into what they used to call 'deep.' Maybe it's because the women in James, you know—well, it's just impossible for them to love. Or be loved."

The famous woman sighed moodily, and as she did, Bud thought he heard the shoe dropping. It was the hour of the turn of the screw, a kind of prosaic epiphany that signaled his exile from Caitlin Wurtz's complicated, overgrown landscape. What the hell had he expected, anyhow? His passport would be stamped and returned without malice; from then on, the country would be closed to him. He held his breath until the critical moment passed. Then, with complete indifference, Caitlin said: "She slept with her mother, you know."

For the next few weeks they saw each other every day. Bud loosened up. He was as quick and charming with Caitlin as he'd ever been in his life. They inhabited a kind of hyperspace, each goading the other to outrage and profanity, to darker definitions of the memorable. He took her places she'd never seen: racetracks and dirty beaches, moribund shopping malls and hidden lakes, rickety amusement parks, airport strip joints and windswept outlooks. He even showed her his orange-bricked elementary school with its vast asphalt playground of old devotions. She stayed away from pay phones. Caitlin never talked about the movie she was writing or rewriting or whatever. Bud wanted to avoid the show biz angle anyway, and took that as a sign of newfound health.

She spoke with dreamlike fluency of psilocybin and preparation for death, of vaudeville, pyramids and butoh dancing. Where she'd lived: the hotels and walk-ups, Palladian villas and pieds-à-terre, garrets and asylums. She was a monologist of awesome power. Just at the moment he couldn't take anymore, when the sun blistered his lips and he found himself drifting from the ship, out of sight, Caitlin threw him a rope and pulled him in. And she wasn't just using him as string for her pearls. Bud told her some ideas for scripts that he'd never followed up on, projects stillborn because he had had to make a living, be the hack. He mentioned *Bringing Down the House* and her eyes lit up at the title, consumed and consuming. When he sketched it for her, it seemed like a favorite story she was hearing again for the first time in years, something precious, sweet as his *Secret Garden*. He told her what he'd never told anyone—that he'd failed as a hack, that he hadn't even been offered a chair at the game.

The Academy Awards were getting close and Bud soon understood he was to be her escort, not driver. Caitlin said she was worried about herself because she was actually starting to get excited, especially about dressing up.

Spending time with her made Bud feel like he was writing prose again. He went through some old files for inspiration and pulled an outline he'd written for a hospital drama about Brian and County General. It was ambitious and unfinished. Maybe he'd pick up the thread again and turn it into a novella—he could always adapt it later for the screen. *Bringing Down the House* had been a dress rehearsal; now Bud was truly feeling *literary*, for the first time since he was a teenager. His whole "case" with Caitlin Wurtz, as James would say, lent itself to novelistic reflections.

He thought of the madwoman with the burning nails and twenty-four-hour bra, and went to the shelf to get reacquainted with a few of the Master's books. He thumbed the worn paperback. If Bud had shown the perversity of Isabel Archer in resisting a marriage to Jeanette, he was now sure he felt like Merton Densher, banished from the Venetian palazzo of that awesome invalid Milly Theale in *The Wings of the Dove.* Yet his conscience was clear; he'd betrayed no one. The only conspirator in his quest for the script doctor's respect was the desire to be acknowledged by someone as great as he secretly hoped himself to be. Maybe there was more. Was he in love with Caitlin Wurtz? Was she a little in love with him? "He was too innocent and she too experienced to make anything of love." He wrote this on a slip of paper, just to see how it looked. He wondered if the sentence was any good. Finally, it seemed borrowed and pretentious.

MM

Penny Reich called the next morning and they had a nice talk. Bud was relaxed and even used the bit about thinking he saw her at a Joseph Harmon party. She asked what he was doing and he mentioned *Toy Soldier* and the Gothic script, leaving Daedalus out of it. Reich sounded enthused and seemed to like it when Bud said he was between agents ("I use the lawyer Don Bloom"). She told him to send her the scripts. Something stopped him from asking if she wanted to meet for drinks.

"Well—see you at the Academy Awards."

"I don't think so," she said. "I don't even watch them anymore."

"Neither do I, but someone asked me to go this year, so I thought it might be a hoot."

"You're *going* to the Awards? With who?"

"Caitlin Wurtz."

"I'm impressed," the agent said. "I really love her."

"You know her?"

"Only her work. I think she's wonderful."

Bud knew he'd scored major points. Respectfully, she didn't probe.

"Well, then, I'll have to watch. I'll look for you."

"I'll wave."

"I'm glad you're doing so well, Bud. Gotta go."

MM

The final day for submissions arrived and Bud went over his polished forty-five-page script again, checking for typos and errors in continuity. He'd planned to pay a messenger service, then decided to bring it to the studio himself. He called the Daedalus office from a phone at the gate and they told him to leave his script with the guard.

On the way back from his errand, Bud stopped by Bookz for the trades.

"Hey, I think Derek left something for you," said the girl behind the counter, rooting around for something below. She pulled out a book—Derek's own copy of Caitlin's memoir, annoyingly dog-eared. There was a Post-It attached: "Vaya con Caitlin!" Bud was embarrassed, and worried that the girl might think he and Derek were soul brothers. Still, he asked when the playwright was due back from Mexico.

"Mexico? He's not in Mexico."

The screenwriter reveled to himself. "His job fell through?"

"No! I thought you knew—Derek got a 'genius' grant. Two hundred and twenty-five thousand dollars."

Bud lurched for the door.

The clerk shouted after him like a cultist: "He's the youngest recipient ever!"

Bud came home to a message from Raleigh on his machine. She's really hanging in there, he thought. *Maybe she thinks I'm a fag.* Every starlet worth her salt was tight with some queer— that was traditional. AIDS had become just another tool for craft, a boon to acting class crying jags. Bud laughed at his blackness. He called and Raleigh invited him to dinner.

When he pulled up, she was doing a funny go-go dance at her front door.

"I quit my job."

"That's great. Why?"

"I got a part in a movie."

"You're kidding me! That's *amazing,* when do you start?"

"Three weeks. I'm the first one they cast."

She pretended to play his body like a beatnik on the bongos, then yanked him inside. They drank champagne and Bud kissed her, wondering to himself if he'd ever feel sexual again.

She said she was starving and sardonically suggested Mortons. Bud thought that was a great idea and Raleigh said the new maître d' was a friend and would probably get them a "power" table.

He was glad about having Dolly's credit card.

Raleigh was a little nervous about being there because she'd quit without notice, but no one seemed to give a damn. Her replacement graciously brought them to their table, campily cautioning her to "behave"—she was high from the incongruity of it all. Bud wasn't about to look around to see who was there, not just yet; he didn't want to be a tourist. Better to be watched himself for a while.

He was about to suggest they have caviar when out of nowhere sprang the feral, unctuous Wylie Guthrie, cupping Raleigh's hand in his.

"Congratulations, young lady."

"Thank you!" Raleigh exuberantly turned to her date. "This is Mr. Guthrie. He wrote the movie I'm going to be in."

They shook hands like debaters on a dais.

"What a *pleasure*. I've tried to reach you, Mr. Guthrie," Bud said, feigning pique. "Did you get a chance to read my script?"

The canny guru was strangely cool.

"I had some problems with it. We'll discuss." He swooped down on the actress again, his jaw unhinging lasciviously. An aside, to Bud: "This is one hell of an actress." Guthrie abruptly moved on, like some legendary host table-hopping an eponymous celebrity boîte.

Raleigh downed her glass, then fast-switched it with Bud's, as a joke. "God, you know *everyone.*" She started working on his drink.

"He's just a writer," Bud said. "We always swap scripts and give each other notes. So Wylie Guthrie wrote the movie you're gonna do." He nodded thoughtfully. "Did he get you into bed?"

He knew it wasn't the brightest thing to have said and she punished him with a look that said: *not exactly your area.*

"Look at him," Bud said, watching Guthrie snake his way through the restaurant. "A regular Swifty Lazar."

They fell asleep in their underwear. Bud woke up and stared at the luminous hands of the clock. It was 3:00 A.M. He lay there trying to remember if that was the hour of the wolf. He cuddled her and she smiled in her sleep. It was better this way, without the pressure. He'd wait until he felt genuinely sexual again or at least until he had one of those piss hard-ons that took forever to go away. Why force it? He wasn't a machine. Raleigh was the kind of girl that wanted a guy who wasn't afraid to explore his feminine side. He knew she probably found it a relief to meet an interesting man who wasn't obsessed by conquest; it was even erotic. They would build trust, then everything else would follow. Sex was the easy part.

Her eyes still shut, Raleigh turned to face him. She stroked his hip and purred. She got something from the nightstand drawer. Then she slipped her panties off, drowsily inciting him, daubing the tip of his cock with gel. She put some between her legs and guided him in. Finally inside her, Bud felt his anxiety dissolve. As Bobby Feld would say, it was a done deal. It felt good to be out of development.

They made love again in the morning. Afterward Raleigh seemed shy and sweetly self-conscious, struggling to contain her excitement at what had happened between them. She made coffee and eggs, and he saw her transparent delicacy and depth of feeling for him. She was poised for a relationship; that was all right, even appealing. Bud figured he had to say something to finish off the dangling white lie and casually mentioned that after their first date he'd stopped the Prozac. (Was he becoming a pathological liar?) Raleigh became terribly concerned and wanted to make sure a doctor was supervising. She squeezed his arm to show respect, support and approval of his decision to go it alone.

"Esme—my friend that you met at the hotel?—she's having an Academy Award party. Wanna come?"

"I can't—I'm *going.* Didn't I tell you?"

"No! You're going to the Academy Awards! Are you driving someone in the limo?"

"Sort of. I'm going with Caitlin Wurtz, but more like an escort."

"As a *date*?"

"It's not a date. She's . . . *neurotic* and doesn't have anyone to go with."

Her eyes narrowed. "Are you sleeping with this woman?"

"No. I am not 'sleeping with this woman.' "

"Then I am *definitely* going! I'll stand in the bleachers, it'll be *fun.*" She laughed, then kissed the top of his head, rubbing it with her fingers as if trying to get a spot out. "Look at this pelt, just *look at it.* Look at this sweet dog's pelt."

៣៣

"Gorgeous, Buddy, gorgeous!"

Dolly smiled crookedly as he examined himself in the gold-flaked bedroom mirror. She was in good spirits, insisting her misshapen face was swollen mostly from an allergic reaction to antibiotics.

"He is really the best, Armani. You look gorgeous in it—better than your fucking father ever did. He was jealous of you *in the crib* he was jealous!"

"I'll bring it back tomorrow."

"You can bring it back the next day, it isn't important. Without a *spot* is important, Hoffmann-Dougherty won't take it back with a spot. And I'll have to pay a fortune."

"We won't be around any food. I don't even think we're going to the dinner ball."

"Maybe this woman will thank you in her speech."

"I kind of doubt it."

"Play your cards, Buddy. It's not the worst thing, screwing an older woman."

He changed into his street clothes and Dolly zipped the tux into a bag.

"Remember to stand close to the camera, I'm taping on the VCR. I love you! *E-zih-zinee! Fahr fahr carmintrate!*"

Rosa, agog at his regalia, ushered Bud upstairs. He sat in a chair by the bedroom fireplace as Caitlin dashed from bathroom to dressing closet.

"It's a beautiful dress," he said. It was deep blue, with thousands of beads.

"It's borrowed—*seventeen thousand dollars.* The costume designer got it for me, do you love it? Borrowed, and blue, and seventeen grand. That's about twice what they gimme now *per page.* That means, in the best of all bartering worlds, I could buy this little frock for *two pages.* I mean, all the French painters used to pay for dinner by drawing on napkins, right? But they didn't have per diem, either. I tell you, Wiggins, I got per diem that could *raise the dead.*"

Bud picked up a script as the doorbell chimed downstairs. The title page read: "Another Fine Mess, by Caitlin Wurtz. Final Draft."

"Put that down!"

"So sorry," he said, drolly.

"You'd better be. *Jesus.*" She took a gulp from what looked like scotch, then began futzing with enormous pearl earrings. "Go through my dirty underwear, why don't you? Though you might like that, huh, Wiggins?" A maid stuck her head in to say the limo had arrived. "You want to read it, Wiggins? Go ahead! Go ahead, I *dare* you—"

He played along like they were an old comedy duo. "If you don't want me to read it, I won't read it."

"Go ahead! It's *brilliant,* I *love* it—it's the culmination of my craft, better even than *Banana Republic.*" She was enjoying the "roast"; the words spilled out savagely, cathartic. "I tell you, it's got *everything,* as they used to say, even a kid who's searching for his long-lost dad—a bum who's mistakenly been made the pope! That's great, isn't it Wiggins, don't you love that? What do you think? Eight thousand seven hundred and fifty bucks a page! This poor shit wakes up and he's the pope! Amazing, isn't it? What do ya think? Go ahead, I can take it. Tell me your thoughts. . . ."

When Bud went downstairs, Ramón was sipping coffee from a bone china cup.

"Ah, Señor Wiggins! When the call came in, I demanded it. I hope it does not *distress* you. I wish only to give you and your paramour the red-carpet treatment—the carpet *roja,* pendejo."

Caitlin appeared on the stairs and Ramón stiffened. He made a nervous, formal hello, then darted outside to the car to open the door for its passengers.

They joined a slow posse of limousines gliding through a run-down section of Hollywood. Bud had always fantasized about winning an Oscar, or at least being nominated, but now he was happy settling for the simulation. After all, back at the hotel the doorman was selling black-market tickets to the show for twenty-five hundred dollars. No, everything was a groove; Bud had the dreamy look of an opium eater. Caitlin told him to snap out of it. She asked him if there was any ice and Ramón overheard. He directed Bud to the concealed bucket, all the while calling him "Orson," like he used to.

"You're Chilean, aren't you?" Caitlin asked.

"How did you know?"

"*Porque lo sé.*"

"*Entonces sabes que soy una fanática de* Orson Welles."

She sat back. "Jesus, I'm starting to get nervous. It's the daylight: you imagine these things take place at *night.* But here it is, sunny and dirty and bright, everyone going about his business—right out of Nathanael West. Talk to me, Bud."

She clasped his hand tight. As the puckish driver smiled approvingly from the rearview, Bud began the story about Welles that was the source of his nickname.

He got his first job as chauffeur years ago, when he returned from the Foundation. He was waiting around the hotel garage when a call came in: the private car taking Orson Welles back to his Las Vegas home had broken down, just a few miles away. Mr. Welles would take a limo to Vegas and Bud was to pick him up ASAP. They rendezvoused, then headed over the hill to the Ventura Freeway. Welles said nothing. The driver was paid per mile in a case like this, so Bud stood to make a lot of money for the relatively short time he'd have the massive auteur in tow. Bud soon began to obsess on his bad car karma, with attendant full-blown visions of the limo breaking down in the desert and Citizen Kane exploding like an eggplant in the heat. He was almost phobic about car trouble (he'd never learned how to change a flat)—and this was before the age of car phones.

By the time they reached Mulholland, Bud was so anxious he decided he couldn't go through with it. He told Welles a warning light in the dash went on and they had to turn back.

They were getting closer and Bud could hear the roar of the mob as they greeted the arrivals. His stomach fluttered; engrossed in his tale, Caitlin ignored the scary salvos.

"On the way back to the hotel, I started to have second thoughts about chickening out."

"Liar's remorse."

"Right. I kept thinking maybe I should just overcome my fears, drive the guy to Vegas, then write a short play or a piece for a magazine. I could have called it *Driving Orson*—"

"How about *Ditching Orson*?"

"*Mira!* It is the ape!"

Calabash, the monkey from *Banana Republic,* disembarked from the limo ahead. He wore a tuxedo and tugged at the leash of his trainer, a pretty woman in a gaudy, sequined gown. There were blinding flashes and screams from the crowd as he took the red carpet. Suddenly, hearing the overamplified voice of an emcee greeting the celebs, Caitlin looked stricken; there was an army of valets and one of them opened the door, as if for search and seizure. She gasped as Bud helped her out. They joined the logjam of arrivals.

"Caitlin!"

Someone broke through a cordon and thrust a script into the face of the Nominee—it was the bald-headed girl Bud had encountered outside the pharmacy.

"You—stay away from me!"

"It's my dialogue! I don't want to take *away* from you, I *gave* to you, it's all answered prayers, goddammit! I just want *credit*, I deserve *credit*—"

Security grabbed the girl and she fell down, then was dragged. Caitlin scuttled away, pushing aside the black-tie horde like someone in a conflagration looking for an exit. Bud went toward her but was perversely distracted by his fellow invitees—he wanted to make sure his face would be registered by all the high and mighty.

"Bud! Bud! Over here!"

He looked toward the bleachers and there was Raleigh, waving frantically. The screenwriter waved back and the mob responded with antic pride: hoots and cheers, like he was somebody. He felt on fire, like a lucid dreamer.

"Ladies and gentlemen, the voice of Calabash, Steve Martin!"

The famous comedian, the monkey and his trainer stood on the platform and a mind-jangling roar went up that made Bud want to scream himself. The river of the crowd had washed her up dazed at the dais and Caitlin hedged the hellish ape's bony fingers as she ran the gauntlet: Bud saw the fun-house terror in her eyes as the bodies closed in around her and Calabash lunged again from the heart of darkness, *her* heart of darkness, a hairy apparition, an underworld reprisal for the sellout squandering of her gifts. She made a beeline for the building.

The screenwriter took off after her and suddenly was in orbit; a blur of faces distinct as the oceans and continents of the watery earth. The bleachers tilted, sliding from his periphery. For a split second, he dreamed himself at home, watching the Awards on television, then slipping into bed, under warm covers. His head hit the walkway with a sickening clop.

He felt cold and peaceful and damp, the legs of the crowd surrounding his body like slim, familiar trees. The cypresses again. There was a far-off fanfare of screams at yet another star's arrival and Bud wondered if he'd be trampled like a pilgrim at a shrine. Someone just behind him said, *Asshole,* under their breath, someone angered by his bad form. What kind of vicious person would say such a thing? Maybe they thought he was just another crasher, a nut like the bald girl. Bud tried to stand but couldn't. Finally, a voice said, "Some guy fell and hit his head." Help was on the way, the voice assured him. The screenwriter was ashamed by his state of affairs and pretended to himself he hadn't fallen at all but had caught up to Caitlin and was ushering her to their seats. He was torn from his reverie by the glare of a camera light that lit him up before someone pushed it away. He must have looked like Bobby Kennedy on the floor of the Ambassador Hotel kitchen.

He felt a cool palm on his hand and opened his eyes: it was Calabash, baring its teeth at Bud as he went under.

"Orson? Can you hear me, Orson?"

He opened and closed his eyes.

"Mr. Welles? Do you know where you are?"

A nurse with a chart joined the doctor.

"His name is Wiggins. Orson Wiggins."

"Orson?" the doctor went on, ignoring her. "Do you know where you are?"

"It's Bud." He felt nauseated. "My name is Bud Wiggins."

"Well, the gentleman who brought you in said you're Orson."

"He's the one who fell at the Academy Awards," the nurse said, as if it were medically pertinent.

"How many fingers, Orson?"

"It's *Bud.* Three."

"Do you know where you are?"

"Hospital. Emergency room."

"Who's the president of the United States?"

He thought a moment, then it came.

"Joseph Harmon."

The emergency room was packed. Bud had a concussion and took twelve stitches. Raleigh followed the ambulance and watched the Awards from the waiting room while he was sewn up. After the show, when Ramón told her what happened, Caitlin made him drive her straight over; she appeared in great commotion, clutching her Oscar statuette, just as Bud and Raleigh were leaving. Caitlin explained that she assumed he'd gotten smart and ducked out—who the hell would have thought he fell on his ass and broke his head? She insisted Bud come in the limo. She wanted to put him up for the night, but he asked to be dropped at home instead. Dolly yelled at him because the suit was frayed where he fell and there was blood on the collar.

His mother made a plate of fruit and sat him down on a chair in her bedroom, in front of the TV. The clip was used as a comic lead-in for the commercial break on the late news: it showed Bud falling in slow motion while the anchorman said, "Coming up, we'll take another look at a man who went 'head over heels' for Oscar." When they froze the frame, a title came across the bottom of the screen: NEXT . . . SEE YOU IN THE FALL, HAVE A NICE TRIP!

Bud retired to his room. He sat on the bed and winced with pain. There was a bruise on his back; he should find a good acupuncturist. That would take money. Gone were the days when he'd get massaged three times a week and send the bill through Guild insurance. His head ached, but they never gave you pain pills for those kind of injuries. That much, he knew from the Doctor. Dolly stood outside the closed door nonetheless, offering codeine. When he said no, she started to stammer, a clue she was embarking on a "sensitive issue." She wanted to discuss the possibility of his getting a nose job from her new doctor. It wasn't that Dolly didn't think her son was handsome, he was *gorgeous*. It's just that he could be even more gorgeous. Bud said he was too tired to talk about it and she retreated. He could see her in his mind, docile and bizarre, padding away barefoot, grateful she'd made an inroad, that her son at least hadn't shouted. Sometimes Bud yelled at her, reminding himself of his father. He'd suddenly feel like Morris and say any old hurtful thing that popped into his head. Brian was like that with his own mother, but worse, slamming doors on her and calling her a cunt. Too bad the Doctor wasn't alive. Bud would have stayed with him tonight at the dorm.

He listened to his messages. There were a few that sounded like they were coming from Oscar house parties. There was a long-distancey hang-up and he wondered if it was Jeanette, calling from Rome, or the Godfather, Jerry Fairchild. Maybe it was Dr. Jurgen or Thelma Ritter.

The dark chorus of cypresses nodded at his window. They had things to show him; there would be time to interpret the meaning of their movements. He watched the television as he undressed. There was a documentary on cable about vaudeville—the Linley Brothers and other forgotten men with tragicomic slapstick faces, cigars and baggy pants. He laughed at the kinescope from the generation of his grandparents and felt the birth of a new ersatz nostalgia. That's what he should do: bring back vaudeville, bring it right to Hollywood. Blake Edwards was good at that. He was always trying to do that kind of stuff, revive the classics, the real McCoy, but with a spin. Bud decided to go to the library and research it, then write a script. As he removed his shoes, he thought about the new project to get his mind off the pain. He turned the familiar word over and over in his head, as if becoming intimate with it for the first time: *vaudeville.* If he said it enough to himself, a story would come. Then he noticed a triangle of crud between the heel and sole of his boot and realized Calabash had been the culprit. Bud had slipped on a banana.

11111

"Is this Bud?"
    "Yes, it is."
    "Hold for Penny Reich."
    "Hiya."

"Hi, Penny."

"The one about the house and the guy—what's it called?"

"Bringing Down the House."

"Right. It didn't work for me. It was sick—not that I'm afraid of 'sick'—I don't know, it was pretentious. I mean, the writing wasn't even that good. But I really liked *Toy Soldier.*"

"Great."

"I didn't *love* it, I thought you could have gone further. But it's real interesting. Do you own it?"

"Free and clear."

"I know there's something similar out there and I want to check the status. It's got some really funny lines."

"Tell me, Miss Reich: do you think I have a future as a script doctor?"

"I think you have a future *with* a script doctor. How's that going, by the way?"

"Caitlin? She's just a friend."

Bud was relieved that she didn't mention his pratfall; she probably didn't even know about it. He cracked a few jokes and Reich asked if he'd ever done stand-up. He said he hated stand-up.

"By the way, there's a movie over at AlphaFilm that's in deep shit, it's called *Bloodbath.* Are you interested in taking a meeting?"

"Sure. When?"

"Right away, they're frantic."

"Do they have money?"

"It's not Disney. But they've just got their foreign."

He brought up the issue of commission should he get the job, and when Reich wouldn't hear of it, Bud thought himself gauche. She said she'd get back to him on *Toy Soldier* and her assistant gave him all the *Bloodbath* info. He had the distinct feeling he was on his way to coming "full Circle".

A few days passed and his eye blackened from the trauma. He returned to work and the Chileans were merciless. Ramón and the dispatcher presented him with one of those dime-store

Oscars, "Best Fall" engraved on its base. He stayed away, getting his orders by phone.

At the end of the week, Bud parked the limo in a loading zone on Hollywood Boulevard and walked north on Highland to the cruddy offices of AlphaFilm Productions.

Genie Katz-Cohen blew into the reception area, where Bud sat reading a two-week-old *Reporter*. She was sweaty and hyper and pumped his hand like he was the antidote to failure and chaos—she actually said, "Boy oh boy, am I glad to see you!" She asked about his blackening eye and he said he got mugged. Bud was beginning to think nobody watched the show this year but the assholes at the hotel. Genie led him back to her office, a cramped room with an enormous desk. There were hundreds of eight-by-tens in stacks on the floor, others tacked to the wall in rogues' gallery formation.

"Can you believe it? I leave TTA, I *leave* Wylie Guthrie, one of my biggest clients, and I get a job here at AlphaFilm— *Bloodbath* is Wylie's film, didn't you know that? *Yes*! Wylie wasn't *my* client, I mean I was one of his agents. If I'd stayed around a little longer, I would have eventually gotten a job at a studio. But I don't *want* a job at a studio. So here I am in casting and the wacko Israelis—they're Orthodox, *completely* wacko—the crazy Jews ask me if I have anything to bring them and I remember something Wylie had in his trunk, I read it when I was first hired at TTA, I was a *secretary*. I read everything. So I show it to them and they wanna make it right away. I can't get away from Wylie Guthrie, I'm telling you!"

It was perfect: his cultivation of Wylie Guthrie had paid off. He wondered why Guthrie wasn't doing the rewrite himself. Maybe he was burned out or consumed by other chores. Anyway, the film was low-budget and Guthrie could afford to farm it out to an old, gifted student. Raleigh's involvement was a further bonus. She hadn't returned his calls since the night at the emergency room and he wasn't sure why. When he finally stopped by her house, she stood there smiling like the Joker; then her face went stone cold and she slammed the door on him.

That hurt because Bud thought he was falling in love with her.
It was weird—now at least he'd be able to get to the bottom
of it.

"Is Raleigh Wolper cast?"

"She's *wonderful,*" Genie said. "Gonna be a *big* star."

"Are you producing?"

"Casting—and coproducing, now. But casting is my *love.*"
She scrutinized him with a smile. "I remembered how funny
Wylie said you were—and that you were a writer."

"So it was Wylie's idea to bring me in," he said coyly. "I
thought Penny Reich had her hand in it somewhere."

"That's what's so wild!" Genie seemed like the addictive
type; Bud wondered if she went to Meetings. "Penny called at
the *exact moment* Wylie and I were having a conversation
about you, I *swear to God.* How do you know her?"

"She wanted to sign me awhile back."

"She's *phenomenal.* I call her the Third Reich. I actually
knew two other Reichs before I knew Penny."

She smiled smugly at her own cleverness, then a cloud came
and took the flipness away: Genie somehow *owed* Penny Reich
and it was time for a quickie devotional, time to display the
immensity of her debt and esteem for the greater colleague. Bud
imagined this sort of subtle soft shoe of obeisance took place
hundreds of time a day all over Hollywood, this homage and
prayerful pause, a musical chairs of worshipers and idols. One
must give thanks—with a flutter of the eyelids, Genie mentally
opened the Penny Reich "file" and was overwhelmed by sacred
text. If she could only convey what this woman *meant* to her
(she shrewdly bought reflected glory by the implied intimacy),
if she could only . . . *impossible.* The suggestion being that
Penny Reich, now vice-president of the Circle Group, had
somehow ages ago saved Genie's life—it was that dramatic—
but *that* was another story, another country. That was a whole
movie. She shook her head from its glazy reverie.

"Anyway, I'm glad you're here. I mean, I've been practically
running out on Sunset Boulevard, shouting for a doctor." She

laughed and put her hand to her mouth like a yodeler. "Doctor! Doctor!"

"So what's wrong with the script?"

"We're shooting in less than a week—can't change that. Penny told you we were in trouble. . . ."

"No details."

"The director isn't here, he'll meet with you tomorrow if everything works out today. You're in the Guild, right?"

He wasn't anymore, not "in good standing" anyway. That could be remedied by his first paycheck. Then he thought it was strange she asked—he was here to save the picture, wasn't he? Of course, he was in the Guild, what did she expect?

"The director's an incredible kid, twenty-two years old. And Wylie you already know."

She handed him a script. He said he would read it that night.

"Okay, here's what we got: *Bloodbath* is like *Phantom of the Opera,* but with a crazy plastic surgeon. They want to make the doctor hip, like a Freddy Krueger. Do you improvise, Bud? I mean, have you done that before?"

"Writers use whatever tools they can."

"God, you don't know what a relief it is to have a *writer* in. It brings something fresh." A young man with wire-rim glasses entered with a video camera. "This is Terry, our video operator. He'll be taping a couple of scenes."

"What do you mean?"

"Don't be nervous—tape is cheap, as they say."

"I'm not following."

"You want to be the doctor, don't you?"

"I'm the script doctor," Bud stammered.

"Yes! The doctor in the script!" She dropped some stapled sheafs into Bud's lap. "Page seventeen—we'll read it out loud before we tape. Remember, now: don't be afraid to shtick it up."

〰〰

The money wasn't bad, and the gig got him into the Screen Actors Guild. The health benefits were great, even if they didn't kick in for a few months. Most of the film was shot in a big warehouse downtown, across from the city jail. There were prosthetics and it usually took four or five hours to get Bud ready. He had to walk around all day in the hot makeup, enduring the dumb comments of the extras and the crew about how hung over he looked or how he should do something about "that acne." The good part was it only took about fifteen minutes to take off.

Bud played an insane plastic surgeon obsessed by the girl who had spurned him—Raleigh Wolper. The tortured physician tracks down her ex-boyfriends, removes their best features—nose, lips, skin, hair—and grafts them onto his face. He thinks he can win her back this way. In most of the script she was running from him, so Bud and Raleigh didn't have many scenes together.

She avoided him on the set and he finally stopped making overtures. Life sure was weird—before the Oscars, it looked like the hostess and the chauffeur had real potential; now that they were Tracy and Hepburn, their love was in turnaround. Here he was, barely a month later, a monster looking into her eyes, telling her Eternity was an outhouse and he was going to wipe his ass with her soul. That was a line he wrote himself and the producers thought it was going to go over big.

He closed his eyes and zoned out to the tinny heavy metal on the boom box as a minion removed his makeup. The day had been rough and the screenwriter was looking forward to dinner with Caitlin. He hadn't seen her much since shooting began; he was just too worn out. She left funny messages on his machine like Bud was a starlet Caitlin was trying to get into bed—her impersonation of a producer was spot-on. Finally, he gave in and made a "date."

"What are you doing after *Bloodbath*?"

Bud opened his eyes. The hairstylist, a burly, hairy man in

Day-Glo shorts, fishnet tank top and high tops, had entered the trailer. He had a row of abandoned hair plugs in his head that must have been from ten years ago.

"Going to Mexico and eating lots of mushrooms," said the makeup remover, laughing. Bud felt invisible.

"I hear Wylie's got something in preproduction."

"I know about it. Sounds *really* interesting."

"The Vietnam thing."

"About the journalist. Do you know where they're shooting it?"

"Here in L.A."

Bud spoke up. "A journalist?"

"It's really *fab*. This journalist is doing research for a book about Vietnam. So he impersonates a vet."

"It's a love story, right?" his friend chimed in.

"It's *so* great. He meets this nurse—"

Bud stood from his chair and ran out of the trailer, then dashed back in to retrieve his bag. The makeup boys looked concerned and asked if he was okay.

"Everyone has the shits from craft service," they concurred as Bud again made his exit.

When Wylie Guthrie answered the door of his Hollywood Hills lair, Bud took a swing. The screenwriter was still partially in makeup; the stunned Master reacted in time to get grazed. The older man gut-punched him and pinned him to the ground.

"Jesus fucking Christ, are you crazy! What's the matter with you?" Bud couldn't speak. "Come on, get up. Jesus Jesus Jesus. Come on, on your feet. You scared the piss out of me."

He leaned on Guthrie as they went inside.

"It's totally different," said the savant of story structure from his capacious living room. Bud was bent over on a fifties couch, trying to catch his breath. "I've been playing around with the same idea for years, man! I got a treatment registered at the Guild a *decade* ago. I'll get it from my files."

"Why didn't you *tell* me?"

Bud straightened up, feeling the painful pulse in his solar plexus.

"For just this reason! See how you reacted? The similarities are *surface,* I'll show you the script. I'm not afraid, I have no *reason.*" Bud stood up and shuffled to the door. "Jesus Christ, I'm sorry I hit you. Take your script back." He suddenly got testy. "You want to sue me? Sue. You come to my home and attack me! I should call the fuckin police! Jesus, Wiggins," he said, contrite. *"Surface similarities at best."*

Guthrie gave him the script and Bud left. He called out as the screenwriter got to his car. REVERSE SHOT: The Wizard of Exposition looked soft and benevolent in the light.

"I enjoyed reading it, by the way. Very well done. I made some notes on the pages, in pencil."

He drove straight to Caitlin's. A woman in a Jaguar pulled up beside him at a light.

"Fuck you, Michael!" she screamed into the car phone. *"Fuck you and your nigger wife."*

Another car took the Jaguar's place; a little boy in the backseat stared at the discolored latex flap on Bud's cheek and the violet smudges on his neck. The part-time actor made a twisted face at the riveted child as he turned up Benedict Canyon, but only managed to scare himself.

Caitlin answered the door and led him upstairs. She seemed a little stoned. Bud lay on the bed while she took off the rest of his makeup with Noxzema and a warm towel.

He pretended she was a nurse tending to his soldier's wounds—he used to have that fantasy all the time when he was ten years old. He had a friend named Jimmy Willow and they played handball against the white wall of the Beverly Hills Mortuary, north of Burton Way. They'd do scenes from movies, switching roles of soldier and nurse. Sometimes they romantically kissed, but only after covering mouths with towels so their lips wouldn't touch.

"Criminy, Wiggins, did Olivier go through this?"

"He's probably going through it now."

"Guess who I signed with today?"

"Who."

"Mr. Robert Feld, of TTA."

Bud felt the top of his stomach pulsing again like an intruder's heart, taut and sickeningly warm.

"I needed a pimp, a Mack the Knife. Especially after the Oscar. Fuck that shyster lawyer with his six percent. I know how to read a contract. Ever read *The Plumed Serpent*? I might just adapt it—I'll get TTA to package it, too, but they'll probably make me stick the ghost of Freud in there! *Quetzalcoatl*...
Quetzalcoatl had an evil brother who got him drunk and tricked him into bed with his own sister. Quetzalcoatl called down a rain of fire to kill the world and the survivors were changed into birds. Do you think we'll be lucky enough to become birds at the end, Wiggins?"

"Are you still taking the pills?"

"No. Should I, Dr. Wiggins? Medication is a *fad,* its effects illusory and dangerous at best." She stroked his forehead. "But if you want me to, Dr. Wiggins, I'll swallow some more."

"Whatever makes you feel better, Cait."

"There he goes with that 'Cait' again. I love it! Listen: take the pills, don't take the pills—who gives a shit, R. D. Laing dead on a tennis court? Merton fried in the tub? Barthes and the bakery truck? All I care about is getting my ass to Mexico. Hey, you oughta come. Wanna? You can minister to me there, Señor *Dr.* Wiggins. Feed me pills, I'll swallow anything you got. Nudge nudge wink wink. Come on, come go with me. We'll stay at the much-talked-about Casa Que Pasa. Do you love me, Bud?"

"Yes."

He was tired and a little bored by her mania. Maybe it was a good idea to go to Mexico, though.

He felt a serious hand on his thigh and looked in her eyes. It seemed completely wrong at first, then completely right. She spoke unintelligibly while they rocked together, sighs and low-toned sadnesses, untranslatable forgive-me confessions. It moved and excited him, so very close now, feeling her breath, lovingly noting the translucence of her skin, her hairy health, the spidery delicacy of the hands and the simple, sensuous boldness of the features. It was the best kind of lovemaking for him, the kind where he knew he'd stay hard.

WW

Dolly was furious—the dry cleaner's could only do so much with the tux and Hoffmann-Dougherty wouldn't take it back. She knew Bud was making good money as an actor, but when he offered to pay for it, she humiliated him by spitefully shouting, "How? *How!*" Like they were paying him in Monopoly money. He tried changing the subject to her malpractice suit, but she wouldn't get off the tux. He decided it was time for him to move out.

He spent a lot of time in his tiny dressing room scanning Friday's trades for rentals. He circled the ones that looked promising (the usual lies: *canyon/writer's Deco hideaway guest-house/cathedral ceilings/fireplace/parquet floors*) but mostly fantasized about moving into a local hotel. He called around and was discouraged—smallish rooms started at twenty-five hundred a month, and that was with a monthly rate. He'd love to live at the Beverly Palm itself; a few permanent residents paid about a hundred and fifty thousand a year for the privilege. Maybe he'd scale down and settle into a motel, lower his sights a little. Too bad the Tropicana wasn't around anymore. He knew of a cheesy place in Beverly Hills called the Four Oaks House, an anachronistic zoning anomaly that had somehow escaped developers over the decades. Back in the sixties, people used to check in while doing their Primal Scream therapy. He'd look into it. Might be a script there—a crooked landlord is put under house arrest in his dilapidated Beverly Hills motel. Or do a "period" comedy about people holed up and waiting for Primal, like an old Mazursky movie. It'd be cheap to shoot, one location. Could be hilarious.

He tried reaching Caitlin all week, with no luck. She was never in at night, and when he called from the set, Rosa said she was "busy"—Bud took that to mean spooked, embarrassed, conflicted. Who knew? Caitlin Wurtz wasn't the most predictable woman on the planet. For himself, Bud was feeling pretty good. Maybe this was the Big One after all. Why not? It was just improbable enough to make sense.

The afternoon was drizzly. Bud wanted to send her a note and went to Bookz for inspiration. He'd do a hiply self-aware parody of a Rilke poem or something. The screenwriter wanted to make her laugh, like he always did; to be lugubrious or postcoitally sentimental at this point would be a fatal misstep. Anyway, there was always the possibility Caitlin wasn't interested, and was warming up one of those better-if-we-hadn't mea culpas that bittersweetly finish off a "special time." Crazy people were always acting out, and to hell with the consequences. Yes, there was the chance he'd never see her again. He'd been prepared for that from the start. Even though that seemed a little extreme, Bud didn't want to get hurt and decided to do some emotional backpedaling. What will be, will be.

He was circling *The Duino Elegies* like a buzzard when Penny Reich suddenly stood before him.

"Bud, how are you!"

"I'm good," he said robustly. "You look great!"

A familiar voice called from "off camera."

"Buddy! What's going on?"

It was Derek. Reich watched wide-eyed, exaggerating her surprise that the young men knew each other.

"I thought you were in Mexico," Bud lied.

"I had to pull out of that. I suddenly got busy."

"He got busy," said Reich worshipfully, her eyes on the former bookseller.

"I heard you won a prize or something," Bud said, casual to the point of near death. He knew it was about to come up.

"It was a grant."

"The Steiner Grant," Reich proudly amended. A deceased

insurance magnate had set the famous foundation in motion. Each year monies were dispersed in Nobel-size chunks, often to unknowns. The media tirelessly kept the public informed of the recipients—jazzy Rhodes Scholars of the nineties.

"I got lucky," Derek said, with a reserve that could almost be taken for genuine.

"Yeah, you got *real lucky,*" said the agent, all sex and husky irony. If Derek Johansen was lucky, she seemed to say, then so was the wind, and so was rain and so was fire.

"So tell me," Bud said, discreetly sliding the Rilke back on the shelf; let no one accuse *him* of being pretentious. "What does a rich young playwright do with his time?"

"Actually, I'm directing a little film."

"Great," Bud said. It never ended with this guy.

"Derek's doing something for the Daedalus Program."

Reich said that the selections had just been announced and Derek was *in.* It was turning out to be a "motherfucker" of a year all right. To top everything, he'd just signed with Reich here and if Bud wasn't crazy, he'd do the same—in a hurry. Bud thought it nice that Derek put him in the same league, the league of the *hot.* Maybe he'd given the kid a bum rap. Derek made a bad joke about "life, pre-Genius grant" and roughly kissed the agent's neck. Reich blushed and told Bud she heard he was doing great work on the AlphaFilm project. She turned to her stellar client.

"Bud went in to pitch a project and was so funny that they cast him in the lead."

Was that what happened?

"Oh, I heard about that." Derek nodded his head indifferently.

"It's been lots of fun," said Bud, like a celebrity chitchatting at a fund-raiser.

"You know, you'd be great for that Mexican thing I was gonna do," Derek said, brightly charitable. "The script's a mess—I could even get you a copy. Would you let me call and give them your number?"

"Sure."

"Do you have an agent, or—"

"Offers are handled through Don Bloom."

Bud thought that sounded pompous, and jokily pretended he meant it that way. He gave Derek permission to give out his home number. He wasn't sure if Derek even had his home number, but the Steiner inductee just smiled, bobbing his head. Bud said he had to go.

He was out on the street when Derek yelled, "Oh, my book! I want my book back!"

Bud nodded his head while Reich, unable to restrain herself any longer, put her arms around the genius's neck and dragged him off, whispering something into his ear that made him laugh.

Caitlin never responded to his Rilke parody.

He'd messengered it to her home that Wednesday and now it was Sunday night and he hadn't heard a word. He was about to drive up there and see what the hell was going on when Dolly showed him the photo in the social section of the *News.* There they were, in ferocious black tie: Joel Levitt, Dick Whitehead and Bobby Feld, faces frozen in laughter, aimed directly at Caitlin Wurtz. The caption said she'd been feted at the Beverly Palm Hotel in celebration of the start of principal photography on *Another Fine Mess,* a Joel Levitt/Mother Tongue production. There was no mention of Billy Quintero, and Bud thought about the meetings he'd taken at Universal—who was involved with whom, on what and from when? Not that it made any difference; it was a closed society. He stared at the picture. The foursome made a tableau vivant, the effect of which was a fuck-you Valentine to the world. Bud suddenly went cold with the thought she'd left town without calling. The cloak of surprise and hurt was settling onto his shoulders when the phone rang.

"Come right away." The voice sounded forced and damp-ered, like she was sneaking a phone call while her kidnappers slept.

"Are you all right?"

"You have to come—I'm leaving tonight."

When he got to the house, there was a limo in the driveway. The motor was running and he didn't recognize the driver. The front door was open.

The place was empty, stripped of furniture and fixtures. The clock had struck twelve.

"Bud?"

The voice came from upstairs.

"Bud? Is that you?"

He found her in the bedroom, standing by the window and smoking a cigarette, very film noir. She looked dead in the dark.

"I'm going away for a while. Please don't ask me where." Bud opened his mouth to say something, anything. "Just listen! I wanted to see you before I left because I wanted to give you something."

She reached in her bag. His pulse quickened; instead of a gun, she pulled out a script.

"I've been working on this for twenty years. I never talked about it to anyone. *Nobody.* Do you understand?"

"I understand."

"I've done some thinking. I'm going to give you this and I want you to make it your own." He was a blank. She handed it to him and he knew better than to look at it just then. "It's missing something—it's missing *you.* I can't fix it. Maybe once I could have, but now I need the monkeys."

"But how?"

"It's a fabulous structure I've made and dammit, I want you to do something with it! *I* want you to—no one else. Now please just take it and walk me downstairs."

They said their good-byes in front of the chauffeur. Bud felt like he was "doing a scene"—as if on cue, a movie wind stormed the trees and skittered leaves on the driveway, gluing them to his pant cuffs. Caitlin pressed her cheek against his, then climbed into the car like a widow hurriedly leaving a cemetery. Bud superstitiously followed the limo down the mountain, as if to lose sight of it was to risk detaching from the earth and floating into nothingness. They parted ways at Sunset, Caitlin turning toward the ocean, Bud heading back to town, to Ship's. He was starving.

He ate steak and eggs at the counter of the coffee shop and examined his bequest. Caitlin Wurtz had given him a screenplay of Henry James's *The Wings of the Dove* and there was alchemy in such a gift. Though it was several years since Bud had scaled its imposing heights, he could still remember the book's intricacies—had she read his emotions?

If the novel represented the crowning achievement of the Master, the script was the jewel in Caitlin's own crown, a decathlon winner in the as-yet-unsponsored Olympics of screenwriting. The story of the American heiress who came to Europe to die had been fashioned into a melodrama of heart-stopping transcendence. The sometimes abstruse rationale of the secret lovers who connived for the heroine's heart and gold had been made radiantly, monstrously bright. Oh, the infelicities! How Caitlin had done it was impossible to know—like any great work, it defied analysis. Its end was visible in its beginning; it was brand-new modern and very, very old, a timeless statue unearthed, what they call an "instant classic." *Wings* was like no script he'd ever read and for a moment Bud saw the awful price Caitlin Wurtz had paid as Bride of Calabash.

What was he supposed to do? *Improve* on it? Twenty years of work and "It's missing *you,*" she'd said, looking square in his eye, a cranked-up, febrile Olivia De Havilland. Suddenly, the script was more a curse than an offering and Bud wanted to drive a stake through the heart of its title page. She'd ignored him for a week after making love and now he had this consolation prize, like a loser on *Jeopardy!* "Dammit, I want you to do something with it!" She was like some witchy cartoon character, an aged she-wolf making melodramatic exits wrapped in the tiresome cape of mania and mystery. He felt thoroughly jilted.

The bestowal seemed prankish, a cruel and quirky gesture whose message was she didn't want his love or his fuck. He'd make it his enemy, to diminish its power and beauty. He would make it nothing. After all, it was only a script.

The screenwriter found a drawer and threw it in like an old phone book. When it was finally out of sight, Bud felt a terrible sadness. He thought he loved this woman. He didn't want to start obsessing, and tried to focus on his anger. He was in pain, and conjured Macon, then the whirling eucalyptuses of the Arbor, *Time Machine* matinées and *kloping* Mrs. Kent, knee-socked Cora and the Secret Garden. Soon he would be indifferent. That was always best; the rest was an energy drain. One day Caitlin would come back and learn that Bud Wiggins hadn't laid a finger on her precious script, nor had he been thinking of her.

Bud got in bed. He thought of their trip to the desert, the windmills turning. He heard her voice and felt the warmth and substance of her body. He missed her. He saw the "figure in the carpet" and it was he, entombed in Caitlin's weave.

3. The Weight of the Human Heart

There was a week of *Bloodbath* left and Bud was exhausted. The night shoots played havoc with his system. The company tried to wrap around seven in the morning, but that usually meant eight-thirty or nine. Bud found it difficult to come home and crash in the daylight; if he didn't get enough sleep, work was hellish. He'd lie down in a cold, empty room off the set and sweatily nod out, until a production assistant would wake him up to tell him he was needed on the set. Dutifully he'd come and sit through forty antsy minutes of delays; then a sheepish PA would tell him to go back to his room and sleep. Hurry up and wait. Ten minutes later they'd wake him up again and rush him back to the set for another hour of waiting. When he finally did his bit, it seemed to take forever to get the tiniest scene onto film. Bud began to pray for the shoot to end. At the end of each night he fought the impulse to tear the makeup mask from his face. Driving home, even to sleeplessness, became an ecstatic maneuver.

Early Saturday morning Bud finished his last scene in the movie. When the first AD announced he was "wrapped," the cast and crew applauded, per tradition.

He went to the Four Seasons for a fifty-dollar brunch. Bud exulted—*Bloodbath* was over. Yet aside from the waiter, there was no one to wryly share the experience with. He thought of the Doctor and became nostalgic. He should probably visit the grave, though he'd never really had the desire; graves didn't move him. When he left the restaurant, the screenwriter found himself on the Santa Monica Freeway heading down to County General.

He drove by the emergency room with its big sign outside: NO ESTACIONAMIENTO. (That used to stick in his head all the time like a mantra.) Brian had some great ER stories. The girl with the flu who slashed her throat because she was tired of waiting to be examined, the psycho med student who did a yeoman's job of removing his own gallbladder—it would have made a pretty good book. While the Doctor was still alive, Bud toyed with ghostwriting one of those year-in-the-life-of-an-intern perennials. Then he thought of something better.

Bud parked outside the dormitory where his friend had died and remembered the few months he'd stayed there as the Doctor's guest, back when he was deep into planning the big Chayefskyesque "hospital" movie. Maybe it was time to take another swing at it. He still had his old notes. Bud wasn't sure why he had abandoned the project but recalled that the story he'd come up with—based on real characters and events—was too dark, more like Huston's *Wise Blood* than anything else, and that wasn't what he'd intended. The screenwriter wanted something crackling and angry and mainstream, dark like *Network* was dark. But at the time it just wouldn't come—he had tried too hard or something. He was going through his sick-of-comedy phase then. What had comedy ever done for him? The week before he moved in with Brian, he had a dream: what they used to call the cold, outer reaches of space, the cool, classical blackness of space and Bud flying like a wisp in a stellar wind.

An *interesting* dream, a pivotal one. When he awakened, comedy was dead inside him. He would do a dramatic genre piece, a hospital story, a smart Big Theme soap opera, signed, sealed and delivered within the Gothic walls of County General. His best friend in the world was down there waiting for him, like some Virgil. It was perfect.

So he moved in with Brian and tagged along on rounds, hovering over emergency room dramas like a stenographic angel, loitering in the halls during morning "Morbidity and Mortality" lectures (good title for something), hanging with impoverished clinic outpatients, cultivating the jail ward, absorbing sickroom babble, employee tics, the rhythm of the wards. Actually living "at the plant" provided him with much-needed discipline. He felt like Billy Quintero preparing for a role—the resultant script couldn't help but be the real thing.

It was a strange time. Brian was on night shifts and popped into their room during breaks, jammed on speed and untold other personal favorites. The two fell asleep as the sun rose (the Doctor assisted in this regard by big green pills and sinister bathroom ablutions) and Bud watched his stertorous friend nod out, ringed by the votive candles of cheap alarm clocks. Brian slept with his good ear buried in a pillow; he was on a never-ending quest for the perfect wake-up device and kept at least a dozen candidates handy. His greatest fear was missing rounds.

Every few weeks Bud cleaned the Doctor's side of the room, faggotry on the scale of *The Odd Couple.* The screenwriter was careful not to prick himself with needles as he went along; bloody syringes were everywhere, amid foam burger boxes and discarded vials. The drug companies sent the tyro physicians pills, welcome wagons of meth and opium. Somehow Bud couldn't *see* what was going on, didn't connect. Then he read some articles about the disease of "codependency" and went to a Program Meeting because that's what he heard a lot of people in the Business were doing. Bud didn't see anyone there that he knew, but he did talk to some people who said he was in denial. "Denial is not a river in Egypt," they said. *Pain is optional.*

Bud asked the Doctor to come to a Meeting and Brian promised he would if Bud helped him cash some more triplicates—cash *scripts,* he said, that's what dope fiends called prescriptions. Bud smiled at the irony. So the Doctor wrote *scripts* in Bud's name and that's how Bud got to AA. They hit all the Thrifty's for Percodan and Placidyl, legal drugstore cowboys, and the Doctor's breath acquired a sickening metallic waft, like an android. Bud the codependent, Bud the enabler.

The first few weeks of his dorm residence were purely gestatory and he preferred to think himself a writer of books, rather than scripts. Sometimes being a screenwriter embarrassed him in the same way he imagined Brando or Richard Burton were embarrassed to be actors. That's what he'd read, anyway; they were ashamed. County General was a teaching hospital affiliated with the university; living within its bosom filled Bud with a phantom nostalgia for the collegiate days he never had, days that most certainly would have been antipathetic to the art of crafting screenplays. Academia was a nest for novelists. In keeping with his role as dubious man of letters, Bud usually carried with him something from the Stolen Library, a talisman that marked the seriousness of his enterprise—sitting in the cafeteria, say, with *Out of Africa* on his tray. He played the literary man and it pacified him, when Bud went into town to get his mail, he pretended to be on furlough from Yaddo. He felt mature, ready to do something "major"—being close to all that morbidity and mortality filled him with sanctity and ambition. From this, he was sure, would come a fountain of light. And that something finally came.

During Bud's stay the Doctor introduced him to a man who blew half his head away with a shotgun in a suicide attempt. This apparently happened to enough poor souls—the recoil altering the fatal trajectory—that it was a Grand Guignol cliché, a joke among the harder-core hospital staff. They choppered the Shotgun Man in from Oxnard, where he lived in a trailer park. They knew little about him except that he worked in an auto supply warehouse. For days the man wrote the same scrawly note to the nurses, over and over: WHY DID SHE LEAVE ME? WHY? WHY DID SHE GO? SHE WAS MY LIFE and so on. The Doctor relished the horror of the scene—watching Bud watch.

He was thinking about getting out of the car, taking the elevator up and knocking on the door of the old room. The thought was enough.

Bud left the hospital, driving past Union Station and Olvera Street. He was wide-awake, high on having finished his acting chores. He thought about writing a witty little piece about the experience for *Fangoria* and calling it "An Actor Prepares." Driving through Little Tokyo, he noticed a building with a giant mural painted on its side—the so-called Temporary Contemporary. He pulled into the sunny lot, feeling like a tourist.

As he parked, the homeless jockeyed to wash his car. It was filthy, the interior a littered mess. He waved them away.

The museum was impressive. A clean cathedral-size space held the main installation—an exhibit of blurry photographs, clusters of dead-faced people staring out as if from an etherous family reunion. There were chambers one could disappear into, cramped and cavelike and full of candles, more Holocaust faces; he got vertigo passing from the catacombs back into the yawning art hangar. And always the photos, as if these people were certain that you had helped kill them.

Bud noticed someone walking slowly through the dark rooms. She was relaxed and attentive to the artist's work and he sensed she was alone. The girl had dark brown hair and wore a crisp white blouse, short denim skirt and low black heels. Her legs were bare. Bud couldn't see the face clearly because of her hair, but liked what he saw. It was an hour of faces: the watchers watching the dead stare back, a mute and shadowy community of solemn, admonishing looks. The show ended at the gift shop, where the exit was. He went there to wait, so he could check her out. He was finally getting tired.

A few minutes into browsing, the screenwriter looked up and saw a girl with a disfigured face. He glanced away, flipping vacantly through a book of neon artists. When he was certain he wouldn't be seen, Bud looked again. The man behind the counter was handing her a folk-art necklace retrieved from a glass case; he was cheerful as a first-class steward and made no sign of noticing the girl's deformity. Bud scrutinized her while she ogled the pendant. She was about twenty-five; half her face looked like it was angrily champing a billiard ball. What *was* it? Had to be a tumor. For a second he heard the deadpan voice of the Doctor drolly pronounce an etiology. Bud the layman classified and assessed: the left side smart, saucy, blasé, a little cynical . . . tough, sexy, even endearing. Then the right—a Francis Bacon housewife who made him cringe. For relief, his eyes moved back to the unmolested side, a city with laws and parks and fountains next to—*there it was*—a broken-bottled slum lot, the thrown-out body of a little girl dead in its weeds, the screaming eye invaded by a purplish flower, cheek stretched over wild bone. The chestnut hair hung casually over the devastated area, its offhandedness lending her a kind of grotesque sex appeal, like one of those decomposed honor students from *The Night of the Living Dead.*

Bud suddenly remembered the girl he saw inside the exhibit and reflexively turned to intercept her; it occurred to him he might have missed her during his cosmetic peregrinations. Then he looked again at the bare brown skin and black heels and realized that the two girls were the same. He approached.

She was standing now beside a stack of catalogs, more dead, blurry faces staring out from the covers.

"Spooky, aren't they?"

She smiled, taken aback, covering her bad side with hair as they spoke. From habit, he thought.

"They're really wonderful."

"It'd be hard owning one of them. I mean, being stared at all day." *Brilliant, Bud.*

"That could be creepy."

"What's your name?"

The girl smiled again, warily this time, as if bracing herself for another faux pas.

"Vivian. What's *your* name?"

"Bud. Bud Wiggins. Nice to meet you."

He shook her hand and made certain to look straight into the calm harbor of her eyes, not wanting his gaze to slip.

"Listen, you wouldn't want to go for coffee, would you?"

She laughed at his boldness, then softened. "That's very nice, but I don't think so."

He plowed ahead, nothing to lose. "I thought we might discuss doing a vaudeville act—you know, 'Bud and Vivian,' like Bud Abbott and Vivian Vance."

It was lame, but would do.

"Were they a team?"

Vivian smiled and he wondered if she'd ever been picked up before. She was probably drawing on movies to know how to handle herself, Grace Kelly in *High Society.* Bud asked if he could call sometime and she tried to shake him off, just like a fifties ingenue fielding a pass. Then she grew prim and "lady-like"—most likely changing reels. *This is silly,* he imagined her saying, *I'm twice your age and very married. You really made my day!* That was her demeanor, though she couldn't have been more than twenty-five. He kept pressing and she surrendered, unsteadily giving him the number.

As he left the gift shop, Bud turned and saw her resume browsing, glowing and bemused, like a girl mistakenly asked for an autograph.

He thought about her the next few days. Just what was attracting him, anyhow? Was he bored? Was it the anomaly and if so, was that "wrong"? It's not like you could separate her from the disfigurement, and why should you? It sounded corny, but everyone was maimed in his own way. The obsessive macho pursuit of "beauty" as a prize was clearly perverse. Was his self-esteem at such an all-time low that he desired Vivian be-

cause the possibility of rejection seemed remote? Or was it the
writer in him again, craving to score on the experience front.
He heard Jeanette's voice: *this is a human being,* she warned.
There could be repercussions. Why didn't he just leave the poor
thing alone? *Thing* is right, said another, churlish voice. Bud
knew he could be compulsive about women; he had talked
about it in the Meetings. *Go pick on someone else.* Then he
made the voices stop. It was probably just his fear of intimacy
talking. He was only beating himself up, as Jeanette's shrink
used to say. Bud was attracted to Vivian, he felt a tenderness
that had nothing to do with pity, and in the world that was
enough. Why should he run? He could be hurt, too, as badly
as anyone. Vivian might have things to show him. He could
learn from her. He wasn't a womanizer and he wasn't a Bluebeard—"protecting" this woman was classic codependent behavior. Protect her from what? From involvement? From life
and from love? She'd been in the world this long without Bud
Wiggins and would survive if their little romance didn't work
out. He dialed her number.

A woman's cheerful voice answered. Vivian picked up.

"It's Bud."

"Oh, hi!" she said, like he was an old friend she was happy
to hear from. "Mom, I have it."

The extension clicked off. Vivian said she lived with her
mother. She was refreshingly unneurotic about it—Bud almost
felt like fessing up about his own living arrangements. Some
other time.

"How are you?"

It had been awhile since he called a girl out of the blue. The
screenwriter felt a little stiff and "prearranged," like he'd been
chosen on *The Dating Game.*

"I'm good," Vivian said, bright and *up.* "How've you been?"

"Oh, all right. Taking it easy. You know—trying to relax."

"Sounds tough."

"It's brutal, I wanna tell ya."

He liked promoting himself as a gentleman of leisure.

"Where do you live, anyway?" he asked.

"Brentwood. My mom calls it Brentwood, anyway. It's really West L.A. Why?"

"I don't know—the prefix was weird. Still, it's really kind of a coincidence."

"What is?"

"Well, my family developed Brentwood. We still own all the land between Barrington and Bundy, from Wilshire to Olympic."

"You're kidding."

"I am kidding."

She laughed. They talked about the exhibit and Vivian asked if he liked the museum. Bud said it was actually his first time there; the mural had caught his eye on the way home from County General.

"You're not a doctor, are you?"

"No. I was just doing some research down there."

"I know about that place," she said slyly. Bud let it go. "What kind of research?"

"I used to have a friend who worked there. A surgeon. I'm thinking of writing something."

"You're a writer."

"For the movies, mostly."

"Wow! I *thought* you were a writer."

"Really? Why?"

"I don't know exactly. You're really funny—I mean, not that writers are funny. Some of them are, I guess." For the first time Vivian sounded a little nervous. "So, did you see your friend?"

"No, he died a couple of years ago."

"I'm really sorry."

This girl knew about pain and death and Bud was certain his understated comment made a bridge between them.

"What do you do?"

"I work at the Observatory."

"Griffith Park?"

"Uh-huh."

"Rebel Without a Cause. What do you do up there?"

"I'm a guide—you know, for schoolkids and adults. Mostly kids."

"You're the one who talks about constellations in the dark."

"Right."

"I've been to those things before. Was that your voice I heard?"

"Might have been."

They hung there in comfortable silence a moment and Bud remembered going to the Observatory when he was young, sighing when the star machine threw out its dusky amazements. He asked her out for Wednesday, but she had night classes at UCLA during the week, so they made it Saturday.

"What do you take?"

"Creative writing."

↯↯↯

Bud thought more about the Shotgun Man.

It was finally learned that the sad, stained notes the would-be suicide was writing to the nurses—true *disjecta membra*—were about his mother. She was the one who died and left him. They lived together all his forty years and he put the shotgun to his head a week after her coronary.

Bud used to sit in intensive care and scrutinize the survivor's face like it was a Rosetta stone of misery. The nurses showed him how to change the Shotgun Man's sheets and make sure the IVs and cavity shunts were clear. Saint Wiggins had found his story.

A week after his arrival from Oxnard, three people appeared at the room of the unfortunate.

A young woman named Rialta, her hair pulled back in a bun, acknowledged Bud with a nod, then gazed at his droopy charge; the Shotgun Man looked back with the martyred eyes of a dog who'd fetched a bone from hell and lived to tell about it. The other visitors, a stoic, leathery man and a skinny woman, lingered cautiously in the doorway. The skinny one looked terrorized by what she saw lying in the bed.

"Hello, Henry," Rialta said to the Shotgun Man.

All of them were employed at an Oxnard auto supply warehouse and the trio finally arranged to visit their hapless coworker. Rialta fearlessly motioned the doorframed couple to come closer. The man stepped forward, then the woman, who trembled before giving Rialta a look like a mountaineer with an embolism forced to turn around with the peak in sight. She quickly left the room. The stoic man stood bashfully at the bedside of his decimated friend and said, "Treatin' you well, Hank?" The Shotgun Man could only nod. Rialta was already straightening the bedstand and asked Bud where she could refill the water pitcher. She was dark-haired and beautiful, with the robust, unruffled presence of a missionary. She brought balm to the air and Bud didn't give a damn if she was a Christian cultist, Scientologist or closet codependent sexaholic—let it be about New Religion or necrophilia or whatever it was that got you to a face like that, so pure it provoked prayer.

Rialta visited the Shotgun Man when she could, sometimes commuting three times a week. It was a drive, and she wasn't even kin. She ushered reluctant others, then came alone. "If the Lord does not abandon," she asked of Bud, "why should we?" The Big Hospital Drama was unfolding before the screenwriter's eyes and the amused Doctor listened between visits to the bathroom.

It seemed so long ago and now the Doctor was dead.

MMM

On Saturday night Vivian suggested they go to a certain bistro in Venice. She knew the bartender and all the waiters—it seemed to be her "place."

The café was dark and homey within. Bud wondered what it would be like to walk with Vivian in the daylight, holding hands. He was pleased to feel a kind of feisty, rugged pride in being with this girl, mitigated by the slight twinge that he was possibly patronizing her, looking for honors from the world for being cool enough to court someone so outrageously damaged.

She was curious about Bud's career and he talked easily, keeping the details at a minimum so not to appear showy. When he asked about her own writing, Vivian passed it off as nothing.

"I'd love to see something you wrote."

"Maybe," she said. "In about a hundred years."

Now and then her face looked like something out of *Beetlejuice* and Bud had to suppress a smile, beating back the pestilential observations of a mischievous inner voice, more of the rank harvest sown from his fear of intimacy.

"Where are you from?"

"Camarillo—up near Oxnard."

"There's a nuthouse up there."

"Right. That was always the big joke. My mom would say, 'If you don't behave, we'll send you to Camarillo for the summer.' "

"Did your folks work up there?" He always said "folks" when first asking about someone's parents.

"My father worked in Redondo Beach, aerospace. But he got tired of commuting and moved us down when I was just starting high school. My grandma still lives there, though. In Camarillo."

A new school presented formidable difficulties, but she loved living in a beach town. After classes Vivian would walk down to the water (she called it the "sea") and at night she'd lie in the grass of the dark border fields of the giant airport, watching jets take off for Europe and New York. They arced over the ocean, joining the black cavern with its tarp of stars; she loved the roar of oblivion and the cool certainty of the earth while the sky fell away.

"Is your father still alive?"

She shook her head and smiled, and Bud knew his death had been the greatest trial of all.

"Cancer. That's when we moved to Brentwood. My mother

couldn't stand beaches anymore, I was surprised she didn't relocate to the desert. She didn't want to go back to Camarillo, either. You know, full circle, without her husband. It would have been like failure."

After dinner they strolled on the boardwalk. Vivian unselfconsciously took his hand and led him across the dark bike path to the sand. There was a warm, gusty wind and Bud thought of the underground ocean from *Journey to the Center of the Earth.* He felt like they were two jets heading into the blackness. His heart sped up as they trudged and his mind jumped— what a strange thing was the "sea." Once in a while he needed to watch waves break, a crustacean urge; he knew it all had something to do with the pull of the moon. A few times a year he'd make his migration. Watching the water roll back over the glistening sand reminded him of kids' books about marine things—starfish and sea horse and one-celled life, manta rays and man-o'-wars, fat white gulls and briny pier stumps, beached jellyfishes and polypy seaweed spinach, surfboards and wet suits and bonfires and grunion and luminous lanternlike creatures that lived in the deepest gorges of the earth, watery pits that could swallow up the Empire State Building. Bud would stand at tide's edge, ankles rooted in the sand, watching the dizzying pane of rippled glass recede, dreaming of mudfishes hauling themselves to shore and into the textbook pageantry of lavish, lovingly illustrated evolutionary charts.

They lay down on the sand. Bud was aware she was keeping him to her good side. Why the hell shouldn't she? He thought of angry seas on other planets.

"Tell me what you say at the Observatory," he said. "What you tell the kids."

She cleared her throat with a stagey ahem.

"When a star explodes, it sends elements into space," she began, deliberately using a "lecture" voice that sounded vaguely ironic. "That's why the earth is embedded with gold and other elements. We humans have traces of elements from exploded stars. That's why it's often said that people are made of 'stardust.' " She pointed to the dark sky. "See? Orion. Orion was a hunter. He was killed by a scorpion. The gods put him in one part of the sky and the scorpion in another: when one rises, the other sets. The scorpion can never sting Orion again." Bud was captivated by the simple myth and wanted to take her hand, but couldn't. That first moment was always hard for him.

Suddenly Vivian was talking about the tumor. It was benign, she said, growing since birth. The doctors said surgery should wait until she was older and her bones had settled. By then it was so invasive its removal would have caused a great gaping hole in her face; surgically stuck in the maw, holding everything together like the pin of a grenade forestalling a blast, would sit some dadaist prosthetic, a toupee of flesh like a parasite stuck nostalgically to a burned-out host. Doctors and pain terrified her, so instead, she wrote poems about worm-eaten sunflowers.

It was Bud's turn to confess, she said.

"Well, I guess it's okay to share it with you: I'm on dialysis."

For a second Vivian thought he was serious, then she laughed, swatting him. The water sizzled the sand as it pulled itself back into darkness.

"Tell me about what you do. You're so modest. You're not one of these famous screenwriters who make millions a year, are you?"

"They'd never let me in that club," he said, with heroic disdain. "I'll tell you the truth. I've been working on some serious projects—spec scripts, they call them—"

"The one you were researching at the hospital?"

"Among others. With a spec script, you're on your own. No one pays you to develop it. The bills started mounting up, so I had to take a job—are you ready?—writing a horror film."

She squealed with delight. "I *love* horror films! Which one is it? Is it a sequel?"

"It's called *Bloodbath.* And that's my little confession."

He couldn't bring himself to tell her he was doing a John Carradine, not so much because he was playing a monster, a man with a face sewn like a quilt from borrowed body parts;

it wasn't the unfortunate aptness that bothered him, but rather the simple mortification of it, that he, Bud Wiggins, a screen-writer who wrote more like a poet—well, it was just too much.

Her eyes sparkled. "It's work, isn't it? Lots of great film-makers started that way. Didn't Coppola make a horror film? And Polanski? I think it's amazing you're even in a position to be paid to write. Do you realize how lucky you are?"

All at once Bud felt the panic of his empty career and wanted to be anyplace but there, sitting on the beach with Vivian, listening to her gush. What was he getting himself into anyway? He should be home writing, like everyone else. He should be home having a career. He felt like a famous driver who'd blown an engine on the first lap, a track star with a ruined tendon, a heavyweight without a main event. Then he looked at her and the panic dissolved like a dead star, light-years away. He liked this girl.

When they got back, her mother greeted them with a weak smile, then disappeared. She had the real American look—the cheerful hostage. He kissed Vivian's cheek and said he'd call soon.

That night Bud dreamed the Doctor was knocking at the door.

He looked like Leonard Nimoy during a Vulcan crisis— Brian always had a thing for Mr. Spock. He said he was having trouble getting back his job at the General and Bud gently reminded the Doctor that he was dead. The screenwriter awak-ened from the dream refreshed and fulfilled, like he'd spent quality time with his old friend. The human brain was primi-tively wired that way. Mr. Spock was right about one thing: in the great village of the universe, emotions rendered humans the town idiots.

The awakened dreamer lay there on Dolly's designer sheets, saturated by the visitation. He floated back to the day of the funeral. He'd insisted on seeing the body and stood beside it behind the curtain at the mortuary, attended by an impatient rabbi. Bud felt like his fingertip was a scale; he could measure the Doctor's weight by lightly touching the cold cheek. A patch of morgue cellophane showed from under the collar at the throat. The attorney Don Bloom sat in the congregation, cowed by grief. He told Bud he'd written the County in order to get hold of the autopsy report—he relished playing detective. The conservative litigator couldn't believe the Doctor had over-dosed, and suspected foul play. He was going to mail the document to Bud as soon as it arrived.

From out of the depths, have I cried unto thee O Lord . . .

After the graveside ceremony Bud walked down the slope with a casual acquaintance, one of the Doctor's med-school compadres. He sidled up to Bud and, apropos of nothing, asked: "How much did you know?"

What did he mean? What *didn't* Bud know? Wasn't the Doctor his best friend? Hadn't the two of them spent the last twenty years together? Wasn't Bud the keynote eulogizer? (He'd spent two days poring through the stolen collection for literary excerpts.) Wasn't it Bud whom the Doctor's mother called with the news, before the siblings? Wasn't *How is Bud?* the question on everyone's lips? Just like you'd ask of a brother or surviving twin. With the classmate's cryptic feeler, the griev-ing screenwriter was thrust into a quandary. Maybe he was talking about the theft of pharmaceuticals. That's it—the old chum was a bagman and Brian a kingpin smuggler, the Mob's connection inside the hospital. Bud had been deliberately left in the dark, protected. Or maybe the classmate was referring to the ancient incident, the death of the little sister that no one ever talked about. That's what really killed the Doctor, if anyone wanted Bud's opinion.

"Everything," he answered, cocksure.

The friend kept quiet.

"Well, what do you mean?" asked Bud.

"I went through a period where I wasn't too interested in women," the perspiry confessional began. Don Bloom joined them, cutting him off.

Did the interns have an affair? Did they secretly marry? Did they go cruising together and read Cavafy? Were outpatients and Jack in the Box night shifters recruited for orgies, young boys shackled to floorboards and eviscerated? Why hadn't Bud been told the details, why had he been excluded?

He was hurt and angry and decided to ask nothing further of the pallid companion because every secret was a potential ambush threatening his significance. Maybe Brian craved Bud's body all those years—could Bud actually have been so blind? Morris always told him to probe "the facts behind the facts" and he had dismally failed the lesson. His best friend was tragically in love with him and the secret had ended in suicide. Bud tried to calm down, telling himself he wasn't the center of the world; narcissism was tough on the nerves. Brian was gay, that's all. That didn't mean he was fixated on Bud. Even if it was true, did the Doctor think that Bud couldn't take it, that he would have rejected him? It wouldn't have changed a thing, aside from maybe enlivening their ongoing acidly affectionate dialogue. The detail would have brought them closer, couldn't Brian see that? The unwillingness to admit his gayness—in hindsight—seemed sadly anachronistic. But the Doctor was ashamed, like millions before him, and couldn't confide, probably because the screenwriter, full of the hubris of someone who earns his keep by dint of self-proclaimed fearlessness, a professional unflinching gatherer of truths, had—unbelievably—*never seriously broached the issue*! Bud hadn't given the gay thing much thought, it was true, and suddenly he felt like a fraud, and absurd prude to boot. The covers had been pulled and Mr. Gonzo Wordsmith was a wimp, asleep at the wheel.

He told himself that the Doctor's sexuality had never been defined, it was always too clouded by drugs. Sex had never been a major theme. No, instead of concealing a double life all these years, the better likelihood was that Brian had merely acted out in the last few months while "circling the drain." He knew his death was rushing up to him and the perversely priggish Mr. Spock needed a less intimate player than Bud to share the mystery of his sundry final engagements, someone who couldn't reject him on a scale that had any meaning.

After all his reasonings, Bud still felt left in the cold. They'd breathed each other's darkness for so many years—wasn't it he who gave Brian *The 120 Days of Sodom*? When the Doctor never mentioned the book again, Bud knew he'd made it his.

He began working again in earnest on the script about Rialta and the Shotgun Man. Most of the characters and events were real; maybe he'd speak to Bloom about getting clearances. It was still more Flannery O'Connor than *St. Elsewhere*, but to hell with it.

Rialta had a seven-year-old niece named Violet who used to keep her company on the drive to County General. She had red hair and white skin that shone. Whenever he saw her, the Shotgun Man came alive. Violet's aunt gave her money and let her go to the cafeteria while she prayed in the chapel.

Bud sometimes accompanied Rialta to worship. At the time he thought he was falling in love with her but never got anything back. She liked him well enough, he reasoned, mistaking his interest in the Shotgun Man for empathy. But he was a paranoid Jew and what was that to Rialta but another way of having half a head blown off, half a soul, half a life. Maybe what she wanted all along was a Jew. Life was like that.

In the script Bud naturally had the Doctor walk with her to the chapel instead and watch as she knelt. The screenwriter kept the reality of his drug problem, for pathos, and added a marriage that wasn't going so well; he gave the Doctor two kids and a house in Pasadena. So much for Homo World.

₩₩₩

Vivian called and asked him out. Her friend Sandy was visiting from Camarillo and they were going to a dance club on Hollywood Boulevard. They picked him up that night at Dolly's. Bud finally admitted he was staying there while his mother recovered from a bad surgery.

Sandy was pretty, with yellowish teeth that made her a little outside. The girlfriends laughed like ornery specialists in the same field, fluently familiar. They shared a constant private joke, the brazen bond of their girlhood otherness. Of Vivian's face, Sandy threw a reckless redneck so-what to the world. Their local friendship was on holiday in the Basin's far frontier and they felt a little like celebrities. Bud enjoyed being the third wheel; he felt like a hitchhiking foreigner, a tourist picked up by a lusty all-American duo.

On the way to the club they detoured through Beverly Hills for the sights, and when Vivian told her friend it was Bud's old stomping ground, Sandy was impressed. They drove up Rodeo Drive and into the residential flats. They passed around a flask and Bud gave them some of the old chauffeur patter, pointing out homes of the stars as they goggled.

"Do you know where Dennis Quaid lives?"

"Sorry."

"That's who I'd like to meet."

"Sandy's obsessed with Dennis Quaid."

"*The Big Easy,* did you see it?" she asked Bud. "That scene where he goes down on Ellen Barkin?"

"Sandy!"

"I'm telling you, I coulda been her stand-in. Hey, if he'd go to bed with Ellen Barkin, he'd go to bed with me. I look better than Barkin, she looks like a *dog.* You sure you don't know where he lives? Man, I'd like to leave a little note. Two little words is all I'd need, and my phone number." She leaned over and stage-whispered the words into Vivian's outraged ear; they screamed like wild alarms.

The car passed the corner where Bud used to get egged on Halloween, the streets called Bedford and Elevado. While the girls cut up old touches, he thought about the Day of the Dead. He used to work at Fun Fair, a novelty shop on Beverly Drive. That was over twenty years ago. When October came, the owner would pay him a buck and a half an hour to walk up and down the street wearing a monster mask. He couldn't believe his luck, being picked from all the other boys. Brian thought the whole enterprise vulgar and preferred to work behind the counter, demonstrating the brightly stenciled tubes with their disappearing scarves, the wands that jerked magically in the air, the trick card decks, rubber coins and floating balls. His hands were already huge and thick-fingered, unlikely for a future surgeon. On Saturdays the Doctor did his sleight of hand for the throngs under the owner's proud, watchful eye.

Bud envied his friend's privileges, while the Doctor allowed him complete domain of the masks. He wore the store ad sandwich board and walked up and down Beverly, his face sweltering, breath warm against the latex, enraptured by commerce, watching pedestrians make their token fright faces. His first real job—drummer and street performer, monster-salesman—awaiting Halloween with its melancholy winds, its edge and its color, its pumpkin and witches' cutouts and read-alouds *(Something Wicked This Way Comes)* at school, its carnival of curfews, cops and boys bigger than he. One Halloween, right before the Doctor died, they went to the Elevado corner. They were nostalgia freaks and often made cynical postmodern jaunts, forays to old landmarks, expecting to find nothing but ghosts. This time, they shook gaping heads at the mother lode continuum—the whole city seemed gathered there: hundreds of parents with bewildered, decorated infants, self-conscious teens on their last trick or treat, ninety-pound bullies with mentholated shaving cream, police cars that looked like engineless props. Nothing had changed the great pageant of their childhood. They got out of the car and joined the river of the parade, their hearts racing from the Methedrine and memories.

He was jolted from his reverie by the girls' guffaws. The cool and ordered streets receded as they pulled onto Sunset Boulevard.

Bud hoped he was still seeing Vivian when Halloween rolled around. He imagined her made up, a peacock on that day, a

Mardi Gras queen of deformity. On that day were her catechism and confirmation, her bat mitzvah; how she would rule.

They danced a few hours at the club. Sandy met a stuntman and
he asked if she wanted to go barhopping. She kept wanting to
know if it was okay to leave with the guy. Vivian said she was
tired and didn't care, so Sandy left to go drink.

Bud and Vivian walked to the car. Vivian reached in and
pulled some typed pages from the glove compartment, handing
them to Bud. Some of her writing. Then she squatted in a bush
and peed.

Instead of going home, she drove to the Observatory. They
parked and Bud followed her to a windy niche of stone steps
that faced the city glitter.

"Did you know that a round trip to Andromeda at near the
speed of light would take half a century?"

"That's helpful information."

Vivian looked at him like she knew they had a future together
and he smiled uncomfortably.

"If we went on a round trip to Andromeda, four million years
would have passed on earth when we came back."

She looked toward Brentwood, and points beyond, lost in
thought. Bud was suddenly tired and wished he were at home,
alone in bed.

"Do you want to come back with me? My mom's up at my
grammie's and I have a feeling Sandy won't be coming home
tonight."

She led him through the darkness like it was a forest of her
familiars; he thought he heard the mother's respirations. They
took their clothes off, chaperoned by the room's tender walls—
allies of her segregation—and fell into bed. Vivian twisted her
bad side away and he kissed her long neck. Bud suddenly
needed her, and as his mouth moved closer to hers, she
squirmed in his arms. He wanted to kiss her full face. He would
make her trust him; he would prove his delicacy and his

arousal. He would talk to her like she talked to the stars. He pinned her arms and began the colloquy by whispering her name. She looked like a scared girl in a hideout, about to take an oath of blood.

"Just fuck," she said, and the bad side presented itself, scuttling and abandoned. "Just fuck me."

₩₩₩

He worked some more on the outline for the hospital script.

In the third act he had Brian leave his Pasadena wife and go cold turkey. He would marry Rialta and adopt her niece, vanish from the hospital and go to Oxnard with his love, a bigamist in the country of the Shotgun Man. It was coming along. Bud was almost through blocking it out. Soon the writing would begin.

The screenwriter took a break and picked up the pages Vivian had given him. There was a short piece about a young girl's response to her father's death, clearly autobiographical.

Bud Wiggins, author, did not feel particularly threatened.

They saw each other a lot over the next few weeks. The sex was good, her room high in a castle that hung in the air, the tenebrous landscape of bed quilt lit only by available lunar light.

When Bud asked about old boyfriends, she was evasive. She alluded to someone in Camarillo, but he was sure it was an unrequited love, the kind of romance a young girl carries on in her diary. No, Bud was certain he was the biggest thing that ever happened to her. Still, he wondered whom she'd gone to bed with. Maybe an early counselor at school or a bus driver or a shrink or a nun or a gynecologist or a consulting plastic surgeon. The whole world wanted a taste, particularly of the vulnerable. Bud observed that her acutely sexual temperament had probably been exacerbated by the misfortune—Vivian's need to connect had become monstrously carnal. She was *experienced,* he thought, but that didn't make her a bad person. That's right. While Bud was still looking for his skates, Vivian had already been around the block about a thousand times, like a freakish *Candy.* She'd probably been "done" by Bobby Feld himself.

₩₩₩

A month after *Bloodbath* was in the can, the production company finally got it together to throw a "wrap" party. Bud felt guilty for not inviting Vivian. It was silly, but he never got around to telling her he'd done *acting chores,* as they said in the trades. At this point, having lied about it was even more damning than the truth. So be it. He'd go by himself and that would be the end of the whole minor charade. The party promised to be a real low-dollar affair anyway—lots of nonunion poverty-level party animals and grungy crew girls dolled up like game-show-hostesses. Bud wanted to show up because it was a good opportunity to talk to Genie Katz-Cohen about writing and directing the sequel.

The party was down on Pico, at a tacky thatch-roofed restaurant with a South Pacific motif. It was loud and no one recognized him out of makeup. Finally, one of the assistant camera girls approached and stroked his smooth cheeks like he was a cat while a grip made a joke about how successful the plastic surgery had been. Then someone said he looked the same as he did in the movie and everybody laughed. Bud looked around for Genie but she wasn't there—no one from above-the-line had attended.

After about twenty minutes, he left. He ran into Vivian's friend in the parking lot.

"Sandy! What are you doing here?"

"I'm with Cody."

"The stuntman?"

"The very same."

"Sleeping your way to the bottom."

"Very funny. So what about you?"

"I did a rewrite, to help them out."

"Mr. Good Samaritan!" She was loaded. Still, Bud knew she was impressed. "That was very nice of you."

"The producer's a friend."

"They probably pay pretty good, huh?"

Yeah, a million fucking dollars.

They walked to her car. Sandy lit a joint.

"I hear you and Vivian are getting along."

"It's nice."

"She really likes you."

"She's great. You gonna move down to L.A.?"

"I should. I'm spending enough time here."

"What do you do? Up in Camarillo."

"I'm an optician's office manager. Real exciting."

"Uh-huh."

"That was supposed to be ironic."

"It was. It is." He paused. "You know, you look pretty good."

The bad teeth broke her mouth open in a smile. Bud's heart sped up like he was on a holdup. He moved closer, smelling the liquor and the pot. They kissed crazily, the secret handshake of betrayal, her hand around his neck like a high school slut, their tongues wild kids in shallow water. He dropped down, sliding his face along her chest, nuzzling the shirt down on one side, catching the nipple. He knelt on the ground and raised her skirt; she wasn't wearing panties. He kissed her there, his knees aching from the concrete. She groaned. They heard some people coming. He stood up and Sandy straightened her skirt, laughing.

The screenwriter brushed his teeth and stepped into the shower. It would be all right. Poor impulse control, Jeanette would say. Didn't matter who was responsible, it was wrong. As the water pounded him, Bud decided his indiscretion might have a positive effect after all, forcing him off the commitment fence. Vivian had been angling for that, anyway—commitment was coming up fast on the agenda. Jeanette was a long time gone and he was ready now, ready to take a chance again on love. Why not?

Bud turned the water off and toweled down, wondering if he'd always have to hurt and betray, even after the exchange of vows. He was really beating himself up now, feeling the panic of conscience. He told himself it was okay, he was too sensitive, nothing really happened anyway. He doubted if Sandy would ever say anything to Vivian—she didn't seem like the compulsive confessor type. For her, it was just a drunken thing, no big deal. You never knew. He was powerless over what that girl confided or withheld. Sandy was loaded, Bud could say he was loaded, too, or maybe taking pills for depression that made him crazy. Back on the Prozac. If Vivian did somehow find out, it would likely be down the line—they'd have already traveled light-years together, by then it would be irrelevant. Vivian would understand what it was, what he did for love, a kind of exorcism of his fear of intimacy, a moving toward her, a crucible. Bud's guilty lucubrations made him realize that Vivian should be his wife.

He turned on the TV. He felt better and wished she were beside him. It was too late to call—it would be a little weird, especially if Sandy were staying with her. Bud decided to tell Vivian what had happened, then ask for her hand. He'd do it tomorrow and get it over with. There would be fireworks, then all would be forgiven. She would see the bravery of his confession, evidence of his profound intent. It would be madness of her to let such a foolish indiscretion jeopardize a lifetime together. They'd find an apartment, someplace near her beloved beach. Vivian would see less of Sandy, that's all, something that might have happened naturally. Sandy was a confirmed bachelorette; the married seek other marrieds. So there would really be no loss. Vivian would never tell Sandy she knew, it would give her power and pleasure to know and not to tell. One more way to bond with her man. Her husband.

As he sat in the cafeteria at Cedars-Sinai the next morning blocking out the third act of the *Shotgun Man* opus, Bud had a brainstorm. It came to him as a perfect prenuptial: he would ask Vivian to collaborate on a script. It would be a trial marriage, a creative vessel of healing and forgiveness. They would write their story, with a few alterations—a rich young prick falls in love with a burned girl. They might even work in Sandy and the traitorous kiss. Like most of his best ideas, this one came with a title. They would call it *The Gravity of Stars*.

Bud and Vivian began, and were good together. He put off his confession and the guilt began to fade.

Vivian loved the process, loved rolling up her shirtsleeves and getting stained with the ink of art and synergy. They often worked in the park bluff overlooking the ocean and Pacific Coast Highway, taking long walks while improvising dialogue. She was impassioned, a fast learner. Bud scribbled on legal pads as they argued at lunch over motivation and structure, character and resolution, arc and intent. They made love and fantasized about selling their script for millions of dollars. She wanted to use the money to build a house in Big Sur, high above the waves.

Would he betray her again? Now and then Jeanette's talking head dangled in the air beside him like a hammy, wicked witch: "You're sick and you're dangerous!" Maybe his ex was right. The screenwriter found himself wondering if he was amoral— no, an amoral person would never have agonized as he had. Maybe that was bullshit; even Ted Bundy said he went through heavy guilt trips after the first few kills. Bud laughed to himself and thought he should probably start going to Meetings again. Meetings or the shrink, for a tune-up.

In the script they had the girl with the burned face working at the Observatory. The rich kid takes her to the beach on their first date and she talks to him about the stars. Bud thought Vivian came up with a great character, a little boy named Artie that the girl met while she was in the hospital. Artie's dying of leukemia. Vivian wrote a scene where the burned girl and the rich young prick show up at the hospital on Halloween with a bag of costumes and Artie chooses the skeletal one of Death. They sneak him out to trick or treat, ending up at an unfinished housing development where the houses are skeletons themselves, silhouetted against the sky. Artie makes them pretend they're a family and the three of them pantomime dinner. They sit in the unfinished living room watching *The Simpsons* on an invisible TV; then pretend to put Artie to bed. Vivian thought the scene might be too maudlin, but Bud was amazed by it. She really had a flair. She wrote another scene where the burned girl says, "I know what goes faster than the speed of light—the soul. Because the soul is the birth of light."

Bud and Vivian were halfway through the script. He felt like they were running to paradise but he had a rock in his shoe. They were sitting in a Westwood restaurant when he told her about Sandy. She went cold and asked what it was exactly that they did, but before Bud could answer, Vivian hit him in the face, breaking his sunglasses. He started to cry, expecting her pity and remorse. Instead, she hit him again and again until he lurched from the table, shielding his eyes like an intellectual caught in a riot. He ran from the place.

A few weeks later Genie Katz-Cohen showed him a rough assembly of *Bloodbath*. She said everyone was high on it. Bud thought his acting was a little over the top, but Genie kept saying how great he was, he was the best thing in it. When he brought up the idea of writing and directing the sequel, she seemed to take it seriously. She would run it past some of the AlphaFilm execs when they got back from Israel.

Vivian sent Bud the sixty pages they'd written together, without a note. There was a scene enclosed that she'd added since. A dream sequence.

The girl dreams she's on the beach, beautiful and unburned. Artie's in the water and she warns him not to go out past the waves. The rich kid is walking with a girl named Sandy (Vivian didn't even bother giving her another name). The rich kid says he and Sandy got married and she's "regnant" with their seventh child. He tells the burned girl he still wants to marry her, that it's completely legal so long as Sandy gives consent. The burned girl declines and the rich kid says she's stubborn and will go on making mistakes until she dies. The burned girl gets defensive and lies. She says she can't become engaged because she's already married—to Artie. Then they hear a scream and it's Artie in his skeleton costume, weirdly bobbing in the waves. "I am the Minotaur," he says.

Bud put the material aside, thinking: *overwrought.* He wondered if he should try to finish it alone. The script was without a third act and God knows third acts were the hardest to pull off. It occurred to him that relationships were a lot like screenplays; beginnings were easy.

He didn't feel all that inspired without her. Everything was a mess now and that was a shame because he'd been thinking the two of them could take a shot at revising Caitlin's Henry James script—now and then the town really liked to "throw money" at man/woman writing teams, if the timing was right. He'd give her a call after she cooled down. Maybe everything would work out and they'd get back together.

††††††

Dolly was getting better and Bud concentrated on finding an apartment. Over the next month he left messages on Vivian's machine but never heard back.

He couldn't get the ending right, so abandoned the hospital script in favor of turning the saga of the Shotgun Man into a short story. In the movie outline all he'd managed to come up with was the Doctor leaving his family and heading up the coast with Rialta and her niece—what seemed like a cop-out third act in a film was actually an evocative, lyrical finale for a grimly elegant novella. At any rate, Bud needed to get the whole thing out of his system and move on to something commercial. He still liked the genre; he might even write a vulgar comedy about doctors and nurses. Why not? Whatever he came up with, the screenwriter was going to have to pay some bills, and soon. For now, the idea was to publish the Shotgun Man story himself and sell it out of Bookz. That was the classy way to go. Anyway, you never knew who might pick it up during a browse—a studio executive, a Barbet Schroeder—the bonus being that the slim volume was really just another pitch, but one that wouldn't fade away at the end of a meeting.

Bud went to see his old shrink. When he asked if she'd heard from Jeanette, the woman smiled enigmatically, ever the smug keeper of confidentialities, the "professional." He liked that about her. He told her about Vivian and his remorse and how he'd thought about going to Brentwood and forcing a meeting. Did the therapist think that was *appropriate*? Bud was an adult, she replied, and could do what he wanted. He wasn't so sure Vivian would want to see him and the shrink said, "How long have you had this crystal ball?" Bud said he'd only just begun to realize how much he must have hurt her. The shrink said something trite about the durability of the human heart and told him no one was stopping him if he needed to see Vivian for "closure." Forget the closure, Bud said, I want to marry her. He thought the shrink would laugh, but she didn't even flinch. She was deadpan and gently pragmatic: You'll have to gain Vivian's trust again before she'll want to marry you. Bud asked if she really thought there was hope and the sage therapist said anything was possible. But Vivian may not be ready to see you, you have to be prepared for that. What if she's involved with someone else? he asked. Then she's involved with someone else. You don't have any control over that—you're *powerless.* I want to be her friend, Bud said, schmaltzy and self-pitying. Then you have to act like a friend. And you have to accept that she may not want to be *yours*—not just now. You hurt this woman. But now isn't forever.

When Bud wanted to know if the shrink thought he could get her back, she just stared at him and said, "I refuse to play the game of reassurance."

He drove over at the end of the week, but Vivian wasn't home. Her mother said she was visiting her grandma up north. Bud thanked her and left.

He began the drive to Camarillo. If he had any chance of getting Vivian back, it was by an outrageous act; he'd have to shanghai her to one of those twenty-four-hour chapels in Vegas. She just might go for that. The meeting in the museum, the courtship and collaboration, the slap in the restaurant, the estrangement and elopement—it would be a great story, one for their grandchildren. A real love story. They talked about having kids once, while on a drive high in the Malibu hills. They sat on a bluff (*The Big Bluff*—another good title) and pretended they were old marrieds, just like the scene from their script with Artie in the skeletal house. After the vows Bud would take her to the Mirage to see the white tigers and gamble with hundred-dollar chips. They might even come up with the third act of *Gravity* on their honeymoon.

As the romantic screenwriter headed to points north, his thoughts drifted to the saga of the Shotgun Man. He recalled sitting in the chapel with Rialta and putting his hand on hers, nervous as little boy Bud at the Saturday matinée. She let it sit there. He went to kiss her and she stayed still, looking straight ahead. He kissed the corner of her mouth the way he'd first kissed Vivian's, and Rialta's head turned slightly toward him, her tongue darting into his mouth like a lizard's. Like she'd never kissed before. She quickly left the chapel and from then on avoided his eyes. She stopped visiting the Shotgun Man and Bud moved back to his apartment soon after.

He passed Topanga—driving along the Pacific always lightened and cleansed him. He began composing text for the Shotgun Man story in his head: the Doctor had thrown away his syringes and was in the car with Rialta and Violet, rocketing toward Oxnard, away from County General and all that he'd known. By the time he arrived in Camarillo, Bud had the last paragraphs committed to memory. As yet those were all he had, but he figured that was okay; he'd read somewhere that Truman Capote always wrote the endings first.

He pulled up to a gas station pay phone, tore the page with the grandmother's address from the book and went back to the car. He wanted his arrival to be a surprise and would have to ask the attendant for directions. But first, he excitedly pulled a notebook from under the seat, found a pen in the glove compartment and hurriedly wrote out the end of the story.

They stopped for hamburgers at a stand by the ocean. Rialta and Violet looked superreal to the Doctor. Maybe it was the quality of the sunlight; everything was defined by light, like a filigree with no end. Rialta noticed his eyes brim up and put her hand on his, thinking the tears a poignant emanation of his old sacrificed life. But the real source of his trembling was the recognition of a fountain, a deep spring at the root of his soul's Garden, water, water, human water, and like an eternal pond in a living park his eyes overflowed as it came to him that the light dusting his companions, the cliffs, the beach, the birds, the aging asphalt highway, the waves of water and littered sand—the awesome sunlight basting and tangling the world was millions of years old.

Rialta sensibly knew when to remove her hand from his; Violet was eating her hamburger and saw none of this meager drama. The salt air blasted him and he knew no one in the world, not even himself. He felt vulnerable, female. Some of this he knew was the first, flulike symptoms of withdrawal. Another part, the sentimental part, came from the fountain, whose deep clear water he imagined contained in a thick stone well, the cold gray stoniness of the Mother well.

It was time to go.

"Shotgun!" the little girl shouted at him beside the car.

Now he remembered who he was: he was the Doctor. He had left his wife and children and the Shotgun Man behind.

"Shotgun!" she repeated. "I want to ride shotgun!"

"You both can ride," Rialta said. The little girl said *No,*

then clambered onto the Doctor's lap as they pulled from the
gravel to the highway and fell asleep.

He looked through the dirty windshield to the brambles of the
vacant lot beyond and felt bored and unwelcome. The place was
like the Doctor's grave—it held no interest. He watched the
phone book page lilt to the ground.

Bud took the inland route back to L.A. It was faster. He'd
be out of Dolly's soon and in his own place. He blasted "Na Na
Hey Hey Kiss Him Goodbye" on the radio and put his hand
on the fresh notebook scrawlings, like a benediction. He liked
what he'd written—the rest would be simple because now he
had an ending that worked. Everyone knew that endings were
the hard part. Beginnings were easy.

ʍʍ

It was a rainy Sunday but the screenwriter decided to drive
around anyway, jotting down numbers off rental signs for anything that looked appealing.

For years he'd had his eye on a certain apartment building,
a stately château on Fountain Avenue. From the street Bud
could see towering ceilings and chandeliers. He assumed there
was an impossibly long tenant-waiting list but decided to check
the veracity of a brass sign out front that always read VACANCY.
He would satisfy his curiosity, if nothing else.

The place was owned by a wealthy Mexican family and
managed by a Jewish grandmother. Bud was astonished when
Bertha said there was a bachelor available on the second floor.
She quaintly described it as the former "servants' quarters."
The room had wine-red carpeting like the seats of old movie
houses, rich wood furnishings and a view of the street. There
was a minifridge and a hot plate. It was too small, but it was
cheap and refined, quirkily grandiose; Bud imagined it within
a tasteful three-star European hotel. There was a little garden
in the rear, near the carport, and the building's cool halls were
kept clean and waxed, suggesting an elegant version of the

Foundation residence in the Heights where he used to board, back when he was a "character disorder." Dolly gave him bathroom towels and linen for the bed. She said it was tiny, but "to screw, you don't need a palace."

The room was a nice place to work. He finished the novella that he called *Shotgun* and dropped it off at the printers. They were going to bind it and give it a nice cover. It wasn't costing much and Bud thought he could get the owner of Bookz to put it on the counter by the cash register. He might even have a book-signing party—he'd scrawl *Best Wishes* or *Salut!* on the frontispiece.

He started noodling with Caitlin's script but had to put it aside when he got the call from one of the Israelis at AlphaFilm asking him to write the sequel to *Bloodbath*. Bud was elated. He asked about Genie and the executive said she didn't work there anymore.

Bud delivered a first draft in four weeks, for which he was paid Writers Guild minimum. The money allowed him to buy a portable computer and a Proton TV. He suddenly worried that because of his modest bank balance, he was no longer "judgment-proof" if the collection agencies went after him. Bud hadn't heard from them in years; but old debts still easily wiped out assets. He called Don Bloom and Bloom told him not to leave a forwarding address with the post office. "You're paranoid. Just have Dolly tell the carrier you don't live there anymore." Too much time had gone by, he said. They'd written him off. Not to worry.

That was Bloom—the hustler, the *fixer*. Bud and the Doctor used to marvel at him.

The boys knew each other from grade school. When Bud moved to Bel Air, the future surgeon and future attorney befriended him. Bud and Brian grew closer, but Don Bloom didn't seem to mind. They were a funny trio: myopic Bud, Brian with the dead ear and the ponytail to his waist, high-strung, whippet-thin Bloom with the alopecia that rendered him prematurely bald. Bloom was a real tekkie—an early hacker, he was the neighborhood connection for stolen telephone access codes. That went on for years, even after Bloom had passed the bar and the Doctor was in medical school back east; the three spoke each day, sometimes by conference call. Even Dolly called midwestern relatives for free, just like the good old WATS line days.

It got pretty crazy for a while, back when Bud's first movie didn't come out and the work dried up. He didn't want to go back to boiler rooms or driving limousines, not if he didn't have to. Not just yet. He couldn't ask Brian for money—as an intern, he wasn't making any. So he turned to his old friend Bloom while waiting for a deal to come through.

The lawyer had lavish offices in Santa Monica. His practice was "eclectic," though personal injury and libel were high on the hit parade. He took the insolvent screenwriter to L'Orangerie for lunch and near the end of the meal a waiter broke a glass near their table. Bloom leaned over and told Bud to keep one eye covered with his hand. Then he called the maître d' over and said "my friend Bud Wiggins" had possibly been injured by a flying shard of glass. He paid the check, gave him his business card and said they would be in touch. "I want to get him to my ophthalmologist."

Another time, at a hotel in Century City, the screenwriter slipped while getting off the escalator. Bloom jumped on that one right away. He told Bud to sit down, and when he returned with the manager, the attorney pointed to some debris overflowing an ashtray by the moving stairs. He said "my friend the screenwriter Bud Wiggins" apparently tripped on the cellophane of a cigarette package cover. When the man appeared dubious, Bloom immediately went in for the kill, giving him the old "I'm your worst nightmare" speech, dropping names and citing the legal responsibilities of innkeepers. The manager withered.

The attorney never actually followed up on those incidents; they were executed with a wink, as if to keep his hand in. He did show Bud a few scams, though, like how to buy expensive wristwatches on department store credit and return them the next day for cash. Bloom transferred his own money into the scripter's savings account to boost Bud's credit line, withdrawing the funds when the deed was done. The attorney went on a spending spree, using Bud's cards to charge camera equipment, first-class trips to Europe, even home delivery of frozen steaks—all in exchange for cash, something like thirty cents on the dollar. Bloom got a kick out of it. He said it would be easy to pay the creditors back once Bud got a deal or if worse came to worst, he could file for bankruptcy, like thousands did every day. Bud was depressed, but the attorney kept him in good spirits—it seemed like play money anyway. As unemployment persisted, the scheme snowballed and he starting buying goods for the attorney's friends with his Gold card. Brian thought it was a hoot, especially the time Bud got a postcard from Paris signed *"Expressly Yours,* Don." Bud kept telling himself he'd be working soon, that for now it was good twisted fun. He'd had one movie made and would have another—the town would pay him the big bucks again and the whole madcap life-on-credit period would be something he'd write a comedy about (he'd call it *Charge!*). He trusted Don Bloom; Don Bloom would not let him go down, even though Bud felt like he was "circling the drain." The credit card companies started writing him letters and the attorney showed him how to stall by firing off threatening letters of his own. Bloom counseled him to send tiny dollar amounts back with some of the invoices. As long as you made an effort to pay, they wouldn't slam the door on you. They wanted their money.

When months passed and Bud couldn't get a deal, even the enterprising attorney got bored with the shenanigans and began urging bankruptcy. By then the screenwriter was numb and addicted, like one of those cardplayers who sit at a table determined to lose everything. He took limousines to restaurants and ate by himself, like some legend. One night he got drunk and went to the whorehouse on the hill—Morris's old haunt—

and wound up with crabs. Bloom continued coaching him on what to say in the letters Bud sent to Diners and Carte Blanche and American Express, the gist of them being he was a hapless victim of wild-eyed Wall Street juggernauts gone berserk with delusional allegations of exotic purchases. The minute you demanded they look into something, it gummed up the wheels and bought you time—time enough to get a deal, to get commencement monies on a first draft.

He finally cut the credit cards in half and got back his old job in a telephone boiler room, selling ink and toner for copy machines. Collection agencies sent letters demanding remittance for nearly sixty thousand dollars. Bloom was increasingly hard to reach, so Bud gave the disturbing bulletins to his sometime accountant Zake Bock. Zake was an old SDS face, a Yippie poet who became an IRS novitiate. Zake took him to his own lawyer, the adamantine Louis Shramm. When Shramm heard the whole story, he urged Bud to turn Bloom in to the authorities. "I know you think he's your close personal friend, but listen to me, Wiggins: this guy is *nobody's* friend! He *used* you! He should be *disbarred*! This is serious, Mr. Wiggins. From what you told me, he used your cards to purchase out-of-state airline tickets. That may be in violation of *federal law*! You could go to jail!"

Bud was badly shaken. As they left Shramm's office, Zake told him there was "no such thing as debtors' prison." Bud's problem was business, not criminal. He said Shramm had an unpleasant bedside manner, was all, he was really an okay guy. Weeks passed and the cheapo bankruptcy ads on television looked more and more alluring, but Shramm wouldn't hear of it; Chapter Eleven was against his beliefs, it was "morally incorrect" and besides, filing in Bud's case wouldn't be easy—he'd be subject to the kind of scrutiny that could backfire. Zake agreed Bud should "forestall," filing wasn't yet "timely." Even the people Bud spoke to on the twenty-four-hour Debtors' Hot Line affirmed that bankruptcy was "the easy way out." Suddenly, everyone was some kind of elder statesman of ethical conduct. Why couldn't he file if it would give him relief? Zake told him to lay low, assuaging him with cryptic, "humorous" cantos on money and politics and madness, weird, abstract, macho harangues in the style of Stevens and Jeffers. *Not to worry!*

Bud actually cried for two months, imagining himself in jail. He knew he'd have a "complete nervous breakdown" (went the Miltown-era phrase) if forced to trial. He really thought he was going to lose it. He joined Program debtor groups and met those who'd been driven practically mad by their compulsion to spend. It was almost funny. They made Bud keep humiliating lists of how much he spent each day on parking meters, gum, pay phones, soda, *Variety.*

Then one day, the threatening letters stopped. Zake said the cunning Mr. Shramm spoke to the collection agencies and told them *confidentially* that his client Bud Wiggins was not playing with a full deck. Wiggins was somewhere in Alaska, he'd told them, trying to raise money to pay off his debts. His client had awakened in the middle of the night with a vision; something about starting an ice company. ICE FOR SALE, in the land of aurora borealis.

That was all a long time ago, but the idea of those collections goblins returning to feast on his blood didn't sit well. Now that Bud had some money in the bank from the *Bloodbath* gig, he phoned Don Bloom to ask if it was such a good thing. Should he hide it? When debtors made money, were creditors notified via some secret "found income" warning network? Would American Express suddenly serve him with papers, slap him with liens, freeze his funds? Bloom said the statute of limitations was an issue—pretty soon, they wouldn't be able to touch him. Bud and his credit card–bought frozen steaks and CD players skittered across the state line like the Road Runner, as state troopers bounced off an invisible border wall; he was Cagney, sneering escape artist, consumer-provocateur, dancer tough. If they did serve him (they'd have to find him first), Bud could "settle," the attorney said he would handle it pro bono.

Bloom could afford to: in the intervening years he'd become a millionaire six times over from property investments. Bud started to like the idea of paying his old debts, even with a dime for every dollar—it felt cleaner that way. There was always the chance the dunners wouldn't go along, but if the case ever went to trial, his good-conscience offer might be important to a judge. Bud's old therapists would take the stand and his friends from the Meetings would fill the court, testifying to his pain and his terror and his tears. How could the court rule against him? How could they send him up the river? At that point surely Bloom the multimillionaire would step in and take care of the debt himself. (Bud never told him how Shramm had encouraged him to snitch.) If it came down to it, Bud had decided to do time without plea bargaining to turn in his childhood friend. No one had held a gun to Bud's head; he was just as responsible as Bloom for what went down. He'd tell Bloom about it eventually, during a "you owe me" speech, when he needed money or a big favor. He'd tell him how he held his mud when Shramm put the heat on. "You owe me!" he'd shout. "They wanted me to turn you in! You don't know the pressure they put on me to rat, you hairless son of a bitch!"

ᴧᴧᴧᴧ

It was evening. Bud rented a video and brought some Thai food back to his apartment. There was something wrong with the tracking on the tape, so he watched the news instead: Lou Gottlieb was on his way to averting another writers' strike. Standing on the Guild steps, lording it over the microphones, the local media fixture peered over half-moon glasses, relishing his role as ombudsman, cheerleader and artist's champion.

Gottlieb, a youthful bachelor in his late fifties, was a WGA powerhouse. Though chiefly known as a producer of classy movies of the week, his first love was writing—he had a TV's Golden Age pedigree and never let you forget about those halcyon *Hallmark Hall of Fame* days. He was one of those men who dream of calling their memoirs *Occupation: Writer* or *The*

Noblest Profession. They hear the eulogies from beyond the grave: "We are gathered together to say good-bye to a *writer.*" He sponsored writer symposiums and writer barbecues and writer weekends in Tahoe and was photographed at charity functions with important East Coast playwrights, novelists and PEN functionaries. Valerie Bertinelli, Barry Levinson and Steven Bochco were just as likely to turn up at his famed weekend basketball games as Susan Sontag, Jesse Jackson, Eric Fischl or an Irvine semiotician with Umberto Eco in tow (Gottlieb was producing an Eco piece for PBS). The busy man lent his Montauk beach house to a poet in the final throes of AIDS, and it was rumored he was trying his hand at a play about that moment in time called *Sanctuary.* Larry Gelbart and Harold Pinter would give him notes.

Gottlieb was a tough negotiator. No one liked a strike, and the timing wasn't great for Bud—he wanted to be in the position to work if he started getting heat from his "chores" on *Bloodbath 2.* He was back in the Guild, an active dues-paying member. Bud let himself feel good about that; he was tired of his hollow cynicism. He was out of the bush leagues and back in the majors again, suited up and ready to play. He might even go to a seminar, the ones where they talk about new software or finding the right agent or lawyer or writing partner. A little hobnobbing with the hyphenates never hurt anyone. The screenwriter stood confidently near the dugout and watched the stadium fill up, whacking the clots of dirt from his cleats with a bat. A base hit just wouldn't do. Bud Wiggins needed nothing short of a grand slam.

Reassured by Bloom, Bud went the next morning to deposit his final check for *Bloodbath 2.* The bank was festively decorated. The tellers wore buttons reading FREE GIFT IF I DON'T CALL YOU BY NAME. They looked sour, like a bunch of parolees manning booths in a festival of humiliation. It was all part of a promotion for car loans, a real small-time hustle. While Bud filled out a deposit slip, someone behind the counter asked if there were any potholders left.

He stood there staring at the teller's shiny, pockmarked cheeks that gave way to baby's-bottom jowls. He had dandruff like people used to and wore a Jesus pin. He handed Bud his receipt and told him to have a nice day.

"My name," Bud said.

The teller looked at him blankly.

"You didn't call me by name."

Outside he threw away the potholder.

Things could be worse—he could work in a bank. That would be awful, Bud thought, enough to drive a body to fund-transfer fraud. Good area for a movie, though. He always liked *Dog Day Afternoon.* There hadn't been anything like it in a while. Set something in a jewelry store in Beverly Hills, like the Van Cleef & Arpels robbery a few years back. "Beverly Hills" was still gold. But an out-and-out comedy, no fatalities. Some-one could get wounded, for that surprising touch of realism. If it was handled right, violence in the middle of a comedy could be very effective. The structure was right there in front of him:

> ACT ONE: *Intro ROBBERS (planning heist, etc.), Intro EMPLOYEES and CUS-TOMERS at bank*
>
> ACT TWO: *The ROBBERY (botched) and arrests (a shooting/injury?)*
>
> ACT THREE: *The TRIAL (some acquitted, some convicted?)*

Lots of surprises, that was the fun of a good courtroom melodrama. If being stuck in the bank with hostages made it boring, he could create more of a caper movie, the lives and events leading *up* to the robbery. Maybe the script shouldn't be comedy after all. Maybe it should be about a killer, closer to *Jagged Edge,* or a mistaken-identity movie like *The Wrong Man.* They finally arrest the killer, the one who looks like Fonda, but it turns out the real killer *is* Fonda—the "wrong man" with the sweet wife and kids. The lead could be an alcoholic attorney lawyer like Paul Newman in *The Verdict.* What if finally Newman's the only one who knows his client is guilty—but he finds out *after* the guy's been released? What were the legalities of such a case? Maybe Bloom would know, or counselor Shramm. It'd be good if the killer was a fat cat and suddenly all this pressure is put on the lawyer to let the whole thing go, pressure from political machines or Bohemian Grove–type groups. But the lawyer can't drop it, he's let too many things slide in his life. Bud knew it was getting a little close to the *Verdict* character but that could be finessed. Besides, Newman played a *type.* No one had the copyright on loser attorneys. Maybe the judge is dirty, like the judge in that Cher movie. It would be good to bring in the lawyer's estranged kid: she's lived all these years back east and her mother dies (the attorney's ex; maybe he's only seen the girl once or something, when she was a toddler) and she moves in with him. One of those instant-daughter deals—Bud saw that in a Neil Simon movie. She's seventeen and the lawyer doesn't want her there, but he gets soft and they wind up helping each other out, winning each other's respect. Bud decided to go to the bookstore to do a little re-search. He was getting in the mode.

The two hundred copies of *Shotgun* had already been sitting at home for a few weeks. A graphics guy at the print shop put the silhouette of a double-barrel on the cover and Bud liked the way it turned out. He was sure Bookz would take the volume on consignment, but one of the clerks said the owner was in Europe. He'd have to wait.

He pulled Cicero's *Murder Trials* from the shelf. It contained actual speeches and summations in defense of men on trial for murder in the first century before Christ. The great orator was in his twenties when he represented Sextus Roscius, accused of killing his father. The tension in the courtroom was palpable as Cicero began his blistering defense, accusing fat cats of the day of conspiracy, greed and murder. His client had been framed;

reading about the victorious Roman's awesome thrusts and cool parings did something to Bud.

He decided to go to the Criminal Courts Building and catch a few trials. He was on to something.

The next morning Bud had a disturbing dream. He was on the street and the Doctor yelled at him from the second floor of the dorm. "Help me with this form!" he shouted, waving a piece of paper. Bud went up and scribbled on the paper while the Doctor watched. It was only when he awakened that the screenwriter realized he'd been filling out his friend's autopsy report.

The dream was in black and white and reminded him of that movie *Dead of Night*—there was something campy and lurid and it shook him like a headless prankster shrieking from its gory hole. He called his old shrink and all she told him was that "the Jungians said the second story represented Consciousness." You *quack,* he thought. Maybe he'd put a quack shrink in his mistaken identity movie. He showered and headed downtown.

Sitting on the benches and watching the accused had a mildly narcotizing effect. The enormous building had five or six courtrooms on each floor and Bud wandered between them like a spectator at a wax museum chamber of horrors. Not being one of the accused made him feel secure and oddly decadent. This was one nightmare he could control.

A dignified black was on trial for murder. He was one of those jailhouse lawyers whom the court cunningly allowed to represent themselves. The convict-counselor was interrogating a white woman on the stand, some sort of forensic expert. He was meticulous and plodding; the woman, wickedly restrained.

"Did you fully . . . examine the, uh, document?"

"I've already said that I did, yes."

It was training wheel Kafka, a bad idea for a board game—slow rape.

In another room he was frisked by deputies before joining

the other peanut gallery pundits, brown baggers and mavens. It was a famous serial killer case, all pentagrams and pizzazz. The case had already dragged on for years, costing millions. There were video monitors set before the judge. The defense was claiming the media had biased the case by "trying" its client on the nightly news; the judge was going to scan some clips for a few hours. The lethargic proceedings had left the killer a little jaded. On this particular day he was so bored he even eschewed eye contact with the groupies who mooned over him from the back row.

"He ain't lookin' at nobody today." The old woman tilted over to Bud, her eyes fixed on the prisoner. "Guess he's tired."

The accused had pretty Jesus hair, a sardonic, sensual mouth and a five-point star carved on his brow. Bud thought of a footnote he'd read the night before. In Cicero's time a prosecutor who failed to establish his case was in danger of having his forehead branded with the letter *K,* for "calumniator"—they called it the Remmian Law. Sounded like *Star Trek*.

When Bud left to get a snack, there was a commotion in the hall. He went toward the crowd of news reporters to get a closer look.

In their midst was Joey Funt, the famous young actor. He'd been charged with assault after slapping a car jockey hard enough in the eye that the kid was practically blinded by a contact lens. As it turned out, the victim was in prelaw at UCLA and wasn't about to take any shit. It looked like Funt was going to jail.

"Mr. Funt! Do you expect to do any time?"

"Time?" asked Funt of the air, a smart-ass hood. "We're all doing time."

"Do you expect to go to jail?" asked another insolent video stringer.

"I'm in jail right now. You people put me there, every fucking day."

The place was a frigging cornucopia! Why hadn't he thought of this earlier? All those weeks shooting *Bloodbath,* all those hours they didn't need him on the set he could have dashed across the street and really *rocked*. One drama after another, the stuff of a hundred scripts—for free. He used to read about people who got hooked on trial watching and now he knew why.

Bud wolfed down some cheese crackers and ducked into another court. The founder of a Valley prep school was on trial for molesting his students. Maybe he could do a satirical piece for one of the hipper magazines. The sexual abuse of children was still having its media heyday. All across America it was the Year of the Child, and in this children's hour the kids were beginning to show some mettle. Bolstered and debriefed, the relentless preschoolers confronted their dead zone caretakers: five-year-olds bullied on the stand before stoic, martyred perps, colicky babes backed by dossiers of telltale X rays, gonorrhea and sex warts. *Granny hurt my bottom!* Oh, yes, the women were guilty, too, the women held the children down to be hammer-fucked. A cabal of aunts and stepsisters, sitters and nuns, nannies, nurses and Big Brothers, bankers and priests, moms and dads and role model athletes—a great American Gothic psychosexual horror picnic. The jails were teeming with marooned, gaslit women who'd kidnapped their kids, literally snatched them from the jaws of incesting spouses. Some simply fled with their progeny, aided by a vast underground, a dark wood of sex abuse survivalists who provided money, shelter and new identities. Per usual, the case of the suspicious headmaster had taken years to come to trial; the humdrum witnesses were already in their late teens. Their prurient recitations were strictly by the numbers. Bud was bored and decided to go home.

There was one more courtroom on the way out.

Here was the next tableau: a man in coat and tie pointing a gun to the head of another man in suit and tie. On a table nearby, an elaborate architect's model of a Palladian villa.

"He came downstairs with the gun, and held it, as I'm holding it now. He was startled by what looked like a body lying on the living-room floor. The intruder became aware of his presence and fired one time, striking him in the shoulder. He was able to return the fire, but the assailant fled."

Bud was transfixed. He realized the men were lawyers, staging a gunfight. Grown men in suits (read "togas") holding tagged weapons, presenting their case to a jury. There was the judge, there the transcriber and there the defendant, a grimly handsome young man laboriously writing into a notebook. Whom were the notes for? All defendants enjoyed making such entries, it rendered them civilized, even while doodling pentagrams or preschool genitalia. Innocent until proven guilty. *"Cui bono?"* asked Lucius Cassius Longinus Ravilla. Nobody attempts to commit a crime unless he is hoping it will do him some good. Tell it to the headmaster and the crucified bunny rabbits.

Bud recalled the young defendant's face from the front page of the *News.* He claimed he'd startled a burglar who was in the act of killing his father. The son was later arrested and charged with the murder, the prosecution contending the intruder was a fiction. Wasn't it last night Bud read of such a case, in a trial two thousand years old? He was inclined to think the boy before him was guilty. Mightn't he have thought the same of Sextus Roscius before hearing Cicero's eloquent defense? Millennia had passed between trials; the antediluvian human drama swept him off his feet, he felt a shiver of historicity, the mystic boyhood wind blew through him again, carrying its odor of ineffable memory, deathless, exhausted, inexhaustible.

The model of the house sat there, eerily evocative. Before such a spectacle, the vagaries of show biz paled. Bud felt ennobled by his powers of observation. He'd watched a capital trial of passing interest and had managed to make quantum connections—Bud Wiggins had *synthesized.* The Cicero nexus would be his entrée to Story. For a moment he thought he might actually bring the rhetorician forward in time to help a descendant solicitor try a difficult case, but that was a bit too *Bill & Ted's Excellent Adventure.* Not that he couldn't pull it off. He decided to play it straight with this one. As a whimsical homage, he would name the attorney Tony Cicero.

Amid the storm of these cogitations, the elated screenwriter stood outside the court beside a fountain plotting his immediate future. He'd go straight to an office supply shop for index cards on which to block out the movie, scene by scene. Bud was about to dash across the street when someone shouted after him. It was Peter Dietrich.

"Wiggins! How are you?"

He grabbed Bud's hand and shook it.

"I'm good," he said, wary and bright.

"You never told me what you thought of the piece in the *News.*" The journalist suddenly caught himself and cleared his throat self-consciously. "We got some good response," he filled in. "People seemed to like it. Hey, what are you doing here?"

"Research. I'm working on a story idea."

"Great down here, isn't it? Lots of heavy shit." Bud glanced at Dietrich's notebook. "I'm doing something on the Wyler case—the kid who killed his father."

"You think he's guilty?"

"Aren't they all?" He laughed annoyingly.

"Do you know what the Roman penalty for parricide used to be?" Dietrich's wan face went lax, ready to learn something. "They whipped you, sewed you up naked in a sack with a snake, a dog, a monkey and a rooster, then threw you into the sea."

"Definitely not your slap on the wrist."

"You still working for the paper?"

"No no, quit months ago. I'm actually writing a script. You know, courtroom drama–type thing. For Joel Levitt."

It was late afternoon and Bud wished he had a sweater. He watched the bureaucrats head for the parking lots and suddenly the whole Ciceronian connection seemed forced and pretentious. A courtroom drama was a courtroom drama, genre was genre and what was he doing genre for, anyway? Maybe he could still use the Cicero thing, but in a totally different context.

Leave *Jagged Edge* to the Peter Dietrichs and the Joe Eszter-hases. Although the idea of a *Twelve Angry Men* did appeal to him, but only if it was stylized and hermetic and you never left the room the jury was sequestered in, if it was black and white with lots of tight pearlescent close-ups, like Von Sternberg. He felt better already, as if he was in a balloon and had just dropped a load of ballast onto Dietrich's head.

"See you around," Bud said abruptly, deliberately not calling the reporter by name. He wanted to put out a tougher vibe. Peter Dietrich was not his friend.

"Real good to see you! Oh, by the way, Wiggins, have you heard of Perry Bravo, the dude the Guild got out of jail?" Bud shook his head. "I don't know that much about him. He was in this writing workshop at Terminal Island. Anyway, he wrote this play and someone optioned it for a script—Lou Gottlieb, you heard of him? The Guild got him an early parole."

"So, what about him?"

"I still do free lance. It'd make a good cover story."

"You're really prolific, aren't you? What was he in prison for?"

"Killed a security guard, when he was a kid. Warehouse burglary."

"Just like *Dino.* "

"Dino?"

"A movie. Sal Mineo."

"He killed someone in prison too, but it was self-defense. One of those Aryan guys. Anyway, I thought you might know someone who knows him. It's always easier with a connection."

"Sorry," Bud said as he stepped off the curb. "The only man I know in prison is my business manager and we're not on speaking terms."

Dietrich laughed and started to say something when the new, improved Bud Wiggins rudely took his leave, joining the river of civil servants that flowed to the street.

———

When Bud got home, there was a message on his machine from an upscale ambulance company he'd applied to months before. He liked having a few lines in the water; sooner or later something would bite. He felt more secure that way.

MobileDoc was the brainchild of a slick Beverly Hills businessman who wanted to bring back the house call. His bold idea was to hire real doctors (mostly moonlighting residents) to staff high tech medical vans that would respond to an exclusive subscribership. There were openings for drivers and the office wanted Bud to come in. Someone was interested in him, and that felt good. With the collapse of his courtroom project, he was at loose ends. It smelled like an "offer."

Why not? You never knew about good material; it usually came right out of nowhere. Maybe Bud could keep the lawyer from the Cicero thing and make him an ambulance chaser. The screenwriter had always loved the medical theme but decided his problem was he always wanted to set things smack in a hospital—too on-the-nose.

He brought in a copy of his driving record from the DMV and MobileDoc hired him on the spot. They wanted him to begin work on the weekend, a forty-eight-hour shift. There were bunks in the building where the doctors and drivers slept. Drivers were referred to as "medics" and he was taught CPR and learned how to work an expensive portable EKG machine. One of the medics even showed him how to give intramuscular injections. Bud wondered about the legality of it all, then decided if the company wasn't bothered, he wasn't going to care.

He went to Hugo's for breakfast. Someone at the next table had left a Guild *Journal.* Bud flipped through it while waiting for his granola.

Underneath an ad for an expensive "Writers Retreat/Seminar" in Lake Arrowhead was an item about a performance that Friday night in Mar Vista. Perry Bravo, recent parolee and graduate of the Writer's Prison Workshop, was to read excerpts from *Go, Van Gogh,* his new play. A Q & A would follow.

The reading took place at a private club and Bravo drew a crowd—Harleys, limos, even paparazzi. It was sold out. Bud knew the security man at the door from Film Society screenings at the Guild Theater on Doheny, and the old guy waved him in.

Just inside, Joey Funt chatted with Krizia Folb. He wore a Langlitz highway patrol jacket and had the refreshed, benevolent demeanor of a deacon on sabbatical. Joan Krause, the famous young actress and author, *haw-hawed* with a wry Academy Award–winning screenwriter. Bobby Feld was there with a model; the two were stuck to Penny Reich and Derek, her certified-genius beau. Bud lowered his head so as not to be seen. He entered the main room—a stage had been erected on the small dance space—and surveyed the place for a seat.

Writers were well represented. There was a working-class contingent; a row of man-wife teams; a few flavors of the month; the occasional Humanitas Award or box-office luminary. There was also the homely, stalwart coffee klatch cadre that couldn't get arrested, even if they were writing something for Joey Funt and Billy Quintero. They *were* the Guild and they would never know glory—no doubt this bookish proletariat drew succor that one as downtrodden as Perry Bravo could be thus elevated. Maybe one of them would be next.

Lou Gottlieb stood over Joey Funt, guffawing. The room affectionately watched the hammy activist's every move. He bent down further, spoke gravely, urgently, intimately into Funt's face, then guffawed again. Bud found a spot against the wall, picked up a program and read about the event.

The Writer's Prison Workshop was Gottlieb's baby, and tonight would be the first in an "extraordinary series of readings" culled from the best of the prison lab's works-in-progress. The whiff of the bellied beast was in the air. Gottlieb had galvanized the town's insatiable hunt for the shock of the new with the novelty of incarcerated men and their dangerous unschooled visions. The intrepid rebel manqué had brought back booty from a place even agents feared to tread. Prometheus was bound and onstage, ready to pitch.

The lights dimmed and Bud's eyes lit on a girl in a motorcycle jacket sitting stiffly in the front row. Vivian! He felt his heart beating like a bird stuck in a box, the valves dumb rubbery wings. Her hair was cut short, the deformity resplendent. The room darkened. Gottlieb took the stage.

"Ladies and gentlemen, thank you for coming."

While he spoke, three actors quietly entered, carrying foldout chairs and scripts. They sat opposite the audience, heads bowed like ascetics, scripts in laps like hymnbooks. Gottlieb inhaled deeply.

"Last week, a wonderful thing happened." He paused thoughtfully, as if in prayer. *"We got a writer out of prison!"*

The room erupted in war whoops and applause. The charismatic master of ceremonies applauded back, vigorously nodding his head, baptizing the mob with sweat. Then Gottlieb made a little soft shoe, a nimble turn on one of those standard, writerly "In the beginning was the Word . . ." speeches, dramatically reminding the audience of their sacred trust—*the words.*

" 'A book ought to be an icepick to break up the frozen sea within us.' That's Kafka. Well, that frozen sea now covers the earth. We are living in an arctic zone. We light our torches, if we have the courage, with our pens and pencils—and *word processors*—and we try to hold back the frozen night. We do not abandon our posts. We chip away at the cold world, for redemption and for truth. Whether we use that ice pick from within the warmth of our homes or the coldness of a jail cell makes no difference."

An early parole had been secured with the intervention of the Guild; *words* had gotten a man out of the joint. In an epoch that had declared a bounty on the head of a novelist, the power of the Word had been reasserted. Writers had awakened. If Rushdie was invoked, then so was Havel—the lowliest profiteer in verbiage could feel the sap and the sacrament, his threadbare roots pulsing of the same tree as, well, Tolstoy or Márquez, Nabokov or Dickens. All were cousined: caption writers and *Granta* poets, studio "readers" and postmodernists, admen, editors, sitcomers, deconstructionists and variety show one-liner hacks were all one. Tonight they congregated to renew their faith and their vows, and it was beautiful. If Lou Gottlieb was the rabbi, Perry Bravo was the high priest.

He left his seat and jumped onstage, punctuated by the fisted salute of Joey Funt.

The applause was nervously respectful, leveling off quickly. With his brawny tattooed arms, the ex-convict was formidably alien. He put down his beer and began reading from the script, without any introduction.

"Ralph Waldo Emerson got dicked all the time by a bull named Nietzsche. One day in the showers, Nietzsche the bull is ripping off Waldo's backs, like usual. And the big dumb con they call Van Gogh because someone bit his ear off in a fight kills the bull. With all the sperm and blood and Minotaurs, it looked like bad Picasso. They hooked up with Charlene Manson, who hated her father the warden. She smuggles them out and the three begin their adventures on the road, into the warm tear-jerk rhythm of the cool come-drunk ribbon of the night."

He paused to sip from his beer and the audience, led by the stouthearted Funt, began to clap. Servility and sexual tension filled the air. Bravo turned the finished bottle upside down and mimed a bear trying to extract the last drop of honey from a jar. The mob was in love. From the darkness, Vivian obediently thrust a fresh bottle at him and Bravo examined it quizzically. He finally seized it and chugalugged as she retreated. When it was drained, he held the empty at arm's length and intoned, *"Magic."* A voice shouted, "You're the magic, Perry!" He acknowledged that with a belch, then resumed reading amid stuttering laughter.

It was time for the ensemble part and the actors finally showed their faces. In the part of Charlene Manson, Raleigh Wolper mimed coming home after a hard day on the lam.

Waldo and Van Gogh were supposed to be couch potatoes, watching old *Sky King*s on a motel TV.

"Hi, honey, I'm home!" she shouted, sitcom shrill.

Everybody howled.

Bud had to admit that once Genet's clown show was brushed aside, Bravo really had something: an original form and kind of idiosyncratic lyricism. The poor bastard had done a lot of reading, *Candide* and Whitman and Melville, Céline and Thoreau, Baudelaire and Swift. Bravo was smart and his characters had depth; he wasn't afraid of emotion. His wasn't the half-vaudeville, half-minimalist bad boy revue that Bud had expected—the Nick Nolte *Weeds* number, with Beckett's smeary turds for greasepaint. His theater felt as epic as thirty minutes of something read from the page could feel. There was an amazing sequence where Van Gogh lowers Waldo down a manhole by his hair into "Montesino's Cave" (Bravo surrealistically described the landscape of what the boy sees down there) that left the audience in an uproar. Even the stone-faced parolee cracked a smile, ad-libbing how it was "getting hot up here." This got its own round of hip, goosey plaudits. Bud moved his eyes to Feld at the precise moment the perspiring agent mouthed, "Isn't this *amazing*?" to an enraptured colleague. Raleigh seemed to be enjoying the role of Charlene, who lived under the street and ran a "permanent floating" deli. Bud recalled an old *News* bite about Charlie Manson's search for a bottomless pit in Death Valley during those creepy-crawling helter-skelter days. Maybe the cave of Montesino was an allusion. Maybe Bravo and Manson had been cell buddies.

There was another passage where Van Gogh got a job driving an ambulance. It was the weakest section, but the audience ate it up. Bud decided right then to block out a script from his nascent MobileDoc experience.

Right in the middle of it, Bravo abruptly left the stage. The audience thought it was part of the show. Then the lights went on and Joey Funt stood on his feet, pounding his palms together like they were a fire he was trying to put out, his face a hot, funky scowl of admiration. Like the characters of his newfound mentor, Funt was unabashedly sentimental. Everyone leaped to his feet as Bud ducked out.

The screenwriter stood outside the club and smoked. Vivian's presence gnawed at him; he wanted at least to say hello. It took half an hour for the place to clear. The night was getting cold and he was about to give up his vigil when Raleigh emerged from the lobby, wrapped in a black shawl.

"Raleigh! You were great!"

"Hi, Bud! Did you like it?"

"*Yeah.* It was heavy."

"Pretty wonderful stuff, huh?"

She was doing a little of the *All About Eve,* looking around as if for her "driver." Bud felt like a stage-door johnny.

"Have you heard anything about *Bloodbath*?"

"I just finished writing the sequel."

"Really? I heard they were having problems."

"What kind of problems?"

"I talked to Genie and she said they lost their distributor. And that they were having big problems with the opticals."

A group was emerging from the club and Raleigh started moving toward them.

"Raleigh, can I ask you something? Why did you cut me off?"

"You lied to me."

"About what?"

"You lied about that woman and I don't like liars."

" 'That woman'?"

"*Oh, come on!*"

She looked at Bud like he was a soot-covered arsonist proclaiming innocence, the flames still flickering in his eyes.

"I knew it anyway, and your 'friend' just confirmed it. The night at the emergency room."

"Caitlin? What did she say?"

"That she was fucking you."

He told her it wasn't true (not at the time anyway; he left that out) and Raleigh said it didn't "remotely" matter anymore. She asked if he was still "seeing" Caitlin, and when Bud protested, the truculent actress showed him a fang.

"Did you know I was living with Wylie Guthrie? He's a friend of yours, isn't he? I'm in his next movie."

A final group was leaving the club. Raleigh spotted someone and caught fire; without giving Bud another glance, she said, "I've *got* to talk to Joan Krause!" and was off.

At the same time, Bravo and Funt appeared. Bud wandered over to the curb within earshot.

"I tried to write a play once," the actor said. "The mother-fucker kicked my ass, man." He smiled a twinkly smile, the one that conveyed he'd been whipped by that particular bitch muse and wasn't eager to climb back in the ring.

"You write?" Bravo asked indifferently.

"Poetry."

He said the word with a journeyman's reserve, as if he'd been asked, *"What union?"* Bravo told Funt he liked his movies, they were always on TV in the joint. "Some of them are okay," said Funt, humbly adding that most of them were shit. The actor-outlaw admired Bravo's Indian, then climbed on his Harley for the long drive to Malibu. The kid really scored, Bud thought. Bravo could give him some tips when Funt did his thirty days.

After the actor's departure Gottlieb came over and gave his disciple a quick hug. Then he introduced Bravo to his date, a mute model.

"Hey, Strong Stuff. I wanted you to meet my friend Tina Honnicut."

Bravo shook her hand and said, "Talking Tina."

"Listen, I don't have to tell you—you were kick-ass up there."

"You ever see that *Twilight Zone*? Telly Savalas buys this doll for his kid, you pull the string and it talks. They call it Talking Tina. But the doll's *real.* It wants to fucking *kill* Telly Savalas!"

"I missed that one. Seriously, Perry, it was unbelievable. We should get you on *Arsenio.*"

"Whatever you say, Big Daddy."

"You're a natural performer, is there *anything* you can't do? Any minute I'm gonna have to get you a fucking agent. I'm *serious.* Do you want to do some acting?"

"Yeah. Me and my homeboy, Joey Funt."

"Funt would put you in one of his movies in a *hot second.* I'm serious, three people already came up to me." He turned to Miss Honnicut. "Can you believe this? You look like *that* and he looks like *this* and they're all over him. Maybe you should get a tattoo."

The model smiled uncomfortably.

Then, in lower tones, he asked the jailbird if he was "okay" and Bud assumed that meant was he fixed for cash. Bravo said he was, and the wily sponsor led the leggy model off, then turned and asked if they were still on for dinner Tuesday at Musso & Frank's. Bravo ignored him and stared into the club's entrance, saying to no one in particular: "Where the fuck is Vivian?"

"Baby?"

Vivian jaywalked out of the darkness, holding a cup of coffee.

"What are you doing?"

"I went to the Seven-Eleven."

"They got coffee here," he said, pointing toward the theater.

"Too many people."

Bud nervously turned to go when Vivian spotted him.

"Bud? I *thought* that was you."

"Hi, Vivian," he said awkwardly. "I saw you inside. I was looking around for you."

"Perry, I want you to meet an old friend of mine, Bud Wiggins."

Bud shook his rough hand. The knuckles were tattooed.

"Are you a real asshole or are you a regular asshole?"

Bud said he was a real one and Bravo laughed, turning to Vivian.

"'This is the first honest son of a bitch I've met tonight."

He could smell Bravo's breath; it was android, like the Doctor's. The guy must have been wired. That's a violation of parole, he thought fliply. Maybe I should snitch. Sure he'd be pissed, but later he'll thank me for it.

Bravo asked him to join them for a drink. Bud scanned Vivian's face for some sign, but it was blank. She gave him an address in Mount Washington, then climbed on the Indian, grabbing Bravo's waist. They roared away.

Bud looked in his Thomas Bros. and got on the Santa Monica Freeway.

He was still attracted to Vivian and wondered how she ever hooked up with Bravo. The man could write, that's for sure. He didn't feel particularly envious, though—what was the chance of someone making *Go, Van Gogh, The Movie?* Well, there wasn't any. No, this was as good as it was going to get for Perry Bravo. He was this week's diversion, a sideshow and nothing more. He probably didn't have a clue to what was going on, not that Bravo had anything to lose; he'd been broken long ago, in ways few could imagine. If he stayed clean and stuck to the work, *Papillon* just might survive his encounter with the Business—real writers usually did. Bud smiled a sardonic welcome to the Yard.

A shrieking ambulance passed and the screenwriter remembered his fresh resolution to write an ambulance drama. It was a nice compromise—he could still explore Brian's world, the world of morbidity and mortality, without being ponderous. He was ready now, ready to write about living and dying and make it funny, make it *move.* He didn't even care anymore about working the Doctor in, the Doctor was dead and Bud had used the *Shotgun* story to say good-bye. Even the Cicero thing seemed worthless now, far away, ancient as a ruin. Funny, how one had to go from A to B to C to get home.

Bud felt lucky and a little at peace.

The Mount Washington neighborhood was dark and hilly.

He walked a few blocks past dirty bungalows with no numbers and finally spotted the Indian beside a dark porch. He saw Bravo in the kitchen and rapped on the dirty screen.

"Wiggins! Out of smokes! Can you get some?"

His hairless chest had a pair of tattooed faces, each outside eye a nipple.

"Danny's Liquor, right where you turned. And get some Cuervo."

He turned and shouted to Vivian for money. Bud said he'd take care of it and left the porch. Bravo called after him to get a carton of filterless Camels.

When Bud returned ten minutes later, the cottage was dark. He opened the screen door and went in. The stench of catshit and incense clung to the ratty carpet, a pall on the clutter of books and old newspapers. He heard a cry, like someone finding the body of a loved one. The cry came again; then the trite pants of coitus.

He put the bag down on the cracked Formica dinette and left.

₥₥

Bud got along well with the assorted MobileDocs. They were yuppie types, third- and fourth-year residents rotating through places like Cedars and UCLA—future shrinks, plastic surgeons and dermatologists. They were untried and slightly spoiled, and spent their leisure time at the office browsing Mercedes brochures; right now the cushy, fanciful house call racket suited them fine. Instead of suffering the crash-cart combat zone of emergency rooms and burn wards, they dreamed of motoring into Holmby Hills to mollycoddle dyspeptic celebrities and fluish captains of industry. It was *Lifestyles of the Rich and Famous* with a touch of *Emergency!* thrown in. Each security gate swinging open was an incentive—with a little luck, patience and the right bedside manner, all this would be theirs.

Unfortunately the clientele was less glamorous than expected. The elitist angle wasn't yet paying off—rich folks just weren't getting the *concept*. There was the odd call from socialites with the grippe, but mostly the doctors traveled to the no-man's-land of South-Central L.A., dosing asthmatic kids with epinephrine. MobileDoc had contracts with a few cruddy local hospitals that obliged them to service welfare families and the totally disabled, even indigents. The company had a huge overhead and talk among the medics was that the owners had overextended themselves. Payroll checks started running late and scammy, Bijan-suited moneymen drove in and out of the office suite in dumb, flashy cars—Pantera, Jensen, Ghia, Stutz; one of them even had a portable fax machine that sat in a pimpy backseat mahogany cabinet. The expensively outfitted Mobile-Doc vans were quickly becoming taxis employed for "grunt" calls—convalescent home invalids, sidewalk drunks with DTs, and warehoused spastics the doctors called *gomers* ("get outta my emergency room"). A few times a week Bud found himself back at the County again, on that long ramp to Brian's emergency room. *No hay estacionamiento para automobiles.*

The medics were strange characters, good to soak up. Some were failed cops; some were disconnected and agreeably deadpan, or "rescue" freaks who didn't know when to shut up. Among them was a bald, sober-faced vet who was a make-believe future doctor, a kind of AMA mascot-moron who doggedly audited premed classes on his days off, earning him a measure of respect from the corps. There was a good-looking actor from Corpus Christi who got caught stealing money on a house call and another guy who looked like Ichabod Crane and hustled Bud at canasta between calls. All of them raced to the bank with their paychecks because if you got there too late, the money might run out. There was a lot of gallows humor about the place going belly up and the drivers popped Talwins and Darvons they took from the "kits" and had phone sex with bored nurses on graveyard. Once in a while they convinced one to come over. They were always fat.

Quietly Bud gathered material for his script.

One night he drove the van to the house of a woman whose breasts were impacted. She didn't have a pump, so they gave her Demerol and the MobileDoc kneaded each tit with his hands, soaking a bathroom towel while the newborn wailed. The milk steamed while her hostile ten-year-old watched like he wanted her banished to a barn.

From there they drove to Santa Fe Springs to a stucco lean-to on a muddy cul-de-sac whose knob ended beneath the San Gabriel River Freeway. Inside a kind of utility room, an emaciated woman lay on a hospital bed. There were faded get-well cards and pictures from a distant prom—the night of the accident. She was the only one in the car who got hurt. The doctor asked what the trouble was. "I can't void," she said. The hospital wasn't sending anyone to pick her up for physical therapy anymore and she didn't have any MediCal stickers left. She usually emptied her bladder with a big red-bulbed syringe, but tonight she was having trouble. When the doctor asked to examine her, she fished under the sheet and pulled out a gun. She said to shoot her up with morphine or she'd kill him. The doctor told Bud to get a syringe, then injected her with sterile water. Later he told Bud it wasn't a real gun. They never called the police.

The owner of Bookz came back from his trip and Bud showed him *Shotgun*. He was impressed and agreed to take a trial ten copies. His store carried a vast array of "little magazines" and he enjoyed the idea of sponsoring writers.

Bud was returning from a MobileDoc shift and went to get his mail. There was a yellow slip stuck on the box. A registered letter was being held for him at the post office. The old debtors' prison panic came over him—his heart thumped like a speedboat. Whom could he call? He didn't want to involve Bloom, not yet. Bloom would just brush him off as a paranoid. Yet whom else did he have? Louis Shramm was a callous oddball, an alarmist who fed off clients' fears like a forensic vampire. He'd call Zake Bock instead; his accountant would take care of it. Bock would call Shramm and Shramm would tell him what to do and Bock would relay the message to Bud. He was finally being sued by one of the credit card companies—that had to be it. But didn't they need a process server for that, someone physically to hand him the papers? Could you be served by registered mail? He'd heard something about that being possible. Should he ignore the letter? If he didn't pick it up, it might look bad to a judge, "flagrant disregard" or something. If he retrieved it, though, wheels might be set in motion to crush him.

He threw the notice into the gutter.

Bud kept working on the "MobileDoc" script but didn't get very far.

He came up with two ambitious dropout kids who get jobs driving ambulances. One's gung ho and the other's cynical, the twist being that the cynical one (modeled after Brian) actually goes the nine yards and becomes a doctor. For some reason, Bud kept getting on the wrong track. When he tried to write the cynical one, he thought of Bravo and the voice got weird, violent—"off." He tried to make it funny, yet the scenes were busily, nastily writing themselves. At one point Bud even had the cynical one on parole, with literary aspirations.

A few weeks after the Mar Vista reading, Vivian called and invited him to dinner.

"I never asked you how you met your friend," Bud said. It was better to pretend they didn't have a past.

"I wrote Perry in prison."

"Did you know him from before?"

"The prisoners put ads in the paper asking people to write."

"You know, I drove up to Camarillo to see you."

"You did?"

"I couldn't find your grandmother's address. That's where you were, right?"

"For about a minute. It's in the phone book."

"Are you still writing?"

"I'm studying tattoo arts."

"Really?"

"Yeah. I'm an apprentice at a studio over in Silver Lake. How's *your* career going?"

"Pretty well. I've been driving an ambulance, researching a new script."

"How Hemingwayesque."

He hadn't heard that one since the days of the stolen books. She paused a minute and Bud thought she was going to say something to impugn his character.

"You should let me give you a tattoo."

"Of what?"

"We'll think of something."

"Sounds good."

He'd hire on as Joe Harmon's concubine before letting this old flame exact some Gothic ink-needled revenge. He agreed to meet them Friday night at Musso & Frank's, Bravo's new hangout. Vivian said they really loved it. She said they saw Pee-wee Herman there.

The next night Bud began a forty-eight-hour shift. The moon was like a scary streetlamp and the winds worried his memory.

There was plenty of "material." Bud and one of the Mobile-Docs—a psychiatric resident who lugged around a laptop computer for entering patient histories—took a catatonic streetperson all the way to the hospital in Camarillo. She looked like a dead, dirty starlet; a nurse scissored off her filthy clothes, cutting through the rotted penny loafers. Then they drove back to the city and picked up a dying woman from an emergency room. She'd shot herself in the head and needed to be unloaded at the County General neuro ward. It seems there was a suicide note but no gun, and everyone wondered if the note was fake. When Bud and a nurse lifted her from the gurney, a pistol clattered to the ground; it had been tucked under her body all along—for ease, the firemen had wrapped the woman in the top sheet of her own bed. Everybody froze and a cop picked up the weapon like it was some sci-fi arachnid.

On the second half of the shift, Bud's partner was Dr.

Kennedy, a priggish, compulsively unfunny wit from Boston who enjoyed being vague about the inevitable associations his name provoked. Kennedy spoke to people like he was an anthropologist interacting with the sweet, fly-speckled children of a tribal village. If a mother was talking about her child's flu, Kennedy might say: "The symptoms you're describing are *flu-like,* but I certainly wouldn't make a diagnosis before ruling out *enteritis, thrush, pleurisy*—we'll take a look. But I'm perfectly happy to call it the *flu* as long as we agree it may be anything but. Have I made myself clear? Now"—the Bill Buckley lizard smile—"tell me some more about the little one's *flu*—"

They visited an old man in a shabby bathrobe who lived over by the tracks on Alameda. The smell in the room was overpowering. The screenwriter breathed through his mouth and looked out the grimy window, imagining himself a squatter and a hobo. When he emerged from his reverie, he saw that Dr. Kennedy was still bent over the old man, staring. The haughty physician was in a fugue state, clearing his throat and nodding his head, stuck in a groove. Bud walked over. A crater-size bedsore began in the middle of the old man's thigh and ended above the exposed bone of his hip. The wound was teeming with maggots. When Bud said as much, the doctor shook his head. "No," he said, then, "right—no—right . . ." The benighted Brahmin was in shock, unable to process what his eyes were telling him. Bud put on latex gloves and they loaded the man into the van. At County, the nurses doused the infested wounds with kerosene. The good Dr. Kennedy went home early, with the look of someone who'd been date-raped.

When his shift was over at six o'clock Friday evening, Bud showered and drove to Musso's.

The unchained artist was gloomy and drunk. He'd totaled his Indian the day before and had an ugly ellipsoid bruise that swelled his arm; the tattoo below it looked like aching, fetid fruit. Bud wondered if Bravo knew about his fling with Vivian.

Sitting there with these strange, provocative beings, Bud felt charismatic, worthy of the triumvirate. Others seemed to take them in with special attention; he caught the watchful hunter-hunted eyes of show bizzy arrivals as they ambled past the booth. Once in a while Bravo said something inaudible to Vivian or encouraged Bud to eat. He was hard to read.

Lou Gottlieb walked in with his model friend and stopped at the table. Bud was inclined to like Gottlieb. He liked these ballsy, blustering Jews who still thought of themselves as marines and street fighters. Put them in a cage together and he wasn't so sure Bravo would be the victor. Gottlieb had his share of buried bodies, had to.

"I just rented a gorgeous place in Mount Olympus while they redo the beach house. From Dick Whitehead—he's a director, very well known. I talked to him about you. You and Vivian ought to come up this weekend."

Bravo's eyes raked the model's whorish dress.

"I'm serious," Gottlieb said, moving away. He knew when to make an exit. "There's a pool the size of Rhode Island. Come up and get some sun."

"You go in with your rug?"

"Huh?"

"You go in the pool with your rug?"

Gottlieb laughed uncomfortably, still moving off.

"Never take it off," he said, the good sport. "It's surgically attached!"

"What's it made from, pussy hair?" Bravo looked at the model. "You make it for him, Talking Tina?"

They smiled back as if they couldn't hear, then were gone.

Bud asked his dinner companions over for a few beers.

Bravo warmed to the apartment and Bud guessed it was because the place resembled a luxurious cell, a sanctuary lined with books.

"That cave sequence in your script—was that about Manson?"

"Hell, no," Bravo said, fingering one of the volumes. "I got that from *Don Quixote*. Ever read it?"

"I'm working up to it."

"Saddest book in the world." In fact, Bud had begun a reconnoitering of the work, and had read that Dostoevsky had said the same thing. The screenwriter watched Bravo next pluck *Funeral Rites* from the shelf. "Genet is God. I learned French so I could read his poems. You can't find them in English. I read an interview with him once, he was in his sixties in some shitty little Tangier motel. They asked how he spent his time. He said he smoked, ate, wiped the shit from his ass. Did his Nembutal. Strange cat. He *loved* ripping off the backs of those little Arab boys, that's for sure. Sorry to say but that's where we part company. Fuck the Arabs—I mean, *you* fuck em." Bravo pulled another volume and scowled. "Philip Roth—whoah, all dialogue! How *radical*! And Updike—Updike's writing about heretics and quantum physics! Atwood's writing about heretics and quantum physics! Joyce Carol Oates's two hundredth novel's a sci-fi romance! Marvelous! What cunts. And here's God with his ruined asshole and Nembutals in Tangier. Did you know he's buried in Spain? That's another reason for you to read *Quixote,* Wiggins." Bravo was on a roll; soon he'd be crashing through the door of *The New York Review of Books.* For now, he was thumbing *The Plumed Serpent,* shaking his head worshipfully.

"Jesus, the beauty. Lawrence is one that makes me never want to write again. The guy's too good."

He went on with hell-bent predictability about Nietzsche and Emerson, *Notes from Underground* and Lao-tzu, even throwing in Oswald Spengler. Then he wanted to know if Bud had read Kleist or the short stories of Dylan Thomas (a lot like stories he wrote in prison, he said, without humility), adding that *The Castle* was so spooky he could never bring himself to finish it—"it's like the guy read my diary." He fingered *The Wild Palms* and said it was a title so beautiful he was going to use it himself. Then he spotted Bud's three blue-gold volumes of Van Gogh's letters and held them gravely in his hand.

"Man, these are beautiful. I never saw these—I had this little come-stained paperback in the joint. This fucker saved my life.

He was working in an art supply store, how old was he then, thirty? One day he *decided* to be a painter, *willed* it. Everything Vincent painted—all those masterworks?—he did in seven years, sometimes *two a day!*"

Bud had heard the *Lust for Life* bio before and Bravo was starting to grate; all that tiresome jailhouse horseshit made him groan. For a second he wondered if Bravo was putting the make on him.

"Vincent *willed* it! Those letters break your heart. A masterpiece a day! And before he sleeps, he writes to his brother like no one's ever written before. A thirty-page letter, it's *gorgeous,* man. When they took him to the nuthouse, the landlord used his canvases to block broken windows so the rain wouldn't get in. He paints landscapes from his cell, only he leaves out the bars. Whenever I look at one of his paintings, I see those invisible bars. Is that a metaphor or what?"

Bud wasn't exactly sure; he'd have to run it past Susan Sontag during one of Gottlieb's Mount Olympus weekend pickup games.

They were about to leave when a final book caught Bravo's attention. It was an oversize hardcover called *The Atlas of Legal Medicine.* Brian had stolen it from a research library a few years before his death and given it to Bud as a birthday gift. It was one of those books that became popular with the art crowd; you could buy it at nihilistic galleries downtown. The volume was filled with photos of the recently dead—by drowning, plane crash, deadly assault, fire and autoerotic suicide. The *Atlas* was particularly interesting because the Japanese pathologist who put it together wove in color plates of the fierce faces of ancient, ardent gods, highlighting the similarity between the latter and the human face undergoing postmortem change. The book was a transcendent oddity.

When a second notice was left on his box, Bud called up his warrior spirit and went down to claim the registered letter. He felt good today, tough enough to jump on the Collections dragon and lop off its fearsome head. He waited until he got home before opening it.

It was a notification: he was being sued by the Writers Guild for $12,649 (Guild minimum on low-budget features) or "100% of the amount" he'd received for writing a first draft of *Bloodbath 2*. At first he thought it was a gag. He wondered who was behind it. Raleigh and Guthrie? Vivian? Jeanette? Or was it Bobby Feld and his cruel posse? He carefully reread it.

The letter asserted that AlphaFilm Productions wasn't signatory to the Guild. "Working Rule Number 8" made explicit that it was up to the writer to determine the status of potential employers; union members who accepted money from nonsignatories were considered scabs. The penalty was a fine equivalent to paychecks received and potential ejection from the Guild, if so decreed. The letter asked for "resolution or restitution" within fourteen days and was signed by Lou Gottlieb himself.

None of it made any sense. Bud *knew* AlphaFilm was signatory. That had been the whole point of holding out for minimum—so he could get benefits. It was outrageous! Bud Wiggins was a professional writer and someone had paid him to *write* something—for this, he was being sued by the very group that claimed to be his staunchest ally, the "writer's friend"! It was *crazy-making,* as they said at Meetings. He should have known better. What was the Guild anyway but another dysfunctional alcoholic family? They should have given Bud a *medal.* Did they know how difficult it was for writers with special gifts to earn a living? They knew all right but couldn't care less. The closer you loitered to madness and bankruptcy, the better— that's the way the threatened old guard liked it. Unless you were an important writer like Stephen J. Cannell or John Hughes, you were better off dead.

Bud drew strength from his rage. The *Writers* Guild. What a joke! Just who were the officers of this sacred institution? Most were hacks, "gutless wonders," failed children's book authors, contributing editors of defunct magazines, political gag writers from the fifties—snitches, probably—who now spent their time faxing letters and jokes to the *Journal,* planning picnic "mixers" and persecuting the constituency. He would countersue for bad faith. He would sic Don Bloom on them. The Guild wasn't inviolable; writers were beginning to get fed up with its papal bull. Gore Vidal had taken on the little shits and so, too, could Bud Wiggins. He'd serve the subpoena on Gottlieb himself.

That night Bud went to sleep early. He dreamed he leased a beach house in Malibu next to Kurt and Goldie. He was writing a movie for Larry Kasdan and Sidney Pollack and Ron Howard and Tim Burton and Spike Lee and Mike Nichols and Barry Levinson. The clique had big Sunday meetings on his deck, with bagels and champagne and lots of laughs. Random beachgoers passed by with chary nonchalance; Bud had stuck a NO TRES-PASSING sign in the sandy backyard, guaranteeing a kind of buffer zone between the house and the wet sand where the stragglers, not exactly eager to stir up a class war, strolled with pathetically contrived disinterest, stealing glances at the homes, spinning tales in their heads about the privileged lives of those within. As he ate granola from a crystal glass, Bud caught the gaze of such a gawker. Then, as protocol demanded, the gawker indifferently looked away, as if Bud were part of the natural landscape, as if he didn't at all envy this man (Bud Wiggins, famous screenwriter) who'd contrived to be eating granola on a tiny deck worth untold millions. Bud watched a school of porpoises make their way north in a glistening, cliché arc. He was a success, his mood light and expansive. For some reason, Brian was there to check his breathing. The Doctor palpated Bud's chest and moaned as if he'd felt the cold head of a mackerel protruding from a lung.

"How long have you had *that*?" said the Doctor.

Bud pointed to the water. "Do you see it?"

"It's a surfer. In a wet suit."

"No, it isn't," Bud said. "It's a sea lion!"

The animal disappeared, then resurfaced, bobbing directly in the stretch of ocean in front of the house. The sea lion looked their way as it held itself in place, sad and outside of time; for a moment Bud thought the oily beast was staring at him. When the lion began to float forlornly south, Bud impulsively jumped the rail of the deck and tore after it.

Bud ran wildly, the tumoral lungs outside his body now. He tried not to get any sand on them. A sickening smell hung in the air. He remembered when he was a boy and the class went to Paradise Cove on a field trip. The students saw a gopher that a school bus had smeared; baked in the sun, it smelled like something infected. Suddenly the sea lion was in front of him, right on the sand, and he tripped and fell into it, forcing an embrace. He tried to swing his lungs out of the way of the fetid, purulent pelt—

He began to moan, macabre and unearthly, the bogeyman wail he used to scatter little kids with at the playground, the sound from his throat waking him up.

Bud wondered if the dream was some kind of premonition. Maybe he had a tumor, after all. If he did, he'd march straight to the Guild. In the lobby, when they asked what his business was, the screenwriter would hold a handkerchief to his mouth like a talisman, a fresh bloody blemish on the cloth his price of passage. He'd stride into the office of Lou Gottlieb, seize him by the lapels and belch a rivulet of blood that would stick to his chin like a syrupy cobweb; a bleb would spatter Gottlieb's cheek as the horrified secretary rang for Security.

With a laugh, he shook the dream's dark weight. Then Bud watched the late show, drifting off to dreamless sleep.

On Monday morning he spoke to the Guild's legal department. He was advised to call AlphaFilm. He did, but all the executives were out of the country. He asked to speak to the bookkeeper. She pulled his contract and noted that, indeed, it had been drafted subject to the bylaws of the Guild. The bookkeeper seemed genuinely disturbed at AlphaFilm's delinquency and said she'd try to resolve the problem during the week. For some reason, Bud believed in this woman. File it under fixable bureaucratic errors and omissions. He thanked her and calmly hung up.

Don Bloom had taught him well. He'd gone up against American Express and won; he wasn't about to lose any sleep over Lou Gottlieb and his Gestapo-hacks.

wwv

One of the MobileDoc physicians arranged for Bud to visit the morgue at County General. For some reason, the Doctor never took him there on tour. As a writer he'd always wanted to add a death house to his catalog of experience.

He went down on a busy Monday morning. A commuter plane had crashed near Orange and ten bodies lay under sheets in the hallway. An exhumed coffin dangled from a crane like some black comedy deus ex machina, awaiting the court-ordered examination of its contents. In one of the rooms, gremlins siphoned gas from a blackened, water-bloated corpse, someone's grandfather who had driven his Cadillac into a river during a seizure. There was a huge closet with brown-bagged babies that weirdly put Bud in mind of the grammar school cloakrooms where lunches were kept on the shelf above the children's hanging coats. On rainy days came the pungent odor of damp parkas and sandwiches. Dolly made him soup that he brought in a thermos and the asphalt of the playground had a gamy smell when it was wet. That gopher smell.

He wandered into a great autopsy room where a white-coated lady pathologist stood over a body angrily clipping off an old lady's ribs with pruning shears, like she was demonically tossing a salad.

"I'm going to be late for fucking court," she said to one of the gremlins. "I spend so much time in court I should have become a fucking lawyer."

In the area next to where she was working, another body's organs were weighed, then thrown back into the cavity. One of the gremlins promptly closed the incision with a giant needle and thread: Hieronymus Bosch's idea of elective surgery.

Bud went to the cafeteria for a cigarette. He had a chronic foreboding he would die from something respiratory, that he'd wind up like John Huston (he should be so lucky), at Mortons for dinner, an oxygen tube in his nose. Bud saw himself at the end, lying at home on a hospital bed, respirations shallow, food crumbs on his unshaven cheeks, the larcenous LVNs swiping anything that wasn't nailed down, even his Writers Guild Award. The short, token visits from friends, sick themselves. He would empty his bladder with a red-bulbed syringe and his mother would cop him morphine on the streets like Jill Clayburgh in *La Luna*. He'd move back to Dolly's so he could watch the dancing cypresses. As he lapsed from consciousness, Raleigh and Jeanette and Vivian would read to him from his favorite books in shifts, all forgiven. He'd savor their voices as the waters of the Nile invaded the ruined tissue of his lungs. *Denial is not a river.* His death would be duly noted in the trades; the MGM lion would hang its cartoon head for a week.

Bud felt lost and shell-shocked in the daylight. He decided to go to a favorite old afternoon Meeting in Hollywood. It had been awhile.

The church was packed. It was good to be anonymous again, to be planted in a fold-up chair with all those losers, *real* losers, free to make communal confession of his fears. He stared at the back of the neck of the man in front of him. The man was discussing his "little kid"—Meeting parlance for *inner child.*

"I came to these rooms because I had no choice."

Bud heard the unmistakable voice of Perry Bravo. He confirmed it by moving over a chair; the speaker's face was in profile now.

"It's part of my parole. But the more I come, the more it works on me. They say, 'Take what you want and leave the rest,' and that's a motherfucker. So I'm not listening at first, see, but my little kid is. My little kid's checking everybody out." He made a little movement with his head, like a scared, curious puppy, and the room laughed. "See, I know too much—I'm so smart I spent fifteen years in the penitentiary, that's how smart I am—but my little kid, he's not such a tough, angry guy. My little kid is scared. See, I'm not afraid of nothin' but my little kid, he's a scared little motherfucker. And he's got good reasons. But now he's looking around and I'm trying to tell him it's okay. 'Hey, it's okay, look around, check it out.' See, my little kid's scared because his old lady went after him with a knife." The room moaned empathically; he had them in thrall. "That's right, his mother. See, she loved him, but she was nuts. It took three men—my brothers—to hold her back. She was *serious.* Your mother comes after you with a knife and let me tell you, you become a 'tough guy.' How's something supposed to *bother* you after Ma tries to butcher your seven-year-old ass? How you gonna top that? So you get tough, become a gangster, a talk show host, whatever. But my little kid didn't know about 'tough.' So these rooms are teaching me something." Someone signaled that his three minutes were up; Bravo eyed him coldly. "These rooms are helping me to learn that I am *powerless* over knives and mothers. That I ain't so tough. See, I didn't even know my little kid was *there.* And when I found him, know what I did? I gave him a hug and the little guy shook like a dumb gray ghost because he thought the crazy lady was still around the corner with a knife. And you know, I'm worried, I'm worried that my kid might be too fucking damaged to even hear me. But I don't think so. I don't think so. I think he's like a cat, this little kid, he's got a bunch of lives. He's a motherfucker and he's got heart. I'm going to stop now, fuckface over there keeps winking my time is up, I see you, fuckface, I'll shut up. But I just wanna say a final thing to my little kid: if that crazy bitch comes around the corner with a knife, I'll be there to put her down, to take the blade away. I'll be there. *She'll have to go through me to get to you.* I want my little kid to hear that, hear it loud. 'Cause I ain't never gonna let anyone hurt you again."

The teasing *Grapes of Wrath* I'll-be-there motif was a nice touch and the room responded with robust, heartfelt applause to his self-vigilantism. Bud toasted the protean ex-convict's flair for drama. There were a few more "pitches," but his was a tough act to follow.

All rose for the Serenity Prayer. Arms formed a ring as the ruminative screenwriter felt a hand reach out to his—Bravo's. Bud held it during the recitation, feeling like a mannish boy.

"You following me, Wiggins, or what?"

People were mingling. Bravo was in a friendly mood.

"Who, me?"

"Jesus, you're worse than Vivian. I take that back. No one could be worse than Vivian, she's like a fly on shit. You're worse than my PO."

He invited Bud for a cup of coffee. Bravo was the "star" of the Meeting; acolytes were lining up to take the wafer. A pretty girl approached and told him she always loved hearing him share.

"You talk like a poet. Are you? Do you write?"

Bravo did his jailhouse death stare, saying nothing.

"I just wanted to thank you," she said, embarrassed by his coldness. All those *inappropriate* vibes had to be jangling, especially to her little kid. She got out of there.

"There's a chick who's offered her throat to many men," said Bravo in a menacing undertone. "One day someone's gonna take her up on it."

O dark guru of Woman! Bud smiled at his own alacrity. It was nice being at the stage of life where one can no longer be seduced or awed. Nobody was going to hoodwink him—not the Guild, not the collection agencies, not even Perry Bravo, legend-in-the-making. They walked out to the parking lot with their coffees.

"I know about you and Vivian."

Bud's mind stumbled.

"Relax. I'm not going to throw acid in your face behind it. She's good people. You're not a snake, are you, Wiggins? Naw.

You're not a snake. But you'd fuck a snake, though, wouldn't you? If someone held its head."

Bravo reached into Vivian's car, a falling-apart hatchback. He pulled out a script and proffered it to Bud.

"Yours?" Bud was relieved to speak. Bravo nodded. "You want me to read it?"

"No, I want you to piss on it. Look, you're a guy who gets paid to do this, right? Vivian said good things about you. See, I don't know the *form*. They wanted me to make this into a movie, but it's a fuckin' *play*. Understan' me?"

He scanned the cover—it was the first draft of *Go, Van Gogh*. No one had seen it yet, not even Lou Gottlieb. Funny how things turned out.

"I want to know what you think. Before I give it to the Great Emancipator."

He lay on the bed and dipped into Bravo's creation. The script was rich and baroque, funny and poetic. Maybe it was terrible and he'd simply lost his ability to critique—he wasn't sure anymore. Bud held the script in his hands as if they'd gone numb, turning the pages with unaccountable fragility. Then, for comparison, the screenwriter examined his ambulance script. Awful. He shoved it facedown in a drawer alongside Caitlin's bequeathed opus.

Bud thought: I must use the character of Perry Bravo. But how? The man wasn't so much interesting as inescapable. Maybe he could put him in his true crime parody. For years Bud had toyed with a book about a serial killer that he called *Department of Humor*. He'd only gotten as far as an imaginary table of contents and a preface:

It's a rare thing when one is blessed with so many tireless, able-minded researchers—collaborators, really—whose effulgence is matched only by their tenacity for Truth; rarer still, to have the lot endure with such grace and equanimity the stentorian midnight whining of that rowdy, if not precocious (certainly towheaded), child who eventually came to be called Department of Humor.

Invariably, a work in its infancy regurgitates stylistic or statistical pabulum—the researchers were always there to mop up the narrative vomitus. For this, I am ever grateful.

There were at least six who formed a core group—too many to mention here. There were also others who became impermanent yet vital satellites, each revolving to the beat of his own orbital drum; to mention them by name would be a disservice to the core of which I spoke.

There is another tribe, perhaps more "down-to-earth," but phenomenal nonetheless, that deserves special note: those who posted my lengthy correspondence, fetched an occasional (much-needed) sandwich, or refilled my water glass at a propitious moment; those who tidied up the place with the unobtrusive expertise of domestic engineers; and those who enlarged the square footage of my cottage (a final 4,700 square ft., approx.) so that I might have a more commodious place to birth. To list their names would demean them.

I would also like to thank S., who was always there with a cup of Sanka and ludicrous suggestions to revise certain passages; and F., who kept at bay the weekly baker's dozen of ardent (if misguided) devotees a writer invariably collects if he survives his first reviews. (Though they are not unkind, they are potentially injurious to an author gravid with young.)

Lastly, I must thank the families of the 137 victims. Their candidness, cooperation and hospitality through hours of interviews were astonishing. I will not endeavor a list of loved ones lost. But here are the names and addresses of the surviving family members, along with (last-current) phone directory listings. . . .

He began to laugh. He wanted to read it to someone, but there was no one to call. Bud started to cry, for his life. He rocked himself to sleep.

The next night Dr. Kennedy and the screenwriter transferred a comatose woman from a hospital in the Valley to Cedars.

"Wiggins, let me drive."

Since the maggot incident, the doctor had loosened up. He'd become annoyingly spontaneous, like an awakened fuddy-dud determined to "taste" life; even his liberation was cliché.

"Come on, I want to see what it's like. Can I put on the siren?"

"If you get in a wreck, we'll be fucked."

"I know how to *drive,* Wiggins. Anyway, she's stable. Just keep the airway open, I'll pull over if she gets weird."

They exchanged places and accelerated into the dark, a rosary of electronic bleats and yelps. The woman's black hair was matted with sweat. A silk Hermès scarf was loosely knotted around her neck. She wore a Rolex and Bud wondered why it hadn't been stolen by some "health care worker" along the way. A thick plastic airway was taped into her mouth and he pulled down the sheet to watch her respirations. He could see her nipples through the screen of the expensive bra; there was an old lumpy scar just below. Bud glanced at Kennedy behind the wheel, speeding through the sirened night, full of stupid, adolescent rapture. He pulled a side of the bra down and cupped a breast. Then he drew back his hand, nauseated.

He called Bookz. They'd actually sold out of *Shotgun* and asked him to bring twenty-five more copies to the store. Someone out there was reading his story. It was a nice boost.

MMM

The following week MobileDoc folded. Bud was relieved. He wasn't in a money crunch and had stopped working on the ambulance script anyway. He never heard from the AlphaFilm bookkeeper, not that he really cared. He'd been paid and that was the only thing that mattered. Let the Guild try to collect their blood-money "restitution." They could sit on Working Rule Number 8 and twirl.

Then the story broke. Lou Gottlieb and an unnamed companion had been murdered in the producer's rented Mount

Ólympus home. Two days later Perry Bravo was picked up in Phoenix. He was being prepared for extradition. There was no mention in the news of Vivian. Somehow, Bud was thankful for that.

He tried calling her at the Mount Washington house, but the line was disconnected. He thought of going over to her mother's but finally decided to let things alone.

Bud ran into Peter Dietrich at Hugo's. The free-lance reporter said he was doing a piece on the murders for *Vanity Fair* and wanted to know if Bud could give him an entrée—hadn't he seen him dining with Bravo at Musso's? The screenwriter downplayed it.

"You're a sly dog, Wiggins."

"What have you heard about the murders?"

"*Clockwork Orange* time. There's some rumor now that Gottlieb was embezzling from the strike fund. What goes around comes around."

"What goes around don't come around no more."

"I like that! Great title for a country song." Dietrich moved closer. "I got details the cops wouldn't release. You know what he did to them? He tied Gottlieb to a chair and raped his friend—the model, Honnicut, right? Jesus, I almost had a drink with her once at Le Dôme. He dislocated her arms. Then he set her face on fire—*just her face*—and raped her again. The guy is watching this, can you imagine? Probably in total shock. Then Bravo does the same thing to *Gottlieb,* dislocated arms and all. *Fucks* him. When they found him, he wasn't wearing his toupee. He *always* wore his toup—they assumed it'd been burned off. You know where they found it? In his stomach."

"What about Bravo's girlfriend?"

"The deformed chick? No one's heard boo. I don't think she's implicated. You got anything on her?"

"You're starting to sound like Jimmy Olsen."

"Who's that?"

"From *Superman.*"

"You want to hear my theory? Bravo finishes his first draft, the *Van Gogh* thing. Gottlieb reads it and *hates* it. Not happy with his prize student. He tells Bravo—maybe he's too blunt about it—and Bravo reacts."

"Cui bono?"

"Right. Whatever. Oh, there's one more thing. Nobody knows this; this is completely off the record, okay?"

"What a ham."

"I'm serious. If this gets back to me, I'll deny it."

"Go on."

"There was something torn from a book that Bravo pinned to Gottlieb's face, like a mask. Some picture of an Oriental god. Too bad it wasn't a Greek, I could tie it in with Olympus. I'm going to find a way to use it anyway. It'll be my hook, my Rosebud. I need to find out what that was."

He noted the announcement in *Variety* a few weeks later that a well-known director was developing a script about the Mount Olympus murders called *Mortal Gods*. Peter Dietrich was not attached. Joey Funt, of course, had expressed interest in playing the lead. The whole case became a staple of hotshot magazines, local news and afternoon talk shows. An op-ed artist sketched Bravo in the style of Escher, sitting at a table over blank pages, pencil in his mouth like a tiny aqualung, the pattern on his collar a hundred ravens, his orbless eyelids propped open by cell bars.

Bud got three letters.

The first, from the Guild, said the *Bloodbath 2* people were taking the necessary steps to become "retroactively signatory." Bud was exonerated; he would have his health insurance. The letter was stamped with the signature of Lou Gottlieb.

The second was a collection agency form letter on behalf of American Express "requesting" $71,643, plus interest. The notice didn't really have teeth—each time the amount appeared, it was absurdly entered by hand, like the "Me"-book fill-in-the-blanks Bud wrote his name in when he was little (the hero was always you). He figured the lackadaisical rebuke was coincidental to his recent surge of income. More like a final, attenuated announcement that the self-described screenwriter was a write-off and certified deadbeat, no longer a criminal conspirator.

Caitlin sent a postcard from Buenos Aires. She was returning to Los Angeles in the next few months and looking forward to reading his draft of *Wings*.

He went to the Silver Lake tattoo shop and asked for Vivian. A biker behind the counter said she was sick. Bud could look at her book if he wanted; he pointed to an album filled with Polaroids of her work. There were hearts and skulls and crosses and orchids and tribal designs, Elvises and Freddy Kruegers.

Then he saw it: two faces, each the size of a newborn's head, etched onto a cropped torso—Bravo's. They were portraits of Vivian, one "as is," the other as "might have been," pristine and unviolated. Beautiful.

Bud thanked the man and left.

He began revising Caitlin's script. For seven weeks Bud barely left his room. Instead of a magic trick that could never be performed in public, these days he thought of it as a prodigious blood relative, a gift horse that wished him well. He would make it his own—isn't that what Caitlin wanted? She was an exhausted Olympian, passing the torch to a peer. In James's word, she had been *magnificent.*

He reexamined her South American communiqué; he'd be finished by the time she arrived. It was perfect. The screenwriter typed the final page and turned on the printer. He changed the title from *The Wings of the Dove* to *Broken Wings,* the name of one of James's stories. Caitlin would like that.

Bud realized how childish and petulant he'd been. For what reason? *Lose your self-importance.* They would begin the mysterious relationship anew, unencumbered by the grotesque, traditional expectations of "romance." He missed her terribly, and needed her to like the script; to show he'd been "impeccable," after all her gifts.

It was four in the morning. Bud let the shower water batter him and indulged in some strategizing. He would use Caitlin's connections to get the adaptation to the heavyweights; it would be fun planning the assault together. He fantasized production starting within the year. He couldn't lose—*Broken Wings* was the kind of script that got a writer enormous attention, whether it was made into a movie or not.

When he stepped from the shower, Bud noticed the red light flashing on his answering machine. He played back the message. There was the unmistakable sound of the open street. A voice said, "Wiggins?" but was drowned out by a siren. Then he heard Caitlin:

"Fear and trembling come upon me; and horror has overwhelmed me. Oh, that I had wings like a dove! I would fly away and be at rest."

There were more street sounds and she hung there. Then hung up.

The next day Bud waited at the printers while they made copies of the script. He flipped through *USA Today* and read that Caitlin Wurtz had been murdered in New York. A crazy fan gunned her down in Chelsea, at a pay phone outside Barney's. The bald-headed killer had stalked her for years, and carried two books: *The Catcher in the Rye* and Wylie Guthrie's *Anyone Can Write for the Movies!*

A few days later, *People* magazine reported Caitlin's last words were something about Calabash. The rest of the article was a bio, pell-mell and dubious. Bud didn't finish it.

᚛᚛᚛

He mailed *Broken Wings* to agents and producers, but out of twenty or so submissions, few bothered even sending letters of receipt or rejection. Maybe it was a mistake to put her name on the title page as "executive producer"—the tribute was probably considered shameless. The timing of the whole thing wasn't right. He'd wait awhile. The script's power would not diminish.

Bud thought back on the violence of the months and wasn't sure of their meaning. Perhaps there wasn't any. He never expected to actually know a murdered person—or a murderer. The mailbox bestowed two final items, lending closure to that season.

Bravo must have torn the page from *The Atlas of Legal Medicine* while Bud was in the bathroom. Dietrich sent a blurred photocopy in the mail; it was being faxed around town, agency to agency, as a morbid curiosity.

He stared at the chilling, caricatural visage, captioned "The Mask of Garuda, as described in the Sanskrit." Garuda was the king of birds in Indian myths, the one that carried Vishnu. "The beak of the bird protrudes similarly to the protrusion of the tongue and lips in the decomposed human body, which may be related to the Buddhist belief that there is another life after death." If there was, Lou Gottlieb had better pray it was one without Perry Bravo.

The second envelope's appearance was fatefully absurd, its timing flawlessly ironic. Brian's autopsy report arrived with a note from Don Bloom attached, apologizing for the long delay; it had been misfiled and only recently uncovered. Bud browsed through the toxicology report, arriving at the examination of organs and tissue. The gremlins duly noted that his old friend's heart weighed 360 grams. There was plenty of morbidity and mortality to go around for everybody.

Bud thought that his dreaming about the Doctor was surely done with now—the grieving was over. For an instant he saw them as boys running on the mystic dark field of the playground, foggy and borderless, shrouded by dusk. Brian made a vaudevillian bow, then took his hat and heart and vanished.

♪♪♪♪

Months passed. He took a succession of sales jobs that paid twice the minimum wage. He was too tired and discouraged to write. Coming home one night from a movie, he stopped at the dry cleaner's on Santa Monica Boulevard.

Bud noticed him standing at the same pay phone where he first saw Caitlin.

The screenwriter laughed darkly to himself and sidled up to the bum, pretending to use one of the phones. He was spewing "pigcocksucker" into the receiver, over and over. There was a yellow *Temporarily out of Service* sticker across the slot. The bum finally hung up, incensed, and stormed away like a farmer foreclosed by the feds.

Bud stood there, lost in thought. He traced his hand in the air as the dying Henry James was said to have spectrally written on a windowpane. A man in a business suit appeared and frowned at the yellow sticker. He turned to Bud.

"How long will you be?"

"Huh?"

"I have an important call. How long are you going to be?"

"I wish someone would tell me," Bud said ruefully, and went the way of his foregone fellow traveler.

Once, an angry man dragged his father along the ground through his own orchard. "Stop!" cried the groaning old man at last. "Stop! I did not drag my father beyond this tree."

GERTRUDE STEIN,
The Making of Americans

4. A Mexican Gambol

‹‹‹‹‹‹‹‹‹‹‹‹‹‹‹‹‹‹‹‹‹

Bud cupped his hand and breathed, then quickly sniffed the exhalation—nothing.

Physically it hadn't been a great month. His hand had swelled up painfully from what he thought was a spider bite; then he broke out in random, itchy blemishes. Finally, he went to the skin doctor, who actually said, "Today's folliculitis is tomorrow's abscess," and prescribed antibiotics. By then Bud had a stubborn outbreak on his forehead that felt cyclopean. He was compulsively clearing his throat like his father did, until it was raw and strained, and was beginning to have trouble catching his breath. He used to hyperventilate when he was young. Once, a schoolboy told him his breath smelled like baby vomit.

Indeed, Bud developed a bad taste in his mouth and thought people winced when he spoke to their faces. He began talking in a whisper or turning his head, the comments trailing in a yawn. He took to sipping beer during the day, as a kind of breath spray.

He remembered the times he got sick in grammar school. The nurse would send him home and he'd start throwing up—that was after Morris Wiggins Communications, Inc., and family left the Heights for Bel Air. The doctors attributed their son's distress to the move.

For a time, then, Bud became an intimate of nausea. Usually, when he couldn't stop retching, the pediatrician came over at the end of the day of a siege and gave him a shot of Thorazine. Why he didn't become a junkie, Bud never knew. The doctors did the upper and lower GIs, gave him barium enemas and found nothing. They said he'd "outgrow" it, the way he outgrew the allergies and the hyperventilating and the facial tic his father referred to as "the twitch" whenever he wanted to give Bud a needle—that's the word Dolly used for her husband's sadistic asides, "the needle." Whenever Bud scrunched up his face and looked like he might cry about something, Morris would say, "You don't have to cry—just twitch."

Bud theorized the bad-taste business of late was probably related to one of his old "allergic reactions." He used to have them bad. The junior high teachers threw him out of class for marathon sneezing seizures and he'd awaken in the night with his eyes swollen shut; Dolly would march him to the mirror before putting on the compresses and they'd laugh at the Chinese boy beheld. For a few years he got shots every week from a phlegmatic allergist with a lascivious lower lip—until he "outgrew" it. Yeah, that was probably the answer—allergies explained everything from bum palates to schizophrenia. He read somewhere that's what debilitated Robert Towne and every now and then Bud wondered if "allergic reactions" were even the cause of his depressions.

Then he thought the source of the bad taste might be a gum problem, but the periodontist said his gums were okay. He suggested Bud see a GP. Could be stomatitis.

The GP couldn't find anything. He told Bud that he was probably experiencing the residual effect of a virus that was

somehow distorting his sense of taste. Viruses explained everything. He prescribed a gargle and lightweight tranquilizer, tenderly ushering Bud from the examining room like he was a
neurotic.

"I want to hear from you in a week—and don't *worry* about
it," he said. "It's probably in your head."

Bud went to visit his mother.

The surgeries had mostly healed, leaving her face strangely
angular and a little glossy. He asked Dolly to smell his breath,
and after she did, she said, "Nothing." Bud cleared his throat,
making a little humming noise at the same time.

"Are you turning into your father?"

"What?"

"Jesus, with the throat, Bud! That reminds me of Morris.
That sad little man—like a nut, clearing his throat, day in,
day out!"

She cruelly imitated them both; nothing escaped her.

"You better not, Bud." Dolly fixed him with a melodramatic
stare. "You better not turn into your father." Then she gathered the elements of lunch from the kitchen, bustling from
counter to fridge as the seasoned tirade began. "Your father
destroyed me. Your father was a *disliked* man, a *hated* man!
They *laughed* at him! A dried-up cunt, he used to call me. Did
you know that? That's what he called your mother. Can you
imagine?"

Dolly always said she kept a diary with all the terrible things
Moe said to her locked away in a safety-deposit vault, as if one
day Bud would inherit this toxic grail and know just what the
hell to do with it. She'd been telling him the dried-up cunt
business since he was thirteen—when Bud, under Jewish law,
became a man.

"He hated his *own* father! You remember Grandpa Louie,
don't you? Weak! And crying—all the time. He couldn't help
himself. You'd say good morning and he'd break down, like a
woman. A stupid man. And *vindictive*. And your father—not

brilliant, Bud. Not a brilliant man. I passed his exams for him! Stayed up with him all night. Moe was afraid he'd be stupid like Louie—that's why he hated you. Because you are brilliant."

"Ma, do you have any orange juice?"

Bud recalled how only a week ago he spilled a glass; his mother had scowled like a betrayed and frightened child, then cried.

"It was booze," she said, still on Morris, softening as she poured his drink. "It was the booze."

Bud changed the subject to his old allergies. He liked reminiscing with Dolly. She laughed about the Chinaman in the mirror and remembered the "chelazion"—the time her eye swelled shut with a cyst and Moe wasn't there to take her to the doctor because he was out fucking Gig, the Portuguese secretary, did Bud remember? Bud was so good, she said, sitting beside her as she drove to the ophthalmologist, cursing over the wheel, stiffened with pain. He'd stuck with her through hysterectomies, face peels, ass lifts, tummy tucks, boob jobs and crying jags.

When he left, Dolly gave him a thick sheaf of typewritten pages. It was the manuscript of her novel, *Beverly Hills Adjacent.* Dolly was originally going to call it *Beverly Hills Teardown,* but thought that too inside—"nobody but realtors know from teardowns."

"I can't believe you finished it. I mean—with the hospital and everything that's happened. You're amazing."

He gave her a hug and she broke away, exultant.

"E-*zih-*zinee!" she crowed, and kissed his cheek. "It kept me alive, this book. I'm going to be on *The New York Times* bestseller list, *fahr fahr carmintrate.* Where do you think you get your talent from? Not from that *fuck.* You get it from your *moth-*ra, you better believe it."

If Bud wasn't exactly eager to begin his mother's opus, it was for a reason: he'd at last managed to immerse himself in the incomparable *Don Quixote de la Mancha.* Dolly would think him an inscrutably asinine phony, yet Bud was determined to launch an assault on the stolen library and actually get some reading done. He was going to start with the biggies.

Bookz had a guide to the classics that glibly recommended skipping over the novel's awful verse and "anything about goatherds." Bud ignored the advice—if he was going to read *Quixote,* he'd do it warts and all. He bought the *Cliffs Notes* and skimmed the introduction. The screenwriter felt an immediate affinity when he learned that Cervantes had his own problems with creditors circa 1597, when family "goods and chattels" were seized; popular myth had it the novelist began his great work from the very place Zake the accountant so festively evoked—debtors' prison.

Bud set aside an hour a day for reading. The book was slow going, the language baroque, the pages crammed with text and freckled with footnotes. The narrative often made him think of Jeanette—there seemed to be lots of doomed marriages and "affiances." It took three weeks to read just a hundred pages and Bud wondered why he was putting himself through such punishment. Reading of Quixote's insomnia was enough to set the screenwriter adrift in reverie, a prelude to sleep; with head propped on pillow and novel spread across chest, Bud closed his eyes and imagined himself in the ocean, bobbing in an agate-colored immensity of water—perhaps the underground sea of *Journey to the Center of the Earth.* He'd always feared the water, never even swam in the ocean because it overwhelmed him. But in fantasy he became a floating organism, impossible to drown. In such a state, that of plasma heaving on the surface, at one with the rolling waves like the great transparent lid of a mammoth jellyfish, Bud wondered how he could ever have been afraid. It didn't seem *physically possible* to drown anymore, even in the real world. Maybe he'd go to the "sea" tomorrow and test his theory. The secret was not to resist. You could just float and float forever. How was it that he read about ocean swimmers going under? Bud felt an enormous calm as he drifted, his reverie was showing him a path, something grander than mere flotation, something shining and simple. If one didn't resist . . .

A powerful wind lifted him up off the water and through the night sky, wafting him over the cold darknesses of a thousand unnamed villages, with their treetops and winking lights and death squads at the door. Bud undulated above, aloof, incorporeal. Sleep was coming. While there was still consciousness, he willed himself down to a village, a cheap firetrap boardinghouse, and men in cloaks burst through the door, hooded thugs, their rickety VW bus on the getaway sidewalk, waiting with its helter-skelter muffler—one needn't have to fear the ocean or the torturer. His secret conceit was he could love the torturer if he had to, to save his own skin; the old Genet routine. He'd give up names, no shame in that—in such circumstances, indifference greets the death of heroism. Besides, the thing you could count on about pain was that it was temporary. In the end, a falling leaf, death by electroshock or asphyxiation, a cool wood drawer emptied of its things, a humiliating cancer—all the same.

Sleep swooped down like a warm black bird; Bud felt woozily Zen. He saw there was a way out of everything, an escape hatch—the Road Runner making an exit through a door he drew on a rock—and this simple revelation was the stuff of serenity, the thing everyone in Meetings was after.

Then his attention shifted. His fingers seemed to swell, the skin stretching, an odd sensation, old as the Secret Garden. He stopped his rocking and investigated, eyes still shut. There it was—the tantalizing and familiar feeling, morbidly elusive, indescribable. He'd strangely "summoned" it for decades, once or twice a year, but lately it had encroached by its own baffling volition. So *abstract* . . . He stuck his head up and the halo of air was thick; he kept his neck stiff, gauging the crown's trespass of the heavy space above. A luxuriant weight pressed on each molecule of his being and he held the feeling as long as he could—what *was* this? He'd even told a Hindu girlfriend about it. She said it was his kundalini.

ተተተተ

Over breakfast at Hugo's, Bud scanned the job ads in a discarded *Reporter*. He was running low on money, and if nothing panned out with the writing, he'd have to go back to driving or telephone sales. He dreaded that yet managed to feel optimistic.

Seated next to him was a fortyish man who happened to be reading *Inappropriate Laughter*. Bud's eye Ping-Ponged between the book and the face until he put it together. He'd seen this man before—at Caitlin's, the day he hid on the stairs. The reader laughed aloud at something in the text, then looked up to see Bud smiling.

"Have you read it?" He was spontaneous and appealing, full of nervous energy; Bud nodded his head like a fellow Mason. "It's the part where she's taken the drug, in Peru. Remember? And she buys the rugs, and they're *huge*—"

"And she gets them in the mail two months later in New York," Bud finished for him, "and they're the size of postage stamps."

The man introduced himself as Jake Weissen, a screenwriter from Toronto. Bud recognized the name from the trades. Weissen had short, curly black hair with touches of gray. He had a look that swung easily from an unusual and captivating candor to a scowling circumspection, almost paranoia. Bud liked him right away. Weissen invited him for "a coffee" and Bud obliged by moving to the chair opposite his garrulous new acquaintance, who convivially unburdened himself over granola.

Weissen said he didn't have a real job until he was around thirty-five, meaning a job that paid. He wound up in L.A., writing jokes for a friend who worked in television. Then someone wanted to know if he'd be interested in working on a sequel to one of the most successful comedies ever produced. The studio wasn't taking any chances and had hired three teams of writers to create three different scripts. So Weissen entered the sweepstakes, joining two others on the dark horse third team—a sellout Off Broadway playwright and a wealthy TV writer who faxed pages from his New Mexican bailiwick. Weissen's team won. The playwright regained his sense of self and took his name off the draft, while the TV writer, whose contributions were nominal, lost the arbitration; thus, Weissen received sole credit. The sequel went through the roof and he was *hot.* He wrote a romantic sleeper and fixed a thirty-million-dollar girl-buddy caper picture. MGM paid a fortune for the privilege of hearing him pitch two sitcom ideas per annum. He played basketball with kingmakers (yes, he knew Lou Gottlieb) and white water–rafted with all manner of agents and icons. He breakfasted with Katzenberg, lunched with Ovitz and dined with painters who traded canvases for points in restaurants. He loved to fuck married women; they used car phones to call him from far-flung spas and talk dirty. He had weekend meetings at the homes of powerful stars, sometimes staying in their guest homes instead of the Château. Weissen became a producer on a couple of projects and the studio sent him to scout theater in New York—a Hollywood pimp in a thirteen-hundred-dollar-a-day suite, schmoozing backstage like he was at a horse auction. He wore lots of Yohji, Comme des Garçons and Katharine Hamnett, rented chicly nondescript cars, read *primo* apartheid fiction culled from *The New York Review of Books,* subscribed to *The Nation* and the *Voice* and flirted with dropping out of the Business and founding a radical paper back in Toronto. Producers enshrined at the Crédit Lyonnais encouraged him to direct. Weissen frankly said he didn't like what he'd become— he was a *hack,* a member of the militant *hakdim,* he joked.

Dick Whitehead loomed from behind and impishly "entered the frame." He vigorously massaged Weissen's neck. White-head wore a bomber jacket and his breath reeked of pot.

"There's the cocksucker Jew who won't help me," White-head said to Bud as he kneaded Weissen's flesh. "I'm dying and this fucking Jew don't give a shit."

Weissen laughed, hunching under the director's probing fingers. "I'm not a good Samaritan, Dick. You're the director—tell them to give me my price. That's all I want. I just want my price."

"Your price, your price. You could buy a rain forest for your fucking price." The director gave Bud a look as he massaged Weissen's shoulders. "Canadian Jews are the worst. The cheapest bastards on earth."

"Hey, who's the *landlord*?" said Weissen. "I'm not the landlord." He turned to Bud. "When Whitehead asks you to rent, you know you're in trouble."

"Not funny, Jake."

"Oh, he's got feelings now!"

"You're a sick man, Weissen." He released his grip.

"Listen, Dick, just push them. They haven't even made a counteroffer. You're the director, right? So be a director—tell them how it's got to be."

After he left, Weissen explained he was in negotiations to rewrite a picture Whitehead was directing down in Mexico.

"You know why I said that shit about the landlord? That's where Lou Gottlieb was killed, at Whitehead's house! Did you know that?" Bud nodded. "You want to hear something *weird*?" He thumped the granola-flecked volume with his fingers. "Dick Whitehead wanted to do a script about Caitlin Wurtz. I'm serious. He *loved* Wurtz, thought she was a great character. Whitehead's always trying to do these 'little' movies, you know, personal. And the studios let him, they *have* to. So anyway, he's supposed to direct this movie she wrote, what's it called? *Another Fine Mess*. It fell apart, who knows what happened. He goes to her house for a meeting and asks me to tag along incognito, soak her up. Because he wants me to write this script." Then he told Bud the story of the afternoon Caitlin Wurtz didn't show up.

Now it was Bud's turn.

He began by telling Weissen about a certain woman on a pay

phone. He told him about the call for a limousine, and when he got to the part about hiding from the studio group at the foot of the stairs, Weissen grunted, astonished.

"You were *there*?"

"I felt like Lucille Ball."

"Unbelievable! This is the most *amazing* thing I have ever heard!"

Weissen was incredulous. When Bud said that was only the beginning, it was too much—*this* was the "little" film Whitehead had been searching for. The image of the furtive chauffeur on the stairs was "priceless." As he went on, Weissen listened the way people used to listen to radio. Bud took him through the Academy Awards and up to the phone call before the murder. The screenwriter didn't exactly say they'd become lovers but left enough to the imagination.

Bud told him about the Henry James script and how he'd made it his. It was the first time he'd ever revealed the connection. Naturally, Weissen wanted to read it.

"What a tragedy," he said, clenching his jaw. "It's a great story, though—your meeting her. A great story."

He was going to give Weissen *Shotgun,* then thought it'd be better at least to wait until his new friend finished *Broken Wings.* One way or another, Bud was determined to get something going. They'd hung out over the past few weeks and already the man from Toronto was saying he wanted to "do something together," something ambitious and small-scale, outside the realm of *hakdim.* It occurred to Bud they might write a pop Freudian comedy, a take-off on the psychoanalytic mysteries of the forties—like *Spellbound* or *Lady in the Dark* or *The Dark Mirror* or *The Dark Past*—a mood piece complete with a shrink, loopy dream sequences, a sexy femme fatale hysteric and a protagonist whose crisis was resolved by the bogus revelation of a long-repressed childhood trauma. A supersophisticated *High Anxiety;* they could even adapt *The Psychopathology of Everyday Life* the way Woody Allen did

Everything You Always Wanted to Know About Sex. That would be a goof. You could call it *Sigmund Freud's Psychopathology of Everyday Life!* with the old *Airplane!* exclamation point. Hilarious and smart, a hipper, homegrown *Women on the Verge.* They could set the whole thing in a nuthouse, cheaper that way. Just dress up an abandoned building, use one of those high schools that went bankrupt, there were lots of them. That was cost-effective. You could put the entire production office in there—wardrobe, payroll, casting, everything. Make it about a tennis pro who commits himself to a mental hospital and call it *Breakpoint.* Have a character who thinks he's Man Ray, have a suicidal director, a diva and a socialite and a famous sitcom star, et cetera, et cetera. He loved all those corny old asylum movies—great genre to send up. The potential for "set pieces" was mind-blowing.

Hugo's was empty. As the waitress served their food, Weissen's face twisted in a scowl; the skin itself looked cold and pale. He stared Bud straight in the eye, then looked away, abashed.

"It's brilliant. *Broken Wings* is the single best thing I have read since . . . the *seventies.* And I'm not a piker, Bud. I'm *serious.* It's like—it's *better*—than *Dangerous Liaisons.* Your script has that kind of feel. I was literally blown away." Weissen shook his head and poured honey on the granola. "I'm a hack. Right? Mind you, I'm a *good* hack. See, the difference between me and you is you have a *vision.* I have an original thought maybe once every five years. The rest of the time I repeat myself, I give the town what it wants. And when I say repeating myself, it's not like a great artist doing variations on a theme. We're not talking Tennessee Williams."

He dug at the granola, then made eye contact again and asked how much of the script was Bud's and how much Wurtz's—like he was assessing a property line. A matter of a few feet might signify hundreds of thousands of dollars.

"It's totally mine—I'll show you the original."

"Bud, I *know* it's yours, I can tell by the images, the rhythms, the dialogue, *anyone* could. You know, I saw her monkey picture, what was it called?"

"*Banana Republic.*"

"*Absolute shit,* Wiggins. *Absolute, total shit.* She was erratic, huh? Wasn't she erratic, Bud? She was a hack, wasn't she, Bud?"

Weissen asked again about the genesis of the *Wings* project and Bud reiterated how he'd been given the whole mess as a gift, without strings. Weissen eyed him like a ferret.

"Was there an agreement? Is anything on paper?"

"No. I was going to get something on paper when she came back to L.A., but I was caught up in finishing the script. Then she died."

"Then she died," Weissen repeated. He savored the phrase like a man convinced the project's minutiae would soon be the stuff of legend. "Can I tell you something? Can I tell you what you should do?"

It was nice to have an ally, someone who respected him and understood. Someone with clout.

"I'll tell you what I think you should do. You should write this whole thing down: how you met her, the whole thing with the pay phone—it's great!—and publish it. You know who would publish it in a minute? *The New Yorker.*"

Bud hated *The New Yorker.* What did Weissen mean anyway? What about the script?

"Or *Esquire.* I could get it to someone there with one call. You know what you could do? You could *serialize* it. *Rolling Stone* would do it, Bud! *Rolling Stone*! Didn't they do the Wolfe book? It's terrible, by the way, I couldn't finish it. You know how they say you couldn't put it down? I couldn't pick it *up*! Bud, this is great! Expand it a little—the stuff about the guy as the limo driver, a *great* character. But you know what makes it different? It's . . . *literary.* No one does what you do. No one in Hollywood."

"But the script. Don't you think someone—"

"They'll never make it." Weissen gave him that hard, awry

hawk look again. Bud felt like a playwright being denied a visa. "It's everything they're afraid of. It's everything they hate."

Weissen reached into his pocket to pay the bill. There was a crumpled check among the dollars and he plucked it out, thrusting it at Bud.

"Did I tell you about this? This check? I got a call from my old agency—they *misplaced* it! I've had it in my pocket for two weeks." It was a quarterly residual for the sequel Weissen had written. The amount was $117,940. "Should I go after them for the interest, Bud? Should I, Bud, is it worth the *tsouris*, Bud? They're thiefs! 'Misplaced'! How does an agency like TTA misplace a hundred and seventeen thou? It's Mafia. They're in bed with the studios. And we're helpless. Do you know what would happen if I went after them for the interest? Blacklist. Should I do it anyway, Bud?" He smiled at his quixotic fantasy. "It'd be great, though, wouldn't it? Wouldn't it?"

〰〰〰

Bud's credit problems flared up.

The latest collection agency was frisky and hell-bent and Zake Bock kept up his jubilant "no such thing as debtors' prison" spiel the way you'd tell a child there weren't any monsters under the bed. Look, darling, see for yourself! Should he finally declare bankruptcy? *Not at this time,* advised counselor Shramm. The bankruptcy process wasn't the lovefest of amnesty it was cracked up to be.

Relax. You're two tents.

The screenwriter took to his bed and his *Cliffs Notes* and read about Cervantes, jailed by treasury agents for account shortages. If Genet wrote *Miracle of the Rose* behind bars and *Quixote* flowered there as well, then maybe it wasn't such a bad place for Bud to be. He'd cell with Perry Bravo. The two would sharpen their pencils together, a regular Sartre and De Beauvoir.

Bud went to Program Meetings for people who had "issues" with money: misers and spendthrifts and everyone between.

The groups preached the moral imperative of paying off debts, working with one's creditors. Loving the torturer. And all along Bud felt himself falling. There was something eating at him that he wasn't sharing, something far worse than the chronic low-grade fever of indebtedness: he'd received a call from Don Bloom telling him the Doctor's case was being reopened for investigation.

Bloom was vague and dodged questions about his sources. He was holding something back; he knew someone in the coroner's office was all he'd confirm. Though no one had said it, the screenwriter kept hearing the phrase *rule out wrongful death* in his head. Bud puzzled over this latest development, even calling the Doctor's parents to feel them out. Had someone "spoken" to them? he asked, gingerly. No one had. Bloom was capable of stirring things up out of boredom or perversity, but the screenwriter didn't think he'd go so far as to invent an official inquiry. Maybe it was part of a practical joke.

Still, it was insidious. The Doctor was dead and Bud knew that somewhere, stored away, were a hundred empty prescription bottles with his name on them. Bud Wiggins. Bud Wiggins. Bud Wiggins. The empty vials of death that brought the brilliant surgeon down like so many stones to the skull. When he cleaned the filthy room for the last time, there were only a few discards—that was because the coroner had already been there. They wanted to make sure any medication or contraband was removed before the family went through the room for personal effects. *Bud Wiggins,* said the labels, *take 1–2 every four hours, for pain.*

Who *was* Bud Wiggins? He was the "friend." The friend who owed money to the world, the friend who bought a wristwatch on credit at the Broadway, then returned it for cash an hour later, the friend who drove a limousine, the frozen steak connection and alleged screenwriter. *The alleged self-proclaimed self-styled screenwriter,* the newspapers would say. What did you do with the pills, Bud? agents would ask, examining his arms for marks. Surely you couldn't have taken them all. Thousands of pills, Bud. And these are just the bottles we found. The Doctor had access to anything he wanted—surely, a surgeon wouldn't have wasted his time running around cashing scripts. Surely not. Did you sell the pills, Bud? What did you get? Five dollars a pill? That's two hundred and fifty dollars a bottle. Not bad for a twelve-dollar outlay. Do you have a health plan, Bud? Because with some of these health plans, you pay a dollar or two and that's it. Isn't that right, Bud? Writers Guild has a pretty good health plan, doesn't it? You're a member of the Guild, aren't you, Bud? What do you write, Bud, slasher movies? Anything I might have heard of? Did you shoot up with your friend, Bud? Did you stay over that night? You were his connection, weren't you? Did you turn him out, Bud? The bottle of Placidyl we found under the body had your name on it, Bud. Do you have an attorney? You might want to call him. Don Bloom? Isn't that funny. We've been wanting to speak to Mr. Bloom ourselves. Will you come with us? Come with us, Bud. Come. Now. Let's go. *Move.*

His ruthless captors would know nothing of the theory of codependency; they would take him to Seville to rot among the Moors. There would be those at the trial who spoke in his favor. The screenwriter had suffered enough, they would say. His relationship with the Doctor was unhealthy and Mr. Wiggins had taken steps to correct it. He had directly influenced the Doctor to attend several sobriety Meetings. The record would show that Mr. Wiggins did this out of Love. Mr. Wiggins was working out the puzzle of his codependency. *Know thyself* was his new credo and he wished to pass such sympathies on to his sick friend. Mr. Wiggins was just starting to find his way when the Doctor died. Mr. Wiggins was perhaps only weeks away from staging an "intervention," confronting Brian and arranging a detox—not that saving the Doctor was his mission or responsibility. That was more of the same madness. No, Mr. Wiggins had bravely waved good-bye to such "cosigned" arrangements. What he did—or didn't do—was out of Love. Yes, Mr. Wiggins was about to stage an intervention, exposing his oldest, dearest friend to hospital authorities and family members, whatever it took, but the Doctor died instead. He died so Bud could live.

Until they came for him in their *Missing* microbuses, came in the night and broke down his door, Bud would put it from his mind.

Jake Weissen was back in town and asked him to dinner. Bud needed money and decided to hit on him. What were friends for?

Weissen had made dinner reservations at Chaya. He was in the shower when Bud arrived at his suite; the door was open. He needed a thousand but decided to ask for twenty-five hundred instead. That way, if less was offered, he'd still be covered. Weissen was in a good mood and joked with Bud as he toweled down.

"What's the matter?"

"Nothing."

"You're depressed, I can tell. Is it bread, Bud? Do you need bread?" Weissen still called money "bread."

Bud was embarrassed and said nothing; the words wouldn't come.

"Do you need a couple grand? How about four, is four grand enough, Bud?" The screenwriter began to quake. He wiped a tear that dripped down his face. "Bud! Bud, don't, don't! It's *nothing*, Bud. In the scheme of things, it's *nothing*. Look—I know we're going to do something together, you can pay me back when they cut a check. It's an *advance*. Did I tell you my deal closed? For the Mexican rewrite? The Whitehead picture! Wiggins, it's great! Lots of bread. They're shooting it in Mexico, *Big Tiny Little*, they're in big trouble. Big trouble for *Big Tiny Little*! I don't even want to do it, Buddy, but the *bread*, the *bread*. That *bread*, it's like having a cock up the ass, it's so good. You know what I mean?"

Weissen laughed and Bud felt light-headed. He was still a young nag and time was on his side. He raised his dripping muzzle from the four-thousand-dollar trough and smiled. His benefactor's face suddenly tensed with inspiration.

"Bud, come with me! Come with me to Mexico! Wiggins, it'd be great! The studio will pick up the flight, the room—you won't lay out a dime! Get out of L.A., Bud, that's why you're depressed! It's *L.A.*, it's *L.A.*! I'm telling you! We'll get you some space at the studio, a typewriter—you can *work*. We'll sketch out something on the plane, you'll write it in Mexico. You'd be *insane* not to go."

Big Tiny Little actually sounded like the project Derek had tried to fob off on him, post-genius grant. Funny how things turned out. Not knowing what to say, Bud asked Weissen if there'd be a problem getting him booked on the plane.

Weissen squinted past him like a union guy in on a fix.

"I'll phone the studio. It's *done.*"

When he got home, Bud threw up. The bile was sweet. The image of his father floated up from the bowl, just like they'd do it in the Freud parody, the killer-father theme, Morris with the Zizanie cologne from Dunhill's on his wrist, behind his ears, haunting him from the crapper. At the sink, old Moe was replaced in the mirror by Ben Gazzara, recoiling from Cassavetes's vomit-spattered fingers in *Husbands*. Bud loved all that tux horseplay, fathers and husbands in dinner suits, uniforms of the night, laughing their crazy, bronchial *Losers* club laughs and puking all over each other.

He gargled, then went to bed. He didn't read *Quixote* that night.

The night before they left for Mexico, Weissen asked if he wanted to go to a party in the hills. Bud squeezed into his ten-year-old Armani suit and waited outside the apartment for his ride, feeling almost new.

On the way over, Weissen said the party was for Joan Krause and Bud got excited. What was the story on Krause anyhow? She was supposed to have this ferocious, knock-your-socks-off wit. He'd seen only a few of her movies. Bud knew she grew up in Beverly Hills and was a few years younger than him. Her latest incarnation, as publicists liked to say, was as best-selling author. She was even writing a few films—robbing Bud Wiggins of a job was a regular industry. Krause was never really linked to anyone in particular. Maybe she was available. He felt lucky tonight.

They gave the car to a valet and wandered in. Weissen was immediately buttonholed by a bearded producer and Bud waded into a den. He wasn't ready for the living room yet.

Joan Krause threw great parties. In her early thirties, she was already some kind of mythic, above-the-line doyenne. There were so many famous faces Bud's impulse was to scream or bolt. Instead, he made a pit stop at a silver M&M's bowl, sucked on a Coke and chatted up a long-legged nobody who was exhilarated just to be there. She made him horny; he studied the hair of her arm like a zoologist. When her friend arrived, she excused herself respectfully, in case Bud was some undisclosed heavy.

He still wasn't ready for the living room and bypassed it, moving deeper into the house. He heard a *haw-haw-haw* and Joan Krause appeared down a hall with a tuxedoed member of the Monty Python group. She wore a tight black dress and had smart eyes.

"Hi!"

Her forehead crinkled as if he were an old lover she'd invited but never expected to show. He knew it was just another improv, but Krause seemed to like what she saw.

"Bud Wiggins." He thrust out his hand and she shook it. "We grew up together."

"Yes! You used to show me your penis. It was enormous, even as a boy."

She moved on. It felt like they'd connected, but maybe he was wrong. Maybe that was just that smart thing she had that wowed people. Krause was potent that way.

After about a half hour of meandering, Bud caught up with his date. Weissen was ready to leave. He "hated" the people there, he said, "hated the Business." At first, Bud thought he was kidding, then recognized it as a curmudgeonly-writer pose, the prickly hack from Toronto—Weissen *was* the Business, but occasionally needed to express contempt, to heap invective then retreat to lick his wounds and regroup; needed continuously to turn his back on the town like he'd been spurned, then begin the love affair all over again. Tonight he was passive-aggressive, as Jeanette might say, in the grip of some social and moral malaise. Bud said he felt like hanging around awhile longer and would take a cab back. Someone shouted Weissen's name and the querulous Canadian recoiled, then rushed out, reminding Bud to be at the Château at ten. That's when the car was taking them to the airport.

A free agent, he walked onto the gray slate that bordered the pool. There was a tree house and an enormous Fiberglas cow nestled in the bush. Bud knew one day he would arrive; one day he'd have his own great spotted house cow to be photographed beside during interviews.

Joan Krause lay on a chaise longue in the dark, smoking a cigarette. She watched him approach and he gently took her cigarette and dragged.

"Good," he said, slipping it back between her fingers. "Soaked in DMT, right?"

"The businessman's hunch. Only the filters, though. The rest is ayahuasca, vine of the gods. It's a groovy kind of love. So where do I know you from?"

"I drove you around once. In a limousine."

In fact, he had, for about a minute. Krause had emerged from a party with some people he was waiting for and they drove her down the hill to her car. The meager anecdote made her smile. When he said he was a writer, she liked that even more. He told Krause he saw her at the Perry Bravo thing and they joked evilly about that for a minute. He was doing all right. A funny, vaguely mysterious bullshitter who said he was a writer and copped to chauffeuring her around couldn't be worse than any of the other bullshitters auditioning for her attention.

"Which really brings me to why I'm here tonight." He paused. "I'd like to be your personal driver. I'd also clean, do correspondence and help each day with what you're going to wear."

She laughed and smiled that X-ray wiliness, a supernatural gamine.

"If it doesn't work out," he added, "I just want to go steady."

"With what part?"

He paused, a little drunk. "With your brains, bones and ovaries."

Bud winced at his own preciousness. Then he thought, The hell with it. Nobody's making transcripts anyway. At least he hadn't been boring. Maybe he had. Stop beating yourself up. He told himself he was a good person, funny and bright and not unattractive. He was young and just beginning to make sense of his life—the best was yet to come. Why *shouldn't* Joan Krause want to go to bed with him? He was *significant,* as interesting as anyone there. He was on his way to Mexico, to write. . . .

Someone glow-in-the-dark-famous came over and Krause mouthed, "Don't leave," as she was led away.

He determinedly stayed out of her face the rest of the night.

Bud ran into a few people he knew and a few others he didn't. Each time he resolved to call a cab, that there was nothing brewing between them but the percolations of her flirty largess, Krause would magically appear and slip her arm in his. Then she'd say something loud like "Have you met my driver with the Danny Glover penis?" and everybody'd laughed and Bud's stock would rise and his heart quicken, remembering the voiceless *Don't leave.* People must have thought they were lovers.

Finally, the celebs were all departed. Krause hadn't been seen for at least forty-five minutes. Dull sycophants lolled in the kitchen, warming themselves by the embers of her personality before facing the unlucky night, unknowns again: the boozy ex-wife of a megastar, the ex-nanny of a sitcom queen, a squirrelly private trainer, two "chore whores" and one of Krause's former agents. The latter mulled over the idea of crashing in a guest room, "my old room," he called it, the boastful message being he was still family. Then he framed his hands around the weary stragglers like a photographer, and captioned: "After the Party, Joan Krause's Kitchen, Hollywood Hills, California, 2:40 A.M."

The agent left.

Bud thought about chasing him down for a ride but decided to find Krause, at least to say good-bye. How presumptuous could that be? No one followed as he walked toward the back of the house.

Outside her bedroom, the screenwriter heard the voice and showed himself. Krause was on the phone and eagerly waved him in.

"Well," she was saying into the phone, "I told you. I only have one, and I need it to sleep. So I guess this down isn't big enough for both of us. This gown, this crown, this *flowne.*"

She talked for a full fifteen minutes while he watched *Bigger Than Life* on the silent screen. The room had a kind of miniature coziness, like a place where foxes kept their jewels. Bud heard her say, "I have to go now, my driver is here," then she *haw-haw-haw*ed and hung up.

"I didn't know what happened to you," he said. "I was so hurt."

"You were, weren't you, and it's because you love me."

Krause had changed from her dress to a nightgown. Joan Krause in bed, Hollywood Hills, California, 2:58 A.M.

When she found out Bud was a local boy, they talked for an hour about the way it used to be. Rodeo Drive: the Luau, where all the fathers went to drink, the little pastry shop and tearoom, the toy store with the big tree in the middle whose trunk dispensed lemonade; the grand coffee shop in the Beverly Wilshire called Milton F. Kreis (all the counter coffee shops were gone now) and Ontra's cafeteria; Romanoff's and Frascati's, Lum's and Blum's and the theater on Cañon that showed art films, the domed Beverly with its free matinées, and Wil Wright's, the ice-cream "emporium" with the heart-shaped chairs and complimentary macaroons. And Century City—Jesus, the whole place had gone up in ten minutes in the backyard of Beverly Hills High. They used to go to the fields there and catch butterflies for science class and now they wanted to tear the school down because the land was worth about a billion dollars. She even remembered Fun Fair: giddily, they sang of Elevado, shaving cream and Great Processions.

"God, we sound like fucking *geezers*," she said.

"Hume Cronyn and Jessica Tandy."

"No, they're *geezers fucking*—on a good day, anyway. It's a dirty job, but someone's gotta do it. So, I guess I'm Hume."

"You look like a Hume."

"Hi, honey, I'm Hume. And you look like a Jessica. Jessica Wang."

"Can I kiss you?"

He might have been asking if she liked cream in her coffee. She did. Her mouth tasted like a girl he made out with in an elevator when he was twelve.

"Good," she said. He passed the cookie test.

Joan Krause smiled and told him to turn out the lights.

She left the room and Bud undressed. He folded his things carefully and climbed under the covers. The bed was like a cloud, a fortune in feather bedding and sheets. Everything was probably from Shaxted or Pratesi, he thought.

When she came back to the room, her face was shining like it had been scrubbed.

Krause took her gown off and got in bed. As he drew her close, an old inner voice asked: "Am I aroused?" He pushed the voice away. He caressed her, gently chastising himself for not being fully in the moment. He hated that. He was two tents. Better lighten up. Joan Krause desires you, you are a gifted writer on your way to Mexico on a project. He closed his eyes and tried to sink down into himself, feeling the nude length of their bodies, his cock settling numbly against her middle like a blind dog in a litter, nosing for warmth. He stretched and felt himself stir. It was good, body to body. Then he kissed her and got a little harder and thought he should take her now, the way men do. Her eyes closed dreamily; he could tell she was enjoying the simple submission to the strength of a male. Again the dreaded feeling came, not being in the moment. He wished he were home, then fought hard against such heresy. Maybe it was all happening too fast with Krause, maybe he'd been turned off when he smelled her perspiration. Or that the part of him that was vulnerable, the female part, was making him twist. Too bad he didn't have Dr. Jurgen's number. Sometimes he just didn't feel anything when he was first in bed with a woman. He'd been through this before—why should it frighten him? He calmed himself by deciding to enter her *in his own time*. After all, they'd been in bed only a few minutes. But sometimes a woman wants it right away. He still had a while. If there was real trouble and he seriously couldn't get it up, he was certain Krause would be sensitive—women usually were, because they always think it's them, at first anyway. That's a general rule. Bud would take full responsibility. He'd tell her he had a lot on his mind, he was writing a huge project and embarking for Mexico in the morning. He'd keep it vague. He couldn't say it was *Big Tiny Little,* she might know Whitehead or something. She knew everybody. He'd tell her he was exhausted, that he hadn't even recovered from the last screenplay. He would lie in her arms and unburden himself, modestly talking about the death of the Doctor, as if she were the first person—*partner*— he'd been able to share it with. Desired to share it with. He would tell her he was taking an antidepressant, he was taking Prozac, the prose writer's drug, he'd say, and she'd laugh. He'd tell her he just started taking it and was already feeling better but there were some funny side effects. And some not so funny. If you know what I mean. Then maybe it'd be all right again, just the interlude they'd needed; his copulating rhythm demanded such bottoming out. Their lovemaking would be richer with the confession, the intimacy, the humanity. The fucking wasn't so important anyway. The fucking was the male thing, it wasn't everything for the woman. After all that, if Bud still had "difficulty," he'd laugh, she'd call him a Bud-ist with an I scream koan, they'd laugh some more, *I'll show you mine if you show me Lourdes,* then he'd go down on her. He would make her come, then she'd want to do for him and he would ask her to hold him in her arms while he masturbated.

He flashed on the book of Indian love paintings a girlfriend gave him on his birthday. The Hindus had a technique to overcome impotence; if the penis was soft, you could sort of gently stuff it in. But Joan Krause was no Hindu, and if Bud began diligently to perform such an operation, she might think there was something really wrong with him. He went down on her and became aroused. He saw her face far away in the dark above him, dreaming its underwater dream. The screenwriter got hard and moved toward her like some amphibian dragging itself to shore. Then he flagged.

"Are you okay?"

Bud rolled beside her and took a deep breath. Near the bed, the ambitious Mexican project and the shadow of Brian hovered like a tag team; they waited an obedient moment before entering the ring. In the dead friend's hand, like a tender reminder, was a bottle of Prozac.

He left in the early morning, kissing her cheek. When he said, "Let's not do it again sometime," she smiled and mouthed, *I love you.*

"You're my baby boy," she added, "on his way to Meh-hee-koh. *El Wiggins.* There, I said it: the *el* word."

ﾉﾉﾉﾉﾉ

On the flight down, Bud dipped into *Quixote.*

He was excited about traveling and had barely slept so it was difficult to keep his concentration. Weissen wanted to gab. He told Bud he'd met a girl just as he was leaving the party. He pointed to some stapled pages in his lap and said it was a treatment she'd given him for a TV pilot.

"Everybody's fucking hustling, Bud. That's the sickness of the town." Weissen was still in the contempt mode, and he was tired. He'd been up all night himself. "Dirtiest girl I've ever met," he said, shaking his head. "I put it in her ass and she sucked it, right after I pulled it out, sucked the shit on it! You know what she said when I put it in, Bud? 'No one can get enough of my ass lately.' And she gives this little smile. Weird! I didn't wear a condom, Bud, should I worry? Should I get the test, Bud? Or is the test bullshit?"

They were picked up at the airport by a studio driver in an older Secret Service–type Ford. Bud had been warned about the Mexico City smog, but it didn't seem any worse than L.A. The only things he noticed were statues of horsemen and street children selling useless, brightly colored bric-a-brac.

The hotel was grand, with breathtaking pastel walls and a great sculpted bowl at its entrance, filled with tempest-blown water. The Mexicans sure knew how to do fountains. Bud was almost phobic about travel, but it felt invigorating suddenly to be in this foreign place, unfettered and enthused. The hosannas he flung at Weissen's munificence further lightened his load as they strode through the lobby.

He left his friend at the registration desk and stopped by the gift shop. The "man from La Mancha" was everywhere: wooden statuettes of the forlorn knight with the pointy chin hung on key chains, his portrait embellishing postcards, purses and pockets. Bud bought some stamps and a Spanish-English phrase book. He'd always been strangely resistant to learning Spanish but was worried about getting sick and wanted to be sure he knew how to ask for bottled water. He also wanted to be able to say "Without ice," because Dolly told him ice was a no-no. You didn't eat ice and you didn't brush your teeth with water from the tap.

He flipped through the book as they waited for the elevator, enjoying its stilted, chauvinist mantras: "This glass is dirty. Please get me another. Would you check the bill again? I believe I have been overcharged."

Weissen had to attend a flurry of meetings at the hotel. The producers were there, but Dick Whitehead wasn't expected until Monday. One of the slaves was already working on getting Bud an office and a typewriter at the studio.

Chapultepec Park was in walking distance of the hotel and he set out for it, footloose. The whole city seemed like a great, slow-moving exposition, out of time—playhouses within galleries, martial statuary stuck in fountains, a rustic zoo with rococo cages, a gigantean wooden roller coaster (the guidebook quaintly warned that it carried no insurance)—he reveled in its pastel, pastoral municipality. He saw banal lovers clenching on benches, and was unjaundiced. Everything seemed superabundant, as if dislocation had sharpened his senses; there was life outside the Business. He ducked into a museum theater to watch a matinée of Strindberg's *The Pelican*. Though he couldn't understand the Spanish dialogue, Bud knew the play well enough and was upset they'd changed it so the mother blew her brains out at the end—he had been waiting for the woman to toss herself out the window, as he remembered. Maybe he remembered wrong.

It was late afternoon. The vagabond screenwriter strolled along the Paseo de la Reforma back to the hotel. He'd made enough sweet explorations, and felt a ruddy, auspicious detachment. Perhaps he'd become a globe-trotter, visiting recondite places, penning classy travelogues like a Chatwin or a Theroux. He sensed a calling, the hatching of a wildly unforeseen secret strength: Bud Wiggins was comfortable in the flux, among foreign things.

He passed some soldiers with rifles near the hotel. Their vigilance seemed purely ceremonial.

On Sunday Bud and Weissen had lunch with some of the production team. The movie's DP and camera operator were mellow roommates who rented a place about thirty "Mexican minutes" away, near Diego Rivera's studio. *Big Tiny Little* had been in preproduction for almost seven months and the lovers' combined per diem had transformed their little villa into a *mercado*-laden Xanadu. On weekends, a driver whisked them to a converted sugar plantation in Cuernavaca that had a swimming pool in the living room. They dreaded returning to the States.

After the meal Weissen went to the hotel and Bud took a cab to an art house theater near the Zócalo. He watched the screening of a silent German film about a husband's repressed desire to kill his wife. Some of the pioneer psychoanalysts had acted as consultants and the movie was full of startling, technically wondrous (for the time) dream sequences. Bud thought about his Freudian idea again and got excited—maybe that's what he would work on for the next few weeks.

Dusk was falling and a soft wind gusted the great church square. Mariachi players waited in a queue along the street to be hired for the evening. The city possessed a festive yet solemn dignity and Bud was flooded by ghostly, fathomless expectations.

Big Tiny Little was about a bunch of neighborhood kids accidentally reduced to the size of food crumbs.

Monday morning Bud rode along with Weissen and the unit production manager to the old movie studio called Churubusco. The indoor set was spectacular. They walked through twenty-foot shafts of grass bowed by a discarded candy wrapper the size of a school bus. They were shown a workroom where a giant ant with hundreds of movable parts was having a spastic dry run. Men were poring over it with the prelaunch seriousness of NASA technicians.

Bud wandered outside to the "all-American" set, suburban houses with shingles and shrubbery, gazebos and mailboxes and white picket fences. He always loved the idea of fake houses, a chimera of spiffy façades; they were eerily evocative. Just give him a camera and some actors and let him loose for a few weeks.

They ate lunch a few blocks from the studio. Bud had a turkey sandwich and *agua, con gas, sin hielo.* Weissen had burritos and *agua,* straight up, heavy on the *hielo*—plentiful chunks of frozen water. Bud told him he shouldn't have ice because you didn't know where the water came from but Weissen didn't care. The intrepid benefactor ate pretty much everything in sight, and it hadn't killed him yet. "What doesn't give me the *turista* makes me stronger," he said.

That night Bud couldn't fall asleep. He felt feverish and turned on the light. His stomach was distended. He ran to the john (Morris always called it *the john*) and explosively emptied himself. The unnervingly insipid image of his father, barefoot on the penthouse carpet, was replaced by that of the icteroid Doctor, who would have characterized Bud's subsequent vomiting as "projectile." The demonic image of Calabash floated before him as the room continued to whirl; he felt like Dorothy in her uprooted house. He presumed Weissen was in similar straits and phoned his room. The imperturbable hack answered from a dreamy sleep.

"Your stomach okay?"

"Yeah. Sleeping. What time is it?"

"Two-thirty."

"You sick?"

Bud made a whistling sound.

"Want me to call a doctor? Hotel has a doctor."

"I'll be okay."

"It's just the *turista.* Everybody gets it. Do you have any Cokes?"

"Yeah."

"I'm gonna go back to sleep, I have a killer day tomorrow. I'll call you in the morning. You'll be fine, just drink Cokes."

Around dawn his agonies abated.

A few hours later a glowingly healthy Weissen came to Bud's

room to debate what made him ill. He theorized it was the sauce on the turkey sandwich.

"How the hell often do they sell turkey sandwiches at that place, Bud? It's a fucking *taco* stand. Who *knows* how long the sauce was laying around?"

Weissen's deductions were strangely soothing and Bud took pride in his body's precipitously purgative response. He felt strong enough to go downstairs and have some 7-Up *sin hielo* with toast while his friend wolfed down pastries and runny *huevos rancheros*. After Weissen left for the studio, Bud decided to take a leisurely constitutional in the park.

A tantara preceded a phalanx of soldiers filling the lobby. It was election time and the president of the country was speaking at a banquet in the hotel. He smiled, waving to guests and employees. *El presidente* wore a businessman's suit and looked into Bud's eyes during his sweep, then grabbed the rail of the escalator and ascended, still waving. The bellboys watched the politician, slowly shaking their heads like orderlies in an asylum, the old man an inmate who thought he was emperor.

Bud weaved through the tangle of boulevards in the Polanco, past the rich people's low concrete houses with their satellite dishes, soldiers and garage doors of golden wood; past the baroque homes converted to embassies, restaurants and couturiers; past the statues and fountains and money changers. Through the streets: the *avenidas* Dante, Rousseau, Dickens, Ibsen, Eugenio Sue, Schiller, Lope de Vega, Lamartine, Lord Byron, Emerson, Tennyson, Musset, Verne, Poe, La Fontaine, Cicerone, Sophocles, Molière, Cervantes. He was feeling avuncular and smiled down sweetly on the ludicrous Mexican kultur. Bud filled up with the tender peace of the convalescent as the sun restored his equilibrium.

He walked to the zoo in Chapultepec Park and noticed tiny train tracks disappearing through tunnels around the periphery. He passed the big cat cages and thought of Don Quixote, Knight of the Lions—everywhere they hawked intaglios and caricatures of the gentle madman from colorful stalls. Bud joined a crowd under a canopy and after a minute a small train appeared and disgorged its passengers, mostly families. The screenwriter boarded, feeling foolish because he seemed to be the only grown-up riding the train without a child, or at least without a friend. He fantasized groups of peasants crowding around to ask, as they would of Quixote, who he was and what he was doing riding the children's train around Chapultepec Park alone. He would reply he was a journalist writing about the zoo train for a big American magazine; this they'd understand. They would beg his apology and prepare a feast that would last three days. After much pleading for him to remain in their village and govern as mayor, Señor Wiggins would regretfully take his leave, continuing on his journey.

By the end of the first week their routine was established. They drank coffee together in the morning, then Weissen was driven to the studio and Bud went sight-seeing or jotted down notes for their incipient project. At night they had a bull session over dinner, during which they pitched story ideas and made each other laugh. Weissen wasn't sure about the Freud idea yet and Bud was anxious to nail something down because soon he was going to need more money. He was thinking of asking for ten thousand. Why not? That, plus the four he'd already given him was barely more than Guild minimum. It was agreed from the beginning that Bud wasn't south of the border for his health. Weissen was a rich man and wanted Bud as a collaborator; why *shouldn't* he be properly paid? He wasn't worried. Even though his friend was pragmatic and unneurotic about "bread," the screenwriter wanted to come up with something tangible to justify the outlay. He wanted to work for his money.

It was better that Bud stayed away from Churubusco. The last thing he wanted was to sit in front of a blank piece of paper in some smelly nook without an idea in his head, waiting for Jake $450,000-a-rewrite Weissen to stick his head in during a break to pitch some insane idea he'd had while jacking into his hankie. He seemed to have a notion they were miners hot on the mother lode of Story; if they could just stick with it long enough, there was gold in the hills and redemption from the ranks of the *hakdim*. Weissen's prognostications were always the same: when the duo found what they were looking for, they could pound out a script in *two weeks,* a shining, radical aberration irresistible even to the big-money boys. They'd change the face of the town with the unthinkable grosses of their wild, low-budget visions. Weissen could afford to be quixotic. Like the sidekick Sancho Panza, Bud was pretty much ready for his island and governorship.

He sent Joan Krause a postcard: "Wish you were queer." Then he regretted it—everyone was always trying to outclever Joan Krause. She'd probably throw it in a drawer with all the other idiot-eager dispatches: *wish you were Lear, wish you were Frears, wish you were Richard Gere.*

The next week Bud went to a curious play in the southern section of town, at the Teatro Julio Prieto. It was about a man who was part gorilla and was directed by the acclaimed Alejandro Jodorowsky. It sounded memorable.

Bud sat in the auditorium feebly trying to translate the program. The ape illustration put him in mind of Caitlin. He'd been actively pushing thoughts of her away; he didn't know where to put them. Too soon, he guessed. Her death had been so horrendously surreal. He didn't have anyone to share his feelings with. That wasn't exactly true. There was Jake Weissen, but the screenwriter was cautious about sharing certain intimacies. He was afraid of trivializing her memory. At least when the Doctor died, there were people he could talk to who had known what Bud and Brian had meant to each other. When they killed Caitlin, he couldn't exactly hunt down Rosa the maid for sympathy. It wasn't only about sympathy anyway, he reflected, but that was certainly part of it. No, he hadn't properly grieved for that woman. Along with what was, he had still to mourn what might have been, and that was hardest of all.

Bud shrugged. He'd save the tears and the laughter for a little memoir, he thought darkly. Like one of those people who happened to know Judy or Marilyn near the end.

He watched the civilized gorilla onstage and fantasized Caitlin making an entrance. It was a one-man show and the apish actor had turned to address the amused audience in the middle of his boisterous monologue; the uncomprehending Bud was completely mesmerized. As the crowd erupted with laughter, he felt a stab in the gut and roaring heat in his head. For a moment, he didn't know who or where he was. The sickly traveler got up to find the bathroom.

He looked in the mirror and was startled at what he saw: cheeks white and gelid, like the good dead Doctor's. He threw out his underwear and put paper towels against his backside, holding them there through his pants as he left the theater and climbed into the car waiting to take him to the hotel. The image of the stage actor as Calabash pursued him like an awful melody, chasing the car down, a sportive Winged Monkey on the far outskirts of Oz.

He spent the night in feverish sleep.

The next morning Weissen called from Dick Whitehead's office with the number of an M.D. the production was using. Bud took a cab to the English Hospital.

The place looked like the City of Hope, but inside, the walls had holes and the corridors stank of contagion. Dr. Piñero took stool samples over the next three days, then made his diagnosis: amoebic dysentery. He prescribed a "Flagyl derivative" and the night Bud took the medicine, he was sicker than he'd ever been in his life. Piñero said the pills sometimes caused fever and vomiting and he prescribed another drug to counter the deleterious effects. The inside of Bud's mouth began to ulcerate. Weissen looked in on him but was a little standoffish, having suddenly acquired a morbid fear of becoming ill. He winced during visits, as if his protégé were part of some grotesque pathogenic experiment and Weissen might be next. He tried to be encouraging, telling Bud to "sweat this thing out." The drugs would knock it down, whatever it was. The mine with the mother lode had a slight cave-in, that's all. Temporary setback.

Three days later the screenwriter called Weissen to his room. The Canadian gasped when he turned on the light. Bud hadn't slept since taking the drugs Piñero prescribed. He had lost almost fifteen pounds. He couldn't keep water down, his eyes were blackened and he was passing blood. He began to cry. Weissen stirred from his denial, tried not to panic and called Dick Whitehead's doctor in Beverly Hills. The physician told him Bud should immediately stop taking whatever medication had been prescribed. He said it sounded as if he were having an allergic reaction and that he was dangerously toxic—Bud was being poisoned.

Weissen put Bud on a midnight flight back to Los Angeles, first class. He looked bad enough that they were worried the airline wouldn't let him board, but it was dark and Weissen explained to the stewardess his friend was nervous about flying and groggy from sleeping pills. The plane was only half full and Bud lay down in an empty row as soon as they were in the air. This time he asked for *agua, con hielo*—it was first class and would probably be all right. The Beverly Hills doctor said it was important to suck on ice. . . .

Bud heard a familiar voice.

"He's right here with me now. Looks terrific. No, he's sleeping." He opened his eyes and dimly focused on Joseph Harmon. Harmon was on the phone. "Look, we're having dinner tonight at Mortons, aren't we? Seven o'clock."

The heavy hitters eat early, Bud thought.

He looked around. He was in the cabin of a jet, sitting in a sumptuous black swivel chair. There was a leather notebook on his lap with Bud Wiggins embossed in gold; he took it to be a script. A smartly dressed steward appeared from behind a mosaic screen.

"Would you like some fresh juice, Mr. Wiggins?"

The screenwriter was sleep-heavy and waved him away. Harmon hung up the phone.

"Well, well, he's awake."

Bud looked out the window. They were tearing through a cotton-candy cloud.

"What happened?"

"You were sick," he said, *"you were allergic to the drugs they were treating you with. But you already know that, right? See, the Mexican doctors aren't too bright. Dr. Brian gave you something that kills infection and gets you regular again."*

That was his cue—Bud urgently undid the seatbelt and excused himself.

The washroom was enormous. On the walls were richly framed lobby cards from fifty years of movies Harmon's studio had made. Bud wondered if any of it was real, recalling Sancho Panza's placating words to his frightened master: if Quixote was truly in a state of enchantment, his natural body functions would be suspended. But this wasn't the case, for Bud Wiggins had a perfectly disenchanting movement. He washed his hands, dried them with an expensive towel and ambled back to the cabin.

"I know this is dramatic," said Harmon, *"but when we heard* Broken Wings *was available we just had to move—Whitehead wants you in L.A. for rehearsals and he wants you on the set."*

"What about Big Tiny Little?*"*

"We pulled the plug. And don't worry about your friend Weissen—he was pay-or-play." Bud could barely believe what he was hearing. *"I can't tell you how excited everyone is. For the next two years your shit don't stink—and for all Dr. Brian gave you, it might just be true!"*

This was a more plebeian Joseph Harmon than Bud remembered. The magisterial coat was worn and raffish; the screenwriter felt a certain nostalgia for the cool killer homo of yore.

The pilot appeared and affably told them they were twenty minutes outside the city. He made a little bow before exiting.

Harmon explained there was only one "Estudio" now, run by the Committee of Independents, a watchdog group of art and film school grads who regularly withheld public funds from pro-

jects that smelled of the old multi-Studio system and its dreaded High Concepts.

It was clear that Joseph Harmon had suffered. The executive implied by way of a joke that many of his friends had disappeared during the revolution. Bud reasoned that Harmon's extensive working knowledge of the Industry had probably spared him. As much as the committee must have loathed and even feared Harmon's hoary mogul ways, they undoubtedly understood the inestimable value of his management skills. Bud thought the fallen giant might have thrived in such an adverse climate, appealing as such to his streak of piracy. Instead, he'd become a funcionario de los huesos, a "functionary of bones"—a man who looks at his hand and sees the skeleton within.

El Estudio's decision to film Broken Wings *was considered a great liberalization on the part of the committee. The effect of the announcement was astonishing; the city seemed to breathe again.*

It was on this respiration that Bud's plane touched down.

*As they taxied to the terminal, the pilot returned to the cabin. He spoke briefly with Harmon, then Harmon nodded and the captain approached with a dog-eared, badly mimeographed script—*Broken Wings. *He asked if Bud would sign it as a gift for his girlfriend. The screenwriter obliged, but when the pilot saw the signature, he seemed disappointed. Harmon looked over his shoulder.*

"I'm afraid that wasn't what he was expecting."

"What do you mean?"

"You've become somewhat of a folk hero around here, Wiggins. They're like children. You see, everyone knows the story of what happened with you and Joan Krause that night." Bud was so surprised that he grunted. "And well," Harmon went on, "you've come to be known as el Eunuco—affectionately, of course."

The script was smilingly proffered and Bud signed again, this time to the pilot's great satisfaction.

A military band began its stentorian loop as Bud's foot landed on the floating stairway. Somehow he wound up preceding Harmon and wondered if that was a faux pas. At the foot of the stairs, el presidente *fervidly shook his hand. This time the politician wore a brocaded uniform and sword, instead of a suit. The old general turned to face a crowd of journalists who reached out to him with tiny tape recorders. Before he could speak, he was unceremoniously swept away by a raft of loyalist bellboys.*

Bud felt Harmon yanking on his sleeve. Beyond the barriers of the policía, *the white Rolls waited for them like Quixote's Rosinante. Bud heard a respectful susurration of "el Eunuco" as they swept past crowds of curious well-wishers. A motorcycle escort led them from the private airport; Harmon himself drove the Rolls.*

"Don't worry about the nickname—it's a sign of affection. I, myself, am 'la Harmonica.' " The windows were down and Bud could barely hear what he was saying because of the sirens. "Don't mind them! They'll peel off for Peralvillo once we're over the hill."

That place sounded familiar.

The screenwriter admitted the city had changed in the time he'd been away. There were fountains and statues of men he didn't recognize. The place looked softly colonial and was blanketed by a powdery dust, as if put in a sack and gently shaken. Still, it was good to be back. It was his country and they were on their way to Mortons.

They were ushered to the restaurant's most powerful table. The room took note of their arrival and a few diners approached their table, discreetly welcoming el Eunuco back from his travels. After the well-meaning visitors withdrew, Harmon bade the maître d' run a little interference—el Eunuco was weary and wished to eat his dinner in peace.

Bud was at the sink in the men's room when he heard the sardonic voice: "¿Hay un médico cerca de aquí?"

He turned and glimpsed with horror a living statue he finally recognized—*the nearly departed Brian. The unsinkable physician immediately remarked on Bud's attenuated appearance.*

"I was sick," *Bud managed to stammer.*

"I know," *said the Doctor.* "I flew down with Harmon. Who do you think got you well?"

"I don't understand. I thought you were dead."

"No, no, that was a mistake. They gave me my old job back."

The telltale chemical odor on his breath made Bud gag. He felt slow and rudimentary.

"What are you doing here?"

"I've got the shits. Saving your life gave me the shits." *The Doctor laughed grimly.* "You know why shit's tapered, don't you? So your asshole won't slam shut."

He looked into Brian's bewildered eyes; for an instant they apologized from their miasma of heartbreak and obfuscation. Then they went stony.

"Why don't we get together tomorrow for lunch?" *the Doctor suggested.*

"Where should we meet?"

"At work."

"The hospital?"

"No, the old TTA building," *said the Doctor as he disappeared into one of the stalls.* "In Peralvillo."

They put him up in Weissen's old room at the Château. In the morning Bud's driver brought him to the agency. There were armed guards along the streets, fingers over triggers in readiness. Their stoicism struck him as loony. They were weirdly, desultorily stationed—one stood sentinel in a park beside a children's drinking fountain, as if an absurdist communiqué had threatened its attack or removal.

When they reached their destination, the driver politely gestured at the building and said, "la Clínica." *More soldiers loitered at the entrance of what used to be TTA.*

The reception area was unglamorous and reminded him of

County General. He was led to a room and photographed, then waited in the lobby on a Fiberglas bench welted by cigarettes.

A large hand clapped his shoulder from behind and pinned the newly minted photo ID onto his shirt.

"Welcome to the clinic!" It was Brian. "You look a lot better. Did you sleep? Are you hungry?"

The morning had been terribly busy and there were a few things the Doctor had to take care of before lunch. There was a lot of "talent" today, and he was late for a staff meeting. Did Bud want to come along? The committee knew he was visiting; everyone was clamoring to meet el Eunuco. One of them was "gorgeous"—Brian slyly said he'd already promised the lady a personal introduction. The Doctor was more charming than he'd remembered and Bud was warmed to be with his sorely missed old friend.

The meeting was in progress when they entered the conference room.

Bud shook hands with each of the independents, apologized for interrupting and urged them to continue. He felt like a celebrity causing a flurry in the Senate. A woman was watching him closely and with a start he recognized her as Jeanette. She wore a Louise Brooks–type wig; a nudge from the Doctor told him she was the aforementioned fan.

As the meeting continued, Bud stared at the bubbling aquarium and its wreaths of coral. There were no fishes.

Afterward the Doctor introduced him to the chairperson, a famous poet-activist. Jeanette joined them and the poet put a possessive arm on her. They were married. Bud noted that aside from the wig, she looked exactly the same. Or did she? He wasn't so sure; he was less and less sure of anything. Jeanette didn't seem to recognize him—or wasn't letting on if she did. The poet asked if they'd be seeing Bud tonight at Dick Whitehead's dinner party and Brian answered that they most certainly would.

As he left the conference room, the screenwriter meditated. Strange things were happening, without a doubt. The thought he was going mad had entered Bud's mind, and if that were true, *he'd be wise not to fight it. When writing a script, he mused, the rule was that the audience must "buy" the premise, no matter how outlandish.*

Still, something gnawed at him. What was to prevent Caitlin Wurtz herself from entering the fray? That could be a problem; she had died before deeding him a proper "certificate of authorship." If she did appear, the nature of Caitlin's allegiances—her very form—was up for grabs. The powerful woman might challenge his credit on the script, forcing an arbitration. He was getting ahead of himself. Bud resolved to make a few delicate inquiries as to her whereabouts.

As they waited for the elevator, there was a scuffle at the end of the hall. Bobby Feld was being pulled from his office by brutes in raw silk suits.

"Get away!" he screamed. "Get your fucking hands off me!"

Feld went limp and a guard kept hitting him in the stomach.

When Bud was little, he saw a character beaten to death in a movie and remembered losing some innocence; it was a revelation that people were beaten long after they stopped fighting back, beaten with fists until they were dead. Feld was still being pounded as the elevator doors shut them away.

Brian used a special key, allowing them access to the basement.

The elevator opened directly into a caged area. A pasty-faced young guard on the other side of the grille verified their IDs before unlocking the door. They entered a long corridor and the Doctor told his friend to wait a few minutes while he checked on someone he "represented." A man in a shiny black suit appeared and Brian went with him. The man's tie was loose; he looked like an arbitrageur who couldn't get anything to merge.

Bud heard moaning and wandered down the cool hallway. He peered through the eye-level grate of a metal door. More whimpering, and the back of somebody's head. The head turned and Bud was staring at Joel Levitt. He had no teeth and there was dried blood around the openings of his ears. Levitt spoke, slow and emphatic, with a lunatic's urgency.

"I am glad to see you," were his first words. *"Will this stain come out?"* The producer repeated himself until it seemed Bud understood. "Llame rápido a un policía."

"Do you know who I am? It's Bud—Bud Wiggins. What happened to you?"

Levitt looked at Bud and laughed, then burped some blood. *"This glass is dirty. Please get me another.* He vomitado. . . . *I have broken my dentures, ¡qué aburrido! I'm just looking, thank you. Where is the nearest post office?"*

Brian appeared and abruptly ushered Bud to the elevator.

Levitt's voice roared after them: "Escúcheme un momento. ¿Que hay en el cinema? *Should I tip the driver?. . . . I wrote to you reserving a room!"*

The Doctor told him an informer had leaked the rebel producer's whereabouts to the committee; he'd only been in custody since Bud's arrival from points south. The snitch had also fingered Bobby Feld, who was being held along with Levitt on charges of conspiracy.

When asked about Levitt's bilingual word salad, the Doctor said that one of the rebels' more irritating methods was to parrot Spanish-English phrase books while under the most intense interrogation. The tactic was *"pure Levitt."*

Dick Whitehead's neobaroque style mansion was in a hilly section of the city called the Bosque, so named for its relative verdure. The ever-sanguine director greeted them at the door and handed Bud a drink. Jeanette appeared and led him in, arm in arm.

"Where's your friend?"

"He had to finish up some work at the agency."

"I'll bet," she said sardonically. *"Show business is his life, as they used to say."*

They were joined by the poet, who made a little show of kissing Jeanette, catching Bud's eye. The screenwriter had a feeling the couple enjoyed the tension a potential ménage à trois brought to the marital table; the husband's demonstrations seemed like a cue for other men to establish a triangle in which he could masochistically define himself.

"I didn't get a chance today to tell you how wonderful your script is."

"You told me it was extraordinary," Jeanette said.

"Extraordinary, then. Jeanette is a great fan of yours." The scent of recreational betrayal hung thickly in the air, enlivening his eyes.

Whitehead accused the couple of hogging the guest of honor before anyone had been introduced and shepherded Bud to the bar. There he met a critic, a painter, an actor and a shorthaired young woman who was head of el Estudio. She was Krizia Folb, but only nominatively so; there was no physical resemblance to the Folb that he knew.

"We're so excited about Wings," she said, with classically treacherous good cheer, a show biz exec to her teeth. That was reassuring to Bud—some things a revolution couldn't change. The painter, a stylish mulatto in a suede skirt, gushed at him and Bud asked if she was an actress. She laughed throatily.

"I'm a painter."

"You're a production designer," said Krizia as she turned to Bud. "She's doing your film."

"I'm the actress," the handsome actor interrupted, and everyone laughed. He thrust his hand at Bud. "Merton Densher. Pleased to meet you."

The name rang a bell, then Bud remembered why. Merton Densher was the male lead in Broken Wings. Bud congratulated him; the actor cocked his head like a cat being stroked.

"Go ahead," the critic told Densher, wry and brittlely debonair. "Bask in it now, while you can." He wore an ascot, sipped a martini and looked exactly like George Sanders in All About Eve. He turned to Bud. "Actors are most amusing when they've just been hired, don't you think? They're like children with ice cream—sheer delirium. But when shooting begins—look out. They become grotesque jackals!"

Amidst much laughter, a housekeeper announced that dinner

*was served. As they drifted in, Whitehead prattled on about how
eight guests were the perfect number for a dinner party. Bud
stopped the maid on her way back to the kitchen.*

*"Excuse me, may I ask your name?" She was flustered.
"What is your name?"*

"Rosa."

*"You worked for Caitlin Wurtz, didn't you?" The woman
went pale and conversation in the room trailed off. "I know you.
Don't you remember—"*

*"I work for Señor Whitehead only," she said emphatically,
"only for him!" She hissed something under her breath like a*
bruja, *then broke away.*

*"You're right, of course," the director said to Bud as all un-
comfortably found their seats. "She* did *work for Caitlin Wurtz.
In fact, this is the house Caitlin leased while working on—what
was that thing with the monkey?"*

"Banana Republic," *answered the critic snidely.*

*Bud suddenly got paranoid and wished he hadn't broached the
name. He was still afraid Caitlin might appear out of the blue
and gum up the works. His curiosity prevailed, and since the
opportunity presented itself, he casually asked how she was. It
was Krizia Folb who broke the frigid silence.*

"Caitlin Wurtz doesn't exist."

Bud sat next to Jeanette at table and they caught up.

*Her political involvements hadn't curtailed her career as an
actress. Jeanette had recently starred in two pictures. They were
fifteen-minute* abstractos *and she wasn't sure they would ever be
seen by the public. She didn't care. It was the work itself that had
meaning, she said. That was something the Old System never
understood.*

*"I'd heard the revolution wouldn't be televised," Bud said.
"But I never dreamed it'd be shot and never released."*

*"I see you're still funny." She scrutinized him. "Will you come
with me—after dinner?"*

"Where?"

"Someplace to have a drink."

"What do you think, Bud?" the critic interrupted. *"It seems a certain opinionated executive feels that lately my reviews have pandered to the—what was the word you used, Krizia?"*

"Cretinous."

"Right. And all because I started using a thumbs-up, thumbs-down index in my reviews."

"And it's the language you use—it's crass and exploitive. The function of the critic is to enlighten, not demolish or entertain. You're becoming a certified ass."

The critic turned to Bud as if he were the only one in the room who finally counted.

"She faults my language, but the Committee's official word-lists are absurd! They use cacoethes *for 'mania,' and* persiflage *for 'banter.' They want Art to conform to Reason and the esthetics of the arcane."*

Dick Whitehead puffed on his cigar, expelling smoke. He gestured at Bud. *"I can see he won't let go until you at least give an opinion."*

The screenwriter wished to do right by his host. He frankly thought the critic insufferable but didn't want to be obvious about it.

"May I quote Cervantes?"

Between courses, during a visit to the loo, he'd refreshed himself from the Cliffs Notes which he carried surreptitiously in pocket. Bud cleared his throat.

" 'To eruct means to belch and people of taste substitute eructations for belchings, and though some may not understand certain terms, it isn't important—for time and use will render them intelligible; this is what we call enriching the language, and if the vulgar practice at it, its influence is great.' " He paused. *"Well, that's the gist of it anyway."*

"Bravissimo!" cried the studio head with delight, her wineglass shattering under the smack of a spoon. The humbled critic approached el Eunuco and bowed; then stood before Krizia and curtsied.

She looked through him, cold and inscrutable.

———

*Dick Whitehead thanked everyone for coming. He embraced
Bud and said they'd be getting together soon to discuss the script.*

*Outside, Jeanette told her husband she wanted to show Bud
downtown. He thought that was a good idea; he was tired and
would go home alone. Bud got a creepy feeling everything was
prearranged, and as they went to her car, the poet gave a rigid
little wave as if saluting his wife's first volley of adultery.*

*Jeanette sat quietly next to Bud in the backseat of the cab and
the silence felt luxurious. He recalled her compulsion to fill dead
air, how she always used to take his wordlessness as recrimina-
tion. Often before bed, she maundered about the Problem between men and women. She'd continue from the bowl, casually
ruminative, knees drawn up to her chest like a potty trainer, her
tiny feet on its rim. Bud invariably thought she was talking to
herself until she snapped, accusing him of being a sadist who
withheld speech, an antinurturer. That was part of the Problem—men didn't talk. Bud lamely defended himself and the
argument would escalate until he ran from her house. As soon
as he got home, the phone would ring and it would be Jeanette,
asking him to come back, to bed. By the time he returned, she
was calm and somehow fulfilled. Now only the lovemaking remained to mop up the night's excavation of the man-woman
Problem. Thus she felt herself in the vital, angry, religious waters
of life. Year after year their sex burned like a controlled fire. She
always came when Bud did, "like a boy," she used to say.*

"Krizia Folb is kind of interesting," he said.

"Very. Did you know her father was Joel Levitt?"

" 'Was'? But I saw him at TTA—"

"When?"

"This afternoon. I talked to him."

"I'd be careful about broadcasting that."

*They left the cab and walked a few dark, unfamiliar blocks.
She steered them through a parking lot and down a wobbly set
of stairs at the side of a building. A nondescript man at the door*

recognized her and nodded them in. As they entered, the roar of laughter practically knocked Bud on his ass.

The room was stifling and overcrowded. There was stickum on the floor and the nauseating smell of rancid butter. Jeanette pulled him to a seat.

The print was terrible, hundredth generation, full of jump cuts where the film had been crudely spliced and repaired. The color was badly faded and the actors' voices poorly dubbed, but it didn't seem to matter—much of the audience spoke the words aloud like midnight-show cultists.

On-screen, a man with a mustache was trying to change a baby's diaper. He was having a terrible time. The baby peed on him and the audience erupted.

When the film was over, everyone left in an orderly rush. Jeanette explained that such cabaret screenings—she called them clandestinos—were illegal and their locations changed each week. As they looked for a cab, they ran into the crapulous critic, with a long-haired boy in tow.

"I saw what you did, I know who you are," he said, a campy, sinister eyebrow raised. "Ever see it? William Castle, know him?" His eyes burned into Jeanette's. "Brilliant fucking direc-tor—and you can tell that fascist cunt Krizia I said so, okay?" He turned to his companion; the kid looked like some jet-lagged sex toy. "Do you know who these two are?" he asked him. "It's Mr. Eructation and his Dulcinea!"

"Go home," said Jeanette, "before you get into trouble."

The critic jumped forward and kissed Bud on the lips, groping his crotch.

"El Eunuco, my ass!"

"Get . . . out . . . of . . . here!" Jeanette shouted. She punched him in the stomach and he fell to the curb. As she hustled Bud away, he heard the critic coughing. His lungs sounded like dying engines.

She shook her head as they got in the car. "He's circling the drain."

They sat in her condominium, high above the Paseo. Jeanette and her husband maintained separate residences.

Bud flipped through a magazine while she mixed them drinks. She brought them over and put a glass in his hand. Suddenly she said: "You know, I still love you."

The screenwriter was doleful.

"The man I'm with is bright. He's good to me. He's a decent poet and he thinks I'm crazy. Remember how I always thought you were the crazy one?" She laughed, then grew serious, gathering herself up. "They say that true love doesn't beat you up like you're a redheaded stepkid—that's something else. That's lust and drama, not love. That's obsession. Real love, the kind that lasts, is just sort of humdrum. That's what they say at the Meetings. 'Give it time,' my Program friends keep telling me. 'Give it time, Jeanette. You don't want that other thing, it gets you into trouble.' "

She kissed him tenderly. He started to speak, but she covered his lips with her tiny fingers.

"When I heard you were . . . no longer with women, I—at first, I thought it was some kind of karma for the way you'd lived— your inability to commit. Justicia poética. *Do you remember what I told you once, about women? That you needed them too much? You kept leaving me for the fantasy of someone else— something else. You went from mother to mother. Why couldn't I see it as a valid exploration, a journey? All I could feel was my pain. And the pain of my life was killing me. You left a hundred times, but you always came back. Isn't that what counts? I know you loved me, that you love me still. I had to be strong and close the door. I lost track of you. Then, at Meetings, I began to hear stories of your struggles. Your Old System humiliation and your martyrdom. That the Business reviled you above all others because you wouldn't conform. Did you know you were an early hero of the movement? So brave. Alone and unsung." She caressed his leg. "Do you feel anything . . . for me? I mean, can you?"*

"Yes."

Jeanette kissed him again, with restrained passion; she would not embarrass el Eunuco by going any further. There were limits now, limits they'd always needed but never had. He'd come back and he was pure, devoid of lust or drama, and that exhilarated her. Jeanette began to cry. She used to cry bitterly, in terrible heaves, unable to catch her breath, falling to the floor and sobbing at the eternal injustice of the man-woman Problem. During a moratorium they'd go to the refrigerator and get a cold pack from the freezer for her swollen eyes, like his mother did when he was the Chinaman.

Bud cradled her. She nestled into him, her lips pushed up against his neck. He stroked her hair. Her face was emptied of anger, and Bud tasted the heart salt of her tears as they rolled into his mouth in affirmation. The world truly was a river and it gently stirred around them; they stood up to their hips near the muddied bank. She opened her eyes, undamming more water. A trembling globe hung a moment before schussing down the cheek.

"Marry me, Bud."

On his way to meet with Dick Whitehead about the script, Bud stopped at Bookz. He noticed a display of Shotgun placed prominently in the window and the clerk said it was selling briskly. Inside, he took a closer look: the novella was in two volumes, enclosed in a handsome cardboard slipcover. He shook them from their case. Shotgun's companion was none other than Beverly Hills Adjacent, Dolly's long-awaited opus ("The instant best-seller by the mother of el Eunuco!" read the blurb).

He flipped it open and was astonished to find crude comic book caricatures of himself—"sage hidalgo el Eunuco"—and the Doctor, alias el Médico. A closer scrutiny of the illustrations revealed the two were on a journey to a place called Zaragoza. Just what was going on?

"I heard you were a smash."

The veritable el Médico was at his elbow. Bud stared at him blankly.

"At dinner," said Brian. "Everyone was raving."

"Wish you could have been there."

"Make any progress with the girl?"

"Maybe."

Bud noticed he was carrying a copy of Quixote.

"I heard you gave a sensational little recital," said the Doctor and, so not to be outdone, blinked his heavy lids and spontaneously declaimed: " 'I know as certainly as the sun shines,' "—his voice loud enough to rouse a few customers and the dozing clerk—" 'that Durandante breathed his last in my arms, and after he was dead, I with my own individual hands took out his heart, which must certainly have weighed a couple of pounds.' "

Brian's outburst put Bud in mind of the autopsy report; as if reading his mind, the Doctor said he'd since made up for that indignity by his own incursions at TTA, darkly noting that if he sometimes lacked Montesino's postmortem finesse, his heart was needless in the right place.

"I need your help," Bud said, morbidly aware of his own organ beating within.

"Anything for el Eunuco."

"There's someone I'm looking for. Her name is Caitlin Wurtz."

The Doctor demurred. For an instant Bud feared his old friend.

"What do you want with her?"

"Research, actually. About some of the revisions I'm doing."

"She's considered a great criminal, you know."

"I know."

He didn't care what her crimes were. He just wanted to see her again.

"What's in it for me?" the Doctor asked coyly.

Bud knew he would help him now; the well of their friendship was deep. He stole the book from Brian's hands and held it like a template.

"I will give you an island," said Bud, all charm, pomp and ceremony. The Doctor acknowledged the allusion yet rolled his

eyes to show it was not enough. "Then I will give you a govern-
ment."

"Got more than I know what to do with."

"Then"—Bud paused dramatically—"I will give you Life."

Brian threw his head back, howled with laughter and promptly
dubbed himself ———, which meant roughly "he who was for-
merly a doctor." He was pleased and drew Bud closer; the screen-
writer felt an unworldly chill.

He said that Caitlin lived in Zaragoza, an unenlightened vil-
lage far outside the city; they must leave immediately, to arrive
before dark. Bud begged they proceed in a direction opposite the
route prophesied in Beverly Hills Adjacent, and his friend
laughingly assented. The Doctor wasn't superstitious.

Bud and Brian suffered many strange adventures as they prose-
cuted their journey to Zaragoza. It rained, yet the sun shone
steadily—"the devil was beating his wife."

Needless to say, the landscape was eerily unpredictable, its
dazzled cope full of myriad accipiters, goshawks and gyrfalcons.
They soon descried a dark thing snaking toward them: it was
Ramón, "he who was formerly a chauffeur," in a fancy Moorish
doublet, with two men in his coach, one of whom claimed to be
the Knight of the Charred Monstrance, the other a smug and
baseborn miscreant and proud of it—alternately Lou Gottlieb
and Derek the Playwright, his squire sui genius, granted. These
were accompanied by the celebrated Calabash, loping like a
sumpter mule under the weight of dull pannel and queer furni-
ture, an impertinent curiosity indeed, or at least, a curious imper-
tinence. Brian clung to his crupper and gave the ape the avaunt
while blood-feeding himself sundry opiates and analgesics of-
fered up by the hospitable (or was it hospital) former Guildsman.

On the road again, homeless persons asked for money and Bud
wondered as before if he was enchanted after all. The Doctor
reminded him even the enchanted beg alms to buy linen to wrap
the moieties of their hearts. Bud nodded at his companion's
wisdom as they approached their New Dulcinea's city.

After a time they reached the strange and florid suburb where Caitlin made her home. Built entirely from garish sets that became obsolete with the revolution, at a distance it looked glorious; closer, the city's bankruptcy rang like a clear bell tone.

There was an abandoned guard gate at the entrance. CHURU-BUSCO VILLAGE christened a wall in varying-style letters; rather, one could see the outline where the letters had been, amid a tangle of freshly painted graffiti.

Moving through this overwrought shantytown, he felt a kind of sunny fealty. When a boy, Bud went to school with children who acted in movies and television and he ached with envy. One of them showed up at the end of a school day in a fringy western costume, straight from the prime-time series he was shooting, and the teachers allowed it because the little star had made such a charming effort to fulfill his education. Most of the time the show biz kids were tutored on the set; Bud imagined them carrying lunchboxes stuffed with residual checks and fan letters and little packets of homework, freeze-dried, like astronaut food. He often dreamed of the studios as rich relatives who would one day come to claim him.

As they walked, Bud began to feel strange. The other feeling came, the ancient kundalini, his fingers expanding, turgid, teasing, painful, his neck hardening, his head a thousand-pound weight. Bud closed his eyes and concentrated, about to solve the riddle when it suddenly went away.

They found themselves at the blond wood door of a long, low stone house. Rosa greeted them with her round, blank face and led them through to the backyard. At the mouth of a trellised opening to a tiny arbor knelt a lady he didn't recognize. Brian informed him the woman was Caitlin Wurtz.

"But that's impossible!"

When Brian bade him look again, Bud was in fact astonished at the resemblance, though it seemed for a while a portmanteau visage, with many likenesses playing across her physiognomy. The Doctor assured him it was enchantment that made him oblivious of her true appearance at first and that the variegated *shadows he now saw fall across her face were the hems of such bewitchment being drawn away, their skirts brushing and burnishing her flesh. True to his clever friend's theory, Caitlin's face finally settled and remained aglow with itself as he remembered it, only more vivid.*

"Hello there!"

The empress stood. She'd been tending to a fish pond lined with stones.

"How the hell did you find me?"

"I'm not exactly sure."

"Well, you've *done very well for yourself. From what I hear.*"

"They're making our *script, if that's what you mean.*"

He didn't care if his friend heard this; he knew the Doctor's interests lay elsewhere.

"I keep dreaming I haven't fed you. . . . That I forgot something—forgot to love you!" *She laughed wantonly.* "I wake up screaming *from this dream, Rosa'll tell you!*"

Caitlin knelt again beside the palmy pond and slipped her hand into the water. A wind kicked up and blew the effervescent fronds. She turned to Brian and said, "Get the fuck out of my presence this instant, or I will positively take up this chair on which I sit and make immediate application to your skull."

She continued in a peculiar vein, accusing Brian of attempting to starve her with a bizarre diet of "a hundred confected wafers and a few slices of quinces." *Brian retreated, gesturing for Bud to join him in conference.*

"Your friend is in a dangerous state of mind. She needs hospitalization."

"Isn't there a Cedars?"

Brian sneered. "In the whole of Churubusco Village, there is not even one clínica. We'll have to take her to Peralvillo."

Bud asked for a few moments alone with her and Brian complied.

"Can you hear?" *Caitlin said to the air, as soon as Brian disappeared—like an amateur beginning a* "mad" *scene.* "Can you hear the wind shiver the trees?"

Bud felt the kundalini pressure on his neck.

"Well, I can." She hitched up her drawers and spit out an aside: "It's the sound of extra-fucking-legal executions."

"That message you left on my machine really spooked me. You sounded already dead."

"Yeah, well, it was a tough night all over."

"The newspaper said you bellowed when you were shot, they actually used that word. That really haunted me."

She fixed him with a look, taking his hand.

"They want me over at TTA, don't they? Ha. *I was always pointing out hospitals to you, remember?"*

"We want to get you someplace that can help."

Caitlin smiled weakly. He wasn't going to let her leave him again.

"You can stay with me. I have a room at the Château, with a minibar."

Rosa appeared with an old book-filled hatbox she'd prepared for the journey. Caitlin stood up, her eye proud and pretty.

"Today I will leave the village as I found it," she continued, "with the same streets, houses and roofs that belonged to it when I took possession. Though my intention was to make some wholesome regulations, I did not put my design in execution, because I was afraid they would not be observed. And a law neglected is the same thing as one that never was enacted."

Bud took her arm and they walked to the back door of the tatterdemalion set; Caitlin stopped dead, like going through would be bad voodoo. They went around. The Doctor caught sight of them, snuffed his cigarette like he was Secret Service and opened the car door in readiness. Her knees buckled and he helped the screenwriter get her in the backseat. Before Bud could object, the deft physician gave her an injection and she yelped.

"You know why they hate me?" She looked at Bud like a kid who'd watched a bully chase her cocker spaniel about a thousand blocks. "Because I was an Old System sellout. That's right. I was a Disney hack—a dried-up cunt, like your mother. Yes," she said, groggy and resolute, "that will be my defense. From out of

*the depths, big guy. Until then I remain forever yours, Wiggins.
Peerless and resplendent."*

They dropped her at TTA and Bud went back to his hotel. He
couldn't sleep. *He was feeling sexual again and masturbated to
the images of a committee-produced bondage film on TV, an*
abstracto *"from an essay by Georges Bataille." It was comprised
of two- and three-minute vignettes. A series of women sat on
couches or rugs and with casual persistence struggled to free
themselves to the accompaniment of* Sketches of Spain; *the slow,
shimmying, bug-eyed samba of these failed escape artists aroused
him. It was the isometrics of purgatory and Bud couldn't turn
away. He had several orgasms.*

He dared not tell anyone of his newfound virility, not even
Brian. Leave people their illusions.

Bud awakened disoriented in the middle of the night, the
sheets dank with perspiration. He threw on some clothes and,
avoiding the brightly lit lobby of the Château, left through the
garage entrance.

He walked a few blocks along the grassy concourse that lined
the park, then hailed a cab. The driver waited while he buzzed
the condo; no answer. Maybe Jeanette was at the clandestino.
He needed to see her, to confide, to hold her in his arms and show
his tears. When they reached a downtown area that looked
vaguely familiar, he bade the driver stop, gave him money and
bailed.

He strolled the deserted boulevard. What did he want with this
dank teatro? It was no longer Jeanette he sought. He wanted to
walk through the matinée doors and join his boyhood friends, to
leave this nightmarish place in a well-appointed Victorian-style
time machine with a soft leather cushion. He wanted to be Rod
Taylor and slay Morlocks. Orson Welles would sit in the back
as they shot into eternity—this time Bud would not turn back at
Mulholland.

He passed through a parking lot, finally reaching the deserted
building. As he fumbled with the lock, it fell away.

It was pitch-black and freezing inside, and everywhere was the sound of broken pipes. His hand slid along the wall and flicked a light switch that strobed out with a dull pop. The image of a Fun Fair Circe burned on the bulb of his eye and with each blood pulse branded its white features on the darkness: Jeanette.

"I knew you'd come."

Very film noir. The committee never did know just what to do with film noir. Someone hit him over the head.

Bud awakened in the bagnio, in not very catholic condition. He touched the top of his skull and cried out—it felt like a match was burning in his brain. He managed to roughly translate some phrases etched into the wall: "Would you send someone down to bring our luggage?" and "What awful weather!"

Could it really be possible he was in the basement of TTA, in the former cell of General Levitt himself? By what fantastic error had he been bludgeoned and detained? Was it the credit cards again? Or was it finally for bogus prescriptions and manslaughter that the bells had tolled? On top of everything, he had a painful erection. The cell door opened. It was Brian.

As usual, he was grimly jovial and apologized for being late— as if Bud had been waiting for him at a table in the Estudio commissary. The desperate screenwriter demanded an explanation and Brian became perfunctory.

"I don't think you knew what you were getting yourself into. They really wanted Caitlin."

"But what do I have to do with it? Besides, I helped bring her back." Brian smiled like a hangman. "Why would you do this to me!"

The Doctor snapped his fingers and sang à la Mel Tormé. " 'Why . . . don't . . . you . . . do what you do when you do what you do to me. . . . ' "

"I'm el Eunuco! I have a film in preproduction!"

Bud felt like an actor with lousy lines—he didn't believe his own reading for a minute. What else could he do? The Doctor began a cursory physical examination of his charge.

"What were you doing down at the clandestino anyway?"

"I was looking for Jeanette. What difference does it make? You sold me out!"

The Doctor sneered, unplugging his stethoscope.

"It was Jeanette who got you here, don't you get it? She was using you! All she wanted was to play Milly Theale in Broken Wings! She made a deal with the committee. If she delivered you, they'd give her the part."

Bud fainted to the floor. He felt a savage pulse in his head and saw dirty, mischievous protozoan aftertrails swishing on the windshield of his vision. A guard appeared at the door with two curates; the Doctor pronounced them ineptly named, for they "far from cure." He shooed them away, then bent over and handed Bud some big green pills.

"It's the only way I can help you now."

"Do they work?"

"I'm living proof—they're the kind that finished me off."

Bud gathered spit in his mouth the way he did when they made their pharmacy rounds. He swallowed them down.

Suddenly the cell collapsed, momentarily sandwiching him between the bars of opposing walls; then the unmoored cage was righted and set on the shoulders of the Doctor and his subalterns. In such a way was Bud borne toward the conference room. As the prisoner surveyed the dreary crusade from his tilting vantage, he considered a word fast, until justice was done—he would not write, nor would he speak. He was yanked from his resolve by the sharp pesticide smell of the corridor. The terrified screenwriter clutched his Cliffs Notes in earnest.

As they carried him from the elevator toward the conference room, Bud heard a woman cry out. One of the men's Arab looks made him certain it was the Madwoman of Churubusco.

"Quisiera visitar la iglesia," said a voice, followed by a rude cascade of laughter.

The snickering cortege set down their burden as the bellowing began. The men walked a few yards and peered at the spectacle on the other side of the wall, then came back for Bud so he could *have a better view. The cage was brought round the corner and from there the screenwriter beheld what was Caitlin Wurtz.*

The distaff was suspended by ropes and pulleys over a bronze pyramid, whose sides were run down with all manner of slimy fluids; by artful winching, the body could be made to hover exquisitely over the point or bear down on it with dead weight. The legs, no longer legs as such but rather a weave of splintered pulp, were unconscionably dislocated at the pelvis and braided about the spokes of an old wooden wheel. The breasts and stomach had been burned and flailed to sternum and bone. From an ingredient in the air, Bud presumed the scourge's hemp was soaked in salt and sulfurous water.

Someone was in the process of disentangling the wheel for better trespass to her cervix. For the operation to come, a pear-shaped mechanical device was being unveiled with not a little interest in one corner, while a Manchegan boy heated up a poignard in a brazier in the other.

In this section of the dungeon, a woodcutter carved a sign to hang from the victim's neck, reading MULIER TACEAT IN ECCLESIA. A curate kindly translated the meaning for Bud ("Let the woman be silent in church"), and while admiring the craftman's assiduity, Bud couldn't help wonder if the hard necklace could be finished in time to meet with the poor woman's approbation.

Caitlin was hoisted off the point now and well tended to as they hassled with the wheel—indeed, to an outsider, Bud was certain it would seem the solemn technicians were making heroic measures to right a heinous wrong. She was being freed all right, but only in the most mystical, penultimate sense.

The Doctor balanced on a ladder at akin height to her head, which was encased in a hideous brank with a spiky bit on its inside that gagged and mutilated her. Every few minutes the bit was unlocked and slid out like a broken-down drill so the apostate could confess to the Inquisitor; because of its extreme involvement with root tongue and dentures, such debridement was performed with a wildly facetious caution.

The Doctor was at the peak of his surgical expertise and its application. By his medicinal ministrations (alas, Bud felt the warming consolation of the fat green pills), Caitlin was conscious, and desirous of assuaging her tormentors.

At last, the pitiful woman found an answer to their inquiry and her words were relayed to the witness: I recant. Sadly a curate took this to mean "I can't, again," or "again, I can't," each one or both together being insufficient tribute and a sign of fatal stubbornness; even Bud admitted a simple Yes would have satisfied the most barbarous of the lot, and turned the tide.

Without segue, Bud Wiggins found himself in the conference room, strapped down before the great table. A voice boomed from behind: "What is your name?"

Lights shone in his eyes, and when he opened them, he could make out the hard, golden hat like a halo on the head of the Inquisitor.

"Bud Wiggins."

"And your occupation?"

"Writer."

"You're no writer!" he hollered back.

"I'm a screenwriter," he said proudly. His situation was frankly "political" and Bud resolved to keep his dignity, in extremis. He didn't want to shame himself in front of any future human rights commissions.

The Inquisitor bent to his ear and whispered: "Have you written anything I would know?"

Before he could answer, the prisoner was neatly plunged backward into the large tank that had doubled earlier as a kind of fishless aquarium filled with lily pads and bunches of coral. Bud's head bucked against a heavy pair of hands that barely let him surface before forcing him down again, mightily. He thought of all the unbreathing little boys he'd ever read about in the paper, the ones revived after forty-five minutes under the ice, saved by a reflex. He caught sight of a blighted angelfish stuck in a decorative, branchy crown and wished it were dusk on the playground and he was on his way to a book-stealing rendezvous with Brian; he heard the faraway sounds of airplanes in Macon

*and felt the languor of his boyhood days; he smelled honeysuckle
and Lysol and the polished coolness of Trudy's checkerboard
floors. He remembered the impossibility of drowning as they
raised him out.*

"Do you know why you are here?"

*He noticed the thick wrists, the hairy, manly arms and mascu-
line watch. He vomited water and prayed for the arrival of the
pediatrician. He had an erection and needed to urinate; the
Inquisitor roughly grabbed it and Bud's "inner child" wanted
to die.*

*"Who the fuck are you kidding, cocksucker! Do you know
what this is? You're supposed to be el Eunuco! El Eunuco don't
walk around with* this *in his fucking drawers! The committee
invokes* force majeure*!"*

*Brian's sudden appearance was felicitous, as it interrupted the
dousing. He held a tube of papyrus. Without prompting, Bud
asked the Doctor if what was happening was real and was told
the events "partook both of truth and illusion." He unfurled the
scroll, handing Bud a pen to sign with. The confession began:*
Puesto ya el pie en el estribo, con las ansias de la muerte, gran
Señor, esta te escribo. . . .

*"Do you know why you're here?" the Doctor asked. His smil-
ing face looked like the Mask of Garuda.*

"Where? Where am I?"

"Why, Peralvillo!"

*Bud was in the water again. Something was in there with him,
wiry and translucent, an eel's rugged tentacle. His whole body
was submerged and this time his father held him down, yes,
Morris was going to finish the job, Moe Wiggins with his smallish,
well-tanned fingers, the golden band and bulgy bikini bottom.
. . . Bud felt a familiar pressure on his neck as he tried to surface,
it was the kundalini, he sensed eyeless spectators somewhere off
camera, fixed, implacable, heard the ringing of the dead holy
vastness and the wind beating down on the swollen palms. Images of flesh in tiny squares, tattooed and waffled, cold like the
Doctor's cheek; then a slim, clear placental thing dancing before*

him, his bony fingers around it, pulling it now like a vine. Bud knew this was an enemy that could at last be vanquished, saw the stem was coming from his head and pulled it, then surfaced, lungs blistered, in a room of blinding light, bellowing, the air invaded his chest and he pulled the tube from his nose as a nurse rushed up and the screenwriter shoved her away and she ran for the Inquisitor. A mushy bag of clear fluid dripped into another eel, this one ending in the crook of his arm. Blood backed up to the bag. What had they done to him?

"Mr. Wiggins? Can you understand me?"

He thought of his mother. Dolly would give him a ride to Zaragoza.

"I'm Dr. Saperstein. You are going to be all right. You were in a coma," the man continued. "You were in a coma for four days. You are in Los Angeles, at Cedars-Sinai Hospital, and you're being well taken care of. Do you understand? You are going to be all right."

The assurances were intense and charismatic, signifying Bud was "out of the woods." The young doctor clearly relished the opportunity for such dramatic declarations; it was like the movies. Bud started to sob. The nurse fixing the bag gazed at him like he was a swaddled child, the sole survivor of an orphanage fire. She paused to pat his shoulder. The doctor told her to leave the nasal tube out, Mr. Wiggins would be fine. Then Bud laughed out of nowhere, the sudden hysteria embarrassing him. The physician stroked his forehead.

"Go ahead. It's all right." *Cry a little.*

Bud was starving and pointed to his mouth. The nurse got him some 7-Up. She held the glass and the straw; just a tiny sip irrigated him. He was propped on pillows yet felt himself falling. Something stuck his side and he reached under the sheet. It was a vomit basin, clean, cold and unused, shard of the Inquisitor's cap. He meditated on its coolness and passed out.

ʍʍ

A week later Bud was released. He returned to his apartment with a kind of clammy apprehension, as if setting foot there would awaken him from a final dream and he would realize he was dead. The place was spotless. Dolly had been through it with a cleaning crew. There was even a vase of flowers beside the bed.

Some details of the hallucination trickled back and he thought of writing a memoir of his illness and submitting it to *Esquire* or *Harper's.* That sort of chronicle was popular lately. He was bored and a little lonely and too weak to do much else than watch the soaps. Weissen called a few times from Mexico City. He felt guilty about Bud's trouble and offered to send money.

The screenwriter went through his phone book, dialing numbers. He tried Sunya, a Hindu girl he met a few years ago during a breakup with Jeanette. She was the one who told him about the kundalini.

Sunya was around twenty-two when they first dated, having lived in the States since a teen. Her English was faultless, except for an occasional glitch—once, she asked if an *eyesore* was a prehistoric bird. She was droll, with a sweet, jaunty walk. Savvy, sensuous and a little aloof, her eyes rolled deep back in her head when they made love.

She was surprised to hear from him and impressed by his Mexican ordeal. It was her day off and she insisted on bringing over some Indian food that he couldn't eat. She looked radiant and extradimensional and Bud knew he was of the living again. He'd left the door ajar, so to be in bed when she entered—he wanted to play wounded cowboy to the hilt. When she left, he called her his sacred *wow* and she laughed melodiously.

A few days later she came after work with some wine and CDs. Bud got drunk quickly. When he realized he had a hard-on, he laughed to himself—by definition of *la Clínica*'s hellish attorneys, he was in breach. He was getting his sense of humor back and that felt good. Sunya glanced at the poky crotch of his pajamas. She put down her glass, looked again and said, "We'll have to take care of that."

When she came out of the bathroom, she was naked. He tried to be on top but Sunya forced him back with a smile; then the smile went away as she worked. She couldn't get enough of his lips, his teeth, his tongue. He thought of Caitlin's ruined mouth in the metal brank, then pushed the thought away.

It was nearly midnight and he watched her get dressed.

"Why did we split up?" she asked, as if trying to remember the capital of a country.

He had often wondered but didn't know the answer. They'd been seeing each other a few months when he told Sunya he loved her. The next night they went to dinner and barely talked. It was over. He went back to Jeanette.

"It could have been some cultural weirdness," he said. "Or the age difference."

Suddenly she nodded her head, remembering everything.

"I know why. I know why we broke up."

"Why?"

"You don't want to hear it."

She gathered her bag and brushed her hair.

"But I do. I want to know."

"Drop it, Bud. I don't know what I thought. It's not even the reason."

"Oh, come on. Tell me."

She was getting irritated. Sonya had a short fuse; maybe that was why they broke up.

"Since you're so *demanding*," she said, giving the word an English lilt, "I'll tell you."

She put the brush in her purse and readied to go.

"It was because you stunk." Bud didn't understand. Was it one of her malaprops? "Your breath—it's not bad now, but it used to smell like puke."

He pretended he was Tristan, his poisoned mouth on fire with sores that reeked. What would this ignorant Hindu know of

Tristan's heroism? When she left, Bud would dream of throwing balls against the mortuary on warm-winded evenings; he would wait for Jimmy Willow to heal his wounds with a towel-shrouded kiss.

"You never said anything."

"I know. It was just too . . . *bee-zarre.* Maybe you were going through something physical—that's probably why you got so sick when you were in Mexico. You were susceptible, your immunological system isn't *up to par.*" She enunciated the last few words with a smiling, liverish condescension for the triteness of American idiom. She was villainous and insufferable and he wished her burned on a bier by Sikhs and Muslims. "It's ridiculous, I know it wasn't the only reason. Anyway, it's not like we were *married.*" She narrowed her eyes in recollection. "Sometimes at night you used to sweat. I'd smell the sheets. I mean—really foul."

Sunya laughed, like she'd made a joke. Bud was nonplussed. Was it real, what she was saying? She was a strange girl, dysfunctional as any. He wrote it all off to the vagaries of youth and Immigration.

"I'll call," she said.

"See you."

"We'll go to a movie. You should get out of the house."

She kissed him on his sewer mouth and left.

Weissen called from Mexico to say he was flying directly to Toronto. *Big Tiny Little* was wrapped.

"Listen, would you do me a favor? I bought this leather coat at Fred Segal and I left it at the Château. They're holding it for me, but I'm worried someone's gonna rip it off. Can you pick it up and keep it at your place? I'll be back in L.A. in two weeks."

"Yeah."

"Are you sure?"

"I'm sure."

"I mean, are you getting around? Are you able to drive?"

"What am I, Ron Kovic? Jesus."

"Because if you can't, it's not a problem. I'll just leave it there until I'm back."

"Jake, it's not a problem."

The next morning Bud strolled to the Château. As he approached the front desk, he recognized Jeanette. She was talking to the desk clerk and looked pissed.

"Well, can you at least tell me how I can get in touch with him? He stays here all the time. There must be a forwarding address."

"I'm sorry," said the pretentious clerk. "Even if I had that information, I couldn't give it out."

"*Great.*"

She turned to go and saw Bud.

"What are *you* doing here!" she said, like he was crashing a private club.

"I thought you were in Italy."

"Why'd you think that?"

"You said you were moving there."

"I said that?" Her eyes twinkled mischievously. "I say lots of things, haven't you noticed?"

"I noticed."

"How are you?"

"Great."

"Living here at the Château?" she asked facetiously.

"Picking up something for a friend."

"You look thin."

"I was sick. What are you up to?"

"I'm *great.* I'm just having one of those days. I'm trying to reach this jerky writer, you might actually know him, Jake Weissen, do you?" Bud shook his head. "He's fairly well known. Anyway, I had an idea for a children's television show—a special. A kind of international show, with kids from all different countries? So I gave him a treatment and he never gave it back. It was my only copy and I'm really annoyed."

"Don't you have notes for it?"

"That's not even the issue—the guy was supposed to be back from Mexico by now. There's a little thing called 'giving your word.' I'll get it back. What a *turkey.*"

It always gave him the willies when she used that word; it was something out of *Hee Haw* and Archie Bunker. How the hell had he ever loved her anyway?

"Where'd you meet him?"

"At a party for Joan Krause. Oh, I'll be able to track him down, it's just the thing of it. You spend a few hours with someone who expresses interest in your work, they promise to read it—I mean, I don't treat people like that. Do you?"

Jeanette suddenly realized she'd been standing there venting her spleen, yakking about being stood up; with a spasm of self-consciousness, she abruptly shook the whole matter off.

"So how are you? What have you been up to?"

"The usual. Working on projects."

"You were sick?"

"Yeah. I went to Mexico."

"Turista, huh."

"Yeah. It wasn't pretty."

"Still go to Meetings?"

"When I have the time." He knew she'd ask. "It's hard, though."

"I know what you mean. I got kind of burned out myself."

"Been acting?"

"A few plays. I've been writing, too—"

"The TV thing."

"And a script. It's *torturous*. I don't see how you've done it all these years. If anything ever made me want to drink again . . ."

"I know what you mean. Have you eaten? I mean, do you want to go to lunch?"

"No, thanks, Bud. I have this stupid audition—a commercial. It's a callback."

"Well," he said, "good to see you."

With a fake smile, Jeanette said, "Take care of yourself" and whisked out of the lobby.

wwv

For the next few months Bud suffered a plague of hemorrhoids and constipation as his bowels struggled to rebuild. He also battled a fear of tainted foods that reached phobic proportions and a subtler, more menacing dread of ingestion itself. His doctor said this was relatively normal, considering what he'd been through.

The good news was that before he went to Mexico, his old shrink gave him the name of a criminal lawyer and they finally connected. The screenwriter filled him in on Brian's overdose and the hidden multitude of incriminating prescriptions, then asked point-blank if he was culpable. The attorney was blasé. No one gave a hoot about those prescriptions, he said, "they had their body," the case was closed. The whole *what's done is done* decree sounded a little frontiersy. Still, Bud had to figure the attorney knew what he was talking about—the shrink wouldn't refer him to a flake, she was too "professional." The guy was very smooth; Tony Cicero couldn't have handled it better.

When he hung up the phone, Bud picked up the *Cliffs Notes* and read for a while before a jagged sleeplessness overtook him. Like Quixote, he "could not close an eye, but, on the contrary, rambled in his imagination through a thousand different scenes." He tried lulling himself with the ocean fantasy but it didn't work anymore, so he imagined himself shut up within a tree trunk during a torrential downpour. He floated wistfully from that humid place, fickle and morose. After a few half-hearted peregrinations, Bud settled for the lair of a cool concrete bunker buried in dead acreage, brushy unincorporated land north of the city.

His eyes grew heavy as the secret washed up. When he was ten, the Bakers—the next-door neighbors Dolly called the immigrants—had a Sunday pool party. Morris sat like a pasha, drinking Drambuie from a floating chaise longue. Bud decided to swim beneath his father's chair and surface on the other side. He never could open his eyes underwater, but it was a short haul, he'd "sonar" it out. So the young screenwriter dived, eyes closed, and came up short, right under the floating body. He flailed, knowing his father couldn't feel his swatting fists, retarded by the water. When he thought he would drown, Bud opened his eyes and saw the white, hairy flesh herniating through the plastic braiding of the chair. He tried to overturn Morris with his head, butting him like a goat, and this was the pressure on the neck, the kundalini. He seemed to black out in the water, a dying Huck Finn, then popped up like a buoy; Moe Wiggins had left the watery perch to freshen his drink. No one ever knew his terror.

Bud rose from bed and went to the desk to jot down his deliverance. He couldn't help but laugh—it was just like the original idea he had for Weissen, *Sigmund Freud's Psychopathology of Everyday Life!* That clinched it. He would use his own experience, a perfect back story for the parody. He'd need to beef it up a little, make it that the floating father has a heart attack and dies, unbeknownst to the partygoers. The boy's stuck below, gets confused, somehow thinks he's responsible, his flailing panic somehow *killed* him. Or something. Stick the kid's mother in the pool somewhere to make it oedipal. All that in flashback. Meanwhile, the kid's grown up to be a concert pianist who suffers from stage fright. Freezes in the middle of a performance. Bud saw a movie like that once, only the pianist was a woman. There was an analyst and the whole bit; maybe he'd track it down and use it as a "bible."

The sleepy archivist returned to bed. He never finished *Don Quixote de la Mancha,* though he did linger over the *Cliffs Notes*[1] to the classic, which inspired him to sketch the outline

[1] If it seems improbable Bud's dream drew so extensively from a work it was reported he'd scarcely begun to digest, suffice it to say his earlier impatience

of a "sudden fiction" for *Granta* about a suicidal honors student who jumps from a Pacific Palisades bluff. (He'd call the story "Cliff Notes"; he wondered if calling the protagonist Cliff was pushing it.)

He was skimming the original text, when "Peralvillo" caught his eye—a place prisoners were brought to trial "after execution." He seized for a moment the fading sights, sounds and smells of his visit to that domain. Then they were gone.

Bud closed his eyes and the concrete bunker called to him. A gentle wind wafted him into the desert air, floating high above the desolation of cities, then down through smoky stars to the terminus of a cold stone grave, sheltering and simple.

In this reverie he was finally able to drift to a sound and dreamless sleep. When he awakened, he felt sane as the don himself at journey's end; in fact, he couldn't remember having ever slept so well.[2]

---

and poor power of concentration often bade him skip forward, and in this manner he covered as much ground as the famous steed *Clavileño Aligero*, or Wooden Peg the Winged. He was duly surprised at the impressive thoroughness of the *Cliffs Notes* and made much use of them, navigating between précis and text without orthodoxy. His feverish mind, often showing more ambition than his will, cleverly arranged the excerpted orphans into a stew it is hoped was palatable to the general reader. It may be also noted while his knowledge of Spanish was nil, Mr. Wiggins developed a fascination with tourist's phrase books (and had an old familiarity with one of Dolly's *Your Spanish Maid* pamphlets besides) that served him well.

[2]It can be noted that several weeks later Bud happened to pull a volume of Genet from the shelf and skip, in his fashion, to the last several pages, which bespoke of "prison festivals." He read the following passage: "In the second volume of this *Journal,* which will be called *Morals Charge,* I intend to report, describe and comment upon the festivals of an inner prison that I discover within me after going through the region of myself which I have called Spain." At this country's evocation, he hurled the book across the room, shattering a vase, the flying shards of which nearly demolished a windowpane. Such was his impulse, and a salutary one, for it broke his creative doldrums as well; he began forthwith on the famous psychoanalytic saga of which this next history will treat.

5. Mothering Heights

And . . . *action!*"

Bud was half awake and thought he was dreaming. He went to the window and drew open the curtain; they were shooting a movie right in front of his building. The disgruntled cameraman surfaced from the lens and pointed at Bud. The director—he assumed it was the director—said, "Okay, we have to cut." A few others tilted their heads in Bud's direction and one of the men broke into a jog. Moments later the screenwriter heard a knock at his door.

"Hi! How you doin' today?"

"All right."

"Great. My name's Mark. We're making a movie outside your building here. Could I ask you to keep the curtains closed for the next few hours?"

"Sure."

"That'd really help us out, sir. Hope it's not too much of an inconvenience—your window's kind of in the shot."

The fellow had the courtly "location" demeanor down pat.
He saw right away Bud wasn't some asshole he'd have to pay
off.

"No problem. I'm in the Business myself."

"What part?"

"I'm a writer."

"Really? We could use you down there." He laughed. "Oh,
and would you mind keeping the windows closed? In case your
phone rings, or something. For sound."

"Not at all."

"Thanks again, sir. You're welcome to come and have a look
if you like."

Bud lay down on the bed again.

"Rolling!"

"Speed!"

"And . . . *action.*"

He showered and left the apartment. A PA stationed at the
front entrance nervously motioned for Bud to be quiet, then led
him through as soon as "We're cutting" came over the walkie-
talkies.

He sniffed around a bit and watched the goings-on. It was a
love story for cable. The stars were a couple of TV actors, and
that was enough to make Bud lose interest. He was about to
leave when he noticed the name stitched on the director's chair:
Witold Kracz.

Kracz was a poet, critic and art school grad who was already
a famous director of the "international" theater when he made
the jump to film. He shot his festival favorites in Europe, on a
shoestring. A few years ago, someone from a big studio "classics" division managed to woo him to the States, where he had
since languished. Bud recalled a recent interview with Kracz in
Film Quarterly. The director said his original intent was to
come to America and "shoot bigger game," but he was unable
to find a project his benefactors would approve. With the development money he'd received, Kracz bemoaned, he could have
made three films already. The interviewer asked why he didn't

return to Europe and resume his career, and Kracz said he was tired of all that. Besides, he had four ex-wives and seven children to support. For now he was simply taking "the famous advice of Sam Peckinpah": be a good whore and go where you're kicked. From the looks of things he'd been kicked pretty hard.

Bud got tired of waiting for the director to emerge from his trailer. He had an important meeting at the studio and didn't want to be late.

Jake Weissen knew a former Paramount production head who'd recently set up shop as a producer—one of those on-the-lot first-look sweetheart deals that guaranteed heavy development monies and lavish offices, for a few years anyway. Weissen also happened to know Andy Mayerling, the producer's new creative exec. Mayerling was once the requisite abstruse film theorist for a leftist art rag in Toronto. Weissen said that the former pundit was currently meeting with writers for a project called "The Worst Movie Ever Made." At first Bud thought he was kidding, then noticed Weissen's rigid, deadpan expression—the look he always got when he smelled "bread."

The screenwriter arrived early and a young man brought him cappuccino with a black linen napkin. He was hoping the meeting would go well; Weissen had given him another five thousand and he was starting to feel the pressure. On top of it all, his sugar daddy was leaving for Germany soon to work on a picture—another opportunity, no doubt, for Bud to explore "abandonment issues." Weissen would be gone for months.

Bud was ushered to a plush, well-lit office and the executive stood to greet him. Andy Mayerling was a genial, bearded intellectual who'd decorated one of his walls with a large *Taxi zum Klo* poster, as if in homage to an old uncoopted self. There was an enormous Dreyer and the usual Hitchcock posters, smaller and in French. Mayerling seemed slightly abashed by his own lavish setup.

"So how long you known Jake?"

"Not too," Bud said. "We're working on some projects together."

"A crazy-man. *Very* talented. You were down in Mexico, right?"

"Right."

"*Big Tiny Little*—word is, Jake saved the picture. It's *amazing.* I've seen dailies, on cassette."

"The sets were great."

"Jake said you got sick down there."

"Yeah. It was a little hairy. Flew me back to Cedars."

"Thank God for Cedars. Jesus. That's the thing that always terrifies me—getting sick in some third world hellhole. It's so Paul Bowles. Anyhow, let me tell you about 'The Worst Movie Ever Made.' It's kind of an *Animal House* at film school."

"I love it."

"Yeah, I think it's a cute idea. If it's done in an unconventional way."

"You could do it half Lubitsch, half Almodóvar."

"That's *wonderful!*"

"I mean, have fun with it—lots of *homages.*"

Bud realized he'd pronounced the *s* and hoped Mayerling didn't pick up on it.

"Did you see *The Freshman,* Bud?"

"I really liked it."

"I had problems with the *movie*—"

"Everyone did."

"Brando was unbelievable."

"Unbelievable. The ending was like Chaplin."

"But the film school professor. Remember the guy that played the professor?"

"Hilarious."

"What was his name, why can't I remember his name? Do you remember how mean and pretentious he was?"

"He was hilarious."

"That's kind of the spirit of what we want. *Animal House,* but *smart."*

They commenced a little highbrow chat about Film, and Mayerling really came alive. Bud even talked about his Freudian spoof and the executive pulled Sartre's *Freud Scenario* out of a briefcase with a whimsical flourish—he'd just bought it at Bookz.

The meeting lasted a full hour. Mayerling sent along his regards to their mutual friend and said he'd be in touch. Bud told him his contact was the attorney Don Bloom.

On the way home Bud stopped at the bookstore; he wanted a closer look at *The Freud Scenario.* The owner asked if he'd heard from Derek and the screenwriter shook his head.

"Did you know he got married?"

"No, I didn't," Bud said.

"He married his agent. That's got to be a first. Why would someone marry their agent?"

"To force them to return your phone calls."

"That's pretty funny, Wiggins. I like that. That's very funny. Say, we sold a few more copies of *Shotgun."*

"That's great."

"What are you working on now?"

"Couple things. I might be doing a script about a film school."

"Comedy?"

"Yeah, but more like a thirties farce."

"You know what would *really* be funny? You should do it like *Animal House.* Wouldn't that be funny?"

₩₩₩

When Weissen left the country, Bud started gaining weight. He was afraid exercise might cause a relapse. Instead of working out, he compulsively checked muscle tone each day by pinching his arms. They were turning to mush.

His dreams became prolific, always the sign of oncoming depression. Maybe it was hereditary. Morris used to get depressed and once even got shock treatment. When they brought him home, he was disoriented for days. That was a year or so before the end.

The last office his father had was near their apartment on Rexford Drive, on Wilshire, between Frascati's and the old Beverly Theater. There was a building farther down—closer to Doheny—called CEIR, named after some company, big gold block letters on its upper corner. It had one of those anonymous third-floor employee snack shops the kids from junior high somehow discovered. The place became a hangout. One day after lunch at the Luau, Morris Wiggins walked over to CEIR, went up to the gravelly roof and stood on the ledge. The guard found him there and called the police. The cops drove him home.

Another time, right around his bar mitzvah, Bud trailed him to the same building. Morris was on his way into the lobby when Bud shouted after him. His father smiled. He took the boy's hand and walked him home. It was the only time he could remember Morris taking his hand. By then it was getting dark and they looked over the roofs of the houses and saw a tiny, remote-controlled hot-air balloon, a short-lived neighborhood fad begun by hobbyist Don Bloom. Morris talked about going away together. He liked to plan trips, the antidote to all those mother and son dance trophies accumulating in the closet. They'd take a cross-country train, he said, one of the *Zephyr*s, with big private bathrooms and glass-dome viewing cars and Pullmans and Negro porters. The *Zephyr* took two routes, one north, one south. They'd go to New York through Canada, stopping in Quebec to see the virid Plains of Abraham, where Bud would later go to school one summer; ethereally, they would waft above the home of the screenwriter's future impotence. On the way to Manhattan, Morris would teach his son about living in the City of Immigrants. He would scrupulously show Bud the sights, treating him to manicures and Circle Lines and horse carriages, concerts in the park and sedan tours of Harlem and museums filled with art Moe didn't understand because *your father was a stupid man.* He would stay in New York City and send Bud home on the southern route, the one that went through New Orleans. Bud would have a private sleeper, within which to read the short stories of Capote. A fag reading a fag, Morris would mutter, but that was later, and he was drunk.

His father spoke of renting an enormous boat with full crew. They'd sail the Indies, the Indie-Prods, the two of them, captains courageous. Would he like that?—Moe wanted to know. Because Morris Wiggins was just about ready to cancel everything, say *Up yours* to the world, and do a little voyaging, a little globe-trotting with the Only Son. They communed like this, walking home from CEIR, home from the ledge, as the wind stirred around them and the young Dr. Brian passed by on his ten-speed, just days away from watching his little sister die in the street in front of his own house. They passed the Cadillacs and Jaguars in their Wilshire showcase windows and Bud felt his father's finger with the heavy wedding ring, then clutched the whole hand again unabashedly as the sidewalk wind made a riot of leaves and little mysteries. Dolly waited for them to come home.

Bud lay there on the bed thinking some more about the ledge, worrying that his father had doomed him to a life of grandiosity and depression. He reflected on those first, blushing years of therapy, when he used to bring a copious diary of dreams to Dr. Jurgen, the white-haired analyst prick. The nascent scenarist would sit in the waiting room with his sad, carefully typed dadaist sheaves, imagining they were worthy of the *Paris Review.* (Jurgen looked them over and said, *"To-hu-vo-hu,"* huffing and puffing like a roguish shaman. "Do you know what is *tohuvohu*? It is the Yiddish word for 'chaos.' ") He didn't have the patience to write his dreams down anymore. He seemed to have lost the facility. Bud felt inept.

Now there was no letup. He stumbled into more mazes until the once-pleasant pastime become a burden. Each night Bud dreamed the world, and its next-day inventory—toothbrush, nod of the head, quality of light upon a shelf—was a déjà vu, redeemed from the nocturnal catalog. At first the index filled a kind of mundane prospectus: things to do and things should have done (*"Should,"* his therapist used to say, "is not a word for grown-ups"). Then the landscape became brazenly Freudian, with the requisite *tohuvohu* thrown in, for laughs. Bud, carrying Dolly's purse through Hoffmann-Dougherty's, through Bonwit's and Bullock's, Neiman's and Robinson's, the dead escalator fields of Haggerty's, Ohrbach's and Seibu. Honoring his father at the Directors Guild—Morris flown in from "Son City" in a coffin with a cutaway head, for display—a liar, lying in state, intestate. No will ("to live," someone says) and the same someone says, *I don't love you anymore,* and suddenly it's bear-washing day: dangerous fabulous bears with antlers. Dr. Brian diagnosed a sleeper's "facial coma," blistery cell blocks and skittish blacks, fourth-dimension talk shows and waves of taffy and quartz rolling under sound stages. Flat branches and skidding motors, a bougainvillea'd centenary of rapes and romances. . . .

Bud began dreaming remorsefully of Jeanette. He could never remember the details. Sometimes Derek and Genie were there; the announcement of their marriage had probably set him off. Within the dream he heard a moan that grew until it rattled his insides and burst from his throat. He woke up howling and blanched at the inhuman sound, a caterwaul, a threadbare keening, a coronach from a rank and homely place. He thought of buying one of those voice-activated recorders so he could capture the wail (something the Doctor might have done) but didn't, because his voice in this instance was damning. It disgraced him. Now, waking up to a testy, alien howl, he was embarrassed again and a little scared because there was something uncontrollable below it, something rumbling the earth. Suddenly he knew the source of his mortal agitation: he'd let Jeanette get away and she was gone forever.

Bud let this notion sit for a week or so. He didn't want to make any sudden moves. Considering the past, the idea of getting her back seemed fantastic, almost revolutionary. He had traveled full circle; the utter impossibility of attaining his love made it romantic again. He thought of Derek. Perhaps Bud had underestimated him. The former clerk had actually married and thus had been ennobled. Now it was Bud's turn. Life was a great cotillion: on one side of the ballroom were the stalwart, stubby-fingered, cliquish little boys with their musky smells and fears of darkness—on the other, the mystical white-gloved girls like fields of flowers. He saw Derek advance and select, and the other boys fall in, Bud among them. Jeanette waited at the silver punch bowl to be chosen.

He thought about his revolutionary idea a few times each day and felt his physical strength return. Maybe the inspiration was nothing but caprice. Whatever it was, the world was fresh and bountiful, full of reason. He went to Bookz and got a copy of *Tristan and Iseult.* That was one of Jeanette's favorites. They used to read aloud from it at night. She loved *Ondine* and *The Little Mermaid* and *The Prophet*—anything about romantic love.

Bud brought the thin book home and read it in one sitting. He felt reclaimed. The oft-invoked Freudian parody looked tired and sophomoric—he'd do an "impossible" love story instead. Bud was certain he wanted Jeanette back, yet the whole enterprise was so astonishingly bold that he wasn't quite ready to admit it. He approached it sidelong, telling himself the "impossible" love story script would be a recovery tool, a welcome back to the world and nothing more. Still, he knew he'd be writing the script for *her* and that the work itself would be a courtship. If he did his job right (joining the lovers at the end of their torturous journey), Jeanette would find his creation an irresistible offering. Until she was his again, Bud's pain would be transmuted into Art and thus be bearable. The notion was foolproof: the script would be his dowry, a shining journal of their rugged beautiful destiny.

He needed time to live with his wild resolution. He didn't want to put either of them through unnecessary pain. He had to be sure. That was the smart, mature thing—to be prudent. Let it settle. When—if—the time finally came to contact Jeanette, Bud wanted to radiate absolute certitude and determination. She would demand nothing less. He knew that by now she was probably involved with someone but pushed the thought from his head.

For a few weeks he poured himself into mapping out the "impossible" script. He looked over *Romeo and Juliet* and found it beautiful but laborious to read. Maybe he'd look at *West Side Story* again. It was difficult to concentrate. He wondered where Jeanette was, whom she was with. The sentimental screenwriter wanted his ex at least to know he was toiling in her great shadow, honoring her. Contacting her just yet was out of the question. Bud knew he was obsessing but avoided going to Meetings. He wasn't in the mood to have his flirtation with Eternity stomped on by jargon-crazed lonelyhearts.

What he really needed was some kind of triumph. Why had that been denied him? Bud wished he'd become controversial or rich or *something* since their last separation—like the returning Heathcliff. A triumph was bound to get her attention. He knew the idea of loving and being loved by a famous man was a secret desire, like flames licking her insides.

The script wasn't enough—he would need to become a knight, a knight of Love. How to begin? He thought about acquaintances from Meetings who cut themselves with knives and recalled the stories the Doctor used to tell him about factitial wounds; he didn't have to go to that place just yet. But he needed to be emptied for the journey to come so as not to be overtaken by depression and darkness. It was all right to be afraid. A knight wasn't a knight if he wasn't afraid.

He would start by fasting. Using the *Cliffs Notes* as a guide, he read the section of *Quixote* where the knight-errant does penance in the wilderness for his ladylove. The don desires to fast, to injure himself, to go mad—like some kind of American Indian purification rite. It appealed to him enormously. Maybe Bud would take peyote, maybe all his suffering was steadfastly pointing him toward the path of enlightenment. He smiled to himself: *those* were the riches he would return with, he'd be Heathcliff by way of Castaneda. Maybe he'd learn Jeanette was only a symbol, that it was madness and death he had feared all along, or fear itself. Yes, he told himself it was even possible his desire for Jeanette would be gone when he returned from such a journey, he wouldn't *need* her anymore. That, of course, would be the precise moment she became his.

Bud paused to test himself, pretending he had her back. What did that used to feel like? The screenwriter shut his eyes like a clairvoyant. To have her back . . . then not to want her. That's what always happened. Would it again? He sank deep within himself, navigating like a diver exploring a treacherous reef. The waters were warm and dark and all he could hear was his own breathing. It didn't seem like the old scenario would recur—not this time. Still, it was a possibility, he would be naïve to say it wasn't. If he got her back, then didn't want her, well, tough shit, he'd just live with it, that's all, and marry her anyway. Husbands and wives often doubted their love. Show me a marriage where they didn't. He told himself it was simply a question of nerve. Put the whole thing in perspective. Doubting, and acting on that doubt, were two different things. He would stay with her out of nerve if he had to and learn from the staying. If he was unhappy, he'd look to an inner flaw, not to Jeanette. Jeanette was Everywoman. He would look within. *I will never consciously do anything to hurt this woman again.* That felt good and sane and right.

"Hello?"

All day he'd gathered courage. Even now, close to midnight, he wasn't sure what to say.

"Jeanette? It's Bud."

"Hi, Bud."

She sounded constricted.

"Did I wake you?"

"Sort of."

"I just wanted to say hello."

There was nothing. He swallowed.

"It's late. And I can't really talk."

"Are you with someone?"

"Yes."

"Okay. I'll talk to you later."

"Good-bye, Bud."

He hung up, then called again, emotional.

"Don't do this!" she shouted, and hung up.

When he called the third time, the phone was off the hook.

Bud took some painkillers from Dolly's bathroom and slept at her apartment for a few days, downstairs in his old room. He told her he was still having stomach problems. She was happy to "take care of my genius."

Dolly's suit against BURTON NAUGAWITZ, M.D., INC., A MEDICAL CORPORATION continued, and the doctor's attorneys offered a generous settlement. She emphatically turned them down. She was going to "screw that asshole in court," and whatever Dolly got, she would leave to Bud, because "your mother's not going to live forever."

Since the disastrous phone call, the image of Jeanette in bed with someone else stabbed at him, but the pills took the edge off. He was feeling a little better. Bud dreamed about a Vuitton hatbox, then remembered the item's origin from his famous stupor—it was the very same Rosa crated Caitlin's books within for the journey back to Peralvillo. He went to Rodeo Drive and bought a fifteen-hundred-dollar replica. He had no income and the purchase used up a good chunk of his borrowed savings, but the screenwriter couldn't help himself. Only good would come from this acquisition. His new idea was to keep a library of books inside the box the way a survivalist hoards weapons and canned goods. It was his trusty Armageddon locker and he kept it at the foot of the bed while he slept. He spent days culling favored icons from the bookshelves of the stolen library. The hatbox wasn't a very large ark, and he sensed the coming flood was great. When he had a workable selection, he rearranged them endlessly, wedging the books by color, size and order of import, stoked by the cedary smell of the luxe accessory. Drifting off to sleep, he imagined himself clinging to his chrestomathic trunk through all manner of adversity and cosmic unluckiness. He might become homeless but still would have his lacquered box. The image of an orphan in the dark holding such a thing was magical—he could see the illustration for a children's book in his head. He would write such a fantasy, say, a "lost section" from that Baron Münchhausen movie or *The Neverending Story*. Wasn't that the one about a little boy and his books? He'd have to rent the cassette. Thinking about himself in the world with the box gave him the same supernal, impervious feeling he used to get when summoning the waves and the concrete bunker. That worried him a little.

He rearranged the books some more in the box, then composed a telegram to Jeanette:

DON'T THROW THIS AWAY! I KNOW IT IS PAINFUL BUT I NEED TO SAY YOU WERE EVERYTHING TO ME. WHY DID I LEAVE YOU? WHAT DID I HAVE TO DO TO MYSELF NOT TO FEEL ANYTHING? WHAT CAN I DO, WHAT WILL I HAVE TO DO TO PUT US BACK TOGETHER AGAIN, TO MARRY? I KNOW YOU'VE HEARD THIS BEFORE. I KNOW YOU HAVE A NEW MAN IN YOUR LIFE. HE CAN'T LOVE YOU THE WAY I LOVE YOU—YOU KNOW THAT'S IMPOSSIBLE. I'M SO AFRAID THIS IS LYING IN THE TRASH, YOU HAVEN'T READ IT, YOU'VE TORN IT UP. PLEASE, JEANETTE! I AM TRYING TO ARTICULATE MY FEELINGS BUT DON'T WANT TO SEEM MANNERED. AND DAMMIT, I AM NOT HELP-LESS! I WANT TO TRY TO RELEARN MY LOVE, MY LOVE. I THINK I'VE ENDURED A KIND OF MENTAL DEBILITATION THIS YEAR (THOUGH I AM DOING QUITE WELL PROFESSIONALLY), A CULMINATION OF SOMETHING THAT WAS NECESSARY TO GO THROUGH TO GET TO WHERE I AM NOW, TO BE READY FOR YOU. I KNOW IT SOUNDS ABSURD BUT I AM READY NOW, JEANETTE! I DON'T EXPECT ANY-THING—I KNOW HOW MUCH I HAVE HURT YOU. PLEASE FOR-GIVE ME!

He thought the bit about debilitation was heavy-handed and wasn't sure about the seeming "mannered," but finally felt it conveyed a kind of delicacy he wanted. The "dammit, I am not helpless!" was ludicrous but had a fractured, ingenuous nobility—indeed, quixotic. He decided to leave it in. Bud liked the fact he didn't mention his Mexican brush with death. There would be plenty of time to fill her in and she'd respect his restraint, that he hadn't played it for sympathy.

Bud waited a few days for a response. When there wasn't any, he sent a Mailgram. It was appropriately less urgent, since he already had her attention. He felt calmer now anyway. Baring his soul had removed some of the pressure.

I WANTED TO APOLOGIZE FOR THAT PHONE CALL. IT WON'T HAPPEN AGAIN. I KNOW HOW MANY MONTHS MUST PASS BEFORE YOU CAN TRUST ME EVEN JUST A LITTLE—IF EVER. I KNOW WHAT I WANT AND THE ACT OF ACHIEVING IT, ALREADY BEGUN (WHETHER OR NOT I FAIL), IS THE BEST AND BRAVEST THING I'VE EVER DONE. I'M GOING TO "DO THE RIGHT THING." I'LL CONTINUE BEING FAITHFUL, NOT SEEING OTHER WOMEN—I DON'T HAVE THE SLIGHTEST DESIRE! MY LOVE FOR YOU HAS REVOLUTIONIZED MY LIFE. I KNOW YOU'LL GO ON, SEPARATE FROM ME, AS IT MUST BE FOR NOW. PLEASE DON'T KILL HOPE IN YOUR HEART! I LOVE YOU AND KNOW PROFOUNDLY WE WERE MEANT TO BE TOGETHER. I HAVE THE STRENGTH TO SEE THAT CLEARLY NOW AND MAKE IT HAPPEN (FROM MY SIDE). I SEE WITH ABSOLUTE CLARITY WHAT MY MISTAKES WERE, HOW I WAS ACTING OUT, UNCONSCIOUS. IT ISN'T LIKE I HAVE NO SENSE OF WHAT I DID. THIS MAN YOU'RE WITH COULD NEVER LOVE YOU THE WAY I LOVE YOU! NO ONE COULD. HOW COULD YOU LIVE WITH YOURSELF KNOWING YOU DIDN'T GIVE US A LAST CHANCE? YOU ARE IN HIS TERRIBLE ARMS! BE MY ISEULT OF THE WHITE HANDS.

He waited a week, then called. He made sure it was an "appropriate" hour—the afternoon. She was friendly.

"Did you get my letters?"

"Uh-huh. One of them was delivered by this cute young boy. 'Telegram for Jeanette Childers!' I thought somebody died."

Bud's nervousness went away. He said some things he thought were poetic and Jeanette sighed, like she was bored.

"I'd like to see you. Do you want to get together?"

"I don't think so."

They talked aimlessly another minute; then she dive-bombed him.

"You know—I don't feel like I'm talking to an adult male." Suddenly Jeanette sounded a million miles away. "You're commitment-phobic *and* a negaholic—you should start going to Meetings again. I don't even know why I talk to you in the first place, I *really* have to examine that. I'm gonna go. And *don't call me,* okay?"

He immediately wrote a longhand letter to his love: *My soul is sick. Should I be condemned? Am I the first to have a sick soul? I think there's more than the small part of a coward in me. I have to redefine love. I dreamed we lived in a tall wood house in a swirling prairie of wheat, I saw us there like a timeless anchored ship, with our baby. There was an electrical storm, mystic winds and wet drapes of darkness. Oh, Jeanette, Jeanette!*

Cry a little.

He thought the "more than the small part of a coward" line sounded like Norman Mailer. The stuff about the storm and the baby was just too wacky and he held off sending it. He was determined to keep his dignity. What was happening to him?

That night he drove by her house; it reprimanded him. The pale moon shone in its window like an impossible boarder. It was a plainer version of the midwestern house he'd dreamed of amidst the swirling prairie of wheat, the Wyeth house with the baby and the picturesque, worm-eaten sheds. Twisters dangled dark legs on the horizon; he felt like someone locked out of the storm cellar. Inside Jeanette lay in the healing arms of her lover.

Bud stepped from the car and peered into the hearth of the kitchen, like Paul Anka did in *Look in Any Window.* He became Tristan and dropped some leaves in the gutter as a sign for her to come, but the gutter water did not flow through those hidden rooms—he'd sing no hymns to the night. He thought of knocking, but it would be like rapping on a tomb. Nothing looked real: not the sidewalk or the streetlamp or the light that glowed within. It came to Bud then that he would never have a wife, a house, a sidewalk, a gutter.

There was a park at the end of the street. He bolted for it the way he galloped home in the dark as a boy, pretending to be encased in a black otherworld aircraft, dropped down from the stars. He jumped a fence and was scratched by the wire. He fantasized he would keep on running, always to the next small town, like the doctor in *The Fugitive*. He'd be a grease monkey (Brian Donlevy in *Impact*) at a garage owned by a widow and her tomboy daughter in a town with a church and a Main Street and regular cops. He would stay in a guest room of the widow's house and arrange his books in scented drawers. The tomboy would love him and bloom as a woman (the first time he saw her, her head under the hood of a Chevy pickup, he thought she was a boy until she shook her long chestnut hair out from the greasy cap) and together they would run like cybernetic heroes into the night.

When Bud got home, he was speeding. He dreaded sleep because he'd developed a horror of waking up to a wrong-headed world. He remembered feeling that way the first few months after the Doctor died. He knew he was becoming seriously depressed and decided to take Jeanette's advice. It was important to do what she wanted—aside from anything, she was smart and knew he was in trouble. Bud had to regain his equilibrium if he expected to compete with her new lover. "You've got to do your homework if you want me back," she seemed to be saying. He would go to one of their old Meetings. He might even run into her; more likely someone she knew would see him there and report it back. That would be a good thing for Jeanette to hear. It would help his cause.

———

An envelope came from Don Bloom. Stuck to the letter inside was a yellow Post-It with the handwritten words *B—Is this a joke? D.B.*

> Dear Mr. Bloom,
>   I'm really sorry it didn't work out for Bud on "The Worst Movie Ever Made." Strange enough to be the case, he takes movies too seriously to be right for the project. But I really mean it when I say that I hope we can do business with him in the future.
>
>   *Andy Magnuson*

‹‹‹‹

For a few weeks Bud sat at Meetings in a warm coat, rejoicing among the legions of the borderline. Everyone in the rooms seemed to have done a stint in the psycho ward. From his chair, the drone of pitching and sharing all around him, the screenwriter meditated on "psychiatric confinement," the hospital as a white wondrous pavilion, a poetic crucible from which come clarity, passion, direction. All the rich kids from high school used to get shipped to Menninger, itself a great house in the Kansan wheat fields. Bud had been denied such a luminous, wrenching rite of passage. Now he felt he'd earned the prize— he was finally bottoming out. It was a pivotal moment, a turning point shared by men who go on to greatness.

His old love became merely an ache among the new thoughts, a wound on some further frontier. He'd admit himself to the hospital without even telling her. It was his journey, his alone. When Jeanette found out, she'd want to go to him. She'd first seek counsel at Meetings for a proper course of action—that's how she worked. Her friends would tell her to stay away. Let him be, they'd say, you can't save him. Her respect for brave, injured Bud would grow and each day she'd feel more like the dignified wife of a political prisoner jailed for a wondrous cause.

He was handling it, whatever it was, and that was Jeanette's bottom line, what she respected most—the *handling* of things, the facing of one's worst fears and weaknesses, the rolling up of sleeves and wading into the muck of the man-woman Problem. Or what have you. Now she would cherish those telegrams, thank God she hadn't thrown them away. They were already in the garage somewhere in a box; she'd have to fish them out. She knew Bud was at last face-to-face with his demons, he said he'd handle it and there he was *handling* it, doing the unflinching terrifying inner work only few were up for. She would *see* he was made of such stuff, and be proud. After all, it made sense—they'd met at Meetings, hadn't they? That said everything. They'd met in the real churches of the Meetings. She had chosen well, and had been so chosen. How exquisite.

When Bud got out of the hospital, he might not even want her anymore. The tables turned. Could happen. Maybe they'd end up working together, lay therapists, healers, but not *being* together, one of those situations life throws you where two people "used to have something." Now both married to others. The old lovers and their current spouses dining together, golfing together, sharing investment portfolios. Jeanette and her husband have kids and Bud and his wife have kids and they all share summer camp and sleepovers. Or maybe Bud would marry and Jeanette would be the one without, Jeanette having twice divorced while Bud's roots grew stronger and deeper in the earth, Jeanette having miscarried and in vitroed and adopted during Bud's effortless procreation. Maybe Jeanette would finally be the one who couldn't get it right, after all her husband-hunting superior pain. Jeanette the high-strung commitment-phobic hillbilly negaholic.

The recourse of hospitalization was balancing, yanking him back from the chasm of life without her. He was grateful for that. Bud exhaled and wondered: *When will she marry this new man, the one who sleeps in her bed?* She probably wanted babies already. The picture of her wedding party with its faceless, dancing groom floated up and Bud felt the vertigo again and pushed it away by remembering when he used to go down on her. She liked to make a little display, spreading herself like the vellum of a sacred, miniature book, winged-moth Mysteries of the Illuminati, eyes closed, a backwoods scamp showing off her bestest, beautifulest bug. It fluttered there, waiting for his mouth. Now she had another man and Bud would cut himself with razors "in the manner of knights-errant who have been too long absent from their mistresses"—that's what the *Cliffs Notes* said. He'd starve himself and be a slashed-up wraith, engraving his arms to atone; this would assure admittance to the white hospital pavilion. Factitial wounds just about made you a shoo-in. He had to do something dramatic because the last thing he wanted was to be turned away and referred to some community mental health service. That just wouldn't do. He'd put his fist through the window of Hoffmann-Dougherty's and crap the bed if that's what it took.

The day arrived for Bud to go to the hospital. Whenever he felt a loss of nerve, he told himself he was doing it for research—a script would come of it. Whatever happened with Jeanette would be a bonus.

"I'm going to the desert."

"For what?"

Dolly hated the desert. It was the place that Moe and his George Hamilton tan used to go and *whorefuck.*

"To write."

"Where are you going to stay?"

"At Two Bunch."

"What is that?"

"Two Bunch Palms. It's a spa."

"Doesn't that cost money?"

"They give me a price."

Bud had always wanted to go write at Two Bunch, with the heavies.

"How long you going to be away, Morris?"

He realized she wasn't being facetious and chose not to correct her.

"I don't know. A few weeks."

"Maybe you can read my novel while you're in the desert at your spa for two weeks. Why don't you get a job, before you go to spas? I never heard of such a thing."

She called him Morris again, but this time he pointed it out. Dolly was taking pills for her blood sugar and Bud was worried about her. A few days before, he'd found his mother loitering in the hallway, just outside her front door; she didn't recognize him. She tried making a joke of it, but he saw she was scared.

Bud went home, packed a bag and showered. He had decided to base his "impossible" love story on *Tristan and Iseult* and write it from the hospital. From everything he'd heard, Chrysalis House was almost like a health ranch retreat; designed by a famous Venice Beach architect, the place was chock-full of Hockney photo-collages and Rauschenberg lithos. Bud thanked God he had insurance.

He toweled himself off and went on a crying jag. *Let's go, let's do it!* He made wild faces in the mirror and wondered if he should cut himself with a knife. He could always do that on the spot, if they didn't let him in. He wished he could close his eyes and be carried into Chrysalis on waves, like the journalist in *Shock Corridor* who has himself committed so he can solve a murder. Bud made himself think of Jeanette with the other man and the pulsing pain came back, so acute it was almost interesting. He made another *Marat-Sade* grimace and slammed his fist into a wall, bloodying it; he needed to gather the energy for hospitalization. If he didn't go through with it, what were his options? Move back to Dolly's permanently? Stop bathing and put on fifty pounds? Win a Golden Globe? At the very least he'd get a script out of it, if not the "impossible" love story, then a souped-up, reconditioned *Cuckoo's Nest.* He practiced his flattened affect in the mirror.

For a moment he thought he should scrap his plan and start writing but knew that was just callowness, a dead end. To jolt himself, he thought of Jeanette's new friend with his new mouth down there. Bud thought of cutting himself again while he got dressed; his skull was a hot, cluttered closet. He was going to go through with it. He felt like an actor already cast in a role—the audition was only a formality.

He took his bag and hatbox of books and called a cab.

The screenwriter cried all through intake but kept his eyes averted. The woman was kind and he grew confident they'd let him in. He was insured by both Writers Guild and SAG; the double coverage made him an attractive candidate.

"You're tired, aren't you?" He wasn't quite sure what she meant but figured it was shorthand platitude of the weary-traveler-shelter-from-the-storm variety.

He belonged to two unions. Of course, he was tired.

Bud was grateful he'd done the *Bloodbath* movies. The Screen Actors Guild gave you something like four months of psychiatric hospitalization. You could check in and out of there like it was Le Mondrian. For a writer, though, things weren't so cushy. You were lucky if the Guild picked up three weeks, lifetime total. It didn't make sense, but that's the way it was. When he went to hell, he'd bring it up with Lou Gottlieb.

While the woman worked at the computer, Bud hung his head low and pictured himself in some old *Life* layout on mental illness, an "unable to cope" cover boy representing millions of depressed Americans, the star subject of a pre-Prozac ensemble of shattered lives grimly depicted in rainy-day-gray photographs with cry-for-help, lives-of-quiet-desperation captions chronicling suicidal vets, adolescent arsonists and suburbanite Miltown-fueled breakdowns. Snapshots from an encounter group: *first moments on the ward . . . Bud laughing wildly . . . Bud smoking and listening, the ash burning long . . . the blurry vérité of him raging, the surfacing of old hurts . . . comforting a troubled friend . . . Bud facing himself . . . Bud*

collapsing in tears . . . Bud being hugged. The boys on cheap
fold-up chairs, with dreary skin and bad haircuts, the girls with
fallen beehives and confiscated mascara. But there is hope in
this house. Final photo: a shot of him leaving the Unit, embracing a doctor, a Negro male nurse watching while the fortified
young artist moves tentatively back into the predatory world's
bright unknown.

Sitting there, he was beginning to feel like Olivia De Havilland in *The Snake Pit.* A movie tear rolled down his cheek as
Bud closed his eyes, feeling the poignancy of his predicament.
Don't let them take away my dignity! He was a fallen gunslinger
and the widowed homesteader rushed to kneel beside him in the
dirt. Bud wanted to thank her; he tried to speak but felt the
smooth edge of her finger sealing his lips. *Don't talk.* They'd
give him whiskey while they poked around for the slug and he
would pass out from the pain. From his sickroom Cowboy Bud
heard the widow's hem brush the floor as she scurried to boil
a pot of water. She pressed a cool towel to his forehead and felt
her devotion to his wound, to his maleness, obsessing on the
stubble and the roughness of his cheek. When Bud was healed,
he would marry her in the fields in the middle of a storm, ringed
by prairie schooners. As she went to lay another cool square on
his forehead, he'd grab her by the wrist and call her by an
unfamiliar name, in his delirium.

Jeanette—

The name would scorch her very being! That there had been
another . . .

The woman at the desk handed him a patients' rights brochure. You had the right to refuse medication and Bud couldn't
understand that. He guessed the brochure was only for "voluntary admits" like himself. The thing went on and on like it was
prepared by Amnesty International.

"Mr. Wiggins?"

A fortyish man in street clothes told him they were finished
with his paperwork.

He was in.

____

Bud got assigned to Deirdre Feder, a staff doctor who gave him pills for his "agitated depression." She had pale skin, a voluptuous mouth and different-colored eyes. Her uneven beauty captivated him. She let the screenwriter keep the hatbox of books in his room and he continued rearranging the volumes within; the doctor said such urges would diminish as the medication took hold. Some of the side effects were blurry vision and trembling hands, but Deirdre—that's what she liked to be called—assured him these symptoms would diminish as well.

He unpacked his things and put them in drawers. Bud gently shook his head—he'd made it over the wall. The room was pleasant and the "cuisine" probably better than average; all this for nearly two grand a day, and that left Two Bunch Palms in the dust. At Two Bunch you'd have to be massaged twenty-four hours a day to get even close to such a figure.

Bud read aloud the part about the magic dog Tristan sent Iseult, the one with the power to make you forget. He remembered the last time he left her, Jeanette got a dog so she wouldn't be alone. That was good—he needed to start drawing parallels between the legend and his life with Jeanette, even if they seemed outlandish. Everything was fodder for the script.

He thumbed the slim volume, then threw it back in the box. He would do good work during his stay, and learn a thing or two about himself in the process. He might have to give Jeanette a call sooner than planned—if he put it off, the urgency of purpose might "diminish" along with everything else. He wanted to make some headway on the script before trying to get in touch. Better not to contact her directly, he decided, not at first. He'd need a messenger, a squire, to tell her that he still loved her above all women.

Bud fell asleep. When he awoke, night was falling. He wondered why he hadn't been disturbed and guessed they were probably easy on you the first day. He was hungry. As if on cue, a counselor came in and told him supper would be served in the dining room at six-thirty. Before leaving, he asked if Bud needed anything.

"Yeah—a third act."

The counselor smiled and left the room.

Moments later a shuffling, unkempt young man appeared, carrying a dirty brown knapsack. His eyes were glazy and his complexion was sallow. Without looking at Bud, he shyly introduced himself as "the new roommate"—Derek the Genius. The vanquished book clerk arranged a few belongings on his bedside table and made some minor adjustments to the sheets. His movements were slow and exemplary, as if for an unseen arbiter. He pulled a giant notebook from the sack.

"Derek, it's Bud. Do you recognize me?"

"Oh, right, right. How you doing?"

He still didn't look up.

"Bud Wiggins."

"Right, I know. Interesting. How you doing?"

"Did you just arrive?"

"Been here a week. Lockup. They give you points—you have to earn your way out." He smiled ironically and looked at Bud for the first time, making a connection. "So what are you doing here, working on a script?"

"Depressed," Bud said. Derek nodded, still smiling. "Have you talked to Penny?"

"Not since I broke her jaw."

Derek told Bud that after he got the Steiner Grant, he found himself colossally blocked. It was understandable at first—things were moving very fast. He married Penny and honeymooned in South America. They were on their way to the Galápagos Islands when Derek dropped thirty thousand dollars at a casino in Guayaquil. Back home, he cast around for the next Big Idea but came up dry. He bought a Rolls-Royce Silver Spirit, then promptly developed a driving phobia, so the thing sat. Penny begged him to sell it but he liked the idea of it there in the pristine garage with pans underneath to catch the oil. He was going to put carpet in there, just like a car museum. He

tried to believe his erratic behavior was part of the creative
process, that soon he'd disgorge a play. He stopped bathing and
Penny's friends started hauling her to codependency Meetings.
One day they went to City restaurant and were about to be
served when the maître d' became aware that Derek was shoe-
less. He ran to the bathroom and Penny intercepted him, steering him out. As they waited for her car they were greeted by
Bobby Feld, who knew them both. He pointed down at Derek
and said, "I remember that from *Barefoot in the Park.*" No one
laughed.

A week later Derek dreamed of the pyramids. In the morning
he punched out his bride, flew to Tel Aviv, got an Egyptian visa
and went to Cairo. It was there he discovered the theme for his
great romantic epic—a Bedouin *Tristan and Iseult.* He had the
outline right there in the giant notebook. As soon as they let
him out of Chrysalis he was going to turn it into a play. He still
had some money left and was going to check into one of those
stucco fleabags by the Harbor Freeway and churn out the
pages.

"When was all this?"

"The Egypt thing? A few months ago." He nodded toward
the notebook. "Wanna hear a little?"

A Bedouin *Tristan and Iseult*! Bud felt only goodwill—there
was room enough for everybody. Funny: outside he never gave
Derek the time of day, he'd flayed and excoriated him in his
heart, but now he was ready to root like a soul brother. They
were *writers,* dammit, and it took the boyish grant recipient
with his felonious marriage, Egyptological weirdness and big
dumb manic-scrawled diary to remind him. Bud was moved.
A romantic epic, he said. There was synchronicity there. The
Tristan of Two Bunch regretted ever treating this boy so badly.
What gave him the *right*? Derek had some wiggy spunk, that
was for sure. Bud had merely milked the blues, but *Derek—*
Derek had cracked bone and ridden the scarab. There was
something to be said for a little good old-fashioned acting out,
Meetings notwithstanding.

Bud wished to make heartfelt amends. He was truly lone-some. Weissen was a friend all right, but not a peer; Weissen was a hack. Besides, it was hard to be intimate with someone you owed so much money. But Derek—how right Bud was about coming to Chrysalis House! He was already reaping divi-dends from the Unknown. He would listen to his roommate—*roommate!*—then share his own projected epic. He would even make Derek his liege and messenger of love. Jeanette suddenly appeared in his mind as Janet Margolin and it was then, as he made the *David and Lisa* connection, that Bud knew where the treasure was buried. That was it: he'd do a *David and Lisa* for the nineties, gritty and erotic and obsessive, part Strindberg, part Stoppard. He would go back to the "play-for-film" of *Bringing Down the House.* It was time to write for the Theater; he'd listen and learn, as if attending a workshop. Bud was excited, and wondered if it was the pills.

Just as Derek began reading aloud, the counselor stuck his head in and said it was time to eat.

After dinner there was Group. Attendance was mandatory. The nightly sessions were run by counselors, but Deirdre occasion-ally sat in as a kind of facilitator. Bud knew about Group from his days in the Foundation, back in the seventies—they'd had them three times a week and called the facilitators whips.

The room was brightly lit. There were about a half dozen patients and Bud was embarrassed. He didn't look at anyone because he had the terrifying certainty the room was filled with people he knew. He squinted a lot and imagined being stared at. The counselor hadn't yet arrived.

"Aren't you Raleigh's friend?"

The voice came from the shape sitting next to him. Bud cocked an eye; he couldn't place her.

"Drugs?" He was still a blank. "You here for drugs?"

"Depression."

She nodded at the password.

"How do you know me?"

"Aren't you the guy who served dessert? The clown at the Beverly Palm?"

"I'm Bud. What's your name?"

"Esmeralda."

He remembered meeting her outside the hotel that afternoon. Bud didn't give a shit if Raleigh found out he was on the Unit; right now he was glad to have someone sympathetic to latch on to. He would take Deirdre's advice and do some "anchoring."

Esme was a troll-faced auto parts heiress who dabbled in acting, decorating, fund raising and bulimia. She'd evidently been there awhile and delighted in acquainting the newcomer with fellow inmates, sotto voce.

"That's Franklyn," she said, pointing to a ruggedly good-looking cowboy type with Sam Shepard teeth. "He's an actor, *paranoid skitz.* He was a valet—stole a Porsche from a party, drove it to Joshua Tree and set it on fire. He hallucinates, though not all the time. You should listen to him, it's trippy. He's *real* damaged."

She moved on to a pasty-faced fourteen year-old boy who was wearing an I'M STILL AT THE CANYON RANCH T-shirt. He looked like he had the pox.

"He's really fucked up. Doesn't talk, likes Michael Jackson—the usual. They put a helmet on him once in a while when he rams his head into the wall. Probably fetal alcoholic syndrome. His brother's Lawley Raitt, the kid from *On Our Own.* " He was blank again. "The sitcom."

Bud nodded at a bald guy, around fifty, who was having trouble standing still. He blinked a lot and looked stranded, a wobbly Minotaur evicted from the maze.

"Who's Mr. Fidget?"

"That's Burty Naugawitz, plastic surgeon. Third time here in eighteen months. They just moved him over from the medical center—he was detoxing methadone. They call him the Butcher of Bedford Drive."

Bud laughed, mostly to himself, then thought: *Free nose job.*

What better way for Naugawitz to settle the old score with Dolly? He'd be damned to leave Chrysalis House without a new nose, a new script and a new wife.

Esme became distracted when the counselor arrived, so Bud completed the survey himself. He was staring at a flustered, powerfully built man whose long, slow blinks were like those of a sleepy cartoon character. White hair sat on his head like a nest-in-progress; one nervously awaited the bird's return. He caught Bud watching and self-consciously smoothed down a cowlick. That's when the screenwriter recognized Witold Kracz. Barely a few months ago he'd fruitlessly waited for a glimpse of the maverick director—now, Bud drolly noted, they were "working together."

The topic of the day was self-esteem. Everyone had a story, Esme whispered. When you shared it in Group, it was called "pitching" or "running story." Witold had a good one. He was in postproduction on his latest film. One day he had lunch in the Polo Lounge, then went for a short walk. When he returned, his room was empty. He complained to the manager and was told the police had been looking for him—his "short walk" had lasted three weeks, of which he remembered nothing.

When Esme finished this last debriefing, Bud brought his full attention to the room. The counselor was facing Witold, driving home a point.

"The *details* arc unimportant—it's what those details *evoke*. Someone made a stupid comment to you. You felt offended. Why? Something triggered you. It's all about how we *perceive*. If someone points a gun at you, and you've never *seen* a gun, what are you going to feel?" He laced his fingers, tapping the thumbs. "Take a step back and look at it. You're a smart man, I know that for a fact. I've seen your movies."

Witold flinched at the last comment, like a peddler whose horse had been shot. He shifted uncomfortably on the hot seat.

"It is poor self-esteem," the director stammered dutifully, with a thick accent.

"You're not answering the question. If someone points a gun at you and you've never seen a gun before, what are you going to feel?"

Witold Kracz trembled, a spy in the House of Mental Corrections.

"No-thing! Surprise, maybe."

"Well, you might be more *curious* than surprised. But I think you're starting to *see.*"

There was something cagey and endearing about the amnesiac auteur. Witold seemed to be playing the oaf, with a dollop of polite child, as if to insure his eventual release. Bud speculated that Eastern Europeans were probably "on to" psychiatric hospitals and could be forgiven a nagging paranoia. These were the protofascist badlands of Disney World, with or without the Claes Oldenburg soft sculpture in the lobby. Though the bright American manner and methodology amused him, Witold wasn't about to let his guard down, not for a Looney Tune second—these were the same people who'd lobotomized Jack Nicholson.

₩₩₩

So it went: the days filled with caffeine, cigarettes and *Donahue* reruns, crosswords in the sun, boredom, Ping-Pong, panic attacks, and sporadic thrusts at his play-for-film. Writing was difficult, because of the almost complete lack of privacy. Everyone ran story; the most bizarre quickly became ordinary. Bud jauntily befriended Burty Naugawitz, even mentioning the Dolly connection. He wished he hadn't—afterward the defrocked surgeon looked bereft.

After a week he was given a pass to leave the grounds. He took a cab home and got his mail. The answering machine had a few frantic messages from his mother saying she'd called "Two Brunch" and he wasn't registered as a guest. Bud left his own message: he was fine, she was right about spending too much money, he was staying with an old girlfriend in Twenty-

nine Palms—that would really confuse her. Maybe he should
have said he was staying at Seventy-six Trombones.

The screenwriter walked the three miles back to the hospital.
He wondered how long he could keep this up. The "impossible"
love story wasn't going so well. Still, he was compelled to finish
the script from within hospital walls. If Jeanette knew he was
there, it might act as an incentive to the work. Yet if she found
out, and Bud remained "blocked," he'd feel like an indulgent
fraud, a loser. He just didn't want to do the thing half assed,
that's all. That's what Morris used to say. "You're a half-ass!
Don't half-ass it! You're taking the easy way out!" The words
still stung; he should probably talk about it with Deirdre or one
of the counselors. Might as well take advantage of the place and
do a little catharting.

Bud had to admit he was feeling better depression-wise, but
not great. The pills had to be good for something. When he
reached the Pacific Design Center, he was tempted to turn
around and go home. If he left the hospital without writing his
Tristan and Iseult, his *David and Lisa,* his whatever, he might
get depressed all over again, only this time do a Moe Wiggins.
No, the only reason he'd leave the place now would be if Jake
Weissen called and said the two had been offered three million
for a script or Jeanette pulled up in her Jeep and blurted "Let's
get married!" Whenever a patient went AWOL from the hospital, the counselors called it eloping. Bud imagined himself and
Jeanette long married, telling the funny story of how he'd had
to elope twice to marry this gal. Though maybe there wasn't
such a thing as eloping when you were a voluntary admit.

When he returned to the room, Derek was sitting on a chair
by the window, reading from the notebook. Bud looked over his
shoulder; the pages were filled with a crampy, hieroglyphic
scrawl.

"This is what I wrote in Cairo," he began. "It's more of a
short story—sort of a hybrid. Whatever."

When he said "hybrid," Bud lost a little interest, then remembered to be kind to his friend.

"See, I'm using it as the basis of the play. I'm in it myself and it's still pretty awkward. I haven't done anything to it yet. So I'm sort of the narrator. You'll get the gist."

Bud settled back with a pillow as Derek began. He was enthralled with the playwright's voice; it possessed extraordinary confidence, like a famous actor reading from a classic.

*"Derek Johansen sat on the toilet of a papyrus store near the pyramids, watching an ant move on a yellow tile like a crazed Bedouin. A boy was talking incomprehensibly through the wall; the playwright—*that's me, I'm either *Derek* or *the playwright—the playwright remained unaware he was offering toilet paper at a price. He thankfully had a box of Kleenex from Joey Nasser's car, so did not have to part with his smelly Egyptian pounds. Nevertheless (and apart from the boy's offer, of which he remained indifferent), he did some rapid calculating, mostly to distract himself during painful spasms of the colon, and concluded that if he did not have his precious Kleenex, he might do well enough with his multitudinous notes.*

"Outside in the dirty village, a woman was selling cows' heads, two rows of three, like a raided children's picture book; flies bearded the heads, the magnetic shavings of an Etch-A-Sketch. Why was he sick? He'd been careful never to eat outside his hotel. There were the expected lapses: ice cubes, and tap water to brush his teeth. He remembered reading about the bowels of death camp survivors—a swig of soda and it rushed out their backsides, still fizzing.

" 'You are okay?'

"It was Joey Nasser, Derek's young Egyptian guide, he of the let me tell you a question.

"Again: 'You are okay?'

" 'Yes.' A moment later the playwright made his way to the car, walking like a man with a grave, fragile mission. He was going to ride a camel right up to the Great Pyramid and noth-

ing—not the death of bowel or the slavish gamesmanship of Joey Nasser—would stop him.

"They drove up a hill and parked at a parfumerie *at the base of the pyramid. It was cool inside. The owner ordered a young boy to make peppermint tea. Joey said to Derek, 'You cannot worry, it is boiling, it is okay.' Derek lay back on the couch. He assured the owner he would buy something after he rested. He wanted to say,* I am a millionaire from America. I will give you ten thousand dollars if I can use your toilet whenever I like. *The owner said he could stay all day if he wished. He felt the gracious host quietly observing the femininity of his visitor. All Americans had this female side and one must hoist these discomfited middle-aged women delicately onto cool stone tables to get the pink back in their legs before slaughter.*

"The camels waited for Derek and Joey Nasser in front of the parfumerie. *He hadn't had a spasm for twenty minutes. They went out. As the camel stood on its legs, he had the feeling he might fall. The camel's owner sat on a donkey. 'Donkeys are from Egypt,' Joey Nasser told him, 'as is the game of chess.' Joey Nasser was a liar. The playwright thought:* I am in Egypt for as long or short as I wish. Can I be taken by this man? I do not have very much money. Can I be damaged by this man? No, I cannot, because I have been graced by this trip.

"He'd dreamed of the pyramids and, under their aegis, had flown to Egypt after trouble with his wife. The small ones were so cool, so personal. He was unprepared for their elegance. Joey Nasser said there were hundreds of them and for some reason this time Derek believed him. He saw them recede into the millennial sandblown fog of the military zone.

"Derek's camel was led behind the huge cafeteria that faced the monuments, through an alley that eventually allowed one to make a grand entrance to the postcard majesty of the great Cheops. Occasionally the man on the donkey dismounted and made some studied, irrelevant adjustment of the reins while clicking his tongue against his teeth, a bloodless Brueghel. The

*camel did the requisite guttural protesting, and if it could speak,
Derek had no doubt it would demand one hundred Egyptian
pounds for its exertions. They passed some scaffolding where
workmen were preparing a production of* Aïda *for which cogno-
scenti from around the world would spend thousands on tickets
alone. Derek imagined himself delirious, lying in his own excre-
ment in a side ward of a ratty Cairo hospital while planetary
billionaires wept for the captive princess.*

*"As the camel trekked toward the burial chamber, the play-
wright went over the story Joey Nasser had told him that morning
on the way from the hotel. That was earlier, when the guide was
still in good form, before his blood sugar dropped and his anomie
became so dark and heavy and bludgeoning.*

*"I am going to tell you now a Bedouin story," he began as they
bounced along in a Jeep beside the Nile. Yes, it was the Nile, and
the fact seemed absurd. Derek smiled eerily, his eye fixed somewhere beyond the river."*

A counselor appeared and told Bud he was late for his one-
on-one. Dr. Feder was waiting for him.

There were two serigraphs on the wall of Deirdre's office,
brightly colored aphoristic washes in the style of Sister Corita.
The first noted that the Chinese symbols for "crisis" and "opportunity" were the same. The second one read: "We cannot
put off living until we are ready. The most salient characteristic
of life is its coerciveness; it is always urgent, 'here and now,'
without any possible postponement. Life is fired at us point-
blank." Tell it to Caitlin Wurtz.

"I understand you know Derek." He nodded. "Small world."

"It is a little strange."

"Do you like each other's work?"

"That's a tricky question for a writer."

She smiled. Bud liked this woman with the heart-shaped face
whose job it was to understand him. Her arms were pale and
he wanted to dampen their black hairs with his tongue. Maybe

she was the other Iseult, the one Tristan found when his true love was in the arms of another.

"Creative people have a special set of problems and sensitivities. And I guess none of it's helped by the nature of the circumstances under which you work. When they say it's a crazy business, they're really not exaggerating."

"I thought you were the one in the crazy business. Professionally, anyway."

She smiled again. "My job is to get you to detach, in a healthy way, from the parts of your job that *are* crazy—the ups and downs, the financial uncertainties—so you don't get depressed. There are wonderful parts of your job, too, or I assume you would be doing something else."

"Hotel manicurist is an option. Or kosher deli work."

"Are you a comedy writer?"

"On a bad day."

"You're very funny."

"That's not a good sign. I'm supposed to be depressed."

"Well, I think the medication we've given you has helped. Do you know what depression is, Bud?"

"Anger turned inward. So says my ex."

"Well, your ex is very smart. It's important that we find the source of our anger. Anger can be a powerful ally. It can also be a destructive force. You know, the average stay here isn't conducive to any kind of extensive psychotherapy. But in the short term, I think we can show you some new ways of using your brain that will help you break old patterns."

Bud said he was having a hard time working. When she asked if anything had been on his mind he brought up Jeanette—in the spirit of things, he referred to her as a "kind of obsession." Deidre told him to close his eyes and picture Jeanette in his mind. When he had the picture, she instructed him to put a "frame" around it. She asked if the picture was in black and white or color and when he said it was color, she told him to fade the colors out until it was black and white. Then she told him to take the framed black-and-white picture and very slowly let it recede, so that it went from close up to very far away until it was only a speck. She had him repeat the cycle about ten times, slowly at first, then faster, until the pushing away of the picture was fluid and instantaneous. The final thing she had him do was look up to the right-hand corner of the room and visualize himself standing there, without Jeanette, in a beautiful place. Then she made him repeat the whole picture-pushing business again but with the added upper-right image of himself "feeling good in a beautiful place." She told him to practice this simple hypnotic technique a few times each day and his obsession would begin to lose its power. She shook his hand and Bud left. The next time he would give her a hug. A long one.

In the midst of his holy mission, Bud's attraction to Deirdre was vexing. He found himself fantasizing about her, reading into innocent remarks. If she had leaned over to kiss him, he'd have betrayed Jeanette without hesitation. Was he just a womanizer after all? For a few months now he'd been faithful, asking nothing in return, knowing all along she was with another. Bud had no other choice—when Jeanette came back to him, he needed to be untainted, a block of celibate months behind him like a log of contrition, a prayerful affidavit of his love. He was now within the cautious prelude of those religious months, yet if Deirdre leaned to kiss him . . .

He shared his secret shame with Derek.

"Don't you see? When Iseult the Fair forgot about Tristan— when Jeanette forgot about you—Tristan met someone else."

"I know, I know. Derek, I need to ask you something."

"You want me to call her, right? You want me to call Jeanette."

They used the pay phone in the hall and Bud listened in, jamming his ear against the receiver whenever Jeanette spoke. Derek introduced himself as a friend of Bud Wiggins, from the Program. When he told her Bud had been hospitalized for depression, she really seemed surprised. Taken aback. Moved and anxious. He spent a minute or so assuring her the screenwriter was all right. Bud strained to hear the tinny voice.

"Talking to you is strange. I mean, I feel like I know you. He said that you were a great actress."

"Did he tell you I hardly ever worked?"

Derek laughed. "Welcome to the club." He playfully moved away so Bud couldn't hear.

She must have asked what Derek did because he said, "I'm a writer," and made a few disparaging remarks about the Business in general. Bud closed in again.

"Anyway, I can't really talk. I'm at a pay phone."

"How did you get my number? It's unlisted."

"From a Meeting phone list."

"Where is he, by the way? NPI?"

"Chrysalis House."

"Does his mom know?"

Bud shook his head adamantly.

"Absolutely not. I probably shouldn't even have called."

"Don't beat yourself up about it."

Before he hung up, Derek softly said their mutual friend seemed to be undergoing some kind of brave and dignified transformation. Bud thought that was a bit much but what the hell. Jeanette thanked him for calling and told him he could probably use a Meeting. "I know *I* could," she said. Then Franklyn walked by and Bud got sidetracked. When he turned back to Derek, his friend was quiet and held him at bay, watching Bud with a cunning little smile as Jeanette spoke.

"I don't think you should call, not just yet. He might be angry—he's going through a lot of stuff. I mean, do what you have to, but he's fine—okay, Jeanette—it was good to talk to you, too—I'll probably see you at a Meeting."

Derek eased the receiver into its cradle, an urbane conspirator. He made a hell of a squire.

He was seriously in Jeanette's thoughts again! How could her boring boyfriend compete with a hospitalized ex-lover, a writer driven mad by passion? Bud wondered how she would respond. He knew she would, one way or the other, she'd *have* to—Jeanette didn't call herself the drama queen for nothing. He would think up a game plan in the event she dropped by the Unit unannounced. He might even refuse to see her. One thing was clear: he had to finish his play and he had to finish fast.

ʌʌʌʌ

For the next few days he worked avidly, sitting beneath the lone pine in the courtyard of the Millicent S. Steiner Pavilion. The warmth of the afternoon sun was sobering. He felt brave and visionary, suffused with love.

Bud needed a means to bind the two lovers, some kind of amulet. When he wrote *Bloodbath 2,* there was the same problem—the need for a dramatic device, something arbitrary that repelled demons (crucifixes were passé), a corny contrivance that symbolized Love or Family. The dark forces really hated Love and Family. When the screenwriter finally came up with the gimmick of a locket (a long-buried heirloom with a family photo inside), the producers thought he was Francis Coppola. In *Tristan and Iseult* there was the device of a ring, but he wanted something different. So Bud paced around the sunny courtyard and thought.

An idea began to surface. A gold, halved heart, adorned with emeralds and jasper, bubbled up in his brain like something once real. Where was it from? He would dangle each half from the lovers' necks in the scene at the orchard, before they parted. He'd make them promise if ever a messenger brought to them one of the halves, they would return to this spot in the piney wood. Even if they'd since married, they would leave a husband or wife and come to their true love.

Bud was interrupted by Derek, who brought his notebook.

"Are you busy?"

"I'm just going over my play."

"Wanna take a break?"

"Sure."

"How's it going?"

"Okay."

"Is this going to be your *Ghost Sonata*?"

"Exactly. But hopefully weirder."

"I like that, 'hopefully weirder.' That's like a yuppie Merry Prankster thing. We should put that on T-shirts."

Bud nodded at the notebook. "The next installment?"

"Yeah. We were talking about Tristan the other day, right? What were we saying? Oh: Tristan met someone else. But you know that. There was a duke, right? Remember? You've read the book. The duke had a vassal who'd been courting his daughter. The duke rejects him because he's a servant, so the boy lays siege to the castle. Right? This is what my whole fucking play's about! Ready?"

His play seemed to be about heat and dust and diarrhea. Bud could put a frame around it and push it away when Derek's story was done.

"Okay, so I'm on the camel heading toward the pyramid. My bowels are under control, right? And I'm being led by the camel wrangler, the 'bloodless Brueghel,' remember? Did you like that?"

"Very much."

"And I start to run Joey Nasser's story in my head. You remember Joey Nasser, right?"

"Great character."

"Okay, this is what he says, this is the story he told me that's running in my head as I'm on my way to the pyramid, sitting on the camel."

He looked down for a moment at the page, "becoming" the character, accent and all.

" '*I live in desert for year and a half*'—this is Joey Nasser talking—'*I don't like the city. Why? a Bedouin say to me, Why do you live there? I tell him: because I am a city man. And he tell me I am very brave. He say, Why do you drive a car? It is a machine, it can kill you. I say, No, I am always my mind on the road, what I am doing. Let me go on. I was in the army, I am in the army, an officer. And one day I am with my men and*

*we are on the desert. And we hear a scream. And we see an old
Bedouin and he is running with a dagger. And we see a young
girl, is fleeing from him.'* . . .

"*Derek could tell that Nasser had told this story many times,
from the precious way he pronounced 'fleeing.' No matter.*

" '*A bedouin,* ' " *he continued, 'he can have four, five wives. Of
course. So sometimes there is problems. So we go to take a look.
We stop him. Why you running with a knife? I say. What you
doing with a knife? We stop him, of course. And he say, Help me!
Help me! And we think he is crazy, he want us to help him to
kill this girl. She is my daughter! he say. And he tell us they were
eating and they spread a mat. And a snake it's under the mat
and it bite the girl. And he cut his daughter from where is the
bite of the snake. And she run. So I say, We will help you. We
will catch the girl and I will call and a chopper will come like
that, the army. We will take her hospital. And he look at me and
he say, You are taking a big responsibility, she is* my *daughter.
And I think to myself maybe he is right! What is it I should do
this thing? So we capture the girl and we bring her to his tent.
And he kill the girl!' "*

Derek relished Bud's dismay before beginning again.

"*Joey Nasser inhaled, then laughed hysterically. 'No, I kidding! He sterilize his knife in the fire and he cut her. His wife—
the mother of the girl—she is like nothing happened. She is calm.
She take onions and put it on the where he cut. And I say, What
are you doing? And she smile and say the onion will suck the
poison. At this moment I say to myself: Shut up. You don't know
anything. You must only watch these people what they do. You
can maybe learn something.'*

"*As they loped through the alleyway, a group of boys in athletic
jerseys watched. One of them smiled obscenely. His eyes seemed
to murderously sloganeer:* see the Pyramids! *They rounded the
cemetery and began the slow trip to the great monument. One
of the Bedouins sold Derek a Coke. He opened it in front of him
as if to put the American at ease, to show him it was a real Coke.*

The camel did not move as he drank; the playwright realized they were waiting for his empty. He dropped it down."

Derek sneezed messily into his hand, then continued in the persona of Joey Nasser.

" *'Maybe four or five months later, I have a nice woman from Oklahoma. And I tell her this story I just tell to you. And she tell me, I want to see the Bedouins, you must take me to them. So I go to where their camp is. They stay six months there and they will stay for two more week. And the man, he embrace me. He say, Why you leave so fast that time? I want to thank you, but you leave. And he say, Come, come. So we drink—he give us coffee. And when we go to leave, he give us more. I say we must go and he say, Why? When I see you go, I fill up your cup so you cannot, you must drink. Because there is a great celebration on this day, you must come! And he tell us that this day is the day his daughter, yes, the girl who lived from the snake, it is this day for her circumcision.' "*

A counselor interrupted—Bud had a visitor. It was his mother.

He stormed to Deirdre's office, wondering who had tipped Dolly—he couldn't imagine it had been Jeanette.

"Did you tell my mother I was here?"

"No. A friend of hers who does fund-raising for the House recognized you."

"Great. Did you talk to her?"

"Your mother? Yes. She called."

"What did you tell her?"

"I said you were a voluntary admit and that I couldn't have a discussion about anything else."

"Jesus."

"I told her you were doing fine. She's concerned about you." Deirdre had the stale equanimity of an abbess.

"Well, she's here."

"What would you like me to do? We can't prevent your mother from visiting."

"Tell her I'm sleeping. Tell her I'm doing research."

"I would feel uncomfortable with that, Bud."

"Tell her that I'm exhausted, I'm in for exhaustion. And that I'll call her later in the week."

"You can tell her that yourself."

"She didn't ask you anything?"

"She asked if you were depressed."

"What did you say?"

"I told her I couldn't discuss it. And I told her when visiting hours were." Deirdre squinted at him and smiled. "*Are* you depressed, Bud?"

"I can't discuss it. You know when visiting hours are. You can at least tell her I'm not up to seeing anyone. Could you tell her that?"

"I'll tell her you don't feel like seeing anyone."

"Thanks."

Bud slunk back to his room while the deed was done. A stranger sat in a chair between the beds, reading a book.

He introduced himself as Ford Sester-Neff, an actor who'd appeared in a few of Derek's plays. The odd name was somehow familiar, yet Bud couldn't place it. Sester-Neff was blandly affable, with a smooth, handsome face and rimless glasses. His "showpiece"—a stiff, expensive leather jacket—looked like the carapace of a beetle from *Big Tiny Little*. It didn't fit his personality; the screenwriter imagined the coat signaled some kind of character flaw. Joey Funt, he wasn't.

Derek was off with one of the counselors and Sester-Neff was hanging out until he returned. Bud took him to the cafeteria for a cup of coffee.

He noticed an awkwardness that was common to visitors on the Unit—a vulnerability, a maladroitness, a sense that the most ordinary encounter with an inmate would leave them looking foolish and undone. Artistic types were particularly susceptible to feeling inferior; they'd read too much and seen too many movies, and deep down most of them thought psychiatric hospitals were holding tanks for the New Wave—savage conservatories of the real deal. They felt excluded, and vaguely reactionary: If I'm so talented, they seemed to ask themselves, why aren't I here in the bullpen having a little Mellaril with my word salad? Sester-Neff was trying to act "natural" but had that stranger-in-a-strange-land look. He seemed to temper his anxiety with an actor's "soaking it up" demeanor that was at once guarded and open. He warmed upon learning his temporary host was in the Business. Bud had confessed his trade with unexpected pride.

He felt above this creature Sester-Neff, who, as it turned out, was really a writer in the middle of his first film script, a story based on his dysfunctional southern family. The visitor enjoyed the "scribbling game"—his last effort had been a one-character play adapted from a magazine article he wrote—and modestly suggested screenwriting was the "trickiest game" of all. Bud disagreed. Tried to write a play once himself. In a sense. Tough going. A family play. A Daedalus submission. More of a proposed filmed play than a movie-movie. It was called *Bringing Down the House.* The actor-playwright-essayist-scenarist effused over the title. Bud reiterated how tough a play could be. Truly a tough game. Anyway, *House* never happened. Other things came up. Sester-Neff smiled knowingly; Life crowded in on writers, waylaid and brutalized them, drank their blood. The whole time they talked, he never asked Bud what he was doing there at Chrysalis. That was one of those faux pas areas that visitors weren't eager to wade into. Better to find out later from Derek. Best now to behave as if they were colleagues in a VIP lounge.

He asked if Bud was working on any scripts and was told about the *Tristan and Iseult/David and Lisa* thing; the loquacious inmate found himself impulsively describing the work-in-progress as a play in five acts about Family and Madness and Romantic Love. Sester-Neff nodded his head gravely, alluding with a subtle glance to the asylum walls, with their terrible perfect power to christen such a work. He was playing the visiting game well.

They talked about the insanity of the Business and Bud loosed a few stories from his Hollywood treasure trove. He told him the one about betrayal and Billy Quintero, ascribing it to someone else. The visitor laughed with inappropriate ferocity.

Derek finally joined them. He bragged about what a good writer Bud was. Bud suddenly felt guilty he wasn't working on his play. He shook Sester-Neff's hand, then left them there.

On his way back to the room, he passed Franklyn. The actor was standing by the pay phone as usual, smoking a cigarette. Bud thought he was an interesting character and had spoken to him at length about the Joshua Tree incident. He had set the Porsche afire to kill the voices coming from the car phone. Franklyn was psychotic, but at least he wasn't confused over whether he was an actor, playwright, screenwriter or essayist.

"I'm working on a play and I wondered if you'd be interested in reading a scene."

"Acting or reading?"

"Read-through."

"I love a cold read. What's it like? Ayckbourn? Orton? Ionesco?"

He was grinning like a telepath who'd had too much caffeine.

"I'm not sure yet."

At this, Franklyn showed his bad teeth and whinnied like a horse. "You know what? If you're not part of the Final Solution, you're part of the pogrom."

Deirdre stood at the end of the hall talking to a counselor. Franklyn nodded his chin at her, then whispered conspiratorially.

"I searched and searched and all the time her vagina was right under my nose."

"I'll get you the pages, Franklyn. I really appreciate it."

He started to break away, but the actor held his arm.

"Do you have a title yet? I got a great one, like one of those hokey Preston Sturges jokes. It's about a dude ranch-sanatorium out in Arizona, right? *Where the Ease Meets the Rest.*"

Franklyn whinnied again and Bud just smiled and walked

away. Somehow he had the feeling as long as Franklyn was acting a part, he'd be fine—like people who stop stuttering when they sing. Bud started getting excited about his work being staged, even in raw form. It felt like the beginning of one of those legendary stories: the play that had its birth in an asylum.

Now all he needed was a scene.

That night he dreamed a confederacy of maintenance men was mopping up the halls. The floods came, a river of shit, like that movie *Shock Corridor,* where the newspaper writer goes undercover in a mental hospital. A girlfriend poses as his sis and the guy tells the intake people he's having "unbrotherly" feelings toward her. They lock him up and after a while he snaps and imagines water pouring through the halls, better than the elevator blood in *The Shining.* In the dream Bud wore a long stained skirt, a kind of monk's robe, and the floor was a corrugated sandbar of turds; the toilet exploded in a hail of porcelain. It was six-thirty in the morning when he awakened from his visions and began the acrimonious section of his Romance:

BUD: The plumbage. The plumbage is ruined in my beautiful apartment.

JEANETTE: It's an actual break in the pipe.

BUD: I can't understand what you're telling me. Have them come out again.

JEANETTE: They've come out twice and they said we'll have to pay for the third time.

BUD: We'll sue the landlord.

JEANETTE: The plumber said, "I understand your landlord's a real Jew." Just like that, without thinking! I just can't take it! If we'd bought the house, if we had our own—

BUD: If we'd bought the house, we'd still have the *fuhcocktuh* problem with the fucking pipe!

JEANETTE: He said it's a big job, Bud. It's a three-thousand-dollar job—

BUD: I don't believe this is happening.

JEANETTE: Well, it's happening. It's happening. It's a break under the slab, right under the slab, six feet down. But it might as well be a *million miles.*

BUD: Did he run the thing all the way out to the street?

JEANETTE: It's right under the slab, Buddy, and it's gonna cost three thousand. At least.

BUD: How far did he run the fucking snake out, I said!

JEANETTE: *(hurt):* I don't know. Whatever.

BUD: "Whatever"?

JEANETTE: Whatever it took! All the way.

BUD: Ninety feet?

JEANETTE: I don't know, Bud. I'm not a plumber. He's the plumber.

BUD: They'll have to come out again.

JEANETTE: They won't do it.

BUD: What do you mean, they won't do it? That's what they fucking *do!*

JEANETTE: He put the biggest thing on the end of the cord, or whatever it is. It chops through everything, it chopped through everything and it was still backing up. A razor-sharp blade—

BUD: Were there any feminine napkins down there?

JEANETTE: Not this time, Buddy, uh-uh. And he said, You better get a jackhammer, lady. 'Cause there's mud in the pipe, it wasn't even feces, it was mud, and it slides back through the crack and there's nothing you can do. They can go and blow the pipe out and it costs three or four hundred dollars, but what's the point if there's cracks in the pipe, Bud? What's the point! And what if it backs up through the faucets, Bud, what if all the—Jesus! The carpets, my beautiful thick white carpets!

BUD: Would you just shut up! Nothing's gonna back up anywhere.

JEANETTE: How do they change a pipe, Bud?

BUD: They just change it, Jeanette.

JEANETTE. IIow du they reach under the ground and change a pipe? All the damage, the digging, months, it could take months, Bud! Where would we stay? How would the house be secure? It's too much, I can't take it anymore! I'm gonna have a nervous breakdown.

BUD: *Have* it then. You *cunt.*

JEANETTE: I wouldn't talk to a dog the way you talk to me!

It was the Moe and Dolly show, real *tohuvohu*—he would navigate the lovers through the shit! Old Butoh Wiggins had to bottom them out, needed to show Jeanette their love was durable enough to be stripped away and rebuilt. He'd create a New Myth, using masks, tattoos and a starkly simple set: a sprawling penthouse—no—a house like the ones from the Arbor, a *pavillon* with Corinthian columns and scarified boiseries. Offstage would be the rustling of a grand, skeletal park, an orchard made of cypress colonnades, of oaks and acacias. He'd add a singular pine and scent the theater with oranges to kill the effluvia of the shattered pipes.

Why had it taken so long for him to write for the stage? He'd always loved it, conceptually. He'd find a way to do the play on the outside—and he wouldn't need six million dollars in prints and advertising. That was the beauty of it. If he could publish a book himself, he could damn well produce a play. Bud felt like he was regaining control of his life again. Movies had subjugated him and it was time for a coup in the palace. Versailles needed some barbarous remodeling; this time he'd get the plumbing right.

The play became a living thing, gliding toward him like a lost love across the ballroom. The work was what mattered now, as it should be, in spite of the artifice of its inception. He serenely reflected that his true marriage was to craft, vision, words—that's where his spirit lived. His talent was there for him, faithful, steady and true. Jeanette was with someone else, and in his pain Bud had wandered to Chrysalis House, a broken-down *folie d'amour,* a pavilion of the nearly living. The inmates there were a company of lost children, the healing chorus of his creation.

What a tapestry it was becoming! He watched it weave: Tristan would go far from his love, to forget. He'd meet another, with pale black-haired arms—a *psychiatrist!*—and marry. After the ceremony he'd feel the stone-studded locket hanging at his chest, remembering with horror the vow. His sworn love wore the other half. When Jeanette learned he had wed, it would cut like a thousand knives. When he felt the necklace and remembered, he wouldn't—couldn't—consummate the marriage (just like the legend). As a cover, he would tell the psychiatrist what he'd told Joan Krause, that he'd recently lost a friend, though he couldn't use the one about the drug with its side effects because she'd ask who prescribed it or offer to change the medication. No, he'd have the reluctant groom simply say a project was weighing heavily on his mind. And that would be the truth. What kind of project? she'd want to know. *Something for the movies!* Maybe Bud would set the whole thing in the Business, do a *Tristan and Iseult* in Hollywood, a real Peter Brook. Why not? Every time Bud picked up a magazine, Mozart was cast with Trump Tower arbitrageurs, Brecht was in Beirut, Aeschylus in the land of Dutch Schultz. Now Bud was in the running, with his *Tristan and Iseult* in the nuthouse, complete with shrink ladyloves and shit-spewing plumbage. *That's Entertainment!*

♦♦♦♦

Bud talked a lot about Jeanette in his one-on-ones with Deirdre, panning for insights that might add rapture to the as-yet-unwritten scenes of the play. He recalled the agonies that came like clockwork each time he left her; Bud would do well for a while, then one day be like a man on the street who suddenly remembers a cigarette left smoldering on the sofa of his crosstown condo. He'd run back a hundred blocks, images of the orchard on fire, the roof of the pavilion scouted by sparks for incandescence. Once, a few months after a breakup, he had the gall to show up on her doorstep with an engagement ring from Tiffany.

She endured the embarrassment of submission and abandonment in front of her parents and friends because she loved him and it was already the middle of her life. Sometimes she would panic and agree to marry him, dysfunction and all. She wanted a child. On a good day Jeanette managed to be cynical and cavalier about their predicament. She knew people who had crazy marriages, she said, bigamists even, maybe that was all "people like us" could hope for. But she was never really serious about any of that, that was just doomsday flirting, honeymooning with the void. Such an amoral arrangement would be demeaning and unromantic, irreligious. And to have a child on top of it . . . She settled for a few hopeful months together before he walked out again. It was worse yet somehow easier each time it happened, leading to the time it wouldn't happen anymore. That's where they were now, complete remission. Only now Bud was trying to make it happen a final impossible time. He wanted her to dream with him again and that would take extraordinary measures. She would resist with all her strength. Like Tristan, he would need to come back to her with a different name, a different voice, a different face. Crisis = Opportunity.

Deirdre said the relationship was toxic. Bud needed to start looking for women who weren't poison to him. He needed to imagine himself and Jeanette joined by an umbilical cord, then observe himself slowly cutting the cord until it was severed. When that was done, he should fade the colors of the picture to black and white, then put a frame around it. He needed to take the picture and move it away until it was the size of a speck. He needed to do this in rapid succession, then look up to the right and visualize himself alone, in a beautiful place.

He finally called his mother. He pictured her sitting in the kitchen, ashen and incomplete.

"Do you want me to come?" Her voice was weak.

"No."

"Why didn't you tell me!" she quavered. "It's no shame, Morris. You cried for help. You're in the right place."

Bud said he was suffering from a chemical imbalance related to his bout with dysentery. The imbalance had manifested itself as depression.

"I knew it," she said. "I knew you were depressed."

"It's no big deal, Ma. It's like being mildly diabetic."

"It's not something else, Buddy? You can tell your mother."

"No. It's all because of the dysentery."

"It should rot in hell, that whole fucking country."

He asked about her own health and she ignored him.

"Do they have you on pills, Buddy?"

"I'm taking some stuff to correct the imbalance."

"So how long are you going to stay in that place? 'Palm Springs'—I *knew* there was something funny. It's two weeks already."

"Not much longer. It's a lot better, but I'm still exhausted. I could have gone to a regular hospital, but the doctor said I'd get more of a rest here."

"Do you have insurance, Buddy?"

"I'm double covered."

"A fortune it must be costing. Well, you stay as long as you need to, Buddy. As long as you're not paying for it. Screw the insurance company good." Then she grew philosophical. "There's no stigma anymore, Buddy. Look at William Styron. He wrote a best-seller. Maybe you could write about what goes on there."

"I actually am doing a little work."

"It was different with your father," she said quietly, as if to reassure herself.

She asked her son if he needed anything, and when he didn't, Dolly said he should write an *Awakenings* and win an Academy Award.

She didn't sound right. It wasn't that she called him by his father's name, though that was something fairly new. It was probably her blood sugar. That, and the stress of talking to her

son, the *nut.* Bud felt guilty: there he was, useless and prevari-
cating, while this old woman with legitimate ailments took her
ruined face to work each day and worried herself to death. He
almost told her about Naugawitz and was glad he didn't.

Bud said he'd be out soon and take her to dinner at Chaya.
Dolly's voice broke as she said good-bye. She told him she loved
him.

"I love you, too, Ma. I'll be fine."

Ford Sester-Neff was now a regular on the Unit and took his
mundane acceptance by its denizens as a source of pride that
the screenwriter felt bordered on fatuity. Anyhow, the guy was
a good audience. When Bud wasn't working on the play, he sat
around with Derek and the Jacket, regaling them with fractured fairy tales. He even brought up being cruised by Joseph
Harmon, leaving out the punch line, so to speak, and they
listened like housewives starved for gossip. He felt a certain
divestiture as he entertained, a lightening of the load, a storyteller's joyous exorcism. Derek had recently spoken to his wife
and was in good spirits. Bud liked making him laugh.

He finished the "broken plumbage" section. After lunch,
Franklyn and Esme did a read-through in the courtyard. A
curious Witold wandered over, followed by the notorious plastic surgeon, then Derek and one of the counselors and, finally,
Deirdre. Bud was right about Franklyn. He was focused and
funny, with a natural feel for the rhythm of the material. And
though she couldn't act, Esme made some interesting choices
and possessed a winning exuberance. By the end of the five-
minute scene's final recitation, there were at least a dozen curious onlookers. They burst into applause.

Deirdre commended the actors, then touched Bud's arm.

"You're very talented. You know who your work reminds
me of?" She stared at the ground and shook her head. "Now
why can't I think of his name? He also writes for the movies."

"Mamet," Witold said, using the tolerant smile he reserved
for laymen.

"Yes! The language is very . . . *direct*. Were we watching part of something?"

"It's from a play I've been working on."

Esme ran into the building, as if on urgent business. Deirdre touched Bud's arm again, then left the courtyard.

Witold stood before him like an old sourpuss. "You You You are saying something. What you are saying is quite serious, it's right? You are not playing, yes? You should be aware not to cuten it up. Why Why Why Why Why you make it cute? You diminish. There is great pain there, it's right?"

He made a few bold suggestions, reminding the budding dramatist that he'd directed theater for ten years before making a single film. He'd like to see more pages, he said, then walked off.

The freshman was pleased the impromptu performance had created such a stir, not that it meant much—everyone was bored shitless and a break in the daily routine was welcome. Derek waited with his giant notebook until the director was out of earshot.

"The The The The The Master approved?"

"He had some pretty good ideas."

"I liked what you wrote, Wiggins. Real fucking good."

"It's not finished."

"Nothing's finished. Can I go on with my story now?"

"Sure."

"I mean, only if Monsieur Artaud has the time." Bud smiled and Derek opened up the notebook. "I ended with the circumsion, remember?"

"I remember." He wondered where it was all leading. He should be working on his—

"The tourist lady wants to meet the Bedouins, so Joey takes her and they're gonna circumcise the girl. Big celebration, right?"

He resumed.

"They reached the foot of the colossus and stayed barely a moment before Derek's camel was led back to the parfumerie.

The whole thing was over that fast, like the time the playwright spent an hour climbing stairs inside the Statue of Liberty when he was a boy, just so he could blink a moment out the visor before heading down again. Joey Nasser mentioned another exhibit, some kind of boat buried with the pharaoh that had been unearthed and put in a building at the pyramid's base. But he said it was too late to see it or the building was closed for repairs or whatever. Derek suddenly remembered he'd had no trouble from his stomach, and was gladdened. Joey Nasser spoke up dramatically: 'I will tell you what happened to this tribe that it ended in murder.'

"*The sullen guide seemed rejuvenated by his tale. For the first time Derek realized the story might be one every guide tells his charge to insure a tip. He couldn't have cared.*

" '*A boy from another tribe fall in love with this same girl who was bitten by the snake,' the guide continued. 'He ask her father to marry. The old man say no. The boy, he offer many camel more than need to marry. The old man he still say no. So one day the girl, she is at the oasis for water and the boy he is with friends. And he see her and he take her and tear her robe like this to humiliate the father. He don't do nothing to the girl. Of course! He still love her. When she go back to the tent, the old man see her dress and think she have been raped. The girl says she is virgin, but the old man too angry to hear her words. Suddenly the boy who tear the dress, he jump into the tent! The old man can do nothing but attend to him.'*

"*Joey Nasser paused majestically—this was the moment for the audience to express dismay.*

" '*You see,' he continued, a congenial magician revealing the secret behind a small sleight of hand, 'when a Bedouin enter another Bedouin's tent, he is that man's guest. And this old man, he must treat him like a guest. If the boy wanted, he could remain for many days and the old man—this is tradition—could not even ask what it was his business to come here. The old man must even feed him and offer him tea!'*

*"Derek had heard this one before. Still, it was not without
hoary, Kiplingesque charm.*

" *'But the boy he say right away that he no harm the girl, he
only tear her cloth because he angry with the old man. The boy
and the daughter convince the old man to get a woman to check
the girl to see she is still virgin. She check and this they see is true.
So the boy go away. But it's not over. The old man he say to his
people, we cannot let this boy go away the same way he come. By
tearing the cloth, he has insulted me. So they decide to go after
him and break his thumb.*

" *'At the river where he tear the girl's dress they catch up to
the boy. They struggle; the boy don't know what they are doing,
he think they kill him. He fight hard, he is strong. In the struggle,
he fall and strike his head. The boy is dead.'*

*"The sun was dropping. Derek's attention was riveted on the
Sphinx. They moved toward it. There was a barrier and Joey
Nasser told him if he gave the men some pounds, they would take
him to the other side. They passed a few more boys in jerseys, with
their desultorily ancient stares."*

"Derek Johansen?"

A girl in torn jeans handed him an envelope and left. Derek
read the letter and smiled like a sophisticate. He kept his smile
and handed Bud the document. It was a petition for divorce.

A few days later Esme invited Bud to her room for an "exciting
announcement."

Exploiting her fund-raising connections, she had made a few
well-placed phone calls to the Golden Monarchs, the group of
socialites and decrepit actresses who threw an annual black-tie
ball for Chrysalis House. It was the typical charitable affair:
along with dinner and dancing, there was usually a raffle of
donated goodies. But the highlight of the evening was a kind
of burlesque wherein the Monarchs belted old show tunes with
specially penned lyrics and shamelessly displayed fishnetted,
gerontic gams during the unsavory cancan finale.

Anyway, Esme's brainstorm was to have Bud's play, or at

least part of it, presented during next week's benefit at the
Beverly Palm Hotel. A little authenticity was just what they
needed to liven things up. To her surprise, the steering committee agreed on the spot to stage the work-in-progress. A *marvelous* suggestion. Besides, she added, it wouldn't hurt Bud's
career—big names like Mike Nichols were expected to attend.

Esme had lost weight during her stay and was starting to look
good to him. She sure had energy; she was like a good agent that
way. Maybe Esme could manage his career. Bud was wondering if he should make a move on her when a counselor appeared
in the doorway.

"Deirdre wants to see you. We've been looking for you!"

On the way to her office, Bud fantasized this was the moment
he'd been waiting for: Dr. Deirdre Feder was going to kiss him
full on the mouth. He laughed at his horniness.

The door was open. He knocked to get her attention.

"Hello, Bud. Come in. And would you close the door behind
you?"

She probably wanted to talk about the play. Maybe she
wanted a part; a private audition could be arranged.

"What's happening?"

"How do you feel about going home?"

He was unprepared.

"I'm doing a lot better, that's for sure. But I'm really learning
about myself—in Group, and one-on-ones. I, well, I'd like to
stay awhile longer."

"I don't think there's any question you've done well in the
environment. You know, Bud, when people come to Chrysalis
House, it's usually for an acute problem—substance abuse,
depression, eating disorders. They've reached the point where
it's difficult for them to function, hold a job, whatever. One of
my patients once described it as being stuck in a dark hole in
the ground. Part of being in recovery is recouping the strength
to climb out of that hole."

Bud felt like he was in a bad documentary. Deirdre smiled
and said with tender irony that the hospital wasn't a workshop

or an artist's studio either. His productivity of late was a healthy sign; the medication had clearly made a difference. It was time for Bud to resume control of his life again. His real life, not his hospital life.

He was nervous and deflated. Deirdre touched his hand.

"You know, all patients develop an attachment to the hospital, a dependence and trust that's essential to the healing process. It's normal to have mixed feelings about leaving."

"I'd like to stay just another week."

"I'm afraid that's not possible."

"But why not?" He felt like a student arguing with a teacher over a grade. "Esme's been here for almost three months, and there's nothing even wrong with her!"

"There's a problem with your insurance."

He was incredulous. "How can that be? I'm double covered."

"Evidently, you're *not* covered by SAG—and you'll have used your Writers Guild maximum in just two more days. You can have a discussion with the business office if you like. There could be some error."

"Fucking AlphaFilm."

"Beg your pardon?"

Bud was silent; he was now a bum. If you were a bum, you got the bum's rush, and that's all there was to it.

"That issue aside, Bud, you don't really need to be here."

"What about the play?"

"You're welcome to come to the Unit and rehearse, as long as it doesn't interfere. Esme told me they want to put it on for the ball and I think it's *wonderful.* I'll support you in any way I can."

She went around her desk and hugged him; he thought of Michael Corleone giving brother Alfredo the kiss of death. Bud decided to leave in the morning. He went to his room and slept.

When he awoke, it was well after dinner. Bud felt refreshed and alive. Of course, Deirdre was right: he was ready to go home. He couldn't imagine why he'd been so upset. Then the screenwriter allowed himself to rage about his alleged double coverage. He'd worked hard and AlphaFilm owed him the bloody benefits. They'd egregiously failed to make the proper contributions—did they expect the actor-screenwriter to roll over and die? He took his anger as a sign of health.

The fight in him was back. He was suffused with unneurotic energy, the old life-force. He would finish the play but already had his eye on bigger fish. A play was a good thing but could get him only so far. He needed to write a movie—Bud Wiggins was a *screenwriter.* When he finished his labor of love, he'd start to work on a script about inmates in an asylum who put on a play: a play within a film, love story within love story. He would tailor it for Jeanette, she'd be back in his life by then, in a big way—he'd make her a star. Maybe he'd set it during WWII, to get some distance. Or better, a nameless and future war, mythical. He'd call it *Asylum Piece.* He already had a jump on the script because the Chrysalis play would be the one actually performed in the movie.

He shivered at the image of Franklyn and Esme onstage at the gala, reading his words. Extraordinary! He was sure to get Witold to direct, that would be a definite plus. The production would be a throwback to avant-garde—did anyone remember *real* avant-garde? Well, Bud Wiggins was going to bring it back alive. He'd have Peter Dietrich profile the thing for the cover of the Sunday *New York Times Magazine.* He thought some more about the title: *Asylum Piece* didn't risk much, wasn't movie-scale; as a play, it was too proudly pat. *The Eternal Return* might be good—or *Performance Heart,* a partial allusion to the bisected jewel. Theater history in the making.

It was after ten and the halls were darkened. Bud got some pudding from the refrigerator and went to the pay phone. He wanted to call Jeanette while still "inside."

She sounded bright and amiable, as if expecting his call.

"How are you?"

"Good. I'm good."

"Are you still in the hospital?"

He played dumb, asking how she knew. Jeanette laughed mischievously.

"A friend of yours called me, didn't he tell you?"

"No. Who?"

"Oh, come on. I'm sure you put him up to it. Didn't you tell him to call me?"

"No."

"Your friend Derek?"

"I didn't."

"I'm sorry, then. He sounded sweet. Bizarre but sweet. Was he someone you met in the loony bin?"

"No. I knew him from a while ago."

"I shouldn't say 'loony bin.' That's really inappropriate. When'd you get home?"

"I'm not yet, but I will be soon."

"You're still at Chrysalis House?"

"Yeah."

"How is it? I mean, are you okay?"

"It's been . . . strange. *Interesting* strange."

"I'll bet."

They laughed together and his tension dissipated. His mission felt unfathomably abstract; his goals ephemeral, fog-shrouded.

"How are *you*?"

"Great!" She was always great. "I'm doing a play, not acting for a change but producing. It's hell. The work is *torturous,* but you really grow, know what I mean?"

"Yeah. That's funny—I've been working on a play since I've been here."

"You've been able to *write* in there? I always admired that about you. It takes me *forever* when I try to write something. You always had that discipline."

"We may perform it."

"Really? What's it about?"

He paused.

"It's kind of about you and me."

She ignored the comment and that was good. He was an expert at reading the signs.

"This play I'm producing—it's Dürrenmatt, do you know Dürrenmatt?"

"A little."

"It's pretty amazing. We're opening soon. In fact, I'm half out the door now to go meet this publicist for a drink."

Bud accepted this as a probable white lie—she was on her guard. He would respect that.

"I'll let you go then."

"When did you say you were going home?"

"Tomorrow."

"You sure about that? Don't people go into those places and never come out?"

She laughed cattily, then apologized pro forma. Years of dull, expiatory Meetings and rigorous Self-help catechism had taken its toll: Jeanette was a compulsive maker of amends. You could say the worst little diggy things to people, as long as you showed them the hairshirt of for-the-record contrition—"I'm sorry" was a Hail Mary that guaranteed admittance to a sober heaven.

"By the way," he said quickly, "how's your friend?"

Bud hadn't meant to bring it up; at least he wasn't sarcastic about it. Jeanette knew just who he was talking about.

"Who, Mark?" she asked blithely. This was the first time Bud had heard his rival's name. "That's pretty much over. We're trying to be friends, but I don't know if that's going to work. Life's so hard, isn't it?"

"Yeah," he fleered. "Tell me about it." The suave cynic made a sound somewhere between a grunt and a snicker.

"He's sweet. Treated me really well. He wasn't crazy enough, I guess. But I don't seem to do so well with the crazy ones either, huh?"

"Maybe we can get together soon."

Bud winced at his words—he hoped it didn't sound like he wanted something from her.

"That'd be nice. I really have to run. Take care of yourself!"

On his way back to the room the screenwriter thought: All is well.

He would have her back.

↯↯↯↯

At the end of morning Group Bud announced he was leaving.

There was surprise, and some consternation about the fate of the play's gala performance; a grimacing Witold Kracz seemed particularly crestfallen. The ball was little more than a week away.

"But what about our rehearsal schedule?" Esme asked unhappily.

Deirdre assured everyone that the author wasn't so much leaving the ship as going ashore. She turned to Bud. "Would you say that was a fair assessment?"

"Absolutely. I'm just worried about finishing the play in time."

"All we need is two scenes," said Esme.

"The The The one about the pipes isn't in bad shape," Witold said. The director volunteered to "put it on its feet" and work with the actors while Bud completed the other piece.

"You might have trouble writing out there," Derek said. "Lots of distractions."

"Like acting sane," said Franklyn. "That'll make you crazy."

"If you get writer's block, you can always sneak back in. We'll leave the light on—just like Motel 6."

That got a laugh. Morale was high.

As Bud was leaving the Unit, Derek gave him a black binder.

"This is my play—I lied to you when I said all I had was an outline."

Bud looked at the title page: "Everything Must Go, by Derek Johansen." Derek said the protagonist of the piece was a retailer who falls in love with a homeless girl. It all took place in Los Angeles.

"What happened to Egypt?"

"You'll see."

"Is this your only copy?"

"Just bring it back. I want your notes."

Bud was moved. The playwright had always been generous; it would feel good to give back. The roommates hugged.

"Can you do me a favor, Derek? I want Jeanette to know about the ball—I mean, the date and everything. But if she thinks she has to go to a fancy dinner to see the play, she'll never make it."

"Have you talked to her?"

"Last night."

"Why don't you just invite her?"

"If I put her on the spot, she might say no. I need you to call and say it's this amazing *thing* and she can stop by to watch without getting dressed up. I already arranged it with Deirdre. I mean, if you can tell her there's a whole group of people who aren't going to the dinner, they're just stopping by to see the play. Can you do that?"

"Done."

Derek did a pretty good Bobby Feld.

They shook hands and Bud left.

It was around noon when he got home. The place looked as if it didn't quite belong to him, like he was visiting a strange city and a friend had left him a key. He sat down on the bed a moment and vacantly tested its springiness, the way you'd kick a tire. He went to the desk and familiarized himself with a few books. He wandered into the bathroom. He opened the cabinet below the sink and removed a bucket of rags, a bottle of Windex and a can of Lemon Pledge. He wiped the bathroom mirror, then started on the furniture with the Pledge.

The smell of certain cleansers always brought him right back to Macon. When he was five, he used to trail after Trudy with a rag, mimicking the patinating movements of her fat hand on the wood. Then Trudy would fix him lunch and they'd watch commercials on the kitchen set, housewives with more rags, parched cabinets lapping up the liniment. The smell of cleansers on cool linoleum: he owned the daytime world of women.

Bud lay down on the bed and drifted. His strange sojourn at Chrysalis House was over and done. The smell of Lysol faded to eucalyptus trees and the railroad tracks of the Arbor, and the mystic winds born within the trellised Secret Garden.

Like a sleepwalker, Bud went to his desk and sifted through his pages.

He hoped the "shit scene" would demolish Jeanette's nervousness, get her laughing, expel the poisons from their bond. He had to take her by the throat and wildly impeach her defenses. She was already somewhere in the ballroom as he wrote, a bruised and elemental nth-power critic; there she sat, skeptical source of the drama, atremble in the royal box. His first duty—like any showman—was to make her *watch,* like an enthralled child at a musicale. It was a helluva job.

For heightened effect, he would follow the *Virginia Woolf* broken plumbage extravaganza with a scene of tender frailties: at the moment the embarrassed Jeanette could take no more of the stercoral penthouse and its hellish plumbage, he'd reel her in and show her the stars and celestial mechanics of the love scene. When it was over, he might even leave the wings and walk onto the stage, like the final guest on *This Is Your Life.* This is your wife.

Bud sat with the blank page. Nothing came. If he was going to write a love scene, he would have to forget about Jeanette's coming to the ball. He had to remove that pressure. Besides, he didn't want to set himself up. Jeanette might well decide not to show; maybe she got back with Mark. Or, she could be in Mexico when Derek called. She liked going to Mexico when she broke up with people. Suddenly that seemed like a real possibility.

With Jeanette tucked south of the border, he began the scene.

Bud lay dying (he'd eventually have to give the characters different names) in the castle of Carhaix near the cliff of the Pen Marks in the village of Prozac. Jeanette has been summoned: she is on the way with her half of the bejeweled memento and he awaits its completion—the lover holds the heart half in his hand, clutching it so fiercely his nails draw blood on the palm. He was counting on Franklyn to play "wounded cowboy" to the hilt. Bud would make the suggestion to Witold that they keep the actor shirtless, like a Bruce Weber poster boy, just boots and Levi's and a silver-buckled belt. A little Bruckner over the speakers, some Sondheim and *Sympathy for the Devil* . . .

He'd peer at the audience from the wings. Was she there? Derek would stand in the back of the ballroom, wearing the prearranged signal: white tie for Yes, black tie for—

Bud knew she would come.

Witold left the hospital, but generously made himself available for rehearsals. He was returning to Europe for an indefinite period, but staying for the ball—he wouldn't have missed it for the world. Seeing this play *on its feet,* Bud sensed, was the denouement and crowning anecdote of the director's "American breakdown" period, one for the memoirs. He hoped that's all it was anyway, hoped that Witold wasn't secretly planning another *King of Hearts.* That's all he needed, to be scooped by this stammering East bloc son of a bitch. No, it was more likely Witold Kracz's next gig would be a remake of *Closely Watched Trains,* for TNT.

The day before the event, Bud sat at an outdoor table in the Farmers Market going over his notes. The area had a pleasant, patio feel and a low-key show biz vibe that was somehow reassuring.

"Bud!"

He stared at a colorfully disheveled woman in front of him who was juggling plastic bags stuffed with food and magazines.

"It's *Genie.*"

"Oh, hi, Genie."

"God, I'm your *hugest* fan, I give you your *biggest* break—and you don't even *recognize* me!"

"I'm working on something." He smiled. "I was distracted."

"I know about you writers."

"Just haven't been myself lately," he vamped.

"Writers are never themselves, or they wouldn't be writers. So how are you? Happy? Healthy?"

Bud told her how wonderful life was, then asked about *Bloodbath.* Genie said that AlphaFilm was in "deep shit." When Bud told her he'd written the sequel, she was surprised.

"And they *paid* you?"

"Yeah."

"I mean, you cashed the check?"

"Yup," he said. "Cashed the check."

"Well, more power to you. I'm in the middle of suing the sleazebags for back salary myself."

"Wow."

"Real assholes. Boy, am I glad I'm outta there. Did you know I was producing now? With Sara Fidell—The Katz and the Fidell Productions, do you *love* it?" She was smiling like a pumpkin.

"Good for you."

Genie started moving; the bags were weighing on her.

"Hey, listen, we're having a party tonight to celebrate our first acquisition, you should come."

"Anyone famous invited?"

"I don't let the unfamous in my house."

Bud arrived at the Hancock Park duplex around ten. Genie grabbed him, gave him a drink and hustled him to the kitchen to meet the "acquisition" itself.

"Mr. Wiggins!"

Ford Sester-Neff violently shook the hand of the new arrival, courteously reintroducing himself as if Bud were potentially amnesiac; they had, after all, met in the confines of Bedlam.

"Jesus, you two *know* each other?" Genie was aghast. "Bud Wiggins knows *everyone.*"

The Jacket solemnly pointed a finger at Bud while looking his hostess in the eye.

"This guy has the most *amazing* stories."

Sara Fidell came in drunk and Genie introduced him. Bud was a wonderful actor and a wonderful writer and Sester-Neff seconded her. Sara stiffly saluted him.

"I'm *stinking,*" she said, à la Bette Davis. Then she hauled Genie away.

"When'd you get out?"

"About a week ago. I'm much better now. Tony Danza stopped talking to me from the TV."

The guest of honor laughed and pulled on his beer like they were a couple of incognito desperadoes. His leather groaned. Bud asked about the "acquisition."

Sester-Neff said he'd met Genie at an IFP seminar and given her his southern family script. She liked it but was interested in something else of his, an apartheid piece called *The Response: A Fiction.* (Bud recalled scanning the "fictional essay" in *Harper's* awhile back.) It was about a white schoolteacher defending himself against charges of terrorism, and the story had stayed in Bud's mind because it got the right kind of attention in the national press. Apparently Genie thought *The Response* would make a great movie, a kind of Pretorian *Kiss of the Spider Woman.* The industrious Sester-Neff had already adapted it as a play and she didn't think it needed much "opening up." The drama was politically attractive and cheap to produce; Genie was confident that with the right elements, she could "make it fly."

He casually asked Bud about current projects and was told about the Chrysalis play: when Sester-Neff learned there was an actual performance at hand—*tomorrow night! directed by Witold Kracz! performed by the patients themselves!*—he was boggled.

"I gotta be there, Bud."

"It's this big charity thing, Ford. It's black tie."

"Listen to me."

He grabbed Bud's wrist and dragged him to the utility room next to the kitchen.

"I'm serious, Bud—I want to go. I *need* to go."

The Jacket was overdoing it—probably coked up, Bud thought.

"I don't know if I can get a ticket. It's one of these five-thousand-dollar-a-table deals—"

"Don't worry about it. I'll get in. I just want to know you'd be okay with that."

Bud laughed, humoring him. "I don't have a problem with it, Ford."

"Where is it?"

"The Beverly Palm. In the ballroom."

"I'll be there." He straightened up and the leather came alive, like the trestles of a great bridge giving way. "You realize what you're doing is genius, right? You've become an exalted impresario of the surreal."

What with the ardent "acquisition" breathing in his face, Bud started feeling claustrophobic. He excused himself for a drink.

He walked outside to the small patio. The cool air felt luscious—it was good to be out of confinement. "What a long, strange script it's been," he said into the air, and smiled. Bud realized he hadn't thought about Her for a few days, probably because Derek had told him Jeanette was going to "try to come" to the ball. That's what she said, anyway. Bud took it as a Yes; the cat was in the bag. It was a relief not to be obsessing. He dared admitting it was possible things wouldn't work out between them, even if Jeanette loved the play and was deeply moved. As he stood there in the sweet night air, such a prospect seemed manageable. He was "powerless."

Bud went in and cruised the living room for pretty faces. He told himself it was all right to flirt. No one got his attention. He was about to leave when Sara ran in, waving a brochure.

"Here it is! Look, I saved it, it's *so weird.*"

She held the glossy leaflet before the eyes of a girl with silver-purple streaks in her hair. There was a photo inset and the girl gaped at it with pretend shock.

"Who *is* she?"

Sara snatched it back.

"I'll *tell* you! She is none other, so it says"—all of this in a mutant English accent—"than . . . *Dr. Deirdre Feder*—now get this: *'Psychiatric Script Consultant'*!"

"How bizarre!"

More people wandered in with their drinks.

"Listen! Listen!" the associate hostess cried.

Sara Fidell struck Bud as a plain, boorish, unpopular girl who liked pulling a wicked rabbit or two out of the hat, for attention. She kept the "funny" accent up while declaiming from the text, making occasional adjustments to an imaginary pince-nez.

" 'Dr. Deirdre Feder is a respected psychiatrist, panelist and radio show commentator. She has consulted on feature films and movies of the week for the major networks, public television and cable—' "

At last a wry young man in black yanked the thing from her hands and held Sara off while reading for himself. The streaky-haired girl peered over his shoulder, examining the document like it was a Chinese puzzle.

"It says she went to medical school in Puerto Rico," he said suspiciously.

Someone started singing *Puerto Rico, you lovely island* and the flyer was passed from hand to hand like a balloon that was losing air. When it landed with Bud, he unfolded it. There was a glamorous, soft-focus head shot of Deirdre inside.

"We got a mention in Army Archerd about our acquisition of Ford's script," Sara explained, rhapsodic. "And we get this in the mail from some praisery. So I tell Ford about it, and he *loves* it, thinks it's *hysterical*—you know, a 'psychiatric script consultant.' He actually *calls* her! Says he's the *big writer,* wants to know more about what she does, the whole yakkety-yak. They have a drink at *Mortons*—"

"Let me see if I understand," said the wry young man. "Ford has a drink with Dr. Deirdre Feder . . ." He paused dramatically for effect. Right on cue, a half dozen guests chimed in, *"Psychiatric Script Consultant!"* and everyone broke up.

"Yes! They go to Mortons and it turns out she's this frustrated actress who kind of fell into the medical thing and can't stand it! She's literally a shrink and she's *married*—to one of these Drexel types, is there still a Drexel? *Some* money-type person, anyway. So they go for a drink and Ford asks if he can see a tape of a sitcom she worked on."

"Consulted on," said the girl with streaky hair, initiating another clamorous verse: "Dr. Deirdre Feder—Psychiatric Script Consultant!"

"He wants to see this tape, but all her cassettes are over at the hospital. The *hospital*—her *day* job, isn't it *hilarious*? Me and Genie want to pitch it somewhere. I mean, this psychiatrist-*adventuress,* it's *perfect*! It could be a spoof—"

"Not a *spoof,"* her partner admonished, passing through with a bottle of wine and some dip. "Studios hate spoofs."

"Whatever. It's like Indiana Jones. Wouldn't Sigourney Weaver be wonderful? Oh, my God, Sigourney Weaver!"

"What about Goldie?"

"Too old."

"Oh bullshit. The studios are 'skewing' old."

"Julia Roberts."

"Too young."

"So what happened?"

"So they go to the hospital and he fucks her, right there in her office. It was *such* a turn-on, he said. He always wanted to fuck a shrink."

"I'm in shock," said the wry young man. "Who would've thought it from Dr. Deirdre Feder . . ."

This time the whole house thundered with the refrain.

ꞍꞍꞍꞍ

The afternoon of the ball Bud drove over to the Unit for final rehearsal. He realized he still hadn't looked at Derek's play. He would in time; for now Bud had his own vision to worry about. He knew he was lucky—some had no vision at all. He'd always been afraid of "the book clerk's" talent, worried it was greater than his own. Somehow Bud wasn't worrying anymore. There was no "greater," there was only inspiration and the bounty of honest labor. He was getting so stable he scared himself.

When he entered the Unit, a counselor looked at him strangely, then told him to wait. The screenwriter sat and flipped through a *People*. Joan Krause was in a "Chatter" section photo, standing between Madonna and Ed Begley, Jr. He should probably find a way to let her know about the gala. *Should is not a word for grown-ups.*

The perspiring Dr. Naugawitz came around a corner and told Bud that Derek hanged himself. He was dead. Bud walked quickly to his old room. It was a mess. Someone from maintenance was brooming hair off the floor. Bud left the room. Another counselor was whispering to Franklyn halfway down the hall. Franklyn's head hung down like a paralyzed man watching an army of leeches advance on his chest. Bud asked to see Deirdre, but was told she was away from the hospital and had been paged.

He went home and spent an hour looking for Derek's play. He couldn't find it. He hadn't cried yet but was feeling a touch of bathos. As Bud hunted for the manuscript, he acted out the variation of an old movie scene in his head, before an imagined audience—the one where the dazed heroine frantically searches for her dead husband's tobacco because he always smokes his pipe after dinner even though the doctor says he shouldn't, *he's waiting for me and I've got to find it for him, can't you see?* Finally, a family friend slaps her from delirium and she collapses in his arms, convulsing with grief.

Deirdre called a few hours later and asked how he was. He

told her he felt empty and she said that sounded pretty normal, under the circumstances. She asked if he wanted to talk about it; he didn't have much to say. Everyone still wanted to do the benefit, she said. In fact, the patients were adamant. They wanted to dedicate the performance to Derek.

When he hung up, Bud thought about her encounter with the Leather Jacket. He ruminated a little on the logistics. When did it happen? Probably just before the therapist called him to her office to go over his insurance problem—Sester-Neff's semen leaking into panties as Deirdre revealed the Blue Cross betrayal. Blue double cross, Blue panty shield. Could have happened earlier, though. That's right: Sester-Neff stopped visiting a week or so before Bud went home. Had a leathery quickie with the rutting psychotherapist, then went his unmarried way. It would have been the height of uncool then to bring his unit back to the Unit for a swagger. So the way it happened was, Sester-Neff bumps into her once or twice while visiting Derek, says hello, then Sara Fidell shows him the brochure and the Jacket sees an "in." Doesn't even tell Fidell he knows of this woman. Part of the fun. Maybe Bud would write an anonymous letter to the head of the clinic. Use Chrysalis stationery, only scratch it out so it says Clitoris House.

Bud felt a pang of jealousy. The Jacket was better-looking than him. And the Jacket was smarter, but he wasn't *funny.* Bud was funny and women loved funny men. It was sexy to be funny—Deirdre herself said she liked his sense of humor. He kicked himself; he should have gone for it. Jesus, for a shrink with a husband to pick someone up and screw him right there in the hospital—outta control. *She's gotta have it.* A mere step away from sleeping with a patient. That had to be the operative fantasy. It was all so lurid and obvious, like a letter to *Penthouse.* Maybe Derek had walked in on the fuck-fest; maybe Derek was in love with Deirdre and was so distraught he hanged himself. Maybe she was "doing" the Steiner Grantee, and told him he was a lousy lover.

Bud could call Peter Dietrich and do an exposé, à la *Shock Corridor*. He imagined the shrink and the Jacket and the doomed roommate all going at it, the Sister Corita serigraphs, the cocks and balls slapping like a porno movie, crisis equals opportunity, then Derek and Sester-Neff were gone and Bud and Deirdre were having a one-on-one and Bud was in the middle of an insight when a deranged former case of hers entered with a gun. "I want you to have coitus with your patient," he announced to the startled therapist. The gunman said he'd kidnapped her children, taken them right off the playground and locked them up somewhere and would kill them unless she did what he demanded. Deirdre knew what this man was capable of, he was paranoid-schizophrenic, Franklyn flickered into view on the screen of Bud's lids.

Deirdre told Bud it was all right and shakily removed her things. Franklyn said to hurry up and Bud helped with the bra. Then she was nude and her nipples were hard and she turned a final time to the intruder and said, "Please don't hurt my babies!" Then she lowered Bud down and guided him inside and softly cried while Franklyn masturbated and Bud whispered, "I'm sorry," his tears mixing with hers. Then Franklyn disappeared. Bud and Deirdre were having a one-on-one again when the healer announced she wanted to try something "a little different." Just as he trusted her to keep their sessions confidential, she said, so she trusted him to do the same. Then she said she didn't want him sharing with anyone what she was about to do. She was going to show him her breasts, "to demystify them." She knew it sounded unusual, she said, but it was really quite a common, if unspoken, practice among therapists. As she undid her blouse, she talked to him about unrelated things like how crowded Yosemite was when she was there last month with the kids. That heightened his arousal. She kept talking, her blouse open completely now. She unhooked the bra, still talking about Yosemite and how her husband really loved to camp, how they had to come home early because their boy got chicken pox. Her nipples stiffened and Bud touched himself while she was demystifying. He asked if that was okay. She said yes and closed her eyes.

He kept playing it like a videotape until he came.

Bud rented a tuxedo for the "premiere."

He parked a few blocks from the hotel and strolled over. He'd forgotten that the annual fund-raiser was a minimedia event—there were lots of limousines and faces he recognized from television. There was even a crew from *Entertainment Tonight*. He watched them interview Victoria Principal and Carol Burnett, then went through the lobby to the Grand Ballroom. A cheerful, hollow-cheeked volunteer type in her sixties greeted Bud from a pink cloth-covered table at the entrance. She checked his name against a list, then gave him a table number.

He sat far from the stage. His fellow diners included the woman who gave him his table number and a few of the Chrysalis counselors and their spouses. The place filled up quickly and salads were served. Bud was nervous—he couldn't eat. He went and found Dr. Feder. She was at one of the better tables, in a knockout diaphanous gown. She enthusiastically introduced him ("This is Bud Wiggins, our writer-in-residence—*former,*" she amended) to her husband, an eager, bland-looking man in horn-rimmed glasses. Witold was also at the table. He called Bud over affectionately. He was already drunk. The director dramatically opened the playbill, pointing to "Performance Heart—fragments of a love story, by Bud Wiggins." He clownishly highlighted his own credit: *staged by Witold Kracz.*

The lights suddenly lowered and the orchestra readied itself. Bud could see the Golden Monarchs in the wings, bustling in preparation, their collective show biz sap rising. They stormed the stage and went through their shameless Fosse-lized gyrations, old-trouper smiles stuck on faces like kabuki masks.

After about ten minutes Perry Como appeared in their midst, parting the heaving spider-veined terpsichores to a standing ovation. The Monarchs peeled to the wings like Busby Berkeley biplanes until the stage was empty. A stool was brought for Mr. Como. Bud couldn't believe the singer was still alive. He remembered being nine years old watching Frank Gorshin do impressions. When Gorshin did Como, he'd sit on a stool and fall asleep in the middle of a song. Now there he was before him, Perry Como, beautiful and white-haired and deathless, a golf course apparition, a numinous Hallmark Card grandpa. The Monarchs had gone out and hired him—a person could hire anybody. After the show the trademark stool would probably go back to the Smithsonian. Maybe Como had an apartment there.

Bud thought of Jeanette somewhere in the audience and it jolted him.

He excused himself and wandered backstage to the hall outside the makeshift dressing rooms. Witold appeared a moment later and offered him a Marlboro Light.

"We We We are very brave. It's fan*tas*tic, Wiggins." He was smiling at Bud with wolfish affection. "I wish I can to put this onto film. But maybe it is better to only have in in in in the memory."

Bud was dragging off the cigarette when Esme flew from one of the stalls in a panic.

"You gotta come!"

"What's happening?"

"It's Franklyn!" she shouted, leading them back. "He's really fucked up!"

As they entered the room, they saw him, head resting on the makeup table, arms dangling like a real skitz. Franklyn looked up at them dramatically, softly crying. Esme started rubbing his neck.

"I can't do this."

He was slurring.

"Why not?" Witold asked.

Bud tried a show-must-go-on gambit: "Dammit, Franklyn, we're dedicating this to Derek."

"The haircut!" Franklyn slammed his fist on the table.

"Be quiet!" commanded Witold, an instant general. For a second Bud thought he was going to do a Patton and slap the shit out of the shell-shocked leading man.

Franklyn sat there and sulked. "Hey, I'm sorry! Okay? Fuck all you people. The thing is dead, long live the thing!"

He got up and left.

"He's too stoned to go on anyway," Esme said.

"What did he mean, 'the haircut'?" Bud asked.

Esme sat down on a fold-up chair, tucking her leg beneath her. "Derek shaved a cross on his head before he hanged himself."

Bud remembered the man with the broom.

"That's what our friend Tristan did," Witold said, "when Iseult refused to see him." He smiled enigmatically, as if begetting a secret scenario.

"The divorce papers shook him more than he let on," she said.

"He He He He *pretend* to be a fool, Tristan, to gain entrance to the castle, right? It is a common theme, no? To feign madness? Franklyn, he's for real! But Hamlet . . . Tristan . . . alas, poor Derek—we knew him well. Tonight, we we we demonstrate our expertise!"

Witold laughed cryptically; he reminded Bud of some tenured grotesque at a cheesy junior college.

"He was not *mad,* Derek, that is why I I I I say it's 'pretend.' He was *de-pressed.* Look"—he turned to Bud—*"listen* and *look:* there is only one thing can we do or else we don't show anything. You must play the part, Wiggins. It is not the first time an author reads his words, believe me!"

Esme came to life like an animated puppet.

"Bud, you *can! Will* you? The material's so *wonderful.* With the dedication to Derek and everything—you've acted during rehearsals, I've *watched* you. You're really good!"

Bud shook his head. Foremost in his mind was Jeanette. The thought of her seeing him perform was too much; it made him squirm.

"I'm just not really anxious to *participate* that way."

"Oh, come on!" Esme cried, on the verge of hysteria. She flashed Witold a revelatory smile. "He doesn't want to be *seen*!"

"He is vain," Witold said, and shrugged as if already moving beyond contempt or disappointment. He was crafty. *"Look at me, Bud!* Don't you think I know half the people out there? You've written something *beautiful* and you're worried about being *embarrassed*? Anyway, most of the audience has been *through* Chrysalis—or *some* kind of damned Program—and the rest are fucking eighty-year-old *socialites.* Cesar Romero and fucking Loretta Young! Come on, Bud!"

"Listen, Wiggins: no one will know it is you. Don't Don't Don't worry. Because we can put on the heavy makeup. Tristan is mad in first scene! Right? We We can keep this way for second. The audience is stupid, they won't know, they don't care. You shouldn't care, but okay. I I I I I have the highest award in my country, my last film was here twenty millions to make, and I am here tonight with you, it is *crazy*! But there is a beauty, too. I I I don't give a shit! You do this for me, for you, for Esme, for for for for for Derek, for the beautiful craziness of it! These Golden Butterflies can fuck themselves, are you going to be afraid of them? Of these rich old ladies and their fags? Don't forget, Tristan pretend to be a a a leper, he paint himself, and Iseult she she don't believe is him, she disgusted, she she she she she she drive him out of the church. This 'leper'! So he try again and he shave his head like De Niro in *Taxi Driver* and change the color of his skin, to be mad—even his voice he change, right? When I I am finished with with with you, Bud Wiggins will not exist!"

Bud went over his lines with Esme as the director expertly applied the greasepaint. There would be two scenes, as planned—the first, with the "bad plumbage" in the asylum; the second in the orchard, beside the "celestial pavilion."

The program notes provided an introductory paragraph: in the opening scene, Bud and Jeanette have already split for the "final" time. Bud has a successful career in the movies and

Jeanette is working as a nurse in a psychiatric hospital. She has a new lover, and Bud a new wife, but he hasn't yet consummated the marriage. He goes to visit Jeanette at work, but they don't allow him on the Unit. He gains entry by feigning incestuous urges for a sister. Once inside, Bud proclaims his love and promises to take her away to a great house on a hill with a magic orchard. She tells him to hurry because the plumbing in the hospital is so bad. That's when they do the fractious duet of broken pipes and ruined carpet, a microcosm for all doomed earthly marriages.

In the concluding section—the play's epiphany—the lovers die from desire in "that shining house in the fields whence none return," their halved hearts joined as one. (The inmates had collaborated on an enormous papier-mâché brooch, gold-sprayed and peppered with rhinestones, carefully bifurcated with an X-Acto knife.) It was the scene he hoped would bring down the house.

Again he thought of Jeanette in her seat and experienced a wave of fear and nausea. How had all this come to pass? If a few months ago someone had told him he was soon to be onstage in the Grand Ballroom of the Beverly Palm Hotel before a black-tie audience, starring in a gala, gaga production of a play he'd written on a psycho ward, Bud Wiggins would have howled. And all to win back Jeanette! It was an absurd and strangely glorious achievement. Yet his love had nobly done all that, had conceived this stunning opera buffa. The night would be filled with laughter and mystery and tears.

The understudy was ready to go on.

Bud stood in the wings and peeked into the vast room from behind a curtain. It was the same place he used to dance as a boy, at the cotillion trophy balls.

The audience was blackness. He felt taut and unreachable under the makeup—anonymous. The Monarchs were winding up their rousing cancan; soon they'd jostle past him like a pack of cyborg Gwen Verdons, overheated and jubilant, a flurry of teeth and sweat. Jeanette's face floated up before him like a pin-up pasted over a bombsight. He was Dana Andrews, at last.

The screenwriter felt something brush his back and turned. It was Witold. He paid tribute to Bud's esprit de corps with a smile and silent clapping of hands. The director said he never watched any of his productions from the audience.

There was about a minute left to show time, and to calm his own butterflies, the nervous Tristan began to think about future projects.

"Witold," he whispered, mindful of his collaborator's potential usefulness as exec producer on such a project. "What do you think of making all this into a feature—the whole asylum/play-within-a-play thing?"

"I find the asylum angle boring and overdone." The director's smile became brittle and impatient, like someone coming down from a high. He spoke smoothly, without impediment. "Jesus, you've just done that, Wiggins! One or two scenes, okay. Then: enough! Don't forget what Nabokov said: 'There is nothing more tedious than a protracted allegory based on a well-worn myth.' "

The director of Chrysalis House brought up Dr. Deirdre Feder to introduce the very special entertainment for tonight.

When he joined Esme onstage, Bud felt otherworldly. Words came like chunks of wood from his mouth. He saw Brian, in his surgical greens, shout, "He's fibrillating!" Bud had the sensation of being chased; something awful was gaining on him.

If we'd bought the house, we'd still have the fuhcocktuh *problem with the fucking pipe!*

Amazing how you could be a thousand miles away. Right now, right there with Esme in the middle of the valley of the broken plumbage, Bud was thinking of AlphaFilm, how in the morning he was going to get on their case about the insurance. The thing was chasing him again—

I said how far did he run the fucking snake out?

Then he'd drop back into his body and hear himself given or giving a cue, immersed in the scene again. Panic. Bud shoved it down by imagining himself at home or having dinner at Musso's, weeks into the future, doing a crossword or finally reading *Anna Karenina,* all this behind him.

They were nearing his virtuosic "despair" soliloquy—the hard part was almost over. Bud had the lines to come down cold but could improvise if he blanked.

They said their last words as the light emptied Esme into darkness and bore down on Bud like a laser, as if to separate his skull along with his heart. He counted only a single cough as he began to speak.

"The plumbage in my beautiful twenty-eight-hundred-dollar apartment! With its thousand windows of whiteness. And the landlord's not around: he owns the drawers and the built-ins: he owns the wood that made the drawers and the hands that made the wood and the trees the wood came from—the orchard!—he owns the souls of the men whose hands held the tools that carved the wood. And he owns the thing that is there before the souls are. Whereas I own nothing. Nothing but the insult of the new day."

He was completely unafraid. He had them in his hands and felt the power, the theatricalization of his self. For an instant, Bud Wiggins wished himself back to every place he'd ever shaken, groveled or run away from, so he could father himself and slay the hairy giants. He even allowed himself to feel the nearness of Jeanette. He *knew* she was there, knew he would have her back, if not tonight, then tomorrow, if not tomorrow, next week, or next year, five years, ten. He'd bide his time—he was that powerful. All eyes were on him as he began the exotic, deliberately brummagem speech of Tristan mad, assaulted by bill collectors. The music had been cued; Bruckner rushed in, lifting him up.

"What is prison? I have no fear now, I don't need your Christ! A blue sky always finds its way to a wall, can I solve the equation of walls and blue sky? Rain down the blows, what good's a reflex without a hammer? Tear out this heart and I'll ascend! I see it now: the orchard, blown by wind! The trees do their dead dance and she will come."

The audience was still, the music fell away. It was time. Bud slowly pulled the half-heart prop from his outsized pocket. He would hold it out for all to see, studded and gold-flecked. He was like an athlete now, a front-runner on the last lap.

"She will bring me her half and the wind will bind this heart together. The jewels will become our eyes and our bodies will become hung like constellations in the cope. The wind will knock the tears from the starry blackness as they fall from our sky-hung eyes, irrigating the orchard. But where is she?"

At once a great shout bellowed from the room, followed by a nasty shattering of glass. Bud assumed it was a clumsy waiter and continued, still in high command. A shadowy figure advanced from the audience. With the light in his eyes, it was difficult to see. . . . Might this be a freakish bit of whimsy on the part of Witold's, to have Esme appear among the tables? No—she wasn't due until the "reunion" finale. Maybe they were running long and the director had boldly cued her entrance—still, why from the audience?

No, it wasn't Esme, Esme was large and this one was—Jeanette! Half blinded by the lights, Bud saw enough of the petite figure to be certain. A frail voice came from the dark, frizzy head; but he couldn't *hear*. What was she saying, what was she *doing*? He stalled, ad-libbing a few words so the audience would think it was part of the play. He was stupefied—Jeanette had outdramatized him, and Bud loved her a thousand times more for it. He raised his hand, fingers clutching the ornament, its papier-mâché chain dangling down.

"Iseult? Come! I am in the orchard. See how the palace is lit?"

She was almost upon him; there was commotion as a few startled diners at the nearest tables stood up.

"Buddy? They wouldn't let me in! I don't have a ticket and they wouldn't let me in!"

A man in a suit caught up to her, seizing her shoulders. Bud blocked the light with his hand and saw a new face, that of his mother, swollen and smeared with makeup, a pleading *Baby Jane*.

"I have the heart!" Dolly cried. "Why do I still wear it, from that fucking man? Take it, Buddy! I don't know why you want it, but it's yours, my darling, don't cry! How I love you, *e-zih-zinee*!"

She collapsed.

vvvv

When Dolly opened her eyes, she was on the ballroom floor. The first thing she saw, hovering like some nightmare image, was the face of Dr. Burton Naugawitz—he'd rushed over to offer a little grandstanding ministration. It took the physician a moment to recognize his litigious ex-patient, her cicatrized face an irksome reminder of foggier days. She screamed, of course.

Dolly loved telling that story (ensconced in her semiprivate at Cedars) because its horror was entirely mitigated by a detail Bud provided later on. The repentant Butcher of Bedford Drive may have done some crabwise scurrying after her collapse, but it was the wispy-haired Mike Nichols who broke her fall; she had virtually landed at the famous man's feet. Dolly was going to send Mr. Nichols her book as soon as she found a publisher, with a note attached about how "hard she fell" for him, etc.

After a few days she felt much better. She'd been taking too many pills in the wrong combinations, a fact Dolly blamed on an expensive Victorian pillbox "gifted" her by a client—she liked showing it off, taking the thing out and *using* it. Her self-prescriptions were also the source of eccentricities over the last six weeks or so and what the internist called the "hypercathexis" regarding a particular necklace with jeweled heart; she'd been clutching the bijou with such force the nurses had to pry it from an infected palm. The object of such devotion sat on her nightstand beside the aqua water pitcher and the flowers from the girls at Hoffmann-Dougherty. Bud examined it, opening the latch. There was no photo within. The artifact beckoned him like a puzzle piece—his brain picked away at it until he could remember.

His mother told him the whole backstory. Though Bud had been discreet about his work-in-progress, Dolly's nosy socialite friend tipped her to the benefit's addition of her son's "sketch"—that's what she called it, like it was Rowan and Martin. So Dolly stopped by his apartment after work one day when Bud was rushing to the hospital to rehearse. She asked to stay a few minutes, said she wasn't feeling so great, she'd lock the door when she left, but she was really there to *snoop*, whacked out and paranoid from the magic pillbox combos. After he left for the hospital, she found a draft of the *sketch* in a drawer with its emphasis on the "halved ornament," described with the precision of a writer of technical manuals, right out of Bud's unconscious; there could be no mistaking what he was talking about. It was hard to focus with all the dope, the Lasix and codeine and cortisone and thyroid and estrogen and Xanax, but she *gets* that this "character" keeps looking for the "other half," over and over he's looking. And Dolly wanted to *help*. Why had he been banning her from the Grand Ballroom, site of triumphs past? She had to hear it all from that woman— inglorious. She was hurt. She was his mother, a writer herself, his greatest audience! His best friend and he knew it. She used to take him miniature-golfing after Morris brutalized them, picking up the pieces. Putting a smile back on his gorgeous little *punim*—*The Young Scholar*.

Dolly found it in the closet outside the downstairs den, Bud's old bedroom, in one of the shoeboxes of Polaroids, next to the oil painting of Morris she kept on the wall until just a few years ago, Moe in a serge suit, smiling like a Mussolini. She didn't care about the other half—the *shit*'s half. She hoped it was choking him while he rotted in hell. She didn't want to embarrass her son, but she *had* to bring it to him, she burned to help him on his big night at the Beverly Palm, where they'd won their trophies. She put on her makeup best she could and wriggled into an Adolfo. Her pressure was dropping as she entered the ballroom to give him what he was searching for. *E-zih-zinee!* She could laugh about it now, from her semiprivate.

The fabled necklace was comprised of a locket given her by Morris to commemorate the tenth anniversary of their marriage—a jeweled heart, cut down the middle, each with a tiny photo of the other, Moe's half nestled in a swale of chest hairs prematurely gray. They were living in the Heights. He was a second grader when he first laid eyes on it, a student at Ulysses S. Grant. Seeing the bauble had inspired him to make his own offerings of costume jewelry from Saturday schoolyard bazaars. He spent his lunch money bestowing oedipal gifts while Morris was away on business and Dolly, so beautiful then, oohed and ahed like every one was frankincense and fresh magic.

Derek was buried the Sunday after the benefit. At graveside, friends took turns reading excerpts from his work. No one came from *Entertainment Tonight.* A somber, reflective Sester-Neff was there in his epic coat. Dr. Feder was also there but left early, probably to avoid a close encounter with the grief-stricken stud. Then again, Bud thought, maybe she ducked into a mausoleum to blow a pallbearer. He laughed to himself.

After the service, he was standing outside the chapel with the Jacket when Penny Reich approached. Did Bud know anything about a play her husband had been working on in the hospital? She was sure there was a play; it had somehow vanished. He told her all he knew of was this story about the pyramids Derek had been reading aloud. The truth was, he had searched his apartment for the black binder without success and now thought of its disappearance with guilty, shuddering disbelief. Penny said she had the pyramid story and Bud sighed; at least that was something.

The three of them talked for a while about trivia, in the low tones of mourners. It was time to go home. Bud hoped he'd never see either one of them again.

———

Bud got a letter from Jeanette saying she was sorry she missed the benefit. She was in Mexico. The note went on, informally formal, then took a weirdly vindictive turn: she accused the screenwriter of being a coldly manipulative "borderline psychopath" and threatened legal action if he tried contacting her again. The last part didn't sound like her. Probably one of her harridan friends from the Meetings talking.

₩₩₩

About a month later, there was a full-page ad in *Variety* announcing the Derek Johansen Young Playwrights Fund. Bud presumed the seed money came from what was left of the grant; maybe Reich had auctioned off the Rolls. She'd lost a husband, but won a class-act nonprofit organization—the careerist's Purple Heart. Crisis equals Opportunity. Agents always knew as much.

A few days after the ad appeared, Bud was messengered an envelope from the Circle Group containing Derek's "Bedouin tale." The attached note said the couple went to Israel on their honeymoon (no mention of Galápagos or Guayaquil) and Derek, already showing signs of strain, took a side trip to Cairo; when he returned, his mind was thoroughly disordered. The widowed agent said that she was thinking of printing Derek's "evocative" story herself, as a limited edition in memoriam. She remembered Bud saying he'd published one of his own stories and wanted some feedback. She would be back from Bali in three weeks.

It was night. Bud lay in bed with the Xeroxed pages and thought about his friend's lost play. He began diminishing its potential; the thing couldn't have been too coherent. The screenwriter even began to doubt its existence. Maybe it was like *The Shining:* all work and no play makes Jack a dull boy. See the pyramids, indeed. Everything must go.

Bud reread the business about the accidental death of the lovesick Bedouin boy, then went on.

> Joey Nasser's story was beginning to get interesting. It had a good structure, anyway. The playwright had always been weak on structure—the guide could pitch pretty good. Derek felt himself closing in on something. He knew that getting away from the States would do it: he had felt it in Jericho, with its shticky old aqueducts; in the ravening jewelers of Bethlehem; at the Dead Sea, when he stood on the balcony of the hotel at night and stared out at the nothingness as if awaiting a shuttle to the moon. He had felt it when the creepy Orthodox boys hissed at him for sins he couldn't name. But most of all, Derek felt his story sense returning in the Old City, where he retraced the fourteen stations of the cross.
> It was all laid out for him, like a treatment for a script:
>
> 1. Pilate condemns Jesus.
> 2. Jesus receives the cross.
> 3. Jesus falls under the weight of the cross.
> 4. Mary sees Jesus with the cross.
> 5. Simon of Cyrene is made to take the cross.
> 6. Veronica wipes Jesus' face.
> 7. Jesus falls again.
> 8. Jesus speaks to the women of Jerusalem.
> 9. Jesus falls again.
> 10. Jesus is stripped of his garments.
> 11. Jesus is nailed to the cross.
> 12. Jesus dies on the cross.
> 13. Jesus' body is taken from the cross.
> 14. Jesus' body is laid in the Tomb of Joseph of Arimathea.
>
> So said the bedside brochure.

He set down the pages and phone-ordered some Thai.

Tomorrow was a big day. Ramón had called and said he was taking his family to Chile for a few weeks. He'd hired someone to drive the limo while he was gone, but the guy suddenly got sick, and Ramón was desperate. The gig came just in time— Bud was running low on cash and hadn't heard anything from Weissen in a while. Better to go back to work.

The food came and he made a plate for himself, savoring his aloneness. Tomorrow he'd start a serious diet. Begin exercising again. He was relatively at peace. He was a survivor. All of his problems were faded to black and white, framed, and pushed away. Bud lit a cigarette. For a while, he would be smoking more and eating less, until he got his weight under control. An old *Cliffs Notes* quote floated to him from nowhere: *I was born, Sancho, to live dying. And thou to die eating.* He was sad about Derek; soon he might be able to cry. Not just yet.

He settled into bed with the last passage, skimming over the part about the bloody war between tribes over the killing of the boy. He read out loud, carefully enunciating the words. At last, Derek was leaving Egypt. . . .

On the way to the airport, they passed the quarry where the pyramid blocks were hewn and carried; Derek's tourist mind dutifully knee-jerked, straining to picture the impossible ancient scene. He was tired, and thought again of Joey Nasser's story. He wanted to use it for something. Yes, he would.

This morning, on the way to the pyramids, he asked his guide about the sprawling City of the Dead. Rich families outfitted crypts with electricity so they'd have light when coming to pay respects. Joey Nasser told him squatters tapped into the power so they could have television and it sounded like another lie, but how else to explain this living necropolis? Derek thought he could write a film about it, make it about the homeless, but surreal, the way that Kurosawa movie was set in a dump. No—he'd write a play instead. After all, that's what he knew. He'd write the play of his life and call it "City of the Dead."

But the moment the title came to him, he was deflated.

He'd heard it so many times before, or thought he had. It was pompous, overworked, a poseur's cliché: . . . *of the Dead*—a thousand times he'd heard the ringing of its grandiose literary bell, its dead-end profundity.

They passed the cemetery and Derek told him to pull over. Joey Nasser said there was no time, he would miss his plane. Derek got out to walk amidst the shantytown of mausoleums. The squatters paid no attention to him. There was something there, hovering over the place, something strange and beautiful. Ineffable. If he walked around enough, he might find it. He felt the familiar calm before creation. He felt alive in every cell.

Slowly a title came to him.

It was the only one in the world, and it was magnificent. Such a title came once in a lifetime and would stand like a cool pillar above the text, town-towering. It had waited to be claimed by him—why had he forsaken it? It was born for him, now his and his alone:

City of the Dead.

6. Wild Psalms

Mrs. Steiner's brain-damaged son lived out his days at a famous "school" in Ojai, and Bud had to get her there by noon. He was to arrive at the Towers around nine so they'd have time to visit the orchid nurseries along the coast. One of the flowers was named for a long-dead daughter. Mrs. Steiner wasn't the luckiest mother, but you wouldn't know it; she watered her children, living and dead, and it vaguely humanized her.

Bud had driven her places before—to the Bistro Garden and Jimmy's for lunch, and to the galleries, always the galleries, sometimes accompanied by her curator, a tawny, serious-minded girl from UCLA named Melanie Sharf. Mrs. Steiner had a vast collection of modern art. Most of it was on loan or in storage, and Melanie periodically rotated pieces through her employer's crammed penthouse apartment. The paintings were usually hung without much care, giving the place a kind of clearinghouse effect—candelabra knocking against Rothko, paperbacks propped against De Kooning.

The little he knew about her Bud had gleaned from the prudish curator during idle conversation. Millicent S. Steiner (of the Chrysalis House pavilion) was a widow and philanthropist. She had an even wealthier sister who lived somewhere in San Marino. She had a daughter who died years ago and a son, now in his forties, who was in a bad wreck when he was a teen. The Ojai son.

The Towers was the tallest building on the Strip. Bud stood in front of the designer aquarium embedded in the wall of the dark lobby. He noticed something trapped within the decorative latticed branches at the back of the enormous bubble, fluttering and membranous, floating like a swatch of white chiffon. As his eyes adjusted, he realized the stuff was the ghostly remains of a fish impaled on the barbs. What kind of sadist would decorate an aquarium with a killing machine? Why were there no other fish anyway? Not even a starfish, crab or shell. No one noticed or cared. As he meditated on the seascape's trite, queasy desuetude, the ladies—Melanie and Mrs. Steiner—stepped from the elevator. Bud nodded at them, put on his cap and walked briskly past the doorman to the car. The three began their drive down Sunset Boulevard to the beach.

The day was gorgeous, an auspicious one to begin work on a new project. Bud would work in his head as they drove, letting the themes roost, the dross evaporate. It felt right today. How to convert life to story? The question dogged him like a riff of car alarms in the night. Life *was* story—trillions of scripts were airborne around him, he had only to take dictation like the Surrealists before him. Bud felt "in the mode," on the threshold of something big. Maybe it was his stint at Chrysalis or closing the book on Jeanette that had finally freed him: today the screenwriter was a great, vibrant Receptor, like the feverish time in adolescence when he read Strindberg's *Inferno* and life became a waking dream, a *cosmo-demonic* detective story, as Henry Miller might have put it. All Bud had to do was pay attention to the clues. Everything—this bright day, this rich old woman, this savvy chestnut-eyed curator in her deep blue shift—everything was fraught with meaning and awaited his use. He was on the way to Oz.

As they drove, Bud thought of *Lilith*. The other night he was in the video store returning a tape. As usual, they said he had a balance for unpaid rentals. He didn't keep a record and challenging them wasn't worth the hassle. It was beginning to feel like a neighborly rip-off; Bud felt like firebombing the smug little video store and its spike-haired thiefy clerks. On top of all this, he was thumbing through a printout of available cassettes when a counterperson with pierced lips told him it was free. So he took two—one for Dolly—and the girl smiled and said: "You must be Jewish."

On the way out, *Lilith* was on the ceiling-hung monitor. Bud stopped to watch.

Warren Beatty was a veteran who got a job as a glorified orderly at a ritzy sanatorium. Jean Seberg played Lilith, a schizophrenic nympho with her own private language. Beatty was so handsome the nuts were practically peeing in their pants. There was a scene where they all took an outing and sat by a rushing creek and Peter Fonda mooned over her while Seberg furiously sketched the water to a beatnik sound track. Beatty squinted at the two like they were doomed, holy children while Fonda said things to her like "If I trust my hands, would they really lead me to things I love?"

It was pretty bad, but stayed with him; he started thinking again about *Asylum Piece*.

"Did anyone ever see *Lilith*?"

"What's that?"

Now and then Bud liked breaking the silence with chitchat, even though he sensed it irritated Mrs. Steiner—it made him feel charmingly subversive. As long as he kept the interruptions to a minimum, she suffered them valiantly, as if such homely communion were the unhappy by-product of recent workers' legislation.

"It was a movie, with Warren Beatty."

Melanie piped up while Mrs. Steiner stewed.

"Did that take place in a hospital or something?"

"Right," Bud said.

"Who's the girl in it, Bud?"

"Jean Seberg."

"Beatty's pretty good," said Mrs. Steiner. "I took my grandson to see *Dick Tracy*. He liked it well enough."

"Are you thinking of writing something like that, Bud?"

Mrs. Steiner looked at Melanie as if she were insane.

"Bud's a writer."

"I thought he was a driver." She spoke as if Bud had vanished.

"He writes for the movies."

"Let's have quiet awhile, okay?"

Mrs. Steiner stared at the sea while Bud watched her in the rearview and made faces. He remembered the words of Warren Beatty's boss man, the shrink, who spoke of the poor inmates: *I often compare them to fine crystal which has been shattered by the shock of some intolerable revelation. They have seen too much with too fine an instrument.* Too fine an instrument! It was like blowing Jean Cocteau.

It was at this moment that Bud decided to do his own *Lilith,* making the Beatty character a guy just back from Vietnam. Maybe he'd mix it with *Toy Soldier,* his old script about a journalist impersonating a vet: the man's never even been overseas and comes to this posh psych hospital looking for a job, saying he was in "the Nam." When people ask about his experiences, he talks about the Mekong Delta or whatever and the film could actually go into phony flashbacks—we'd be able to *see* his trumped-up pastiche of what it was like "over there"; that would be great fun. Bud had run all the war flicks and was bored out of his skull. He was tired of smug symphony-scored slow-mo rice-paddy carnage, all that hopped-up hammy Horrors of War high drama. Time to do a little serious debunking, something outrageously comic and expressionistic, an *immorality play*—he'd falsify language (he was gonna puke if he heard one more soldier talk about *Zippo raids* and "being in the world") and thumb his nose at the pious liberal politics of agony and death; if he was "reactionary" then so was Swift. Bud Wiggins would liberate the form with an antiantiwar movie that would out-ante them all.

He grunted with confidence, then caught Mrs. Steiner staring at him in the rearview.

"It's nice to be able to entertain yourself."

"If I learn to trust my hands, would they really lead me to things I love?"

"What?" She was scowling.

"It's from *Lilith.*"

"You know, you're getting too cute."

They rode the ten minutes to the nursery in silence. Mrs. Steiner and her companion were inside the glass building for about half an hour. Bud stayed in the car, tripping; moviedom's dreamy new guerrilla.

They arrived at the Brennan School before twelve. The group of white adobe buildings that housed her son had been around since the forties. It resembled the *Lilith* hacienda and Bud imagined Jeff Chandler or Brian Donlevy driving up in a cream-colored roadster and dropping off some harelipped incest child. Mrs. Steiner excused Bud for lunch.

He drove into town, sucking on some jerky he pulled from the glove compartment. It was tough and sweet and vinegary. To hell with lunch. Life was definitely better when he wasn't eating—he wrote better when lean. Food really clung to his ass. He hated the idea of being struck down in the road someday and laid out on a slab at County, his gut cram-full of half-digested Big Macs. He'd made the resolution to fast, as best he could. It would be exciting to get thinner than he'd ever been before. To be a hunger artist.

He bought a fifth of Stoly and a six-pack of Diet Cokes for the backseat bar. As the clerk took his credit card, Bud noticed the numbers tattooed on his arm. While they waited for the approval code to flash, the screenwriter stared. It was a long time since he'd thought about those numbers, years since he'd even seen them—the old guy was a relic. The whole world was an atrocity zone now, and the Cadillac of them all, the once Blue Chip Holocaust, was losing its zip. Like all Jewish boys, Bud and the Doctor were compulsive readers on the subject. In one of the used-book stores, they found *The Theory and Practice of Hell,* a thick yellow tome, Auschwitz-porn with a centerfold of grainy, lurid photos; that was one volume they might actually have paid for. Still, it was hard to get too worked up. Bud grew up among Jews and never experienced the prejudices Moe and Dolly had been exposed to, the kike stuff—the Holocaust remained a kind of lurking epic out of Brothers Grimm. They made jokes about it. *"Six million Jews walk into a bar—"*

So they waited for the approval, and when the number came, it had the same amount of digits as the old man's tattoo. There it was, the electronic epiphany—Bud was definitely "in the mode." The world was ruled by numbers, he vamped, waiting for approval, numbers and numbers and Deuteronomy. The Doctor was numbers- and phone-obsessed. Six months before he died, he installed a second line in Bud's apartment because Bud always complained when Brian came over and monopolized the phone in his Methedrine-fueled search for illicit credit card codes; he also enjoyed calling New Zealand and French Guiana and Papua New Guinea and Easter Island. *Just send me the bill,* he said, like a high roller. The point being, when Don Bloom finally sent over the medical examiner's report, Bud noticed the autopsy number was 657-124. The second line that Brian installed was 657-1024. *Ruled by numbers.* That was one of those coincidences he rarely told people because it was too obvious—a ghost story that never quite delivered.

On the way back to Los Angeles, Mrs. Steiner was abnormally talkative. Visiting the invalid had softened her. Bud felt

warmly familiar, like an errant nephew doing penance behind
the wheel before inheriting his great-aunt's millions. He had
genuine affection for this uncomely, puzzling woman of many
mansions. Millicent Steiner was splenetic and repressed, like
that movie about the old lady and her chauffeur—you had to
bully your way right through, that's all. He wasn't a career
chauffeur anyhow, so why should he give a shit about slavish
rules of conduct? He'd shake it up, be "loose." He was fluid,
polymorphic, that was the thing that distinguished Bud Wiggins from the other hired hands, the fawning lummoxes who
drove her from points A to B; he was an artist. Maybe he had
some weird kind of future with this woman. You never knew.
It was worthwhile to give a push.

Bud rambled on like the three were having tea at Trumps,
fancying himself a blood confidant, a maverick young heir.
Instead of the limo, he pretended to be driving a stately midwestern sedan, a New Yorker like his crybaby grandfather used
to have, then a Jag, then a Bentley, then a Range Rover and
finally, a Lincoln Town Car. In his mind he saw the chiaroscuro
of branches playing on the hood as the car threaded its way
along dusty treelined roads to the Ranch, the Steiner digs in
Santa Barbara with the Pollocks hanging in the perfect barn
with the commissioned Ed Ruscha horseshoe sign hanging over
the entrance, an ever-hip welcome, green wood lettering on a
blue wood field: STATE OF THE ART. There would be a black-tie
hayride tonight, folks choppered from the airport, a real hoe-
down with blackened redfish and reddened blackfish and western ensembles from Maxfield's and guests who owned priceless
acreage under landmark skyscrapers, whole sections of cities.
Bud Wiggins was once her driver, they'd say, now here he was
poised to marry into the clan. He would sire a damaged son and
make the duteous trip to Ojai in a steel blue Facel-Vega. By
then he'd be fifty and possess a slim, formidable body of work,
essays and poetry and film criticism, the rigor of his output and
the kindness of critics long since endearing him to the flintiest
of relatives.

"How long has your son been at Brennan?"

"A long time."

"I really think that a beautiful place can heal."

"Yes, that's true," answered Melanie.

"When I was at the Foundation—a halfway house in the Heights, up north—I found the spirit of place had an extraordinary effect on the emotions. Extraordinary and phenomenal and irrevocable."

What the hell. He liked playing the lyric fool for Mrs. Steiner; it gave him certain farfetched liberties. He wanted to connect with her on the subject of the son, take her out of herself, *move* her.

Melanie nervously cleared her throat. "I think a pretty place is especially important when one is ill."

"Because the body *knows,*" he went on, the drunken seer. "To be in certain hills at a certain moment of a certain day— Have you heard of Jean Giono, Mrs. Steiner? He was a French writer—*Joy of Man's Desiring*? Let me show you how it begins: 'It was an extraordinary night. The wind had been blowing; it had ceased, and the stars had sprouted like weeds. They were in tufts with roots of gold, full-blown, sunk into the darkness and raising shining masses of light—"

"Hey, you know what, idiot?"

Bud watched the old woman's rheumy dead-genital eyes in the mirror as she spoke up. Her hair was a helmet; she looked like some hellish sci-fi Roman senator.

"Just drive, all right? Just fucking drive."

﹏﹏

After he dropped them at the Towers, Bud went back to the hotel and sat around the TV room. The dispatcher gave him an airport drop-off. He swung out of the garage and picked a businessman up at the front entrance. Bud schmeared the doorman, just to keep the wheels greased. It was already four o'clock. The traffic would be bad, but he knew a shortcut through Cheviot Hills.

He thought about the Vietnam movie as he wound his way along Motor. He knew of a vet center over on Franklin—maybe he'd drop by to get a feel. Keep it simple, though. Don't do too much research, already did a lot for *Toy Soldier.* Just a taste. Ease into it. Start with the sound track. For "the Nam," it was always Hendrix and the Doors, Hendrix and the Doors, tedious steadicam honchos with their weed-sucking acid-rock warrior shorthand—enough already. Bud's idea was to use thirties and forties tunes instead, like something of Dennis Potter's. He'd explode all the hackneyed, nostalgic syntheses of that war.

He dropped the businessman at the curb. The guy looked into Bud's eyes, shook his hand and said, "Thank you." That's how it was with some of them. Instead of giving you money, they looked in your eyes and thanked you, as if it were the same.

There weren't any police, so Bud put on his cap and dashed inside to hustle a ride. He was looking for someone with money. The game was discreetly to approach such a person at the baggage carousel and ask if he needed a car. It was amazing how many were going right back to the Beverly Palm; you could nail them for at least fifty, sometimes a hundred. The practice was illegal and the airport cops were vigilant. Bud acted harried, as if searching for a tardy VIP.

There wasn't much action. The six o'clock from New York—a traditionally "fat" flight—wasn't due for an hour but was worth waiting for. First, he needed to park the car in the lot. As he stepped to the sidewalk, Bud noticed a man with a black leather knapsack and expensive briefcase. He was in his late sixties with a long silver beard, a healthy riot of curls. A heavy blue coat was slung over an arm and his shirt was stained with food. *Get Outta My Emergency Room.* What was he doing with a copper Halliburton? Bud had priced them around the time of the hatbox, and they weren't cheap. Was he a courier? No, he looked too squirrelly for that. He was smiling and his eyes were fierce. He gave the uncanny impression of blithely waiting for something momentous. Bud was pulled to him as if by an invisible cord.

"Are you expecting a car?"

"Young man, I am waiting for a taxi."

His mellifluous voice bore an absurdly thick Yiddish accent.

"You're waiting in the wrong area. Where are you going?"

"I am going to Beverly Hills, to the Four Oaks House. Do you know it?"

The Four Oaks House was an anachronism, a throwback to a different era; in fact, Bud had looked into staying there when he moved out of Dolly's. It was one of the last residential hotels in that city, only a block or so from Rodeo Drive.

"I'll take you there. I have a limousine."

He'd give the guy a treat, for the equivalent of cab fare. Why not.

"A limousine?" Suddenly the old man looked very sly. "A cab or a limousine—this is *sophist's choice*! You must give me a corsage, like prom night. A car like this," he said, "is for a corsage or a cortege."

Bud opened the door and motioned him in. When he tried disencumbering him of the Halliburton, the old man yanked it back with a scowl, like he was cuffed to it. The curious traveler clung to the knapsack as well, and it didn't look light. Maybe he really was a courier. Before he climbed in the car, he looked Bud up and down.

"Why are you so thin? You look like a *muscleman.*"

Whatever. I'm a muscleman and you're the *Treasury of Yiddish Humor.* He already wanted to get rid of him. When Bud started closing the door, his passenger thrust out an arm. He saw the tattooed numbers.

"Are you a chauffeur?"

"Yeah. I'm a chauffeur."

The old man shook his head restlessly and grabbed Bud's wrist with a bony hand. "Are you a *sho-far*?"

The screenwriter looked at him blankly.

"If you are a true shofar, you must blow yourself at Yom Kippur's end!"

His face got rubbery and gleeful as he threw Bud back his

wrist and settled in, ready to be driven. He sat with his palms flat on the seat's velour, like a fragile old king afraid of losing his balance. When Bud shut the door, he saw the numbers again through the window. He noted their appearance as a kind of approval code, though the nature of the transaction was yet unknown.

The old man checked in and Bud loitered in the lobby, waiting to be paid.

The Four Oaks House was on a street sheltered by trees, across from a small park. Bud used to walk through it on his way to a sleepy coffee shop on South Beverly. He'd just dropped out of school and the afternoons were suddenly filled with a bright, weirdly alluring emptiness. He sat by himself in a booth and ate unhurried lunches while his rich friends led the moribund life of high school juniors. Club sandwiches at three in the afternoon (it was intriguing how many ways different chefs prepared a club) and strangely ardent dreams of sailing a rusty freighter to Peru. Why Bud chose Peru was beyond him, but the dropout knew he wasn't long for this place. He would linger over his sandwich and feel poignant at the long lunch's end. His ennui was blamed on Morris, who'd died some months before; he disagreed with the notion, but its universality served him well—it made him unapproachable. He knew he was on a journey, an errand of destiny, unamenable to counsel. It was romantic. He sat in the banquette and licked his skin; it smelled sweetly carnal. His mortality aroused him. At seventeen Bud Wiggins was officially retired.

Seeing the little park brought it all back. The trees smelled ambrosial—then. Intermixed with such heaven was a formless and abject dread. There was something about those lunch-booth afternoons, the memory had *color,* heavy and dream-like—maybe he'd had some kind of teenage breakdown and didn't know it. He remembered the obsessive nocturne of Peru and its blue mountains; he'd run to the ends of the earth, falsely accused, son of *The Fugitive.* A freighter would float him to the

Andes. A boyish Ben Gazzara, he'd commune with the great poet Vallejo and eat the mystical vine—a real bar mitzvah. Maybe it wasn't too late. He could invite his new friend, Mr. Martin Buber. Sir Richard Halliburton the *Zionista*.

The old man interrupted his reverie by handing Bud a ten-dollar bill.

"I am Israel." The screenwriter felt tired and wanted to go home. The money didn't matter anymore. "Israel Levi. It's enough?"

"It's fine."

"If it's not enough, you should say."

He fished out a money clip. There wasn't much there. Bud waved him off.

"Tell me your name."

"Bud."

"You have no last name?"

"Wiggins."

"Wiggins . . ." He stroked his beard like a rascal. "Was this *Wigginitz*?"

"I don't think so. I don't know."

"You don't know or you don't care. Which can it be?"

Bud got a second wind and smiled.

"Do you have a wife? Do you have a daughter or a son? Come tomorrow if you are unfettered. I will speak to some people; then we will have a coffee. Is it all right with you, Wigginitz?" He handed him a scrap of paper with an address. "You come at seven, seven-thirty—tomorrow night. Can you do it, Wigginitz?"

"I'll try."

"He's going to try, he says! You're an amazing man, Wigginitz, don't ask me how I know so much. You, I think, are one of the thirty-six. Do you know about the thirty-six? Soon enough, you will know. Much to learn! You're a high number. Me, I am low, let me *set the tone*. The high numbers work hard, and for what? Exhaustion, like tight shoes, can be fatal. Better a beating. I am the Seraph of Strelisk, but better you should call me the Rav, it's all right."

He patted Bud's shoulder and walked to the tiny elevator.

"You have a good car, Wigginitz. We'll make a *shtibl* of this car, to ride with good conscience. Because it is provocative, this car, yes! Isn't it, Wigginitz? Molotov—*mazel tov!*"

Bud drove over to the veterans center. The night was cool and it was good to be out of his cheap suit. A crowd spilled from the building onto the sidewalk.

The poetry reading was over. The place looked like where he used to go for Meetings—humble, cheery and diehard, with lots of ratty couches, busted coffee cups and king-size starfish ashtrays. There were bulletin board announcements of holiday air shows and alcoholism conferences, Agent Orange updates, BVA (Blind Veterans Association) blowouts and bike runs to the Wall. Veterans were like stupid children with an inviolable obsession; they really depressed him.

He plunked down on a smelly chair and leafed through a mimeo program of poems, dull, denuded dithyrambs of the sardonic *and-justice-for-all* school, moronic roundelays on Canadian deserters, Khe Sanh and Uncle Sam. He half expected a stressed-out methadone-gobbling quadriplegic to roll in with an M-6o and do some damage. The cruddiness of the place already had him hostage—life was one grim, low-rent psychodrama here at the VC: the veterans center, the Victor Charlie, the Mr. Charles of Hollywood. It was a mistake to have come down.

Bud glanced at the program again and idly read a poem about divorce. At least it didn't mention the war—didn't have to. It wasn't bad. He got the sense it was written by a real person. He felt a hand on his shoulder and turned around.

"Oh, I'm sorry! I thought you were Thomas."

The woman was around forty—black hair, blue eyes and a southern drawl—and Bud couldn't speak. She looked like a fever dream messenger: full of darkness and the promise of speed.

"I'm Bud."

They shook hands; then he got a pinched, worried look.

"But I *am* a little concerned."

"About what?"

"About Thomas," he deadpanned. "I'm probably overreacting, but I'm worried he isn't here. I think he's on a death trip."

She laughingly caught on.

"Somehow I don't think so. A little death trip might be good for him, though. It's been so long since he's had a vacation."

"What's your name?"

"Rachel. You want to come outside and watch me smoke a cigarette?"

She wore chartreuse stretch pants tucked into Beatle boots and Bud was in love with her by the time they hit the street. He was hoping she'd tell him she ate fire on the Venice boardwalk for a living; he imagined her swallowing the lights of a jungle runway. He was astonished no one disturbed them, couldn't understand why everyone wasn't trying to talk to her. About ten years ago a friend pointed out Anna Karina to him at the Chalet Gourmet and Bud went and saw *Bande à Part* and *Alphaville* at the Nuart—Rachel reminded him of the Godard actress. She had the same kind of beauty, and the same was-famous/might-be-famous charisma, like a traveler incognito. They stood under a streetlamp and she demurely noted Bud's intensity as she spoke, watching him watch her.

His princess was a registered nurse who'd spent two years in Chu Lai. Rachel was a full-time student now, going for her M.S.W. When she asked if he was a vet, Bud lied with an impostor's facility. She said he looked young, but the screenwriter knew he looked just old enough. Rachel probed and Bud kept it general until she begged off. As good as their rapport was, she didn't know him well enough to press—that must have been her thinking. She didn't know him from Adam. Every vet carries his experience differently and you had to respect that.

It was a foolproof fib; his reticence to "open up" could be interpreted as caution or dysfunction. But what was the point? What was there to gain? Nothing but the perversity of the moment. He almost told the truth, but was seized by an epic boredom of self. If he didn't lie, Bud would have to confess who he was and what he was doing there—at the moment, he wasn't so sure anymore. It didn't seem enough to say he was simply curious about the place. And if he took some sort of coy middle ground, he'd be a petty mystery man. One thing was clear: he wasn't about to start with the nauseating *here-for-research-I'm-a-writer* routine. He should probably just cut out and leave St. Joan to her war babies. Time to *didi mow,* as the Nam book glossaries said: go and go quickly. *Mos koshe.*

She was saying the divorce poem was hers. Bud responded with an uncredited paraphrase of a Vallejo stanza. Rachel was impressed.

Bud asked if she wanted to go have a drink. She couldn't— she was meeting a friend.

"Who, Thomas?"

"No." She smiled. "But someone who *knows* Thomas. Actually."

"Is there really a Thomas?"

"There's always a Thomas."

She gave him her number.

That night Bud couldn't sleep. He went over the transcript of his remarks, hawk-eyed, searching for inanities. His heart sped up when he recalled the way she looked at him. He read her poem again and again, spent hours assembling her face, imagining her body, her life, her smells. Inevitably he came to the comic denouement—*You're a vet, right?*—and his guarded, preposterously affirmative retort.

Then Bud got a brainstorm and laughed out loud: *he'd continue to lie.* That's right! After all, this girl demanded the audacity of a fresh approach. Why was he making such a thing about it anyway? He hated that. He'd gone and implied he was a disturbed vet, so big deal. Who gave a shit? It was gonzo *funny*. Besides, he didn't really make any claims. Never too late. He would lie through his teeth then, cryptically referring to his hitch in the halfway house like the place was some kind of posttraumatic stress syndrome emporium. He'd juggle the balls, do a whole number until it got old, *then* tell her the truth—Rachel would love it.

ᴧᴧᴧᴧ

The address the Rav gave him was a nondescript mid-Wilshire professional building with an airport-style metal detector in its lobby. The young Filipino guard beckoned him through.

He stepped off the elevator into the third-floor hallway. There was a long glass case filled with old dolls. A mosaic hung behind it, missing several of its tiles. A metallic Tree of Life swallowed up a sign: HOLOCAUST MUSEUM →

He followed the arrow into a large room filled with exhibits. There wasn't anyone around. There were wall-size blowups: early censures of the Jews, ghetto life, mountainous piles of spectacles and human hair. One of the enlargements was big as a mural and featured a blurry seraglio whose walls had rudely, inexplicably vanished. Naked women, hands covering genitals, huddled like seraphim over a burial pit.

There was a bank of phones attached to a replica of Auschwitz and its grounds. Bud picked up a receiver. The recorded voice explained the camp layout and the destiny of its arrivals. The prisoners arrived by train, it said, and were immediately waved to the left or to the right—the old and sick and very young toward death, the others toward shadowland. He looked closely and saw minuscule figures disembarking from boxcars and even a tiny SS man with an arm raised, pointing fatefully. There were more figures beside the crematorium, in various stages of undress.

He moved on to an exhibit of martyred children's drawings of ghetto life that segued to a bunch of poems by survivors. Bud thought the verses almost worse than the poetastering of the vets. Muse-wise, it seemed exposure to hell had its major downsides.

Bud heard the unmistakable voice of the Rav, then noticed the leather knapsack sitting on the floor beside a glass case. There were three things inside the display: a striped threadbare uniform, a pair of worn shoes and a dented metal bowl. The old man suddenly appeared and stormed toward him.

"The bowl, Wigginitz!" said the Rav, peering into the case. "The bowl was your God. You wear it here"—he pinched an imaginary loop at his waist—"on a wire. You know still, I think of *Quixote.* Have you read?" Bud nodded. "The don, he sees a man with a bowl—a barber. And he thinks it is a great crown! It is a simple dented basin, for shaving, but Quixote sees a treasure! This is what the bowl was, in the Lager. A treasure."

"What's 'Lager,' the camp?"

"It isn't beer," he said sarcastically. *"Konzentrationslager.* Though it could be Schlitz. *Au-Schlitz!"*

Once on the street, the old man walked briskly and Bud made an effort to keep up. He stuck close so he could hear.

"Are you hungry, Wigginitz?"

"Sure."

"Good, we go to Canter's. Cantankerous cantors canter to Canter's. I was a partisan, that was 1939. Our little cadre called itself the Wild Palms, for the trees of Palestine. Also, there were palm trees on Yatkever Street, in Kovno. And in Lwów, too, believe it, no one knows where they came from. We were captured by the Nazis—by then Wild Palms was full of fugitives and frightened men. 'Woe unto us! For the day declineth, for the shadows of the evening are stretched out.' " He looked back at the lagging screenwriter. "Already out of breath! Make *sparks,* you know what are sparks? *Schnell,* Wigginitz, are your legs of iron? Don't be a muscleman, Wigginitz, *komm, aufstehen!"*

The old man began to gallop. Bud was chasing a mad rabbi

down the street, like in a Hasidic tale, and began to laugh—he
was truly "in the mode."

The two went on like that for a few miles, a roving vaudeville
duo, until they reached the Fairfax district. When they arrived
at the restaurant, the Talmudic Jack LaLanne was barely
winded. He made faces at the cheese Danishes and big blocks
of halvah, like a crazy kid. Bud followed him into the rest room.
Inside, the old man read from the yellow sign reminding employees to wash their hands.

" '*Nach dem Abort, vor dem Essen Hände waschen, nicht
vergessen.*' The toilet *Kommando,*" he mused, stroking his
beard. "A board with holes, we used to sit, side by side, to shit.
You must write this, Wigginitz, for the television. For the Fox
Channel. If you are a true *Scheissbegleiter,* you will 'put it into
development.' *Scheisse macht frei*—learn to speak, Wiggins! Or
you cannot understand my jokes!"

Bud ordered a diet plate and was ridiculed with the "muscleman" bit. The old man ordered lox, eggs and onions ("the nova,
please"), a whitefish plate, kreplach, borscht, a New Yorker
sandwich (tongue, pastrami, coleslaw, corned beef, Swiss
cheese on rye), chopped liver, french fries ("please burn them")
and two black-cherry sodas. He soaked up his dishes with
challah, saying, "You must watch they won't take your food.
The best place for bread is in my stomach—I won't steal from
myself!"

He asked the Rav where he came from and, for the first time,
felt his companion's deeper resonances. The old man spoke
with sonorous passion, and by phrasing and intonation made a
chant, a nigun. The story began.

He was a rabbi from Vilna. As a young man he studied at the
Bet ha-Midrash of the old melamed Zing, a Hasidic master—a
zaddik. On 22 Sivan 5701, Zing was present at the Slobodka
massacre, when they made the rabbis eat sandwiches made
from the scroll of the Torah and the genitals of the rebbetzin;
the zaddik's wife and mother were murdered during the campaign. He never mourned them, never lit the *yahrzeit* candle.

When the Rav asked why, he replied there were so many to mourn—"how could he specialize with these two?"

Zing had a daughter, Miriam, and the Rav was in love with her. When things got bad, the Rav arranged for her to be kept with a family in Lwów.

He protected the frail zaddik, looking after him in the ghetto. They moved from place to place; because of Zing's status in the community, the Germans would have killed him right away. Eventually they were sent to the camp. Inside the Lager, people sought the famed rabbi for counsel in matters regarding the commandments of the Halakah, the book of Talmudic Law. The great scholar formed his *sh'eilos u-teshuvos,* or rabbinic responsa, scribbling them on paper. He gave the scraps to the Rav, whose responsibility was to hide them away for posterity.

"What kind of questions?"

The Rav took a breath, seeming to look through Bud as he spoke.

"May a boy don tefillin three months short of his thirteenth birthday? Because they were especially murdering children and the boy wanted bar mitzvah—so, would the Law allow this early? They had to know. May a man castrated by the Nazis— *God avenge him!*—join a minyan? The ruling, by the way, was he is forbidden to live with his wife but is in all other ways a Jew. May a man whose teeth were torn from his mouth soak the matzoh on Pesach—because he can't eat otherwise—when his forebears forbid this soaking? (A *bayus din* overruled the old tradition and it was allowed.) May a Jew translate Torah for a Nazi beast? May a kohen give blessing with his shoes on? May a Jew kill another Jew when ordered under the threat of death? There are many questions! How to sleep with a woman who has menstruated but there is no mikvah? That's a load of menarche, Wigginitz, no? Because this is kareth, see Leviticus eighteen:nineteen and twenty:twenty-one and Tractate Nida in the Babylonian Talmud."

The old man stopped for a moment, taking a plastic pill box from his pocket.

"This is the Luminal." He swallowed two capsules with his soda. "Those were the voiced questions. There were many more unvoiced, and those we must answer at the hour of Lamentations! What serpent flies in the air with an ant lying quietly between its teeth? What eagle has its nest in a tree that does not exist and its young plundered by creatures not yet created, in a place which is not? What are they who descend when they ascend, and ascend when they descend? Because I'll give you a clue, Wigginitz, the flaw of angels is they cannot ascend; the rapture of man, that he must; his tragedy, he will not 'turn'! *Teshuvah!* Who is the beautiful virgin with no eyes, her body concealed in the daytime, revealed in the morning, bedecked with ornaments which are not?" Bud was pallid, overheated by the old man's loopy exegesis. "Love is strong as death, Wigginitz. Lift up your heads, O ye gates! These gates are two grades, found within. They are *hesed* and *pahad*—mercy and fear. Wigginitz, I am fond of you. You are an orphan. The blood love of a father for *eyn sohn,* this is expected. Where there is no blood: this is a mitzvah!"

He threw down a fifty-dollar bill and bolted.

Over the next few days Bud tried working on his Nam/*Lilith* idea but couldn't get the old man out of his head. He'd have to use him somehow, weave him into the script. The screenwriter was already thinking of writing the film as one long Group—he'd draw from his experience at Chrysalis and the distant halfway house days. That troubled time would faithfully serve him.

He called up Foundation memories: after a final club sandwich, Bud ditched Peru, threw out his wallet and hitchhiked up the coast. He stayed at a hostel, then a commune, winding up in a big stone building where they shaved his head and called him a character disorder. The outfit was heavy into therapy, but not of Dr. Jurgen's effete predilection. On Group nights, the five-story nerve center hummed with apostates, convicts, junkies, saints and humanists. Participation was mandatory, the tribal pursuit of mental health doggedly utopian. The place's poignant compulsion to heal moved him; he felt in the midst of an overwrought, ambitiously tender crusade. Once in a while there were marathon Groups. They were called Dissipations and usually lasted three days. The Dissipations were run by Foundation elders called whips; the whips shot participants with water guns so they'd stay awake. Around the last twelve hours, things got heavy. Those pesky whips used strobes, noise and profane props to egg the members on—coffins and whatnot, even "ghosts" made appearances—by then the dissipators were so tweaked they confessed to snuffing unwanted newborns, tossing overdosed lovers from buildings, robbing churches, raping the handicapped, drinking Woolite, shooting Listerine and masturbating their kids. Bud always managed to dodge the Dissipations; he thought it would have finished him.

The movie—Bud Wiggins's *Lilith*—would be a filmed Dissipation. Three days—three acts. It was perfect. The magnificent face of the Rav floated back to him. He'd make the old man's "character" one of the whips! Aside from some establishing-shot exteriors, the only location Bud would need was a large room.

It came to him that the Foundation had another name for whips. They called them rabbis.

Ever since Bud met the Rav, an idiot essay question beat in his brain like a tired pop song: *What is a Jew?* He hadn't thought about his own Jewishness in a while. He was raised indifferently enough; at least his parents weren't Jew-hating Jews ("Those are the worst!" Dolly used to say). Hanukkah was celebrated, but Christmas won out. He remembered only patches of Hebrew school—the aromatic temple, the vainglorious cantor and the rabbi who looked like Steve Lawrence. To this day he retained a kind of half-wit knowledge of certain Hebrew letters. With a little help, if he stared long enough, he could isolate *Adonai* and *yal-dah*—girl. Bud couldn't, of course, speak the language of his grandparents, though he did pick up on phrases (his grandma called her husband a *momzer*). Dolly and Morris used the phrases, too, but their Yiddish was never fluent.

Another lesson learned at Hebrew school was to kiss a book, if dropped. It was originally prayerbooks that were kissed but that was a ritual easily extended to the famous stolen collection. For a while he kissed anything that dropped—pens, fruit, eyeglasses. Then Bud and Brian started kissing books without having dropped them at all, especially when they fished them out of their underwear. Books needed to be stolen and kissed.

He was bar mitzvahed, a social must. During "the season" he was invited to three or four blowouts a week. The invitations came by messenger, engraved on miniature Torahs in sacks of cerulean velvet. He would pose the question to the Rav, for a responsum: Do we desecrate the Torah with such invitations? When his own time came, Morris the Communicator helped write his big temple speech ("How will I go forward? With pettiness or passion? With vision or with vice? With apathy or empathy . . .") and rented out a big room at the Friars Club for the party. There was a wood-burned sign above the banquet hall that spelled out THE "BAR" MITZVAH in a gluey lasso, and another sign where the drinks were served, THE "MITZVAH" BAR. Bud got fountain pens and a bunch of ten- and fifteen-dollar checks from his friends. Morris took pictures all night and Bud didn't even mind. He usually hated his father's shutterbug mania, and now he realized why: like a tourist, Moe Wiggins was only passing through.

⋀⋀⋀⋀

The following Monday Bud got the call to pick up Mrs. Steiner. He dropped her off at Locanda Veneta for lunch, then drove home, fixed himself an egg and tuned into *Lilith*.

Beatty goes to the boss-man headshrinker to pose a question. If Lilith's so sick, he wants to know, then why is she so happy? The doctor dismisses her happiness as mere "rapture." Beatty likes the word. He asks permission to take Lilith to a country fair, with booths and banners and a jousting tournament in the woods, men on horses impaling rings like wedding bands on their lances. Fast forward. Warren Beatty, occupational therapist, and Jean Seberg, schizophrenic, are walking around a Renaissance Fair, Beatty with his shades. Actor's choice, no doubt; the movie was redolent of Method. Then Beatty's gone and some little boys at the tournament are selling cold drinks and Lilith takes ice like diamonds from their bucket. She tells one of the boys he can see her blood if he touches her lips and sure enough his fingers go to her mouth and he says he can't see any blood and she says it's there, only it's clear, it's white. She tells the nine-year-old his blood is blue—"hot and blue"—and that she has no money to pay for the diamond-ice. Can she give him a kiss instead? Yes, ma'am. And she kisses him on the mouth, right there in the sylvan open, a lingering kiss, and you can see the little boy's heart driving him to darkness. She whispers something like a lover, you can't hear, and the boy's older friend is watching, dead and dreamy, and Beatty looks back at Lilith doing her thing, his mouth does a small movement, he's not yet understanding what he's seeing. It was about the weirdest thing Bud had ever seen.

Who was Jean Seberg anyway? She wasn't Pia Lindstrom or Pier Angeli or Inger Stevens and she wasn't the one Pavese killed himself over. No. Otto Preminger plucked her out of the Midwest and ruined her life. There was something about the Panthers. She had a thing for the blacks, she and Jean Genet: Jean Seberg liked to "burn coal," as Bud's probated friends in the Foundation used to say, the Panthers shoveled snow and Jean Seberg was a come-drunk coal-burning bitch. Married a writer, that's how the sex icons got their kicks. Died in France. He remembered reading somewhere that the CIA killed her. Conspiracy stuff always made Bud lose interest.

Warren Beatty sits in his old girlfriend's house, the one who married Gene Hackman. Hackman's a boor, a domestic bully. When he talks, Beatty winces; he's listening with his feminine side. The James Dean thing, where another man's words are like jackhammers. Fast forward. Beatty and Seberg are stand-

ing outside a hardware store and there's this little kid again and
Lilith hits on him, like a pedophile! Gives him money! A real
chicken hawk. She's making plans to meet him when Beatty
yanks her away.

"Do you think they can cure Lilith?" she says, blistering.
"You know what she wants? She wants to leave the mark of her
desire on every living creature in the world. Think they can cure
this fire? If she were Caesar, she'd do it with a sword. If she
were a poet, she'd do it with words. But she's Lilith. She has
to do it with her body."

He drove back to the restaurant and waited. Mrs. Steiner gave
him a downtown address and they set off. Bud hoped the old
woman wouldn't use him into the evening because he was meeting Rachel for dinner. His heart snaked; excited thoughts of the
nurse were tainted by subterfuge—it wasn't sitting well anymore. There'd be time to thrash out the whole cockeyed dilemma with the Rav—Bud had already left a message at the
Four Oaks House about wanting to have lunch soon. His social
calendar was getting full.

They drove into the garage of a postmodern building near
Bunker Hill. He let her off at an underground elevator.

"How long do you think you'll be?"

"You just stay there, for chrissake," she said contemptu-
ously.

Bud tipped one of the valets so he could park close by and
sit. A few minutes later a woman stepped from the elevator and
approached the limo.

"Are you the driver for Mrs. Steiner?"

"Yes."

"She left a satchel."

It was on the floor of the backseat. Bud felt like stretching
his legs and insisted on toting the bag.

"Are they her attorneys?" he asked as the elevator sped
upward.

"Architects."

"For a house?"

"I really don't know."

Mrs. Steiner was sitting with some men in a conference room. When Bud delivered the item, she looked at him in an abstractly hostile way, as if he were a lame image from a recurring dream. The factotum left the room and got some coffee from the kitchen.

On his way to the elevator he stopped at an elaborate model of several buildings encased in glass. Small white letters spelled out: THE MILLICENT S. STEINER FOUNDATION FOR HOLOCAUST STUDIES. Bud recognized the style as Jilly Frobe's, designer of Chrysalis House and éminence grise of the architectural avant-garde. Frobe had built the famous barn-gallery on Mrs. Steiner's ranch, overwritten about for its "Native American wit and meditative elegance." Now he was on to the Big Project.

A restaurant bridged two buildings: the visitors center and a museum of contemporary art called Psalms. One could commune with the numbing logistics of genocide, then recuperate over cold pasta salad before embracing the pastel *Guernica*s of proven Venice Beach money-makers. Bud got a promotional idea for the gift shop T-shirts: *we put the ART in mARTyr.* He'd tell Melanie, just to watch her burn.

When he got home, there was a message from the Rav to meet him the next day for some shopping. The old man wanted to make sure Bud brought "the wonderful car," there would be "many" packages.

Rachel was an hour late and a little stoned. She had a toothache. She came in, sniffed around, then asked if he had a cat. He asked her why and she said it smelled like pee. Bud was embarrassed and lied again. He said a friend's dog had had an "accident." Did the place really smell? he wondered. The world was a series of rudely improbable shocks, even from people you wanted to love and to trust. He remembered wearing a tux for the first time, at a cotillion ball. His favorite teacher from school happened to be driving by as Bud stepped out the front door.

"You look like a headwaiter!" he shouted, and it hurt. Didn't anyone in a tux look like a potential headwaiter? Or was it only a select few? Sean Connery and Cary Grant and Frank Sinatra didn't look like headwaiters; maybe only Jews did.

They had an early dinner at Musso's, then went to the university for a symposium on films about Vietnam. Rachel had been invited by a guy she met at the vet center who was doing research for a television show he created about the war. He was apparently interested in her book. Bud thought she meant a book of poetry, but Rachel said she'd written a war memoir, the fruit of a writing workshop at UCLA. She flashed the thin, battered sheaf from her shoulder bag, letting him see only the title page: *The Colorized Version,* by Rachel Morrison.

Inside the auditorium the panelists showed samples of their efforts, each sanctified by a "media professor" 's ceremonious introduction. The excerpts filled the monitors: snipers, elephant grass and *boo-koo boom-boom,* diddy-bopping, doo-mommies, Hueys, hooches, Hendrix and horsehit; klicks and lurps, pant-shitting, quiver-throated letters home to granny, tunnel-tossed grenades, roughed-up buffaloes and fucked-over farm animals, short-timers and Saigon hookers, bitching black privates, hip helmet-sloganed lunacy, LZs and APCs, lock and loads, recons, medevacs, dinks, grunts and firefights, number ones and number tens and lots of *I-turned-back-to-him-and-his-head-was-gone-it-just-wasn't-there-anymore!* soliloquies.

Bud went to the rest room to escape the hot air. Standing at the urinal, he pissed on the pretentious medley of clips, each one gorily self-serving, staunchly, inescapably middle-class; everyone kept bungling the burglary. The presentation gave his own project new vigor—no one was on to him, no one was even close. As he shook the tip of his penis dry, a lovely, ironic title rose to the top of his skull: *The Holocaust Museum.* That was it! He'd keep the Dissipation—a room filled with catharting vets—working in the Rav as a survivor of the camps who maybe lost a son in the Nam. The old man would be the fillip, the symbol evoking holocausts past, present and future.

When Bud returned from the rest room, Rachel was at the lip of the stage talking to her panelist friend. Mitch had long, tangled hair and a maroon Mont Blanc pen stuck in the pocket of his, yes, fatigue-style shirt. He seemed a little aloof for someone supposedly keen on her work; probably playing hard to get. Bud had been to enough show biz seminars to recognize the syndrome. The lawyers and agents and casting directors were bad enough, but when Talent got up on the dais, look out. Rachel's friend greeted visitors with the benign, regnant befuddlement of a rishi. Week after week Mitch Traggert was on an Emmy safari, hacking his way through a jungle of insipid programming, carving a historic niche in the annals of the form, dreaming of the transition to features. Week after week he was a warrior; tonight he was showing his feminine side. Tonight he would listen to and nurture, not cathect.

The antsy screenwriter loitered at a careful distance from his date and Mr. Traggert, so as not to be introduced—the last thing he wanted was to suffer an awkward exchange of platoon number niceties or whatever it was vets did on a first date. Traggert's attention was diverted by fresh minions and Bud seized the moment, leading her by the arm to the exit.

Rachel wanted to have a cocktail at the Chart House and they took Sunset to the beach. She insisted on rolling down all the windows and it was freezing. Having her there in the dark had overstimulated him; he didn't feel the cold. They pulled from her flask. He hated scotch, but it went down easy. She recited from her book, screaming passages above the wind.

The chapters were color-coded. As she gave him *Red,* he yearned to see the words on the printed page. Suddenly, Bud was a thirteen-year-old purist again, craving possession, *needing* what was spoken to exist as a volume to be stolen and sequestered in the hatbox-ark. He became ferociously nostalgic for the phantom *text* as Rachel's mouth made the words. Hers was a dream of a memoir, a gorgeous tone poem; he listened with familiar, envious obedience, the privileged capitulation he felt as a boy upon discovering a new stolen Master, a voice so larger than his own. It was obvious she had seen too much with too fine an instrument.

When they got to the restaurant, Rachel grabbed his hand and led him down the side of the bluff. They took off their shoes and the sand was cold. They could see the silhouettes of the diners through the windows high above. The ocean roared, gobbling up and spitting out edges. She chased it back, taunting, and when it was roused, turned and ran, dark water rumbling after her like the bogeyman. She rushed into Bud's arms and they fell down near the bluff. This was their place now, intimate, impregnable. He imagined them alone in a primeval living room, ends-of-the-earth homesteaders.

Her tongue was acrid and Bud remembered the toothache—he was probably tasting infection. Rachel put his hand between her legs, then closed them tight on his fingers, grinding rhythmically. She wanted to fuck in the sand like some teenager, but he didn't; if he couldn't get hard, all that grit and water would make for unappealing farce. His fingers were inside her now and the bad tooth taste went away. After twenty-five years he could still smell the mouth of a girl who pushed the stop elevator button and kissed him during hide-and-seek. The smell was like a color.

ttttt

"Death begins with the shoes," said the Rav as they sat in the waiting room of the custom bootmaker. "Since then I have only shoes made. They have a mold of my foot here. And in Italy and in London."

The well-known store was over on Third. Shoeboxes inscribed with names of celebrities were stacked from floor to ceiling, kinky crypts of a chiropodial Forest Lawn: CLINT EASTWOOD, REGIS PHILBIN, PHYLLIS DILLER, FRANK SINATRA, SANDY DUNCAN, KENNY ROGERS, FARRAH FAWCETT. Mr. DiGiaimo, the sixty-year-old owner, brought out a pair of pointy black demiboots that looked like objets d'art. The Rav fixed him with a crazed stare and shouted: *"Wer hat kaputte Schuhe? Wer hat kaputte Schuhe!"*

The shoemaker smiled like a straight man.

"Do you know what I ask of him?" said the Rav. "I ask, 'Who has broken shoes?' This they ask once a week in the Lager. Then you would go and make your own selek-juh from the shoes of the dead. It was that you could get a *worse* shoe than what you had if you picked wrong. This could be fatal." He held the boots before him, inhaling through his nose approvingly as he nodded his head. "In these I can wait for Him to come. In these I could withstand the abuse of Nachman in Istanbul. Wigginitz, I could walk to Palestine in these DiGiaimo's shoes! With Kafka I walk!" He turned to the Italian. "Did not the *yehudi* say, Signore DiGiaimo, that the best penance is to become a wanderer and a fugitive?"

They drove to Beverly Hills and power-walked Rodeo Drive. The old man truly loved his ruby slippers; he looked natty in his fourteen-hundred-dollar Comme des Garçons raincoat, purchased earlier at Neiman's. The Santa Anas were bothering the trees and the Rav peered at the world as if the winds were doing his bidding, sweeping the sky and streets clean for unimaginable ceremonies, ecstatic parades. On such a day, Bud thought, the harsh clarity of light could well make an old man appear frail and foolish. Instead, he looked visionary.

"In the Lager you don't need head, heart or courage. Well, maybe you need a head. What you really need is shoes, bowl and bread—the gray, gray bread. And to keep warm. And to keep moving." He breathed deeply, propelling himself past Claude Montana toward the Rodeo Collection. He laughingly called the respirations *tohuvohu,* or the "world of confusion."

"Ausrücken! Einrücken! Ausrücken! Einrücken! The *coming in* and the *going out!"*

He spoke of Sabbatai Sevi, the false Messiah; how the Jews were ruled by sacred and secular units of time; of the gardens of Auschwitz he called Canada, where he was once allowed to sunbathe; of living in a forest in Mischantz like a mad Tristan in a world of no Iseults; of *gulden, pfennigs* and *piasters,* Gog, Magog and Gehinnom, Janowska, Lwów and Medzhibozh and the Baal Shem Tov. He slurred some words and Bud didn't know if it was German or Yiddish, Ladeno or Aramaic, or a private language, like Lilith's, or Dolly's—*E-zih-zinee!* Sometimes he called himself Zing and sometimes the "tremendum" or the Responsa. Just when Bud thought he was a crazy-kike Sid Caesar and nothing more, he shpritzed about *Kratzeblock* and *Kinderakzion,* the hallucinations of typhus, Goethe's oak at Buchenwald, ceremonies for the changing of underwear and the Festival of Booths, using words Bud dimly remembered from Hebrew school: *sukkah, lulav, esrog.*

In Auschwitz he got work in a toy shop—"a toy shop, Wigginitz! Imagine it!"—making marionettes for the children of the guards. One week he made a trick cylinder from scrap he "promoted" by trading his hoarded bread rations. He could make a handkerchief disappear inside it; the Rav used to imagine himself in its cool chamber, also vanished. His pastime was metempsychic dreaming.

"Like a gilgul, I would enter this magic tin tube! It must have a soul—after all, I had fashioned it, it was a new thing, Wigginitz, born in a dead place. A new thing that held bright rags and made joy for the children. So: it had a soul. I give it to a Kapo for his son, he must do me a favor in return. The Kapo he is pleased. But I am trapped. From then each week I must invent a trick and the boy is the test. If not amuse the boy, I suffer by kicks and blows. So, friend Wigginitz, I become a thaumaturge by incentive, and Zing he tells me thus I am climbing rungs to heaven."

The Rav bought twenty scarves at Hermès, then Bud followed him across the street as he dashed into Polo, where he loaded up on silver picture frames, riding boots, cashmere sweaters and a thousand-dollar crocodile billfold. He paid by credit card. As they were leaving, he bowed and addressed the entire shop. *"Auf wiedersehen in jener welt!"*

" 'See you in the next world,' " he translated for Bud as they walked. "Big phrase in the Lager. That, and *Morgen früh*—'tomorrow morning.' Which meant 'never.' "

There was a final errand—he was looking for "a very special bowl, Wigginitz." They ducked into a crystal shop on Camden Drive. None of the salespeople could help him. He was looking for a special bowl, he kept saying. Suddenly the old man was perspiring and restless; he steadied himself against the screenwriter and caught his breath. He wanted would Bud please to take him back to Four Oaks.

When they got to the room, he sipped a Diet Coke and quietly regained his strength. Bud talked about being a screenwriter, then brought up Rachel. His dilemma had acquired a picayunish, comforting banality in light of the afternoon's strange and tumultuous confessions. The Rav unfolded a scroll of painted oilcloth while he listened. He pointed to the letters Y H V H in the cloth's center.

"*Yod He Vav He*—see each letter gets a color, ascribed by Zohar: blue and black, then the luminous white. When the blue does not cleave to the white, it is poverty. Israel fails. Without male and female together, there is only poverty. The fire of the Lord descends and consumes the fat and the flesh of the burnt offering beneath—*reines Juden fett!* At such times peace and harmony is reigning." He stood up, beaming at his creation. "This is the prototype. I'm talking to many people about it. You see," he said, brandishing a leaflet, "here I have the rules."

Bud realized the old man was talking about a board game. The leaflet's heading was written in Hebrew-style letters: "Eye of Zo-Har: The Game of Kabbalists." The official rule book was subtitled *The Guide to the Perplexed.* He said to look and learn—*kabbala* was derived from *kabbel,* to accept, and *kavvanah* ("the mystical concentrations") from *kavven,* to direct.

"The wisdom and art of the kabbala means *accepting* the yoke of the Kingdom and *directing* one's heart to God. Everyone in this town wants to direct! No, Wigginitz?" The cloth was full of symbols, numbers and animal figures, some daubed and scrawled, others painstakingly traced. "I conceive this in the Lager. When Zing give me the scraps to hide on which he wrote his responsa, I use the spaces he did not mark to form my ideas of this game. And I write it down and bury everything in a hole. Years ago I dig it up, when back I go on a tour. I am a tourist at Auschwitz at last! It will be great, greater than Monopoly, than even chess."

The Rav took a crystal bowl from an end table, the reliquary of filthy bits of parchment. He placed it on the floor beside the scroll, took a scrap from its mouth and laid it carefully on the cloth like a puzzle piece. He was on his knees, as if hard in prayer, squinting. He took a fountain pen and copied a shape from the scrap onto the cloth.

The screenwriter realized with a shiver what the bowl held: these were the unearthed responsa of Rabbi Zing, buried for decades in a tin box, remnants of the theory and practice of hell. He got light-headed and felt himself falling.

When he came to, Bud was on the couch under a light blanket, a wet Hermès scarf across his forehead.

"*Aufstehen! Aufstehen, teshuvah!* You fell dead because you 'turned.' Do you know what is the turning? It is to turn from one's aberrations to the way of God." He patted the blanket. "You must think of God the way a child is thinking when the father at night tucks him in."

He pulled up a chair and served Bud a cup of tea and a plate of sugar cookies.

"It's not Yom Kippur. You must eat. Why do you fast? You are losing weight, I know. To what purpose? Are you seriously desiring to become a muscleman? In the Lager the walking dead we called the 'musclemen,' to this day I don't know why. I'm listening to you about this woman—this Rachel, the nurse. She reminds me.

"Do you know the favor the Kapo did me for the magic tube? He got a girl out of the frownblock, the whorehouse there. You could get a coupon to go there, to the Polish women—the coupons were not for Jews, a Jew could not go. This girl, I knew from Bielsko. He got her out for me and they put her in the krackenbow, absurdist hospital. You never saw such a place, Wigginitz—an 'infirmary' without medicine or doctors!"

Bud adjusted the pillow, feeling something underneath—the Rav's new boots. The old man howled with laughter, then began to cough.

"This is how you must sleep in the Lager! They will steal your eyes, your whiskers, your breath!" He stood up. "Go home now, Wigginitz, eat something. I must take my *Mittagsruhe.*"

As the Rav knelt to roll up the cloth, Bud rose. The old man was still coughing, pale and exhausted, bedeviled by the fulminations. He carried the bowl of parchment to a cabinet, locked it in, then went to the bathroom and closed the door. A baleful moan preceded violent hacking.

Bud folded the blanket and draped it over the arm of the sofa. He was feeling better but didn't want to leave just yet; he'd wait to see if the old man was all right. He pushed the bag of scarves around the tabletop and thought of the magic tube, its secret compartment choked with hidden squares of patchwork silk. His eye lit on some legal paper under the bag. There were prominent crystal and china shops jotted down, with corresponding rows of four- and five-digit figures. Bud assumed they were prices. At the bottom of the list he read: "MILLI. STEINER." There were numbers after it—"Home" and "Office."

The old man returned to the room with a manuscript.

"This is my *Totenbuch,* my memory," he said. He'd been in touch with a company in Portland called the Survivor Press. They wanted to publish it, but the Rav was unhappy with the book's current form. Maybe Bud, a "professional," could have a look. The old man then spoke softly enough that the screenwriter strained to hear. He said that Moses de Leon, author of the *Zohar,* was called a fraud, a plagiarist, a pseudoepigraphist, a frustrated writer who recycled anonymous works for financial gain, a con who gulled the rich. He looked deep into Bud, his eyes dull and fathomless.

"There was Rabbi Schmoom and there was Rabbi Boom; there was Rabbi Voof, there was the Rabbi of Grip, there was the holy Ragoon and there was Rabbi Oshosha. I am the Seventh. I am the *reshit*—de Leon. The essence of them all."

He held his hand up and scarily showed the palm: *"I am the Sabbath."*

As Bud ran from the room, the rabbi began to sing.

www

There was a lot of work the next week. He chauffeured around an old movie star who demanded they chase a fire truck because it was "newsworthy." He took a black comic to the fights, then over to a speakeasy on 110th where they served five-o'clock-in-the-morning whiskey, grits and eggs. He spent a few days driving one of Ramón's regulars, a man whose wife died the year before. The story was the will stipulated she be buried at the wheel of her beloved Ferrari. The family complied with the request.

Rachel had left *The Colorized Version* in his car. He thought that was deliberate. Between her and the old man, Bud was beginning to feel like Max Perkins. The memoir thoroughly lived up to the force and beauty of its preview. As he moved on to the annals of the Rav, Bud felt his cup too filled with others' wine and put it down; the screenwriter needed room for his own creation. During work hours he sat in the limo sucking on jerky and fleshing out details of the Vietnam project. He compulsively checked his machine for messages. There were a few from Rachel but nothing from the old man.

He thought about stopping by the Four Oaks to see if the Rav was okay. His story about liberating the girl from the whorehouse was intriguing—Bud wanted to hear more. He might be able to transpose it to the Nam script, make it part of something the old man's "character" divulges during a Dissipation.

www

Ramón came back from his vacation. He didn't feel like working much, and that was good for Bud.

The screenwriter sat in the driveway of a San Marino ranch house, waiting in the car for Melanie. There were strips of bright crepe paper tied to posts, and far away he heard a crowd of children. The scene was suffused with peace, and the warmth sank into his bones—voices of the children, the *stitch* of the sprinklers, the gardeners passing like you weren't there. He wondered what the place would look like in a year, in ten years, ten thousand. Bud closed his eyes. The limousine became the throne of the old matinée; the cool breeze of millennia dried the sweat of his neck as trees and house disappeared, replaced by starry blackness. Then, like Rod Taylor in *The Time Machine,* he was encased in mountain, awaiting the dawn of a new world.

The house of Mrs. Steiner's sister looked like it could pass for a sanatorium. It would be a nice place to shoot the exteriors, though San Marino was probably too expensive, permit-wise. The rich cities made you pay through the nose. No, a real hospital would be better, more dramatic. It wouldn't be hard to find one—they were going belly up all over the city. There were probably a few that made themselves available for production purposes. He could get Rachel to ask Mitch Traggert.

When the old man mentioned there was interest in his *Totenbuch,* Bud felt the urge for outside consensus; his experience thus far had been dizzily hermetic. He got hold of the Survivor Press catalog. Aside from Holocaust literature, the small publishing house had issued a new translation of a Borges book, some true crime Americana (emphasis on the grotesque), droll, quirky travel yarns, lesbian erotica from the Jazz Age and a surrealistic profile of an African despot. They seemed perfect for Rachel's book. Bud sent *The Colorized Version* with a letter introducing the "radically poetic memoir of a nurse's tour of duty in Vietnam." He would eventually show Rachel his humble précis, so much like a love letter.

The screenwriter added as a by-the-way that he happened to be an acquaintance of Israel "Rav" Levi, flattering the editors on their perspicacity. Almost immediately after mailing the manuscript, Bud regretted his remarks. There was nothing really to gain; it made the dispatch smack of the small, dumb hustle. He was worried about a backfire—if the old man heard about it, he might think Bud was using him. Still, it wasn't worth getting paranoid over.

Melanie tapped on the glass, startling him. She had a boy with her who wore a sandwich board with a big letter *E* that reminded Bud of *The Manchurian Candidate.* She hugged him good-bye, crumpling the cardboard a little, and the boy groaned at the damage. Melanie made it all right again and kissed him. He seemed to stare at Bud for a moment, or stare through him; the sometime chauffeur thought of Artie—Vivian's creation—bobbing spectrally in the waves. Then he bounded back to the house as she got in.

"Hi, Bud. Hope you weren't waiting too long."

"Not at all."

"You should have come in and had some lemonade."

He pulled out of the driveway.

"Those *children*—it was so sweet!"

"What was?"

"The *birthday* party."

She yanked at her gloves, a little out of breath, like the Royal Nanny after an Easter Egg hunt.

"Where's Mrs. Steiner?"

"Out of town—in Dallas, she'll be back on Saturday."

"Who's the kid?"

"Her *grandson.* He turned twelve today. Isn't he adorable?"

Bud relished the opportunity for details. Melanie didn't mind answering a few questions, as long as they weren't too gossipy; she enjoyed a once-in-a-while fellowship with "helpers," comme il faut.

"So this is Mrs. Steiner's sister's house?"

"Uh-huh."

"Are they close?"

She hung back a bit, primly mindful of her role.

"I imagine. It's her older sister. She isn't well." Her face abruptly changed and she gushed, "They had the most wonderful magic show!"

The inflection sounded familiar—it was that of an ingénue in a forties film, the kind who throws her arms around Spencer Tracy. "Oh, Father, we're going to have the most wonderful Christmas!" Bud knew she was relishing her moment as Mrs. Steiner's executrix; he watched her in the mirror and was touched by the absurdity. The curator was playing a role out of a costume drama—perhaps the French Revolution—and this particular scene called for stableboy and marchioness. Melanie Sharf gave a bloodless, wooden performance. What she needed, he thought, was a good gigolo, a good gigolo to use her up and crawl over her engorged body to get to Mrs. Steiner. Some of the old Casanovawitz, as Ramón used to say.

"I don't know if you've ever been to one of these things," she said, "but the emotions that play over their faces! They sit in your lap, *mesmerized.* Children are really so special."

Now she was playing a wombless priss. Bud decided to change the reel.

"Melanie, I wanted to ask you something. I was at a friend's house and I saw Mrs. Steiner's name on a slip of paper."

"She sure knows lots of people."

"I know. But this man is pretty unusual. That's why it stuck in my mind—I mean, her name being there. He's kind of a rabbi."

"All the work she does with the temple and the museum—did you ask him? Your friend?"

"I didn't have a chance."

"You say he's a friend."

"A new friend. I'm interested in him for something I'm writing."

She nodded her head, as if everything had become clear.

"So you're not that close."

"Not really."

"I can ask her."

"Don't bother."

"Why not?"

"Because it doesn't matter."

"My God, *writers*! They make everything into a mystery."

She suddenly stared through the rear window as if seeing an apparition, and gasped at the loveliness of the blossomy trees that lined the road. The screenwriter knew it was a ruse, that she was posing for a handsome man approaching in a Carrera. The sports car shot ahead and Melanie sat forward again, the smallest shadow of spinster moon falling across her face—now she was Audrey Hepburn in *Roman Holiday* and it was time to go back to the palace. When Bud dropped her off at a little Westwood apartment, she left reluctantly, the way lonely people leave movie houses on rainy afternoons.

She waved and Bud drove home.

There was a note tacked to Bud's front door. He stood there and read it:

A BLACK, E WHITE, I RED, U GREEN, O BLUE:
VOWELS
ONE DAY I WILL TELL YOUR LATENT BIRTH:
A, BLACK HAIRY CORSET OF SHINY FLIES
WHICH BUZZ AROUND CRUEL SMELLS,

GULFS OF DARKNESS; E, WHITENESS OF VAPORS
AND TENTS,
LANCES OF PROUD GLACIERS, WHITE KINGS,
QUIVERING FLOWERS;
I, PURPLES, SPIT BLOOD, LAUGHTER OF BEAUTI-
FUL LIPS
IN ANGER OR PENITENT DRUNKENNESS;

U, CYCLES, DIVINE VIBRATIONS OF GREEN SEAS,
PEACE OF PASTURES SCATTERED WITH ANI-
MALS, PEACE OF THE WRINKLES

WHICH ALCHEMY PRINTS ON HEAVY STUDIOUS
BROWS;

O, SUPREME CLARION FULL OF STRANGE STRI-
DOR,
SILENCES CROSSED BY WORLDS AND ANGELS:
O, THE OMEGA, VIOLET BEAM FROM HIS EYES!

He thought the verse contrived but recognized its power.
Here were the vowels again, and the colors: the *Yod He Vav He*
with its blues and blacks and whites, the grandson with his
lettered board—Eye of Zo-Har. There was more than a touch
of Lilith there, too, *fahr fahr carmintrate*. What did it all mean?
Anyway, Bud preferred Rachel's prose because he didn't understand her poetry. Then he chided himself, recalling what the
Rav had said about the kabbala: "The effect upon the soul of
such a work is in the end not at all dependent upon its being
understood." One day Bud would *will* himself to hear the whole
color spectrum of vowels. This way, the old man said, he would
enter the primal center of innermost light and "the palace of
translucent radiance that enclosed the center." The Palace of
Love that sits amidst the secret firmament of a vast rock, where
the serpent flies in the air with an ant lying quietly between its
teeth.

Scrawled beneath the typed poem was: MEET ME MUSSO'S AT
TEN P.M. *xxxooo* R.

Late that afternoon Bud went to the Holocaust Museum.

As usual, the place seemed deserted. He walked toward the
back room. A large TV sat on a platform. In front of it, a
pink-skinned man with thyroid eyes and a red beard held a
remote. He sped up the image. Bud stood behind him, watching
the rush of images—death trains passing sun-drenched fields
that shimmered with indifference, the diaspora of interviewees
addressing the camera with subtitled *tohuvohu* anecdotes, more

trains and field and Survivors blotting tears with handkerchiefs like silent-film tragedians: trains: field: barbed-wire sun.

The screenwriter introduced himself.

"Staying for the documentary?"

"I'm hoping I can. There's something I wanted to ask you, though. I met a man here the other day, I think he was a rabbi. Strange guy with a big white beard. He had a leather knapsack."

"Him! Yes. *Very* strange. They come—the Survivors. He said he was from New York."

"What did he want? I mean, just a look around?"

He shook his head. "To make a donation. They get old and they come here, who knows. An old woman came two months ago to give a bent spoon she carried with her in the camp. Two weeks later she was dead. Sad. They let go of what they've been carrying. We put it in a case, for display."

"What did he want to donate?"

"Something of his wife's." The man anticipated Bud's next question and remarked, "She died in the camp. These people are strange. What they've been through . . . Last week, we had to remove an exhibit." He pointed to the case that held the bowl and the shoes; the striped uniform was gone. "Yesterday the man who gave the uniform died. He wanted to be buried in it."

World of confusion, he thought. To be mortal was sweet pathos and dementia: the delirium abided in the sacred, loamy soil. He thought of the woman moldering in her Ferrari, Bulgari earrings dropping off peccant lobes.

Bud said good-bye to the red-bearded man and hurried out.

Musso's was still a few hours off. He went into a theater and bought some popcorn so he wouldn't binge at dinner, then drove over to Bookz.

Bud was in a quandary. He'd learned nothing from the *Totenbuch,* a dry, practically unreadable arcanum of impersonal musings and useless theosophy. He returned again and again to the haunting image of the Rav bent over his board

game "prototype" with its babel of outlandish symbols: pure
madness. The screenwriter was astonished at his own reticence—why hadn't he asked the old man a few key questions?
Like, where did he get his money and why did he want to spend
it on a goddam bowl? What about his wife? And where did
Millicent S. Steiner come in? Something had tied Bud's tongue;
he'd been shamanized. Maybe the old man was a thief who
trafficked in religious artifacts—those scraps of parchment, and
further holy writs. Maybe Bud had become the unwitting accessory to fraud. On the other hand, was he suspicious simply
because the Rav was, as it were, unorthodox? More than anything, Bud feared being a prig.

For a moment he felt himself in the queasy grip of obsession.
He didn't doubt the old man's power, or ability to move him.
Yet there was something unsettling and unfinished about the
"rabbi" that the screenwriter couldn't ignore. He had a growing
sense of jeopardy. Maybe that's simply how one felt when in
touch with a remarkable man—a magician, a zealot, a zaddik.

The moment passed and Bud chastised himself. He was on
to something; he was "in the mode." Now was no time to get
square. Besides, the Rav was looming larger in his script. Bud
called his character the Survivor, alumnus Auschwitz, and gave
him a son, a Viet vet who's strung out and writes really *terrible*
novels about the war. (Finally, a vet who can't write.) The kid
winds up jumping from the roof of the veterans hospital. The
Survivor goes to the VA twice a week on Group night because
he's lonely. And for penance. Mistreated the son, never said he
loved him, never held him, et cetera, et cetera. Overwhelmed
with guilt. No family left, wife dead, end of his life now, *Krapp's
Last Tape,* hears voices in his head, the usual ghosts. Reveal the
Survivor knew Primo Levi or Bruno Schulz when they were in
the camp, like Ozick's *Messiah* book and all the rest, do the old
reality-stew number. Make the Survivor the proprietor of a
Lawndale magic shop that's going under because of a new Toys
"Я" Us. Bud had read about Wal-Mart invading Middle American towns, settling on their outskirts—within months, beloved

Main Street was cracked sidewalk and tumbleweeds. That right there was the play Arthur Miller never wrote.

The bookstore owner applauded Bud's arrival.

"Author! Author! When are you going to bring us more of your opus?"

"You need more?"

"I think we're out again." He punched *Shotgun* into the computer and pointed to the screen. "See? We've sold forty-four copies."

"That's great. I'll bring some in."

He was peremptorily introduced to a cashier.

"This is Bud Wiggins, famous screenwriter and author."

She smiled blandly. "Someone on the phone wants to know if we get *Weekly Variety,*" she said to the owner. "Do we?"

Bud browsed the novels on display, reading the jacket notes. *Blue Numbers* was about a man who awakens one morning with a Lager tattoo on his arm. He hits the Holocaust lecture circuit, hiding his deception from a woman he loves. Another was about a former Buchenwald inmate who sells stolen Judaica to universities. A third volume was translated from the Hebrew. It had something to do with a man telling stories to the Nazis to forestall death, like Scheherazade. He flipped through the stylistically imposing work—a character in the novel "knew" Tadeusz Borowski. Bud had heard of Borowski. He was a Survivor, a writer who killed himself before turning thirty. The chapter headings were in Hebrew and the reader was provided with translations: *plagiarism,* for example, which the author further defined as literary theft.

Bud was jittery. He was definitely "in the mode," but so were others, and they had a Brobdingnagian jump; the trail to Mount Analogue was sorely littered. The screenwriter pushed away the negative thoughts—he would find an unknown route to the top. It was the getting there that was important. Anyhow, he was writing a movie. Who read books? Nobody, that's who.

He drove straight to the Four Oaks House. As Bud left his

car, the old man was walking out the entrance, crouching under the weight of his leather knapsack.

"Wigginitz!"

"Listen"—Bud stared back, gathering courage—"I think it's time you told me real things." He mentioned his follow-up visit to the Holocaust Museum and the Rav was abashed. Maybe he wasn't a sociopath after all. "Are you trying to sell something to Millicent Steiner? Are you planning to sell the responsa?"

He stroked his beard and grinned, his face a lantern, glowing within; it was a tad *Karate Kid*. Bud half expected the old man to say, "You've learned well. Now you are ready for the Knowledge."

"A man should pursue the Torah like a lover. Such is the thralldom. Come to my honna-sot orheem Saturday night—"

"Where?"

"Here, where I am staying! This is the traditional time for storytelling." He got a faraway look, as if reading a Tele-PrompTer somewhere in the middle of Bud's head. "I will be a Torah for you: the commandments of the Torah correspond to the bones, and the prohibitions to the sinews of man. Thus the entire Law includes the entire body of man."

He adjusted the knapsack, staggering under its weight, then moved in the direction of the park. He grimaced and Bud saw his death's-head, tightly drawn. The screenwriter reached out and steadied him, wishing them both onto the oilcloth, into the Eye of Zo-Har.

"What do you have in there?"

"The life of man is to carry something that cannot be carried, over an impossible distance. Some must haul the shit of the entire barracks out where it is freezing. They must ascend with it a mountain that cannot be climbed."

He winked broadly.

"Me, I carry Palestine," he said, trudging off.

———

Bud waited for her in the booth, his heart pounding. Love was a garden and love was strong as death, so said the game of the kab-ba-la. He wanted to spear rings for her with his lance. As she slid across from him and smiled, he breathed her in; the night-air coolness clung to her like a jealous, minty vine.

Rachel was drunk. She leaned over the table to kiss him, morosely beautiful, her eyes watery church windows—she'd take anything on the chin tonight, even the end of the world. He imagined her wandering from camp to camp, the refugee of a holy war.

He told her he wasn't a vet. He told her he was a writer working on a script about a writer pretending to be a vet. (He loathed himself for throwing in something about Pirandello.) He was "in character" when they met—that's how he did research, he said. Rachel listened, chain-smoking and stone-faced, then burst out laughing like a dipsomaniac. After a while she closed her eyes, as if trying to find something filed away in her head.

"I read your book," he said. "I mean, *really read it.* It's phenomenal."

"Hey Wig, don't blow smoke up my ass." She surfaced; her eyes opened wide as she gulped a shot. She looked fabulously ruined. "So fuck me, you're not a vet. It's a *hoot.* Stop atoning."

Bud tested the waters by saying he wanted to send the manuscript to a publisher. She didn't mind. She stroked his arm, all transgressions forgiven. He sensed Rachel wanted to unburden herself, if only she could speak. How many foolish men must have bared their shallow contritions while she said nothing, her own sins delitescent in the dark, confessions to kill all others.

Bud needed her to know him. He talked about the Movies and the Doctor and Jeanette—even Morris Wiggins and the way he died. She ordered ice cream and languorously chocolated up her lips. He wanted to tell her he loved her.

She smiled, coquettish and dislocated.

"I have a little boy."

"Who does he live with?"

The smile tightened. "Not with me."

He let it go; he'd circle back to it. They ordered more drinks.

Rachel was from an old California family. She dropped out of college to attend nursing school, shaming her elitist mother by such meager ambition. She was supposed to come into a trust but the woman somehow blocked it. An emergency room gave her a job and one of the doctors showed her how to shoot up; a year later, she enlisted in the Army, to get clean. Rachel used to laugh about that—going to Nam to get clean. She went because she was strung out and bored and wanted to spite this woman her mother, a bitch with the nerves of an assassin. She got hepatitis and spent the last month of the tour as a patient in her own hospital.

Back at his apartment, they drank and watched *Lilith.*

The jousting tournament was about to begin. Beatty was on his horse and the announcement came over loudspeakers: *Charge, Sir Knight!* The movie star won and the officials asked if Lilith was his lady. He said yes. They gave him a laurel and told him to crown her Queen of Love and Beauty. Then the orderly slept with his troubled charge in the woods.

He asked Rachel about her book and she said she'd always experienced words and smells and sounds as color. They called it chromesthesia. She had a brother who was the same way.

How could Bud ever hope to make a bridge to her, to *understand*? He was left out of the mystery, it was too late to learn. Maybe it all just meant Femaleness. There were upper and lower waters, male and female, zaddik and zaddek. He must make his union with the Presence, for it behooves a man to be both male and female.

Fast forward. Warren Beatty catches Seberg in a barn, romping with a lesbo inmate. The possessive junior therapist shows his male side and gets violent. Wacky Zen master Lilith turns on him with ferocity.

"If you should discover that your God loved others as much as He loved you, would you hate Him for it? I show my love for all of you and you despise me!"

Beatty does her right there in the concupiscent cow house.
"This movie is *inspired*!"
"I thought you'd like it."
"Gonna do a remake?"
"Let's say 'variation.' "
She unbuckled his belt.
"Bud? If you discovered that God loved others as much as He loved you, would you despise Him for it?"
He laughed but then she opened his fly and took out his cock. Bud's fingers sank into her hair, tracing patterns on her skull as she groaned and sucked until he came. He led her by the hand to his room and they took their clothes off and got in bed. Rachel had a white wormy scar under a tit, from an old accident; he'd seen it before, that time Dr. Kennedy took the wheel. She called it a keloid. He moved his fingertip over it, the shell of a burrowed, sleeping thing.

They slept and Bud dreamed of the college in Quebec. He used to send home sweetly pretentious letters about the whirligig weather, its storms and sunny calm arriving like "trains in a station." He was playing the literary prodigy, stockpiling juvenilia. Life was full of immediacy, maybe because of his youth; the mind was dimly aware it was minting memories. He met a girl, fragrant with hashish. They went back to the house he was staying at and took off their clothes. He was still a virgin. He put his fingers inside her; the equation of bodies left him spiritless, uncomprehending. He couldn't have known that he needn't understand. It was like the poem or the Torah. Everything must have had a color, but he was blind.

He woke up at four in the morning. Rachel was dressed and alert, like someone leaving for work.

"What's happening?"

"Can't sleep. Going home." She kissed his cheek. "I love you."

Bud listened to the door shut, then drifted off.

ⱮⱮⱮ

At the end of the week, a letter came from the Survivor Press. He was surprised at its promptness.

Dear Mr. Wiggins,
We received *The Colorized Version,* by Rachel Morrison, and have taken it under submission.
I was gratified to learn you are an acquaintance of Rabbi Levi. He is an amazing man who simultaneously embodies and transcends the spirit in which the Press was founded.
We have not heard from him since he submitted a few excerpts from his extraordinary autobiography, *The Toymaker,* five months ago. Our letters to the Rabbi have been returned and we have no forwarding address. He's a little elusive! We know he is immersed in his work and wish to respect his privacy at all costs.
I would greatly appreciate it if you could drop us a line saying he is well, etc. It would be nice—though not essential—to have a current address, P.O. box or whatnot. We hope he is prospering and are confident the Rabbi will be in touch when his schedule permits.
Again, thank you for the MS. We'll be back to you in due course.

It was signed by Gerald Scherick, publisher and editor.
He was puzzling over the note when the phone rang. It was Mrs. Steiner. Melanie had told her of their discussion about "Bud's rabbi friend." As it turned out, he was a man she'd been eagerly trying to meet. The philanthropist didn't evince the slightest interest in Bud's connection to her quarry; that would have been conversational, alien, off-point. Why was she calling herself anyway? The rich were never easy to figure. One thing was obvious: the scraps of paper—the responsa residuum— were apparently of great value. There had already been satirical jabs in the press about the encroaching show biz "feel" of the Holocaust studies project (one critic had referred to it as Six

Flags Tragic Mountain) and Bud knew from the curator that Steiner was stung. More than ever, she needed a *tantarara,* something beyond run-of-the-mill corroded uniforms and photo blow-ups of the doomed—she needed a hook, a goose, a *sitz,* as the Rav might say. She needed the Responsa.

"I'm planning a dinner party a week from Saturday. Would you extend Rabbi Levi an invitation?"

"Yes."

"It will be *intime.* Melanie will be there, and some people from the museum. Of course, you may come if you have no other plans."

Her wooden largess was no less touching for its expediency. Bud was enjoying himself.

"If he's unavailable, we will make it for another night. Eight o'clock. Call Melanie as soon as you know."

He felt like saying, *just fucking drive.*

"Is it black-tie?" he joked.

"For you, yes. For everyone else, it's casual."

He drove some executives from a Midwest tile store giant. During the day the businessmen inspected their franchises. When night came, they wanted to let their hair down, so Bud took them to a strip joint on La Cienega. He went to the bar while his clients were led to tables up front.

The audience of men watched the show with studied aloofness. They hung their money on the low grillwork bordering the stage where the dancer, nude except for black heels, moved her pussy from face to face, hovering before each in suspended efflorescence. The altar of the uterus held high dominion over the watchers' puny paper offerings—this was modern burlesque. A DJ spun records for the routines and talked on a mike. He had names for the strippers like "Clitoris Leachman" and "So Horny Weaver" and "Genevieve Blow-Job." Bud wondered what an extraterrestrial would make of it.

The dancers became waitresses in between numbers, like scumbag Cinderellas, and for some reason Bud was embarrassed for them. They probably did all right. He'd seen the ads in the classifieds for exotic dancers, promising the big money that never came. He used to read the phone sales solicitations in the trades, the ones aimed at out-of-work-actors. *Earn a thousand a day, for just a few hours of work each morning!* A cheesy death world of fringey show biz hype. Like the battered car he used to see around town, with the spray-painted slogan: FOR SALE—A BILLION DOLLARS.

Bud watched a girl serve drinks, then backed into shadow, almost losing his balance on the stool. As she leaned over a customer, he saw the keloid. It looked like a tissued finger riding there, a white, waxen grub. It was dark. Bud's eyes were fastened on Rachel and the man. He gave her some bills and she looked around furtively, like a ham actor, to make sure no one was watching. All eyes were on the stage. She crouched while holding the tray, pulling the tube top down on one side. The man put her breast in his mouth. She looked around some more, the tray close to her body now, above the man's head, concealing the suckling. She looked right at Bud, without seeing him. The music crescendoed and she pulled away, tugging the top back up. The dancer onstage collected the dollars that hung like clothespins as Bud ran into the night.

He sat in the limo with the windows shut, blasting an oldies station. When his clients came out, he was pounding the dash to "I Hear a Symphony." The stoned executives were halfway in the car before Bud even noticed them. He turned the radio off, but one of them turned it back all the way and danced on the sidewalk while the others clapped.

ᗑᗑᗑ

When Bud showed up at the Four Oaks on Saturday evening, the old man was waiting in the lobby. He wore his long black Comme des Garçons coat and looked somber and formidable, his beard brushed to a lucent, pearly fluff. The limousine moved through dark streets, the Rav silently pointing his finger this way and that until they were downtown. Their destination seemed exact. Bud was surprised at how well he knew the city.

They left the freeway at Alameda and drove onto Main Street past Union Station. After about a mile the old man signaled Bud to pull over. He parked and the two of them walked down a slope to the enormous train yard. The moon was bright. The Rav walked with unlikely agility; Bud knew the knapsack he wore like a hump on his back was heavy. He would finally know what was in it. He would know lots of things now.

He struggled to keep up as they scampered around a brambly, unused trestle, then climbed a hill beneath a concrete bridge to reach a vantage point. Bud had never seen such a swath of tracks, never imagined a Los Angeles of trains, like Chicago or New York. He felt the old man's kinship with the dark artery. They smoothed out the dirt, cleared away some debris and sat, overlords of the Yard.

The Rav mentioned that Mrs. Steiner phoned him at the Four Oaks and he had impersonated a saturnine aide who referred "all inquiries regarding the rabbi to that famous, venerable amanuensis-about-town Bud Wiggins." When Bud relayed the dinner invitation, he waved it away like a petty detail that would arrange itself. The old man behaved as if events were unfolding right on schedule, and had been from the moment they met that afternoon in the airport. It gave Bud the chills.

"What is it you carry around in the knapsack?"

The old man drew apart his beard like a curtain.

"Do you see where there is no hair? It is where they tore the beard from my face. No flowers grow in this part of the garden anymore. You wonder why am I here, in this town, this place. You wonder, but you don't ask. It is my wandering, my mortification. To die among strangers, is it so terrible? Is it so different than loving one's enemies? The greatest redemption! In each city there is a rock and a fountain that flows from the rock. In each city one may find His seventy crowned palaces. Each palace has a door to seventy worlds. Each world opens to seventy channels, each channel to seventy supernal crowns. All these things are the heart of the world.

"A tale is told: the girl I was telling you I liberate from the whorehouse, it was Miriam, daughter of Rabbi Zing. The family I hide her with in Lwów turn her over to the Gestapo. So Miriam she end up in camp. It was still not known she was the daughter of Zing. Such beauty, my Miriam, you ache to watch, you cannot look at the face full on. The doomahz, they put her in the frownblock, the place for the whores. This was Auschwitz.

"I find out she is there and one day I make a bribe to the blockletest to see her. I go to her and she looks but my Miriam doesn't know me. She makes herself naked. She thinks I am there for something else. On her backside they put a tattoo, WALK IN DANCE OUT. Around her mouth they put another tattoo in tiny letters, all around: *Nach dem Abort, vor dem Essen Hände waschen, nicht vergessen*—'Wash hands before using. Cleanliness is health,' a louse is death, to each his due. Miriam is without tears, her face is puffy with the clear fluid of the lymph leaking from the ink. They have put numbers and figures everywhere on her face. She is beyond desecration—a living responsa. Out of the depths, have I called unto thee, O Lord! I sit down with her and wash her hair in my precious bowl. She still has her gorgeous hair, they don't cut it till she leaves the frownblock. I 'organize' gray soap—just like the bread, it looks—and dirty water; it is enough. While I wash, I look at her face, her eyes turned to the sky. I say her father is well, but she cannot hear. I rub her scalp to soothe her, it is the most mikvah I can make.

"I am washing and remembering. When she was a young girl, we first met. Always chaste, but we did not like everyone to be around. And we are children, trying not to be. So we sneak from our houses to meet under the wild palms of Yatkever Street, in Kovno. Under the moon, on the street corners Dzika and Chmielna, Ceglanan and Marshalkowska—we met on the New Year of the Trees and kissed on the eve of the Sabbath, on the ninth day of Zut, the anniversary of the destruction of the Temple.

"Do you know what is the bribe I do, what I free Miriam? It is from the tricks I make for the Kapo's kid. Do you remember, Wigginitz? Do you remember the magic tunnel? They release her to the krackenbow, the clinic, and I find out later they let her go not from of my magic tunnel but because she shows sign of typhus. I was thinking how clever and important I am, and what should be my reward! The great maggid! To the World of Illusion, I'm going soon, Wigginitz—*o-lam ha dim-yon*!

"If you are in the clinic, you are exempt from the roll call, which starts sometimes three in the morning. So this way she gains strength. But she is hallucinating from her sickness and her father—Zing—comes to see her, but she does not recognize. 'The Lord shall smite thee with madness, and with blindness, and with astonishment of heart! And thou shalt grope at noonday, as the blind gropeth in darkness and thou shalt be only oppressed and robbed always, and there shall be none to save thee!' She calls me Simeon, from Rabbi Simeon ben Yohai of the sheltering branches.

"They give her medicine and soon she is well enough to be a worker in the clinic. Me I think she knows, but it is a different Miriam now. There is a veil between her and the world—more than a shroud of tattoos. And she is now a great genius: those who pass through, she makes better with her hands. It is like a myth, Wigginitz, yes, it is, this I concur. They wish to be healed so bring to the infirmary their paltry gifts, but you know in the camp a loaf of bread was worth a skyscraper. Miriam she takes nothing from them. The Kapos come to the clinic and this is rare. When the monsters are ill, they come for her hands to be touched. Even the nurses leave my Miriam alone, and this is a *sign* because the nurses are the real shits. They sell the spoons of the dead.

"The holy intaglio of my Miriam's face is a fountain, a well, a Palace of Love! We in the barracks scrutinize the engravings there when she sleeps—where the kisses of the King are kept on the rock in the secret firmament, kisses of Love. 'Every soul

loved by the Holy One is blessed and enters into that Palace.'
So the people come to her before the selek-juhs, because they
must look strong. You know what is the selek-juh, Wiggins?
This is the selection for death. All the time in the Lager it is
going on, lights, camera, *Aktion*! The block-spur comes—the
block-spur makes the selek-juh from the weak—and the ones
who Miriam has touched survive the *schlechte Seite,* they are
not chosen. It is good sometimes not to be the Chosen! And now
they are true survivors—now they think in their heads that they
are blessed.

"I once in a while used myself a technique of Zing's when a
friend falter. This was in the Lager. I would look him in his eye
and say: 'You will survive! You will have a son you will see live
to be twice the age you are now.' Anything would do. 'You will
live to sew a *chuppah* for your daughter's wedding day, and
dance with the badhan in the Seven Days of the Feast. You will
go to Palestine and your husband will make cabinets there, and
your grandchildren raise egg crops.' The simplest pronounce-
ment gave them strength, sustained them. In the Lager one
grasped at anything—hope and despair are merely states of
mind. Neither is rational. But this you surely know, Wigginitz.
Because you are amazing.

"But Miriam's technique, it was something more. She never
had to say a word. By touching them, they transformed. It was
impregnation of soul, *ibbur,* completion. Of course, many died
by bullets and by fire, their flesh rended, as the curtain of the
torah's ark—but with an *'Adonai!'* This is what she gave them.
It was also this time I learned who had put the marks on her
face at the same time fornicating with her, so that she was
burned above and below, male and female, her upper and lower
waters. *The smell of my Miriam is as the smell of a field which
the Lord hath blessed!* It was the Kapo for who I make the
magic tunnel his child. For his son.

"Do you know there were two jobs I was doing at the Lager,
Wigginitz? I was scraping a vat shaped like a pear, so big they
must lower me in. It was in Canada, the section near the crema-

toria. Why this it was called, for me is unknown. And the other thing I am doing, I am thinking a trick for the boy—my second job. Remember, each week I had to make magic, and this time I am worried because I have so much rage for this Kapo. But I am dead if I cannot think of the sleight of hand solution. So I am scouring the vat and thinking like a bastard. And I am suddenly thinking to do something with a little bottle, again the shape of a pear, that first I saw when washing Miriam's hair— you see, to have this thought, I cannot help because all day long I am in the vat, the belly of this idea, this notion. And slowly it is something in my mind.

"I tell the Kapo I need something and he gets for me a bottle of *parfume* from the frownblock, a tiny bottle. I affix a rounded bottom that is weighted within so the bottle cannot lie on its side, only straight up. Now it is a pear, like the vat. Have you seen these clowns of plastic, Wiggins, the ones you knock with your fist and they rise up from the ground to be struck again? Over and over and over? This is what the bottle is like, a little bulb with a small-mouthed opening, a bulb you cannot lay on its side. When you try, it stands up straight, with absurd pride! I make another weight, a thin bar that slides into the mouth. With the bar inserted, *abracadabra!* the bottle lays down.

"So I bring to the boy and I push the bottle on its side while the Kapo watches. He will judge. The boy tries to touch it, but I don't let him. I repeat the movement. The deliberate laying of the bottle on its side. Very dramatic, to show that it is easy. Then I pick it up the bottle and hand it to him, but the weight it slips from the mouth and into my palm without seeing. This is sleight of hand, Wigginitz. And the bottle will not lie down for the boy, only I can make it lie down. The Kapo is amused and makes me tell him the secret. When I do, he delights in withholding it from the boy. He finally tells him, and the boy goes to find friends to demonstrate. I am alive for another week.

"Miriam is not well anymore. It is 1945. We hear bombs. There is a Kapo I fix his boots, he allows me to walk with Miriam in Canada. Like lost lovers, we spend our time in the forest. A sukkahs. Does she know me? She is a wanderer now and I am blessed to hold her hand. Do you know Rabbi Nachman? At fourteen he married; so began his country life. Like Ruskin, nature obsessed him. At the end he slept in a house built from trees, dreaming that he lay in the midst of the dead."

"You are walking, with Miriam. Near the crematoria."

"There is the pit on the other side, but you can't see. Miriam is sick and dreaming—it is time to eat the third Sabbath meal. She cries, 'Mutti!' and I hold her. I rock her, baby girl, and make a lullaby. Then I fall to sleep for what seems three days and three nights. I dream of making beds—and know when I wake up I am preparing for death. There is a wind that carries the voices from the pit beyond like a thousand shofars: they say 'Komm, komm, komm.'

"The three days are the days a man is in his grave before his belly bursts apart. At the end of three days it casts forth its putrescence onto his face, saying: 'Receive back that which you put into me; all day long you ate and drank, nor ever gave a thing to the poor; like feasts and holidays were all your days, but the needy did not share your food and were left hungry. Receive that which you put into me.' And three days more having elapsed, the man is punished in each organ, in his eyes, his hands, his feet. For thirty days then, the soul and the body receive punishment together. Therefore, does the soul tarry during this time on earth below, and does not ascend to her sphere, as a woman is isolated through the period of her impurity, her redness. All this has a color, don't forget it! There is blue and black and the white light of the *Yod He Vav He*. Wigginitz, are you confused?"

"What happened to Miriam?"

"When I awaken, Miriam is dead in my arms, dreaming lymph from her open eyes. It is unbearable! I stare at this face, a useless Torah, I finally read the tautology of the refractory signs: death. That is all it is. This is the bright, dirty mystery of the tattoos! I am ashamed. The man who put them there knows more than me.

"It is summer in the Canadian field and I am going to walk into the pit. This is my resolution; I have made my own selekjuh. I put ashes—they are everywhere you dip your hand in the dirt—on my forehead and remove my shoes. I am ready for the Lamentations. I recite the coal needray and the vidooey. I leave her in the grass, a fading tenement billboard, a seraphita. The roar of insects is divine. I have touched her lymph and they swarm to the clear fluid traces on my finger. The flies are my Sabbath clothes—the Messenger is here and I must be properly dressed! There is new moon; it is a festival day. I will go to the pit with my rooah, then back to the Garden for my beloved. I am a living prayer at this moment, I am a magic tube swallowing up bright silken scraps. Did you know that when the end is near, prayers are heard with more urgency? As doctors hasten a birth in a pregnancy that is overdue.

"I have walked a few yards and I hear a voice. It is the Kapo's son, looking for me. He holds the pear-shaped bottle and cries. It is broken. He has lost the weight, his friends are making fun. He does not see the other broken toy lying in the grass. I take him by the hand and he goes sweetly with me to the vat. I break his neck and shove him like a weight through the tiny mouth. I see the head disappear, its soft hair like a field. *See, the smell of my son is as the smell of a field which the Lord hath blessed.* This is Genesis."

The old man stopped, his breath shallow. After a few minutes he smiled.

"You asked what I carried in my sack."

ɯɯ

It was the following Saturday and the Rav was late. The hostess made herself scarce.

Melanie was there, and a frail, liverish man, the one in charge of the Foundation's "document acquisition." A fiftyish manservant in coat and tie served drinks and canapés; he looked like the security chief of an exclusive department store. Bud sat on a sofa beneath a badly hung Motherwell, which was veneered with hair oil from sitters' scalps.

"Aren't you getting too thin?" Melanie asked. She was on her second martini.

"I've been fasting," Bud answered.

"Isn't that supposed to be terrible for you?"

"I feel great."

"Well, you know what they say," said the acquisitions man. They hoped he would leave it at that, but no such luck: "You can never be too rich or too thin."

"Tell it to Karen Carpenter."

The dated reference wasn't altogether unfunny in such company; Melanie found it hilarious. Bud laughed along with her. The acquisitions man smiled benignly to himself, like someone hard of hearing.

"Seriously, Bud, how much weight have you lost?"

"Fifteen pounds, maybe."

"Was it *voluntary*?" Her eyebrow lifted archly, invoking the dreaded Virus.

Mrs. Steiner swept into the room, wearing an ill-fitting, incongruously formal gown.

"The rabbi knows the address?"

"Yes," he answered.

"Why the hell didn't you come together?"

"He had some business to attend to."

"He's very busy, the rabbi. Think he's too busy to eat? Gary, what time is it?"

The manservant answered it was almost nine.

"I think we should start."

They went to the dining room and within moments a Scandinavian woman was serving them soup. A giant bloodred Gilbert and George called *Winter Tongue Fuck* took up an entire wall; a blackened Nevelson construction adorned another. Mrs. Steiner disapprovingly took Bud in.

"Did you lose weight?"

"I've been dieting."

"You look awful."

"Mrs. Steiner, that's mean!"

The hostess cracked a smile. "Oh, he doesn't care. Did I offend you, Bud?"

It was the first time she'd ever called him by name.

"I'm terribly hurt."

"Join the club."

"Yes," said the liverish man, "join the club."

Fish was served and they ate awhile in silence.

"Say," said Mrs. Steiner, "how do you know the rabbi anyway?"

Before Bud could answer, the doorbell rang. Mrs. Steiner sprang to her feet, beating the manservant to the entrance hall. The screenwriter followed, arriving at the front door as she opened it.

At first he didn't recognize the old man. He seemed to have shrunk in size and had the empty, radiantly beleaguered look of a senile man lost in a public park. The knapsack was gone, and the beard, unevenly curtailed. The screenwriter had never seen him so defenseless. When it occurred to Bud it might be an act, his spirits rose.

Mrs. Steiner introduced Rabbi Levi to her guests. His arrival had drastically altered her demeanor. Bud suffered a wave of credulity, as if in fact the Rav was a world-famous personage all along. She poured him a brandy and made noise about bringing food, which he refused. The manservant asked for his jacket; he declined. They sat him down at the head of the table and put a plate in front of him anyway. Melanie was alert and obeisant, and the dry bones of the acquisitions man grew animated.

Tonight the old man told no stories. He listened as the others spoke of weather, travel, cost of living. He finally agreed to some soup. When he finished, the group went to the living room for coffee.

"I would very much like you to see the architectural model

of our project—the Foundation for Holocaust Studies. Will you be in town much longer, Rabbi?"

"A little longer, yes."

"Then at your convenience, I would like you to see what we're doing. Bud can pick you up in the car."

"I am sure it is a lovely building."

"I want you to see that it will make a beautiful permanent home for your documents."

Bud knew what she was talking about.

"You had alluded to a price for the material."

Mrs. Steiner bristled slightly; Melanie cleared her throat and excused herself.

"A generous price, yes. Upon verification of authenticity."

The acquisitions man grunted and cocked his head like a dog, signifying he was the final arbiter in such a determination.

The old man waved his hand, as if erasing an invisible blackboard.

"I am not to *sell*. I wish to make a *donation* of the responsa, but under only one condition." Mrs. Steiner seemed perplexed. "My condition is: that the gift be memorialized on the Wall of Martyrs in the name of Miriam Zing."

"Rabbi Levi," she soberly began, "I am grateful and honored by such a magnificent gift." Without belittling him, she said the Foundation's mandate was to note such remembrances—in other words, an inscribed memorial was a given. Melanie returned and sat beside Bud.

The Rav was unsteady. He removed his jacket and Mrs. Steiner got him a glass of water. As he gulped it down, Melanie saw the numbers on his arm and glanced at Bud with exquisite pungency. The room became intolerably still and sad for a moment. Then he put down his glass and fished inside the coat, carefully removing a lizard-skin portfolio from a large pocket. He handed it to the acquisitions man: the responsa.

Mrs. Steiner clasped her hands together and set them in her lap, like a prime minister addressing the pope.

"May I ask a personal question, Rabbi?"

He nodded his assent.

"Who was Miriam Zing?"

"She was my wife."

At the door the old man turned to face the guests. He took some paper from his pocket, a *kvittel* for the wall, he said, a poem he wrote that afternoon:

> "See how I come back
> to the wonder of my first word.
> Close the window, friend,
> Shield me from the smallest wind.
> In the dark there are two of us;
> what could be less?
> I am the hearty patron
> Of all the hungry tasters.
> Let us saddle sleep
> and ride off in our private park.
> The mays will kiss
> The must-nots in the dark."

Bud stayed with Rachel that night; he felt emptied out and needed to be with someone. She was ferocious. She ground against his fingers until they were bone-sore, baring her teeth like a wolf caught in a trap. She growled as she came. Through the night, like in a movie, Rachel told him she was afraid, she never said why, and the wind tossed the moonlit trees like shadows of burglars on their faces. She never said why and it would be gauche to ask. Funny word, *gauche,* he thought to himself. Fifties word.

It was afternoon when he awoke to Rachel walking in with groceries. She asked if he remembered his nightmare. He'd cried out in his sleep, she said, skirmishing on the sheets—a low moan first that sounded like someone else. Bud felt feverish, outside his body. He wanted to go to the rabbi. He wanted to write something, something brand-new, to shake the earth. He wanted to butt his head against a wall until he entered the world of confusion: *o-lam ha dim-yon.*

Rachel said she had things to tell him.

〰〰

A few days after the Steiner dinner he received an urgent call from Melanie. She said the so-called responsa the rabbi donated to the foundation were just indecipherable shreds, ballpoint phonies.

"Who is he, Bud? Who *is* that man?"

"A friend."

"He misrepresented himself! Is he a criminal, Bud? Mrs. Steiner is livid!"

"What's she going to do?"

"I shouldn't even be calling. How involved are you, Bud?"

"What do you mean?"

"Her credit card, someone's been charging huge amounts on Millicent's credit card! They think it was that old man! It's terrible, Bud! She thinks you gave him her credit card number. She even suspects *me*! She asked me if there was anything between us—if I was seeing you. Bud, you *have* to tell me—are you involved?"

"I'm not involved in anything, okay, Melanie? Is she going to call the police? Has she called them?"

"It's a mess. It's just a mess," she said, on the verge of tears. "It's *really creepy.*"

"I'm sorry, Melanie. I'm sorry about what's happened. I had no idea."

"You just better not have anything to do with it, Bud. You better not."

Bud drove to the Four Oaks. He took the stairs to the room, knocking on the door. It was unlocked. He opened it, calling out the old man's name. Then he stepped inside.

The room was breezy—the windows were wide open—and

rapturous music came from a portable CD player that sat on the end table. Probably another one of Mrs. Steiner's little gifts. He moved toward the bathroom. The door was closed.

"Rav? It's Bud."

The screenwriter fantasized he was in the midst of a classic horror film "reveal": the old man had probably been hacked to death and was lying in pieces in the tub. He slowly pushed the door open. *Rav?* Nothing. There were clumps of hair in the sink and the floor below, the color of the old man's beard.

Bud turned down the CD and went to the cabinet. It was empty except for colorful bags from expensive Beverly Hills shops, carefully folded and stacked one atop the other. He went through the drawers for receipts but found only matches, from Bistro Garden, Mr. Chow, Chaya, the City.

On the table in front of the sofa was a paper bag from Hollywood Magic. Bud held it upside down and a red plastic bottle clattered onto the Formica. He stood the fig-shaped toy on its rounded bottom, then pushed it over with a finger, holding it down. When he let go, it jauntily righted itself—

"You cannot be in here!"

The manager of the Four Oaks House stood in the door. Behind him loomed a stocky man with a holster visible inside his coat. He spoke.

"Who are you?"

"Bud Wiggins, I'm a friend of the Rav's."

"The who?"

"I'm a screenwriter."

"Ah, the chauffeur," said the stocky man, mostly to himself. Then he turned to the manager. "You can leave us alone here."

"What's going on?" Bud asked.

"Your friend has been arrested."

He introduced himself as Detective Rayburn. He knew all about Bud from Mrs. Steiner and had planned on getting in touch. They sat down at the table. The detective asked how he met the old man. Bud talked and Rayburn listened well, dropping the occasional cogent question. He seemed impressed that

Bud was a writer, sympathetic almost, giving him a certain leeway as the unlikely story unraveled, as if allowing for the "imagination" factor.

"Do you think Mr. Linley used Mrs. Steiner's credit cards for goods and services?"

"Mr. Linley?"

"Mr. Jerry Linley, that is who we're talking about."

"I don't know."

"Were you ever with him when he made a purchase or maybe ordered something over the phone?"

"Yes, but I never looked at a card. Besides, wouldn't her Visa have 'Millicent' on it? How could he sign?"

"Mrs. Steiner has corporate and personal cards. Did Mrs. Steiner have an account with the limousine company, Bud?"

"No."

"How did she pay, cash?"

"Credit card."

"She was a regular customer, wasn't she, Bud?"

"Fairly, yes."

"It's unusual that she wouldn't open an account, isn't it?"

"She's an unusual person."

"She can afford to be."

The detective began poking through drawers and cabinets.

"Did you have access to those account numbers in the course of your work, Bud? I mean, as a driver at the Beverly Palm."

"I don't handle the billing."

"But you have access to records?"

"Anyone that's in and out of that garage does."

"When the dispatcher gives you an order, it's a carbon, right?"

"Right."

"And the order has pertinent billing information on it, such as a credit card number. Correct?"

"That's right."

"And you keep a copy of the order in the car, for your records. Plus, it has the address of your client, their destination, et cetera. All important information. Is it possible, Bud, that Mr. Linley might have gotten hold of one of those order sheets and copied down Mrs. Steiner's credit card number?"

Bud admitted it was possible.

"We found the credit cards of other individuals in his possession. Did Mr. Linley give you any documents or belongings for safekeeping?"

"No."

"Have you ever been arrested, Bud?"

"No, I haven't."

"I was sure you hadn't. It's something I have to ask. Do you know any celebrities, Bud? You must encounter them in your line of work."

"I know a few."

"Have you written anything I might have seen?"

"I've written lots of things. The last one produced was a horror film."

"I enjoy horror. You know, I have a brother who's a writer. Thom Rayburn, Thom with a *T-h,* ever heard of him? He's a journalist, mostly. He was the one who did the quickie book on the Mount Olympus murders."

Bud asked if he was under any kind of suspicion and the detective said he really didn't think so.

"Do you have a holiday coming up, Bud?"

"Every day's a holiday."

Rayburn laughed. "No travel plans?"

"No."

"Well, if you get the urge to go and gamble in Vegas or fly to New York to see a show, hold off for a few days. Boy, that sounds like something cops say in the movies, doesn't it?"

He opened the door and Bud stepped out to the hall. Rayburn closed it behind them, making sure it was locked.

"You go anywhere you want, Bud. I don't care if you go to Italy. Just leave us a number in case we need to get in touch." They started down the hall to the stairs. "Do you ever go away to write?"

"Sometimes I go to the desert."

"Beautiful place. Where do you stay?"

"Two Bunch Palms."

Bud sat on his impulse to visit "Mr. Linley." He felt betrayed and a little foolish but was curious about the old man's motives. He wanted to be cool for the confrontation—better to let a day or two pass before rushing over to the jailhouse. Linley wasn't going anywhere. He made plans to drive up the coast with Rachel.

The day startled them with sunlight. Rachel looked beautiful. She was wearing Keds; her long dancer legs had sweet burnished patches of hair on the thigh. The calves were copper-colored and smoothly perfect.

She was property-watching as they drove—the beach houses on one side of the highway, the hill-perched rancheros on the other. She said her family had a beach house once. They had a place on the beach and a place in town, on Copa de Oro. When she was twelve, her parents pitched a tent in the back-yard on the sand and that's where Rachel and her younger brother lived for the summer. They made a leafy barrier behind the tent, a trellis of vines so you couldn't see the house. They pretended they were on the other side of the world. She got an atlas and they picked the seas: Black, Baltic, China, Caspian. That was when her dad was still alive. He died ridiculously on a hunting trip years later, run over by a Jeep on the veldt. She came home from Williams College for the funeral—Gavin was finishing high school—and they put the tent up again and cried together inside. Gavin stayed close to his sister, watching and taking care of her. She really fell in love with her brother then.

Rachel never went back to college after that. She started nursing school instead and got a job in an emergency room. One of the doctors loved shooting her up. She stole from the hospital and kept the tubercular syringes, with their tiny gauge needles, in a silver box her father gave her when she graduated high school. She stashed the Demerol ampules there, too, they looked like tinkling dollhouse miniatures, glass-blown bowling pins she kept wrapped in one of her mother's scarves. Rachel snapped their heads off, drew the fluid up, pinched the skin between her knuckles and shot it in. She started putting it in the big muscles, too, her thighs and rear end. Gavin didn't like that. Her movements around him were slow and seductive. Sometimes he pushed her away.

Bud asked about the brother.

Rachel told him that a year after their father's death, she drove Gavin to the Hamburger Hamlet. They took her grasshopper green Spyder, another gift from Dad. She was dirty and it crashed like in a movie and Gavin was thrown like in a movie. That's how she got the scar under her tit. Her mother totally shut her out. She crated up the daughter's things—every memento, photograph, reminder—just like she never existed. Relatives wouldn't return calls, not even the aunt who was always her champion. Rachel was broke. She tended bar in West Hollywood, the Rain Check Room, and a parolee boyfriend went and robbed the beach house. Then the two of them robbed the Bel Air digs. The family was house-heavy anyway, she said, and laughed. They were just trying to lighten the load.

She wanted to get clean. Heard the one about the Polish junkie who wanted to get clean? So there she was on the South China Sea, where she'd already imagined herself during sandy peregrinations with Gavin—destiny at work. It made sense, her new locale, she understood its crazy, sweltering algebra. It made even more sense with heroin; life had finally given her a decent job. Rachel Morrison was a scurvy, sassy debutante, the air dark around her like a sibling-tent. She ministered to the wounded, so many of the boys were lanky and flat-stomached like Gavin. The sick young men loved her and she could do things for them. *So many wounded boys,* Bud thought, *discovering their God loved others as much as He loved them.*

Rachel directed him through winding streets and by the time they reached the Brennan School, he breathlessly understood: she was Mrs. Steiner's daughter.

They went inside and her brother's leg spasmed while she held him, foot waxing the floor like a dog whose owner had been away too long. He seemed bewildered. When he tried to wriggle from her arms, Rachel laughed and kissed his face all over and the caretakers cracked up. They liked her. My beach bum, she called him, because his hair was mussed and there were crumbs on his flannel shirt.

Bud went to the car and waited. He thought of calling the old man but decided against it; he'd visit in the morning. Rachel and Gavin left the building and he watched them stroll the grounds. The screenwriter wondered if the invalid really recognized his sister. He was idly curious how he would cope with accidentally running over Dolly.

Rachel was quiet on the way back, shielding her eyes from the water. She'd had enough ocean for today. Bud remembered her say she had a son. He asked if the father was the burglar-boyfriend.

"Jesus, you don't forget anything, do you?"

"It's not exactly a tiny detail."

"I had my kid *way* after I got back from Nam. My mother didn't want to see him. She made it clear that Caleb had no participation in the estate. I didn't give a fuck about his participation in the estate. I just felt it was important for him to meet his grandma, madwoman that she is. I'm weirdly sentimental—or fucked up enough to care about them making a connection. So I arranged to bump into her somewhere, with Caleb. Well, the blood just drained from her face—he looks a lot like Gavin. She even calls him that sometimes by mistake. Sick. She made an offer to me, she offered me a lot of money each month if she could have him. Raise him. I was in pretty bad shape then, really scrounging. I was using again. I had abscesses—could barely take care of myself, let alone Caleb. I signed a piece of paper. My mother basically agreed to pay for drugs in exchange for my son. What a woman, huh? I'm clean now, and I have a fancy lawyer. I'm going to get him back."

That night Bud dreamed he worked in a hospital on a hill.

Detective Rayburn had been shot. He lay in a white bed, hold-ing an *"emmis"* basin like an offering. That was a word Bud's grandpa Louie used to say: it meant luck.

The next morning, Bud decided to visit the Central Jail. He stopped to answer the phone on his way out the door.

"Bud Wiggins?"

"Who is it?"

"Jack Rayburn."

"What's up?"

"Well, I see you didn't leave town."

"Should I?"

Rayburn laughed folksily.

"Not unless you want to. The reason I'm calling, Bud, is to tell you that Jerome Linley passed away last night in his cell. He left some belongings for you to claim."

The screenwriter saw an image of the old man hanging from a pipe, but Rayburn said he had a heart attack. Bud wondered to himself if the Rav had been in "Sabbath clothes." One of his cockamamie riffs was about wanting to be in his Sabbath clothes when the Messiah came.

He made the trip downtown. Everything moved slowly. A marshal finally surrendered a plastic garbage bag with a "J. LINLEY" tag. Bud signed for it without looking inside.

At home he tore the bag open with his fingers and pulled out the old man's leather knapsack. There was an envelope inside with Bud's name written on it. The note said: *I dreamt that the goyim crucified Mozart and dug him a donkey's grave.*

Bud pulled a Hermès scarf from the sack, then a thick sheaf of papers tied with ribbon, like love letters. He undid them. They were pages torn from books—homiletic tales and Hebrew poetry, exegeses of the kabbala, eyewitness Auschwitz ac-counts—their passages highlighted by yellow marker. As he flipped through them, he recognized the old man's iterative, singsong voice in the words; the Rav's memory had been photo-graphic and from this miscellanea he'd mixed a wild-eyed, soul-

ful mélange in the broad bowl of his skull. Here were the old
man's crib notes, a discursive Frankenstein of parables, fractured bon mots and stolen remembrance. From the pages of
Borowski, Schulz and Primo Levi ("The best place for bread is
in my stomach—I won't steal from myself!"), Bud encountered
great chunks of monologue, even the stanza the old man had
recited at Mrs. Steiner's, lifted from an anthology of Yiddish
poetry. From the same source came the cryptic "Mozart and
donkey's grave."

It was apparent the mysterious Mr. Linley's giddy stream of
consciousness was often fed by the deep spring of *Basic Readings from the Kabbalah.* The "Eye of Zo-Har" itself was repre-
sented by a bona fide instruction book—companion of a quirky
Ouija board-type party game from the late fifties. And more:
pages ripped from *Survival in Auschwitz* (Levi); *The Joys of
Yiddish;* Scholem's *Major Trends in Jewish Mysticism* and *Sabbatai Sevi, The Mystical Messiah; I Shall Live: Surviving Against
All Odds; The Nazi Doctors; Parables and Paradoxes* (Kafka);
Fury on Earth; Hello, I Must Be Going (on Groucho Marx);
Hunting Humans (serial murder); *Description of a Struggle*
(Kafka again); *The Street of Crocodiles; Jewish Magic and Su-
perstition: A Study in Folk Religion; Divine Hunger; The Death
of My Brother Abel; The Eagle's Gift; Eichmann's Inferno; Ha-
sidic Tales of the Holocaust; Pico della Mirandola's Encounter
with Jewish Mysticism; The Survivor; The Hour of Our Death;
The Chronicle of the Lódź Ghetto; Deep Dyslexia; Shelley: Also
Known as Shirley* (Shelley Winters); *Moments of Reprieve; The
Memoirs of Bridget Hitler* (illustrated); *Metaphor & Memory;
Wieland, or The Transformation; The Mind of a Mnemonist;
George and Gracie: A Love Affair; Kiddush Hashem: Jewish
Religious and Cultural Life in Poland During the Holocaust;
Paracelsus's Selected Writings; Tormented Master: A Life of
Rabbi Nachman of Bratslav;* even a pornographic paperback
called *SS Horror Chamber.*

From the bottom of the knapsack Bud removed two final
items, a heavy velvet J&B pouch and a book, its spine and pages

intact—*Responsa from the Holocaust,* by Rabbi Ephraim Oshry. It was the authentic source of the old man's myth, the true story of the burial of "questions and responses from out of the depths."

Inside the pouch was a crystal bowl. A crack ran through it like an ugly white hair. He turned it over. The fissure went through zigzaggy scratches at the bottom. Bud tied up the pages and set them in the bowl. He thought of setting them on fire but worried the glass might shatter from the heat. He tried to remember the letters the old man ascribed to the colors of a flame.

MMM

Things were going well with his tragicomic tale of group therapy among the vets. In *The Holocaust Museum* script, the character of the Rav really came alive. The screenwriter realized how much he was already missing him.

Bud felt good to be out of "the mode" and wholly in the work. He fell into a rhythm, isolating himself from the world. He slept deeply and relished his own company. He still challenged himself with fasts, even though his weight was lower than it had been in years. The hunger helped him focus.

When Bud finished the second act of *The Holocaust Museum,* he called Rachel. She was on her way to Arizona, to write and stay sober. It was her time to be alone.

Rachel's manuscript arrived in the mail with a form letter attached. The Survivor Press was not considering anything for publication until after the spring of next year. The book should be resubmitted then.

Gerald Scherick added some words to the bottom in an erratic hand. His wife had become seriously ill and the fate of the press was uncertain. He wished Rabbi Levi well and thanked Bud for his interest; he was optimistic they would be "out of the woods" after the new year. An indifferent postscript noted that parts of Rachel Morrison's book seemed to have been "inadvertently" culled from *Maldoror*.

᠁

A month or so after the old man's death, Bud got a call from Thom Rayburn. It took him a moment to realize he wasn't the detective. He was the brother.

"I understand you're a movie writer."

"Sometimes."

"That's a tough game. Me, I come from newspapers. Write a book now and then, when they let me. Get a lot of ideas from my brother's cases. You ever talk to him?"

"Not in a while."

"You know, the Rayburns are from Massachusetts, North Adams. I was visiting our mom up there—she's been sick. She runs a cab company, loves it, bless her heart, she's a widow, tough old gal, won't take a penny from either one of us. I was up there, and after I spoke to my brother in L.A., I decided I was gonna take me a little side trip to Albany. That was Linley's hometown, did you know?"

"I don't know anything about him."

Rayburn asked Bud to meet him for coffee. The screenwriter suggested Musso's.

"That'll be like old times for me," he said.

The bachelor Thom was about sixty-five and wore rimless glasses, an old legman who looked more like a cop than his brother. He was retired and occasionally free-lanced pieces to travel and historical magazines. He'd written a few books: a straightforward true-crime account of an uninteresting murder and a prosaic biography of an American CEO, commissioned by the titan's corporation. It was true he'd authored a "quickie" on the Mount Olympus murders but was unhappy with the results.

"The editors screwed me around on that one," he said. "But that's what you get when you do it for the money." When Bud asked about Perry Bravo, Thom shrugged his shoulders. "Still in jail," he said. "Let's hope so anyway."

He began talking about the Linley case. The screenwriter was startled to learn that through the detective's leads and the brother's inquiries, a double homicide "on the books" for nearly fifty years had been closed.

"You mean, something involving the Rav?"

"Who?"

"I mean, Linley."

"Is that what he called himself?"

"That was a nickname. He said his name was Israel Levi."

Thom nodded thoughtfully. The ball was rolling: a powerful columnist friend wrote a piece for a Chicago paper about the retired journalist's investigations, called "A Revelation in Albany" and Thom was soon returning to that town, a popular TV newsmagazine in tow. He'd already gotten a respectable advance on a book from a publishing house that did well in this area—it knew how to market. He was convinced a movie deal wasn't far behind.

"My brother told me you spent a lot of time with Jerry."

"Was he a Jew?" Bud wasn't sure why he'd asked.

"No. But his wife was."

"How old was he?"

"Jesus. Had to be mid-seventies."

The waitress brought Thom's breakfast. Bud was only having coffee.

"Jerry Linley had a vaudeville act with his brother Mickey. Jerry meets a girl, Miriam Altshuler, a nurse. This is early-early forties. They elope. Her father's Orthodox and never speaks to his daughter after that. The Linley Brothers do all right. Magic, comedy, burlesquey stuff. Remember that phrase 'Zing me'? Naw, you're too young. It was just one of these phrases they popularized. It meant: go ahead, sue me, 'zing me,' whatever—screw you, it'll roll off my back. It was very big. Culture: nobody knows why everyone's suddenly saying something, what makes a tad. It doesn't last. The point is, they had a following. Everything was going beautifully.

"Jerry and Miriam have a little boy, Izzy. Beautiful, I saw pictures—I got lots of stuff, Linley had crap in a safety-deposit box under a different name, in Yonkers. Sent a check in every year, clockwork. Had the key to the box in his hand when he died. Did my brother tell you that?"

"No."

"Anyway, everything's beautiful, going great. Like I said, the act is doing well, Izzy's three years old and Jerry's sick with love for the kid. Takes him everywhere. Forbids Miriam to work anymore at the hospital. They're not rich, but the boys are comfortable—they got new cars, they go to clubs, Miriam is not wanting for beautiful things.

"But Mick is starting to drink. A blackout drunk, the worst. Jerry tries to get help for his brother because he loves him, but something is funny. Something is eating at Mick. Jerry finds out one day that Mick, the brother, and Miriam, the wife, they're sleeping together. And have been practically from day one. The child is not his—it belongs to Mick. And I think Jerry Linley is dead from this moment.

"He wants to kill his brother, but Mick is in Manhattan on a three-week toot. A few years later he died. But right now he's lucky—he's climbed into a bottle and you couldn't find him with an FBI manhunt. So Jerry goes home. It is late afternoon. Miriam is standing at the fence, talking to her neighbor. Izzy is running around on the lawn. Jerry kisses her and goes inside the house. Izzy follows. Jerry closes the door and kills the boy with his hands. Miriam comes in and he beats her with his fists until she's dead. No one hears anything. He lays the bodies in the bed, under the sheets. He writes a suicide note, pins it to his shirt and takes an overdose of sleeping pills, Miriam had them from the hospital. Remember, she was a nurse. If it was me, I would have put my mouth around the barrel of a shotgun. But Jerry wasn't a violent man—that sounds funny, I know—

he wouldn't have known how to get hold of a gun. I don't think when he came home that afternoon that he even had a plan.

"Sixteen hours later he wakes up. It's ten the next morning, the neighbor's pounding on the door. He didn't take enough pills! I've talked to a few shrinks and every one of them says this is the *true moment* of psychosis. He's lost the will to finish himself a second time. You can see it, can't you? He walks out the back porch, their blood on his clothes, his skin. Before he leaves, he throws memorabilia, what have you, into a pillowcase—I'm guessing about the pillowcase—and he manages to open a safety-deposit box."

"In Yonkers."

Thom nodded.

"Why Yonkers?"

"I have no idea. He puts a few things in the box, walks out of the bank and never goes back."

"Where does he go?"

"That's part of the mystery—I've got a computer working on it. See, the last ten years he started using his real name again, on and off. My theory is that he's wandering from town to town, going through America. Meets people, charms them, lies to them—whatever he has to do. Stays a little in each place like David Janssen, do you remember *The Fugitive* or are you still too young? He works, any kind of job. And he steals. This is my theory. Finally, I think Linley knows he's dying. That's why he arranged for his confession to be read."

"What confession?"

"The so-called Holocaust papyrus—what did he call it?"

"The responsa."

"That was the confession."

"What are you talking about?"

"The note he pinned to his shirt when he took the overdose, after the murders. A confession of his crimes. They put it together at the lab. I can send you a copy."

Thom had some general questions. Was Linley in touch with anyone? Did he ever mention the wife, the child, the brother?

What was in the knapsack? Letters? Photos? Anything of interest? Thom said he was sure his publishers would be willing to
give the screenwriter a "research honorarium" for any materials that proved valuable to the book. Bud said he'd thrown
everything out. It was junk.

"My brother said there was a bowl."

"Yeah, cracked in two. It was dangerous, so I got rid of it."

When the check came, Bud reached for it. He wanted to get
out of there. Thom Rayburn halfheartedly dug into his wallet
for some bills.

"It's okay," Bud said. "It's on me."

"No, my publisher will pick it up—"

"Don't worry about it."

"You didn't even eat. It isn't Yom Kippur, you know."
Then, just in case Bud thought he was a Jew, he added, "Since
I'm on this story, I've had to learn."

The screenwriter left twenty dollars and they walked into the
harsh sunlight. He asked about the tattoo on Linley's arm and
Thom said the numbers were the birth date of the son. Bud
didn't particularly like Thom Rayburn but had to admit he was
one hell of a Sherlock Holmes. He shook Bud's hand and told
him to watch for the show in a couple of weeks.

"Thom, you said the old man had the key to a safety-deposit
box when he died."

"Right. See, Linley's laying in his cell and *bam* he knows he's
dying. He's about to have the heart attack of all heart attacks.
So he panics, starts *screaming* for the bowl—see, he had it when
they booked him, in the knapsack. He keeps wailing and
screaming, nobody ever heard anything like it, and they bring
him the bowl just so he'd keep quiet. When the medics come,
he's already dead.

"One of the cops said he was scratching at it with the key,
like a chicken. Maybe the old man was using it to dig through
the bowl to get to hell. People have done worse with similar
items. My brother told me about a woman who abducted a
pregnant lady from a clinic and cut her baby out with a car key.

Can you imagine? That's why it's a shame you threw the bowl away."

"Why should I have kept it?"

"I had a theory about that bowl. I might just use it anyway—it's a good angle for the book. Sort of a Rosebud variation."

"Go on."

"It was mostly crap in that bank box. We got a court order to go in there. Photos of the kid, backyard stuff, Jerry next to the new car, Miriam dolled up, sitting between the brothers at a nightclub. Random time capsule stuff. Well there was a bowl in there, a baby bowl with 'Izzy' painted on the bottom, you know like they do. See, Israel was the name of Miriam's grandfather. She thought when her dad found out who the kid was named after, he'd soften up and take her back to the fold. She was wrong."

"So what's your theory?"

"I think that's what the old man was trying to scratch on the bottom of the bowl with the key—'Izzy.' It's a shame you threw it out. But who wants to keep a broken bowl? Adios."

Bud was glad to get away from him.

He drove around, to clear his head. He was thinking about what slobs the Rayburn brothers were when he saw the bumper sticker on a beat-up Audi, WALK IN DANCE OUT. It clicked: the phrase was the motto of a popular ballet studio on the Westside. The old man's mind was fertile—the vaudevillian in him regurgitated the cultural landscape right to the end. A real comedian, as they say. *Walk in, dance out.* If the old man were alive, he'd say it was graffiti he discovered on the wall of the gas house while shoveling bodies—etched with a dying fingernail before the "dance" of ascension. More ethereal scratchings against surfaces, more Rosebuds . . .

He recalled a dance the old man did the night Bud took him home from Mrs. Steiner's (he called it his *oy gavotte*). It was in the hallway of the motel, outside his room. Bud was embarrassed at first, then swept away. The Rav had turned his head

toward the sky and shaken it from side to side like a blushing
lover, while his body undulated against space like a sidewinder
through brush, his face frozen in a killer's smile, cheeks sopped
with tears—a sublime soft shoe that seemed like a good-bye.
The dance of the zaddik.

Bud had left him there because it felt too intimate. The rabbi
never acknowledged his departure.

He wondered about the whole Holocaust business; Thom
Rayburn wasn't the only one with a theory. Bud figured that
the old man had concocted a past the way you worked up shtick
for an act (maybe the "rabbi" was one of Jerry's treasured bits),
and the fabrications finally overtook him, yanking him offstage
like a grand Hook. Such was his madness. Maybe at first he
played Survivor for sympathy or money, retreating behind the
beard and the kooky Yiddishisms—on the road, a petty thief
and raconteur, he might have had years of relative peace before
the dark forces came to collect the debt.

Still, nothing could diminish for Bud the power of the old
man's Lager story. It was a phantasmagoria of his own making;
the screenwriter was sure it was not to be found in any of the
purloined texts. One would have to go back more than forty
years to examine the allegory's *etiology,* as Brian might have
said—even then, it might be unknowable—but suffice that a
holocaust is a holocaust and the old man chose one that history
at least deemed dwarfed his own. He was in its grip from the
beginning, the instrument of an elaborate, hallucinatory penance. His life had become an epic, hellish myth and Bud tried
to imagine the sad vaudevillian as a child, wondering if you
could read such a destiny in his eyes.

Bud reexamined the bowl's bottom—he would never tell Thom
Rayburn his Rosebud theory was correct. Why should he? Bud
was the old man's friend and besides, the bowl was for him and
him alone. He burned the ribboned packet of pages in a waste-
basket and put the cracked heirloom deep in a drawer. It was
the drawer of the Henry James script—there the bowl would

rest, the Master's prop, apropos. Bud put a magic scarf from Rodeo Drive in its mouth and imagined it a silken flame, the rabbi hovering somewhere within.

He went to Bookz and found Rachel's vet center poem in a copy of Anne Sexton's *The Divorce Papers*. Then he looked at *Maldoror*. The book was morbid and violent, grotesquely beautiful. It was written by Lautréamont, aka Isidore Ducasse, a grandfather of Surrealism whom no one knew anything about. He died in his twenties.

Bud flipped through it. Somewhere near the back, he read: "Plagiarism is necessary." Yes. *All is plagiarism,* he thought. "You pick your nose like your father," Dolly used to tell him. You plagiarize your father.

He made a pilgrimage to the Judaica section and *The Penguin Book of Modern Yiddish Verse,* finishing the circuit. He found some of the poems the old man had ripped out. Then his eyes lit on a footnote:

According to the Kabbalistic doctrine of *Shevirat hakelim,* the divine light which flowed into primordial space should have been caught and held in special "bowls," or vessels, that emanated from God for this purpose. But the light broke forth too suddenly, and under its impact the vessels were broken and their fragments scattered into the depths of evil.

Bud felt lightened, hungry. His "fast" was over; he would eat what he wanted. It was the Sabbath.

He felt the wind of the dancing zaddik's robes as he stepped into the light.

7. The Mawkish Wedding

he business of Mrs. Steiner and the confidence man naturally found its way to the drivers in the form of bizarre twists and allegations. Bud soon became a pariah. That the detective's inquiries absolved him of wrongdoing only enhanced the part-time screenwriter's status as rip-off artist and coconspirator. Such unexpected boldness was truly shocking and for a few days the men accorded him the kind of sidelong respect reserved for *bandidos.* Still, at the very least he was guilty of a most heinous and unforgivable crime: carrying someone "off the books," joyriding with an old grifter at Ramón's expense. That really made the Indian's blood boil. Who knew how many others had been schlepped gypsy-style to what nefarious, sordid ends?

Bud was blacklisted. He tried a few other limousine companies, but they weren't hiring. When he stopped by the Beverly Palm to do a little goodwill lobbying for work, most of the drivers he'd worked for were out. The dispatcher gave him the cold shoulder. Toward the back of the garage Ramón stood by the limo in his shirtsleeves, holding a rag. A detail crew was sudsing the interior and steam-cleaning the engine. Bud walked over.

"We are exorcising the *grand larcenies* of General Noriega Wiggins. General *Oy-vay* ga. If you wanna job, you're pissing in the wind—nobody gonna hire you."

"Come on, Ramón, that's bullshit. And it's unfair. I didn't do anything illegal and you know it."

"Legal, illegal, that's not the issue, *maricón.* You *played with my income,* Zapata. *Puta.* Better head for the hills. You'll never have lunch in this town again!"

He dropped in on his mother.

He hadn't seen Dolly for a while. Bud lied and said he'd finished *Beverly Hills Adjacent.* He called it a "great read." She told him she was even thinking of mailing it to *that fuck* Joseph Harmon.

He sat down at the white and gold Kawai and noodled.

"Oh, Buddy, play something! Play something for your mother!"

He was rusty. He tried a little Bach, then some Schubert and Debussy. Dolly sat behind, enthralled. When Bud reached the end of his memory, she said there was sheet music inside the bench. She wanted to hear *Moonlight Sonata.*

Bud lifted the wood flap and saw them: three neat stacks of *Shotgun.*

His mother explained that she went to Bookz to get the new Dominick Dunne and saw his beautiful story, right by the register. *Shotgun,* by Bud Wiggins. She almost died. He'd mentioned that the store was carrying it on consignment, but the fact just didn't sink in until she saw it in front of her—she wanted to scream, "That's my son!" Sometimes people idly examined the thin blue volume while their books were being rung up, but no one ever bought it. Seeing them thumb through his creation, then set it down again, was torture. So Dolly watched and waited and browsed and got into conversations about authors. Then she worked her way around to recommending it, without saying she was the mother.

Dolly came back to the store a few weeks later and *Shotgun* was gone from the register. She thought the world had discovered her son, but then she found the volumes buried in the remainder section, some with their corners crumpled. She bought the ten copies to give to rich clients at Hoffmann-Dougherty's and every once in a while stopped in to buy some more. Sales generate interest, Buddy. What was so terrible?

"You had too much punctuation. You should have given it to me to look at. Your mother's a brilliant editor."

"Next time."

"Fahr fahr carmintrate."

She wanted to go to Adray's to complain about her new toaster-oven. They drove in Dolly's car along Wilshire toward the discount store, Bud at the wheel. As they passed the building where Morris jumped, Dolly looked up, staring at its hard edge against the sky, her chin trembling in melodramatic reproach. She always did that when they went past the place, arching her neck and looking up to the fraudulent heavens like Morris had really hoodwinked everyone and *ascended,* a Houdini getaway to that great Whorehouse in the Sky. It was funny actually having a jumper in the family. When Bud saw *The Tenant,* instead of being upset, he'd been strangely soothed: Polanski jumps off a roof, but it doesn't finish him. He hauls himself back up the stairs, broken and bloodied, and jumps again. Bud loved that.

Bud didn't attend school the week of the funeral. When he returned to classes, one of the seniors said, "It's a bird, it's a plane, it's . . . *Morrrrris Wigggggins!*" There was a stain on the sidewalk for months. *Cry a little.*

———

Bud received a letter from the WGA informing him the producers of *Bloodbath 2* had arrived at tentative writing credits.
Since he'd worked on the project, the Guild required he be duly
notified. He stared blankly at the page:

Story by
Loni DeVoto and Mark Ben-Dov

Screenplay by
Moira Leventhal & Jeffrey Berkowitz
and
Ruggiero Pratese
and
J. W. Bosker & Danae Steffling

Who were these people? Why had his name been omitted? Did
this mean that *Bloodbath 2* was in the can? But how could it
have gone into production without Bud's knowing? And how
could AlphaFilm have financed a sequel to a film that had never
been released?

He called the Guild. A woman explained that because proposed credits for *Bloodbath 2* included more than two writers,
the script was subject to an automatic arbitration. That was one
of the rules. Bud told her he'd written an early draft; there was
no record of it. She encouraged him to send in all related
materials. He asked to see a copy of the script on file and the
woman said she would send it by mail. The nervous screenwriter wanted to know if he'd be *testifying*—if he would have
the opportunity to defend himself, present his case. She said
that wasn't part of the arbitration process, but a letter with his
"views" most certainly would be welcomed by the committee.

Arbitration was a tricky, serious game. The difference between a solo or shared credit could sometimes be a few hundred
thousand dollars. He wasn't in that league but knew no good
would come from total absence of acknowledgment—unless
you were one of those fabulously paid script doctors who

couldn't care less, in fact demanded anonymity. Unless you were a Caitlin Wurtz. The official arbitrators were selected from a list of writers, each of whom had more than three produced credits. Naturally there were Guild rules that worked in the writer's favor. For example, if you were a director or producer trying to glom a writing credit, you had to prove you wrote at least 50 percent of the script. Bud read that in the *Journal*. He wasn't in the worst of shape then. He was the original writer, and from what he'd heard, it would be hard to knock him out of the box. The idea of real writers as arbiters was particularly comforting; they'd be inherently sensitive to his case. Nevertheless, as far as he knew, a decision couldn't be appealed. If the committee ruled against you, you had little recourse but to stomp your feet and get drunk.

Bloodbath 2 arrived, full of grammatical errors and smudgy Italianisms, badly translated. They'd apparently shot the thing in Rome. There were no significant departures from his original draft. There weren't even new characters, just old ones flamboyantly recycled from the *Wiggins* script, clumsily expanded, wrongheaded and jerry-built. The names, of course, had been changed—standard operating procedure on any lowlife rewrite (like a child who covers his eyes and thinks no one can see him). Who did they think they were that they could plunder his work and summarily remove his acknowledgment? Did they think he'd cave in, say nothing?

His defense needed to be right and clear as mountain water. He would begin the encyclical with "To Whom It May Concern." There were two things his father had taught him: how to fold toilet paper to wipe his bottom and how to start a letter.

I have just reviewed the first draft and subsequent two revisions of *Bloodbath 2* I delivered to AlphaFilm (hereafter referred to as I, II and III) and the shooting script (hereafter referred to as X) of *Bloodbath 2*, recently received by mail. It is my strong opinion that X adheres to I, II and III in plot, character, imagery and substance. It departs in only a few instances that I will briefly note; the departures are innocuous, in that they do not alter or affect plot or character as developed in I, II and III in any intrinsic way. (I make quick note of one of the typical, petty alterations of X: in I, II and III, Barbara is a *candy striper;* in X, she's a *nurse's aide*—the only difference being that candy stripers are volunteers; nurse's aides are paid for their work).

The main departure seems to be the creation of a new character, a dour and mysterious Mother Superior who reveals to Thomas that Dr. Hacker's "unquiet spirit" must be put to rest by burying his bones in "hallowed ground." I believe this character is in a total of four scenes. One of these scenes (in the bell tower [X, p. 58]) is expositional, and echoes information from III (pp. 54–8) and II (pp. 71–3) in which the voodoo high priestess Trudy Sapphire enlightens Barbara. (Joanna Hacker, the doctor's psychotic mother, is first mentioned in the latter cited speech.) The Mother Superior is, for all intents and purposes, a "catholicization" of the Trudy Sapphire character. Trudy imparts her information to Barbara; in X, the Mother Superior imparts the same information to Thomas. As Thomas and Barbara are sharing information at this point anyway, the alteration is moot. In II (pp. 56–60), Trudy tells Barbara that Dr. Hacker must die "by his own hand"; in X, the Mother Superior tells Thomas that Dr. Hacker must die by the burying of his bones in "hallowed ground." Both solutions are arbitrary, in that they serve to hasten denouement. In I (p. 88), the importance of the retrieving of the stainless steel grappling hook is emphasized over the retrieving of the bones in X.

In X, Joanna Hacker (who figures throughout I, II and III) turns out to be the Mother Superior. The revelation that the Mother Superior and mother are the same person is a kind of coda that does not intrinsically alter the plot or exposition of I, II and III. X faithfully transplants from the latter the details about the mother, the conception of her son et cetera.

The departure of secondary and minimal importance in X is the role Barbara's father plays in helping out Thomas and Barbara by locating the site of the buried bones. Though Barbara's father is absent from II and III, he plays a major role throughout I. He is described as a drunk (I, p. 10) and, as in X, is a source of important information (I, pp. 38–9, 61–2). He still wears his police officer's uniform (I, p. 6). When we meet this resurrected character in X, *he is drinking in a bar, wearing his uniform and badge.* And: *he is in possession of vital information.* In X, he volunteers to Thomas (p. 76) a "spare key" to the sewage plant that leads to hell; in I, he steals the keys so he and Barbara can get onto a locked ward. In I (p. 112) Dr. Hacker assumes the appearance of Barbara's father in order to trick her, after he has decapitated the real dad; X transplants the scene unaltered.

In X, there is a character, Elijah Kreister, who is identical to the character Elias Kroyten in I, II and III except for the fact that he is wheelchair-bound and possessed of a third nipple. Later (in X), Kreister is impaled on a demonic, spiked tractor–lawn mower. This torture device is a version of the spiked "bicycle built for two" in III (pp. 3–4).

JoBeth is the only child who undergoes any real alteration of character in the X script: instead of a troubled black child who "raps" and loves fire, she is a troubled white child who enjoys "rap music" and craves rebellion. She also has a different death than she had in I, II and III. Once again, these alterations do not affect plot; she is simply an altered version of a "troubled girl" character.

The development of the plot in X that concerns the Mother Superior, the holy water, the burying of the bones in "hallowed ground," et cetera, however in keeping with the tradition of films of this genre, is also derivative, it seems, of much of the imagery in I, II and III. In I (pp. 62–3) and III (p. 14), there is a nightmarish religious motif, with writhing crucifixes, Catholic girls with slashed wrists and stigmata. The stigmata of I recalls the bloody letter spelled out on the chest of Elias Kroyten in X, p. 66 (*The Exorcist* notwithstanding).

In X, there is a sudden reprise of its opening scene, where Heather's mother tucks her into bed and is then decapitated by Dr. Hacker. As Dr. Hacker holds the mother's severed head, it talks, scolding Heather (X, p. 84). This is a redoing of the "talking head" scene in II (p. 89) and III (pp. 74–5) where the severed head of Elias Kroyten talks as if it is answering game show questions.

In X, Dr. Hacker reveals his belly, writhing with the "souls of dead children." This is derivative of the child wraiths in I (p. 76) and III (p. 70), the ones who have eyes "like dolls' eyes." The latter two scenes seem to be the source, also, of one of the first few scenes in X where Heather is confronted by Dr. Hacker while she is taking a bath. The tub's faucets become his hands and the drain plug becomes his head, which then floats menacingly between her legs. This bathtub scene and the cesspool scene in X (p. 98) are derivative of the imagery in III, where Barbara is menaced in the sewage plant by machinery that takes on human (Hacker) characteristics.

The vomiting dog in the climax of X also makes important appearances in I (pp. 86 and 88), II (p. 105) and III (p. 87).

There is a new scene in X where the bones of Dr. Hacker become an avenging, animated skeleton. In both X and I, II and III, Dr. Hacker holds Louis hostage (II, p. 81; III, p. 67) and Heather, shell-shocked, is isolated and sedated. This scene in X with the avenging skeleton at the sewage plant may be said to be the only truly new scene distinguishing X from I, II and III.

It may be helpful to note that *the X script contains no new major characters* (other than the Mother Superior, who I have tried to show is an "extension" of the Trudy Sapphire character in I, II and III). In fact, *X contains only one additional, ancillary character,* an orderly. The X script faithfully

retains the entire ensemble, without exception, of I, II and
III. . . .

He sent the letter by registered mail, along with his original
draft. That night he read Cicero, and felt enlivened.

ʍʍ

The owner/operators at the Beverly Palm paid their backup
drivers hourly wages but made them wait for the gratuities,
which always came along with accounts receivable. A few
months had passed and Ramón owed Bud around twelve hundred dollars in tips, some going back almost a year. He went
to the hotel to see his former boss.

The swarthy driver was at the front door, on his way to the
pool to deliver a forgotten Filofax to a "sunbathing Jewish
cocksucker." Bud followed.

"Zapata! Did you come to steal more credit cards?"

"Funny. Any of my gratuities come in yet, Ramón?"

"Not yet, *bandido.* They are very late this month. The bookkeeper is a *Thief,* starring James Caan. I'm waiting myself for
three thousand, *Zapatita.* I will let you know."

The pool was crowded. Everyone was on the phone, like
bookies in paradise; Bud wondered what a farm boy would
make of it. Ramón murmured, "Ah! There is the Jew!" and
headed for a sun-stained bather with great chalky tufts of chest
hair. The screenwriter looked around to see if there was anyone
from the Business.

He noticed a woman staring at him from one of the cabanas.
She wore a white robe, a white towel wrapped around her head
like a turban. She smiled and waved. After making sure she
wasn't waving to someone else, Bud walked closer. Her smile
grew broader. Did he know this woman?

"Bud? Are you Bud Wiggins?"

"Yes."

"I don't believe this. It's *Cora.* Cora *Copeland.*"

"Cora?"

"From the *Arbor.* I *thought* it was you, but I wasn't positive."

His brain struggled to match the little girl he remembered with the grown-up face before him.

"How did you recognize me?"

"You haven't changed that much."

"How long has it been?"

"Twenty years? No! Almost twenty-five."

"Jesus."

"What are you doing here?"

"Visiting a friend."

"What about you?"

"I came for a design show. And I have an aunt who lives here, she's been sick. Can you stay? Have you had lunch?"

"I can stay for a little."

He was relieved that Ramón appeared to have left.

Bud sat with his first love in the white cabana heat and everything fell away at its borders, melting into brightness. They lay on floral chaise longues while a boy brought Cokes and club sandwiches and ice cream in silver bowls. She was the girl whose chair he chivalrously placed on the desk at the end of the school day; he was the boy whose tousled hair she dared stroke in the silent sacred cloakroom. They laughed, astonished.

Cora was living in Napa, not far from the Arbor. Her father died a few years ago, leaving her land and a hotel. She dabbled in antiques and interior design, and went to night school to learn French. She'd been married and divorced early, without children. It excited her that Bud worked in the movies; he told her some stories. She was staying a few days and insisted they have dinner together. When he said good-bye, they shook hands and she loosened the towel from her head, unraveling the yellow hair, its long strands darkened by dampness.

卅卅

The next night they went to a place on Melrose for penne arrabiata.

It felt easy being with her. She was lithe and small-boned and always looked like she'd just stepped from a shower, anointed with fragrant bath oils. Her eyes were clear blue and her laughter was throaty and full of health. When he asked a question, her response was honest and direct. Cora was without guile. She wasn't an agent and she wasn't a lawyer and she wasn't an actress—for Bud, neutrality to the Business had rendered her practically luminous. She was fascinated that he was "an artist," mock-envious, and curious about the goings-on of the town the way a tourist wants to know about native mores. After he told her about *Shotgun,* she begged him for a copy to take home with her. When the bill came, she grabbed it. Bud didn't fight her.

They went back to her room for a nightcap. Robert De Niro was on *Arsenio* talking in hushed, reverent tones about how he always wanted to work with Penny Marshall. Who would have imagined the A List American directors to be the alumni of craphouse seventies sitcoms? They necked a few minutes on the couch. Bud thought: how strange life is. He'd finally caught up to this girl, their roots roped back a quarter of a century and now the tendrils had found each other far beneath the bower's loamy soil. She was unneurotic and lonesome and returning to Napa soon.

Cora whispered, *come on,* and led him to the bedroom. They undressed quickly and made love without wasting a single kiss, movement or caress. He thought of them as the paradigm of "consenting adults." Their bodies excited each other, yet there was something grounded and mature about such passions. Afterward they watched old movies in bed and avoided profundities about their fated alliance. Bud Wiggins and Cora Copeland had momentously come full circle but were keeping their heads. He took that as a good sign, always remembering what Jeanette said about mistaking lust for love. It was sweetly moving, the way she looked at him, touched him, the way he held her. Such tendernesses with such shared history was something amazingly new. Revolutionary.

Cora invited him up north to a bed and breakfast she owned in Sausalito. Maybe he could move away from here now. They'd build a little workshop on the rim of her land where he could write a few hours each morning. What he wrote didn't really matter, it was the *act* of writing that was important, for that's what he was, forever and ever—a writer. He knew he would get good work done that way, do the hard work well, amid such tendernesses, not far from the Secret Garden.

The next day he drove her to the airport. There was something sure and unspoken between them: she would be his wife if he asked. *If he so wished*—Casanovawitz need only say the word. Cora wanted to be married again, she'd said it casually over dinner. She was tired of all the dull assholes who kept taking up her offer to go dutch on dinner dates. She was bored and threw herself into decorating and that was fun, but something was missing. He loved how Hollywood had her wide-eyed, she was a hick who didn't know from *Variety*—to Cora, he was an exotic, ardent being, a *writer* she'd kissed with virgin lips a lifetime ago. Their childhood's communion was magical and wondrous, like a misty castle in a fairy tale, and it touched her deeply; they'd gone to bed with a cosmic long-lost-lovers twist. She looked at him like he was a mortal destination, a beguiling country of soulful hills and mysterious winds she might never return from.

As she vanished through the gate, Bud was certain he'd do it. This one act would yank him to the next phase, like that square dance move where someone pulls you through. He knew a publicist who'd get the nuptials into the trades—not that Cora would care a whit. He'd buy a diamond solitaire at Tiffany (Dolly would be thrilled to front the money), then fly to Napa unannounced and slip it on her third finger, where a vein ran straight to the heart. The day of the wedding would be crisp and clear, banners snapping in the dizzying blue sky above her vast property, friends and relatives flown from the country's four corners. She'd wear a Victorian gown from the place he used to window-shop with Jeanette. The rabbi would sing as they stood under the *huppah,* breaking glasses underfoot. A child already growing within her, their secret, the wedding band thick and golden on his finger.

Bud watched through the glass as the jet began its taxi to the runway. Like in a movie, she waved to him from first-class. He blew a kiss.

He stopped at Bookz on the way home. Near the register was a grainy, grayish book with black lettering, struck through by a stylish red bolt: *Force Majeure: Tales from the Holy Wood,* by Ford Sester-Neff. One of the clerks said it was a limited edition of show biz stories by an up-and-coming screenwriter. Some famous director had already optioned it for a movie.

He flipped to "A Writer's Assignment" and read a few pages. The names were different, but the story was the one he'd told Sester-Neff that day in the Chrysalis House cafeteria, about Billy Quintero and Joel Levitt. Though it was told from the newspaper reporter's point of view, Bud recognized some of his own conversational rhythm and phrasing.

ʍʍʍ

The small title in the want ads seemed almost lyrical: CHAUF-FEUR/HOUSEMAN NEEDED. Bud was running out of money, and even though he knew nothing about the function of a houseman, he figured whoever placed the ad mostly needed a driver. The *houseman* part probably just meant doing errands. Waxing the cars, buffing the floors, fucking the wife.

He called the two-seven number and a gruff voice answered—the prospective employer. He wondered why the guy was answering his own phone. Well, why not? He was answering his phone because he needed someone to answer his phone. Bud drove straight over. As he walked through the lobby of the Towers, he feared running into Mrs. Steiner. The doorman watched the screenwriter wander over to the aquarium before going to the elevators. The membranes of dead fishes still waved in the water.

He got off on the twelfth floor. A door at the end of the hall was open. Sinatra was singing "Night and Day."

Sid Braverman met Bud at the entryway in a voluminous checkered silk robe, accompanied by two poodles that nipped at the screenwriter's calves. He twirled a snifter to the music. Braverman had hair like a white cliff and bragged how he was seventy-six but looked at least fifteen years younger. It was true. He showed Bud the scars from his triple bypass, then picked up one of the dogs and sang "Street of Dreams" into its face. Bud got the job.

"You seem to be a very intelligent young man. I may have something else for you, in sales. What you should really be doing is *canvassing*—the money's in the leads. You make three, four times what you get as chauffeur."

"That much?"

"*Easy.* Sky's the limit. I think you would do very, very well, Bud. Anyone can drive—Jesus, I've had *monkeys.* That's not to say you don't have the job as chauffeur if you don't want to do the canvassing."

"I like making money."

"Then you're normal."

The phone rang and he picked it up in the kitchen. It sounded like he was talking to a bookmaker. When he got off, Braverman poured himself another drink, then pushed the glass at the fridge while it ground out ice. As chunks dropped in, his robe was spattered with Courvoisier; he snapped his fingers to "That's Life."

"Tell you what. I'm going to put you on a draw. You go out with one of my men—you'll catch on in half a day. Some it takes a week, because they're stupid. But you—I think you'll do very, very well. You'll get it in a day—two, *maximum.* "

"I answered the chauffeur ad," Bud was telling Pep. It was the following Monday; his tutelage had begun.

Pep was in his forties. He lived in Valley motels, clean ones with midget pools whose vacancy signs were so discreet they looked like apartment houses or insurance claim centers. He somehow got away with giant, curly-orange rockabilly sideburns on his smooth white face. He had the unflappable, hollow, friendly affect of a DJ, a nervous laugh and too many words for the waitresses. Pep had been through a lot of Buds on orientations but wanted to like him and be liked back anyway.

"Oh, right! The 'houseman' bit! That's how he recruits," Pep said, grinning. "I did that for the Old Man, too, drove him around for a year. But he was right—the money's in canvassing."

Pep was a "character," a textbook loser with clammy skin and bad teeth. He looks like he belongs in a snapshot you'd find in a drawer after an eviction, Bud thought, an old zigzag-edge Polaroid like the ones Dolly kept in the shoebox: standing in front of a stucco duplex, everything bleached and tilted, queasily transient and unmemorable, the fence behind stuck in the mortgaged dirt, a car fin intruding on the frame, American as the weeds.

They got into his car, leased by the Old Man and deducted from Pep's weekly draw, some sort of brougham with puffy velvet seats, a pimp's suburban Sunday cruiser. Braverman had warned him Pep was lazy—he skipped days, cheating the leads and spreading them over the week so he could go to the track and drink. Bud thought he was just sounding off.

He let Pep do most of the talking on the way to the coffee shop (it wasn't hard). He had no desire to divulge anything personal, particularly anything about the Movies, though he was certain Pep would be impressed. Bud's latest avocation had nothing to do with "research" for some future project. It was just a job; Hollywood wasn't in this particular diorama and that suited him fine. Hollywood was fading away, like an island receding into the horizon—Bud stood at the bow of a deserted ship and his gaze was pitiless. Soon he'd set course for Napa. Or maybe do a Jerry Linley and *zing* the world, but with a happy ending: his journey had begun in Sester-Neff's Holy Wood indeed and it was time to depart for mystic parts un-

known, Peru and Spain and Palestine. He felt alive and awakened to all things. As they drove, Bud lapsed, thinking himself
a powerful producer scouting locations with an idiot Teamster
for a big film.

"So," Pep said as they settled into a booth, "what do you
think of the Old Man?" Everything came down to that.

"He's wild."

Bud could have said, "I'm the Bob's Big Boy Killer," and
Pep wouldn't have flinched.

"Yeah, he *is* something. Smart son of a bitch."

Pep feared and admired the Old Man. He perspired while he
rhapsodized, his face taking on a moronic, slavish, ageless grin,
taut and homely and needy. The Old Man was a *thing* that
provided, a *thing* that wouldn't die, a constant in a volatile,
hostile world.

"How long have you worked for him?"

"Four, five years, on and off. I've made the Old Man some
money, you better believe it. See, that's what's good about
canvassing. He needs us as much as we need him. I mean, he
may have the Mercedes and the driver and the condo in the
Towers—but he couldn't make a dime without us, without the
leads. The leads are gold."

"What's the most you ever made in commission?"

"In a week? When I'm not messing around, or at the track—I
like to go to the track—oh, I think there was a week I cleared
three thousand. But then I took two weeks sick and played the
ponies." He showed his yellow teeth, then grew serious again.
"Lost it! Well, most of it. I think I was, Jesus, up to fourteen
grand but then I started drinking. You can't drink if you want
to win. Came back to the Old Man—the Old Man always takes
me back because I'm a proven money-maker for him. So it
evens out."

"You can really make that much?" He wanted to believe it.

"Oh, sure," Pep said, with the insouciance of a miniature gold
champ. "The beauty is that when you sell a job, you get your
commission as soon as the bank loan goes through. No risk."

"What neighborhood are we going to? Do you know?"

"I never like to pick a place, you jinx it. Sometimes I wait for a feeling. Maybe we'll shoot over to Hawaiian Gardens. Lots of Japs there, but I want to go anyway. The Old Man doesn't like Japs because they're tough. Or Jews—you can't sell a Jew. But I like the challenge. The Old Man likes 'em more *moochie*—but don't ever let him hear the word! He *hates* that word, I don't know why. But he sure is something. Once, back when I was his chauffeur, this old lady wasn't home when she said she'd be—widows and old ladies, he'll close them every time, *loves* 'em. He knew he was going to sell her, but she wasn't home to get in the door. We circled the house *two hours* waiting for her to come. Never did. She was probably out of town, visiting her husband's grave, whatever. The Old Man was so mad he walked over and pissed on the side of her house!" Pep choked, laughing up toast crumbs. "See, the Old Man is the best friend you got. He's the *best.* A legend. He used to run gin, during Prohibition, did you know that? He's been in jail, had Duesenbergs. And if you got a half-decent lead, the Old Man'll close. It's true. No one closes like the Old Man. He'll close it, then have a 'mechanic' out there seven in the morning. He gives you ten percent and that's rare now. Plus extras, sometimes fifteen percent, if he puts in stone or steel. He'll close three, four deals a night. And *that's* money. He works six days a week. You know he's had a quadruple bypass?"

"Really?"

For a moment Bud imagined himself with silver hair and parchment skin, his heart suddenly dying within.

"Oh hell yeah, he called the mooches from fucking *Cedars.* I still worked 'cause I knew when he got out he'd need the leads, and it'd be good for me. There was more than one week I didn't go out when he was laid up, but he still paid me a draw. Oh, he'll take care of you. But he's tough." Pep winked and shook his head. "He's a tough bastard. He'll never die."

———

Cora called and asked when he wanted to come north. Bud said he was working on a script and wouldn't be able to travel for a few weeks. He'd have a paycheck or two by then—he didn't want to go up there broke. She sent him a brochure of the place in Sausalito that had a picture of the room they were going to stay in. It looked out onto the bay.

A letter came from the Guild with the final determination of credits on *Bloodbath 2*. His name was not included. He called someone in the arbitration department and was told the decision could not be appealed.

> To Whom It May Concern:
> This letter is in reference to the motion picture *Bloodbath 2* and its recent arbitration.
> I was an actor in the first *Bloodbath,* starring in the role of the Doctor. (I do not believe the film was ever released, though it may have been distributed in Europe.) During the shoot I was encouraged by producers to "write" my own material through improvisation and actual on-the-day dialogue rewrites; in this way I contributed substantially to the resultant script. Though I have been a member of the WGA for years, I was never paid for my work nor did I seek payment. Whatever "writing" I did was within my capacity as an actor.
> Because of the quality of my work, AlphaFilm employed me to write a first draft of *Bloodbath 2*. I was also to reprise my acting chores in the role of the Doctor, a character I helped create.
> I recently received a letter from the Guild expressing its "resolution" of the matter in question (cf. your letter of the 12th). I think that the ruling is unfair, and will not let it go unchallenged.
> Who are these people selected as judges in the arbitration process? You provided me with a general list. I understand that they are Guild members, fellow (supposed) writers. What I would like to know is how I

can be certain such committee members weren't "friendly" with party or parties implicitly challenging my authorship? Shouldn't I be able to learn this through direct interrogation? I would think I had that simple right. When I made a telephone inquiry in this regard, I was elaborately stonewalled—it put me in mind of the Wizard of Oz and his pyrotechnical show. I'm sure the Guild knows its business, but I find it strange to be ruled against by a council I will never see, speak to, touch. It's bizarre! In one fell swoop, my credit was removed by parties unknown; in another, that action sustained by a star chamber whose judgment was presented as a Solomon-like fait accompli.

I was told to send a letter to the Guild outlining my beliefs in the *Bloodbath 2* matter. To what end? Why can't I state my case in person? I knew Lou Gottlieb fairly well: if he were alive, Lou would no doubt add his voice to the growing legions pleading for democratization of the arbitration process.

I am compelled to inform the Guild I have retained counsel to protect my livelihood in these matters. I'm prepared to take the whole case to an outside court. My counsel, Don Bloom (a successful trial lawyer and constitutional scholar), has been in touch with Mr. Gore Vidal's legal defense team; I trust this will make you think twice about your actions.

If the arbitration is ultimately resolved in my favor, I will still lobby for procedural reform.

I anxiously await your response.

Sincerely,

Bud Wiggins

ⱮⱮⱮ

Braverman leased him a sporty new car with a T-top. It made the freeways easier; it made everything easier. He never saw Pep again.

Bud worked six hours a day, earning four to six hundred a week, less car and taxes. The best neighborhoods were the ones that still thought there was a middle class—they greeted the Old Man's acolytes with the insane durable politeness of village peasants because Sidney Braverman was a *thing* that provided, he had something bright and expensive: paint. Some kind of house paint anyway, guaranteed for twenty years, sprayed from a gun in pretty colors right over the wood, the eaves and the dusty cracking stucco, the day new again from a bettered house. Each one had a different look—some were sociable or prettified, others standoffish and indifferent, evil, heat-warped. He kept a log, to maximize his efforts. Beside each house number he'd scribble hieroglyphs: *"pretty wife/return/talk to husband," "no one home/tried four times," "music on/car in driveway/no answer/return," "return/careful! dog," "said come back two weeks/gone on trip."* Whenever he got a lead (a mooch that he'd hand to Braverman for the kill), Bud rated it one to ten according to his "nose." The Old Man usually closed anything over a six. When he finished with a neighborhood, the screenwriter knew it as a naturalist knows a favorite inlet, its rocks, contours and living things.

Saturdays and Sundays were prime time because everyone was home between comings and goings from shopping centers, amusement parks, hospitals, sporting events, gunshops, cineplexes, auto shows, malls and hobby centers. The collective mood was always unpredictable; a friendly neighborhood could suddenly sour for no apparent reason. Sometimes when he knocked on shadowy doors, people acted like murderers being interrupted. Once some kids in a pickup threw a bottle that shattered near his feet.

He worked in the rain. When he got bored, Bud altered his

sales pitch or took painkillers. He pretended to be a machine, impervious to weather, blanketing every square inch of house, yard, curb, sky, armed with spiel and hieroglyphs, working through the night in jumpsuit and infrared goggles. He stood on porches—the little ecclesiastical ornament beside the bell, the Marriage Encounter decal on the window or the sign of the fish that he never understood—inhaling the peeling corners and receding foundations, the chapped fading window frames, the mucky, stale children's shoes on the welcome mat, plastic big-wheeled tricycles on the shag beyond the torn screen door, treacly family smells that blasted through the screen.

At dusk—the dark dropping down through the trees but the light still holding awhile longer, tunnels of dusty light on famil-iar things, sidewalks and bushes and shabby landmarks Bud knew by heart—the neighborhoods were like rank carnivals coming to life: piquant dinner smells, sadistic nightly news, cars raging home, their engines blowing out the disappointment of the day. Campers sat in driveways like bug shells, guest rooms for deranged relatives; fathers used them for workshops, or sanctuary after supper, scary light on in the shell, power tools and poison for the weeds and rats.

Bud worked into the night, mercenary and muscle-toned. When he was done, he rocketed on the freeway, the warm air cutting his face through the T-top. He imagined his car could lift off into darkness. He thought of a book he'd read as a boy about country children who wake up in the middle of the night to meet in a vast windy field. There, a spacecraft awaits them. He was always trying to find that story again; maybe he'd imagined it. He would write something for children. He tried to, years and years ago—

Once there was a bony boy of twelve who tried to write but couldn't so he tried to write a children's story instead. His only attempt was abandoned after a single typewritten page. He took the sheet to a photocopier and had it reduced in size, so he could look at it as if written by another, a discrete, published thing. His eyes kept adjusting to it—still, it remained his—and he had them reduce it again, then again and again until it was difficult to read. Still, it was his. This boy, a prolific gatherer of books, looked at the reduced text of his fresh pages and thought: I will be no Chatterton, no Radiguet. *He played piano at the Academy of Music and danced ballroom style at the after-school cotillion. His teacher was a Russian with bad mascara and perfect pitch and his waltz partners were little girls with stiff white gloves, hairy arms and terrible perfume; the odor of otherness. He vaguely dreamed of "concertizing," practicing scales each day for hours until he was too tired to learn his études. He blanked at recitals. The boy, a youngish mystic, cried in his dark room at the foot of the stairs and thought:* I will be no Scriabin. *Once a year came the cotillion ball and he would dance in competition and win. They gave him great trophies with metal grilles and faux marble bases, and when he got home, he arranged them into an exclusive cemetery on the nightstand. At night, he watched Astaire and Kelly on the late show—one celestial, the other streetwise; the muscle of a swan, the elegance of a tough. And the boy thought:* I will be no Nijinsky . . .

I will be no Buñuel or Sturges, Renoir or Lubitsch. I will be—

〰〰〰

Bud sent twenty-five anonymous letters to the Guild that said:

ARBITRATION ≠ ARBITRARY

〰〰〰

He was lost in thought, standing on the porch of a house with the hieroglyph pad, waiting for someone to answer the bell. He heard a voice behind him.

"No one lives there."

He turned to face a little girl. She stood over her bike, then bumpily rode off. When he looked through the gauze-curtained windows, Bud saw there was no furniture in the rooms.

The next day she came toward him, primly walking the bike beside her.

"What do you do?"

"Why?"

"I can ask you."

Her own boldness made the girl smile. Bud smiled back.

"I sell things."

"Do you sell paint?"

"Sort of. For houses." He started to walk.

"Did you try to sell my father paint?"

"Probably."

"Our house is painted already."

She stayed at the sidewalk and watched him approach the door of another house. He rang, turned around and smiled, suddenly self-conscious.

"I don't think they're home," she said.

"I think you're right."

"Why do men always come to ask about paint?"

A backyard voice shouted: "Aubrey!"

She turned to Bud, said, "Bye!" then pedaled off.

The next day he got started late. People were rude. He found himself skipping houses, then whole blocks, aimless. He walked straight to the car after only forty minutes, knowing this was the worst thing to do. Whatever you did you had to keep going.

He'd parked on the edge of the neighborhood, next to a convenience store. He got some Chee-tos and coffee. It was getting dark. The little girl appeared on her bike.

"I was sick today."

"What's wrong?"

"A cold." She coughed, to show him.

"You shouldn't be out. Where are you going?"

"My mom needs eggs."

"How old are you?"

"Ten. How old are you?"

"Twenty-four," he lied. "Am I too old?"

"Yes."

"You're Aubrey."

She smiled. "How did you know?"

"I heard your mother."

"That wasn't my mother. That was my *sister.*"

They stood by the car under the trees.

"Do you want to go for a ride?" He put his hand on the door. "I have kind of a convertible."

"Okay," she said, and started to get in.

"Put your bike where it won't get stepped on and I'll get the eggs for your mom. Jump in the backseat and hide. If anyone sees you, your mom won't get the eggs and she'll be mad."

He bought a *TV Guide* and a carton of eggs for the girl. His heart was jackhammering and he thought of robbing the place, but all he did was get two more eggs, hard-boiled, from a big plastic water-filled jar next to the register. Eggs on top of eggs. When he left the store, the cool dusk air made him shiver. He got to the car and saw the blurry woolen hump of the girl's sweater as she scrunched down. He got in.

"Stay like that," he said to the air. "You can come up in a minute."

He drove about a mile, then parked in an alley.

"Okay."

She sat up.

"What are we going to do?"

He leaned between the bucket seats and put his mouth on hers. She dodged him a second, then put her tongue in his mouth as he steadied himself, his hands on the front headrests, arms drawn back like wings. She sneezed and laughed and kissed him deeply. They breathed loudly through their noses awhile. He pulled off her underwear and, lifting up her bottom, put his mouth between her legs. She shifted awkwardly, not knowing whether to sit up or lie back. Finally she grabbed his neck with her hands like a carousel horse.

Bud helped pull on her underwear, legs blotchy red where he held them. She went to kiss him again, but he said her mom would be worried. He took her back near the store and made her promise not to tell. He gave her the carton of eggs.

⋘⋙

Bud didn't canvass any leads the next week. He called in sick. The Old Man was kind and asked if there was anything his chauffeur could send over. Bud ripped his phone out of the wall and left the leased car across the street from the Towers, keys on the mat. Then he walked to the freeway.

At the on ramp, a rusty cyclone fence held back thickets corroded by smoke and exhaust. There was a hole in the decaying chain link that he'd watched for weeks, passing on the way to work. He imagined the homeless living inside. He went through, hoping not to have an encounter. He cut himself on one of the wires and worried for a second about the rust.

Beyond the dense, brittle bushes was a rough clearing with an old mattress. He turned it over, but the bed was twisted and wouldn't lie flat. Yellowish brush reached toward the freeway like a dirty meadow. Bud was cold. He gathered debris—cardboard, a greasy quilted vest, a plastic bag—and covered himself with them as he lay down. It was getting dark and the evening air was like a sweet, cool breath on his forehead. The cars sounded like waves. The blackness of the sky seemed to start beneath him, hemming him into its curtain. He thought of the carved-out brambly park of long ago, the one with secret bowers and boyish passageways. He thought of the time machine: he could lie here forever and watch the fast-motion changes wrought by its sorcery. Then he felt the call of the Secret Garden and the wild, sultry winds of his arborescent boyhood. Bud began to shiver and dream.

He was lying in a large backyard that sloped down to the deep blue slate of a huge pool. Bud and the bicycle girl lay side by side on a gorgeous lawn. They'd been married that afternoon in a house on a hill, a white pavilion surrounded by acres of orange blossoms, honeysuckle and wisteria. All Hollywood was there and far away were the powerful voices of celebration. Then he slipped away from the wedding party, awake again in the filthy bower's Secret Garden, praying she would join him among the darkening shapes. The new bride rolled over to face him and it was Cora, young Cora, his first love, only love. She was cold and he gave her the soiled vest to wear over her gown. She asked why they were there, away from the party. He told her what he wanted to do. She smiled at him adoringly—it was so romantic, to say it a second time, away from the crowds and the cameras. She looked deep into his eyes, he was so sweet and loving and nervous, so chivalrous. She touched her finger to his lips, thrilled and grateful to have chosen this man to be her husband for Eternity. They grew solemn. She took his hands.

This is where they exchanged their vows again.